Heart's Home

H.B. PATTSKYN

Dreamspinner Press

Published by
Dreamspinner Press
382 NE 191st Street #88329
Miami, FL 33179-3899, USA
http://www.dreamspinnerpress.com/

Cover Art by Paul Richmond   http://www.paulrichmondstudio.com

ISBN: 978-1-61372-236-7

Printed in the United States of America
First Edition
December 2011

eBook edition available
eBook ISBN: 978-1-61372-237-4

To the friends, new and old, who have stuck by me, family who have believed in me, and to my wonderful fan fiction readers who gave me the courage to do this.

Chapter 1

ONE... two... three, Police Constable James Heron counted the solemn, resonant chimes of the clock in the market square. He pulled out his pocket watch and adjusted its hands so that his timepiece read 3:00 a.m. exactly. Only six more hours until the end of his shift—and only one more night before he was back on days, at least for the next few months. Every constable who worked for Scotland Yard took his turn on the night shift, and every man hated it. The night shift was long, cold... lonely. *At least at three o'clock in the afternoon, there'd be people about,* James thought miserably as he walked the long, narrow corridor between the tenements of Buck's Row on aching feet—aching legs. At 3:00 a.m., his only companions were rats crawling up from the sewers to eat garbage off the streets.

It was easy to imagine how a madman had ripped his way through the back allies of Whitechapel last year, spreading a wave of terror and suspicion in his wake. *Jack the Ripper.* Just thinking his name caused gooseflesh to rise on James's arms. He was new to Scotland Yard back then and hadn't been much involved in the case. Even so, the young constable continued to see boogeymen crouching in every shadow and lurking in every alleyway. There were other murders, of course, London was full of lunatics and cutthroats, but there was something inhumanly grizzly about the Ripper killings that stuck with James—with everyone who lived and worked in Whitechapel.

So far in his tenure as a constable, the worst James had dealt with were drunkards and petty thieves. He was just as glad; he was a slender man and had only just made the Yard's height requirement of five feet, seven inches tall. He doubted he would be much good against the kind of man—monster—he imagined someone like Jack the Ripper must be. Worse still, James had the sort of face people described as "sweet" or "innocent"—not exactly the sort of face that instilled people with confidence or made them take him seriously as an authority figure.

He peeled his helmet from his head and ran a hand through short wheat-colored hair.

"Evening, Constable," came a saucy greeting from the shadows. The boy laughed when James jumped. "You'll ne'er be making that promotion, acting like a scared cat every time somebody says 'boo'." The lilting Irish voice belonged to a slender young man with generous golden-red curls, bright green eyes, and the face of an angel—although as usual, his expression was more puckish than angelic. Either way, he was beautiful. He pushed himself off the wall he'd been leaning on and sauntered further into the amber halo of the gas streetlamp. "Feeling lonely tonight, Sir?" he asked, gazing up at James through half-lidded eyes.

James's cock stiffened in response to the younger man's sultry tone. He cleared his throat. "Isn't it a little late to be soliciting, Rob?"

The other's smile was bright. "Best time, this. Get 'em stumbling home drunk from the pubs or heading off early to work. Or walking a beat." He leaned in closer.

"How about I just buy you something to eat, instead?"

"Whatever you want to call it is fine by me," Rob all but purred.

Ignoring the obvious invitation, James got his purse out of his pocket and handed over a couple of coins. "Get off the streets for a few hours, Robin. It's not safe out here, this time of night."

Rob pressed in close, patently ignoring the mixture of irritation and concern in James's voice. "I prefer to *earn* me wage, Constable. You'd prolly prefer it too." He ran a feather light touch over the growing bulge between James's legs. "Ya canna' deny ya didna like it last time, can ya?"

James faltered. He'd spent nine months trying to forget the one and only time he'd had congress with the other man… boy… teen. He'd never sussed out exactly how old Robin Perris was, or even if "Robin Perris" was his real name. "That wasn't business," said James—he wasn't sure which of them he was trying to convince. The fact that he hadn't paid Robin for his services before only made James feel worse about the encounter. Rob had offered his friendship, and in return, James took advantage of him.

Robin reached out and curled James's fingers over his palm, closing the constable's hand on the coins he was offering. "So keep yer money, James." His tone lost all lasciviousness. "It weren't your coin I was after, anyway. Let me take your mind off your sore feet for an hour. No one will know. I *want* to, James."

James remembered the way Robin had looked so beautiful, lying underneath him, a halo of ginger curls splayed across the pillow as the young man panted and moaned, begging for more. It seemed the harder James took him, the more Rob wanted. But that was just a harlot's stock in trade doing the talking—wasn't it? James shook his head. It didn't matter. "I can't. I'm on duty." He forced the money into Robin's hand. "Rent a room, and get some sleep."

"No rest for the wicked, James," Rob answered, pocketing the coins.

A gust of cold wind came up from behind them, carrying with it the foul stench of the Thames. "I have to be on my way, Rob. Be safe." *Please.*

"Always am, Constable." With a sassy wink, the redhead strolled off into the darkness. It seemed to swallow him up whole.

James shivered and headed in the opposite direction.

ALUN BLAYNEY shot a jaunty grin over his shoulder as he exited the Frying Pan pub. Several of the men he'd been playing cards with were already slumped over their table, snoring off the effects of cheap whiskey and gin. They were all human. Alun wasn't, not that his companions had any idea they'd spent the better part of the night being hustled by a werewolf. Lycanthropes metabolized alcohol faster than humans, but Alun knew how to play the part of the drunkard when he wanted to. Humans got stupid when they drank too much, and when they got stupid, they bet more than they should and stayed in the game too long. Invariably, that meant Alun left the game with a heavier purse than he'd come into it with.

Dropping the ruse, Alun slipped out into the night. He was glad to be away from the pub's stench—stale food, sour ale, and human sweat. Even if the streets smelled no better, at least they weren't crowded.

Alun was tall and broad shouldered. He had a lean, hard build, tawny complexion, and coarse, dark hair that he wore longer than was considered fashionable. He doubted his rugged, angular features were anybody's idea of handsome, either, not that it mattered. He preferred his companionship rented by the hour—but not tonight. Tonight, he had enough money in his purse to rent a room for a week and was looking forward to sleeping on a soft mattress, not sharing it with anyone. Alun picked up his pace; he would have to hurry if he wanted to get to his favorite doss house before the landlord closed up for the night.

As he made his way through the narrow, nearly empty streets, Alun turned his face to the sky and sought out the thin sliver of the moon overhead. She was almost new—he'd been born under the New Moon, the Dark Moon. He snorted. Dark Moon born, during the dark of the year—no wonder he was an outcast.

Tonight, like most nights in the city, the moon was almost completely obscured by smoke spewing from the chimneypots. Still, knowing she was there brought him a measure of comfort, especially after having spent the last few hours in a cramped pub full of loud drunken humans. Like all lycanthropes, Alun considered the moon to be as much of a mother as the woman who had birthed him—perhaps more so, since his own mother wanted nothing to do with him. He hadn't seen her since he'd been banished from his birth pack's land, some twenty years ago.

But he'd made his choices, or so he liked to tell himself. There was no going back. He was *diangen*. Unwanted.

As Alun neared his destination, the streetlamps seemed to sputter, their gas-fueled flames flickering, creating only tiny pockets of faint orange light in the inky darkness. A sharp tingle hammered up Alun's spine. He stopped in his tracks, peering into the growing shadows, straining to hear anything that seemed out of the ordinary.

The only thing he heard was a rat scrounging through the garbage in the alleyway.

Alun chided himself. He had a purse full of other men's money, more money than he'd had in his possession in a long time, and it was making him jumpy.

The wind shifted then, filling his nostrils with the scent of fresh blood. Death. Something… familiar. Alun's gut churned; it was the heated, musky scent of another lycanthrope. He bolted toward the scent, dreading what he was sure he was going to find.

JAMES rounded the corner of Palmer Street and stopped dead in his tracks. Though the light coming from the streetlamps was faint, he could still make out the silhouette of a tall, broad-shouldered man crouching over a huddle of rags on the ground. His stomach wrenched. He knew without raising his lantern that the rags weren't rags at all. He couldn't make out whether the person sprawled limp on the cold ground was male or female, alive or dead, but his imagination immediately conjured up images of Robin lying there, lifeless.

The rational part of James's mind told him Rob had taken the money James gave him and rented a room for the night, but that didn't stop the wave of nausea from paralyzing the young constable for too many long moments. With trembling hands, James finally raised his whistle to his lips to sound the alarm, but before he got it to his mouth, he found himself slammed into the wall behind him. The force of the blow knocked the wind out of his lungs and made the world go momentarily black. By the time James's vision cleared, his assailant had pushed both his arms high up over his head. His grip was like iron! The more James struggled against the impossibly strong man, the higher his assailant pulled his wrists, until James was straining just to stand on his tiptoes. He was certain that in just a few seconds, he was going to be as dead as the person on the ground. Even if James cried out, the other man could—would—kill him long before help arrived.

"I ain't no killer," his attacker growled into the soft curve of his neck, his voice momentarily stilling James's hopeless wriggling. He was so close, James felt his rough lips brushing against his skin. The sensation sent shivers up and down James's spine and made his heart pound harder in his ears. "If I *were* a killer," the other man went on, in a low, husky tone, "you'd be *dead* by now."

James nodded, acknowledging the truth of his assailant's statement. "Who... who are you?" he stammered. He didn't think he sounded very authoritative and could well imagine Sir Robert Peel turning in his grave that one of his "bobbies" was so easily frightened by a common mug-hunter, a street thief. *Or maybe not so common*, he thought, grateful that the other had eased his grip just enough that he could get his footing.

"She's dead," was all his assailant had to say.

James let out the breath he didn't realize he'd been holding. If the dead person was a "she," a woman, it wasn't Rob, because even as flamboyant as Robin could be, there was no mistaking him for a girl. *But that poor woman is still somebody's daughter*, James reminded himself. *Somebody's sister. Maybe even somebody's mother.* "Who are you?" he asked again, his voice only slightly steadier this time.

The other man lifted his head, but James still couldn't make out his face in the shadows. "You can call me a concerned citizen," he retorted. "I was passing by, an' saw...." He shrugged. It was obvious what he'd seen. "Ain't nothing nobody can do for her now but give her a decent funeral."

"What about catching the man who killed her and bringing him to justice?" James challenged—which may have been a stupid move, he realized belatedly. Killer or not, the other man was taller than him by at least seven or eight inches and still had him pinned up against a wall. James was starting to lose feeling in his fingers.

As to his comment, the man merely snorted with unabashed amusement. "You do *that*, Constable, and they'll be making you head of the CID for sure."

James renewed his struggle more from frustration than fear or pain. He knew why the people in East End didn't trust the police, he didn't blame them, but *this* wasn't helping. He said as much aloud.

After a moment's consideration—and without a word of warning—James's assailant released his hold on his wrists. James stumbled forward, barely keeping himself upright as his full weight was returned to his feet. The other offered him no assistance.

"You know that assaulting a police constable is a crime," James pointed out irritably, after recovering his balance.

The man scoffed.

"You never said your name."

"Like I said," came the mocking reply, "you keep making observations like that, an' they'll be promoting you in no time."

With a resigned sigh, James knelt on the cobblestones. He didn't remember dropping either his whistle or his lantern in the "skirmish"—or maybe ambush was more like it—but he found them on the ground nearby. His whistle was fine, but the glass of his lantern had broken when it fell. A sudden flare of orange light filled the shadows, startling James; he turned to see that his assailant had struck a match.

"Thank you," he managed, as the tall man knelt next to him, carefully re-igniting the lantern's wick.

The other shrugged. "Ain't nothing."

In the flickering light, James finally got a good look at his assailant. It was difficult to gauge his years—people who lived in the East End aged fast—but he didn't look more than thirty. His features were rough hewn but not unpleasant, though his dark hair was a bit shaggy. Long bangs half-hid intense, blacker-than-night eyes that were surrounded by dense lashes. James felt his pulse quickening again as those dark eyes scanned his face. He licked his lips and swallowed hard.

"She's been cut up pretty bad," said the man, his gruff voice bringing James back to the gruesome scene before him.

"Yeah," he muttered, half under his breath. Reluctantly, James got to his feet and realized that only dumb luck had prevented him from stepping in the shallow pool of blood on the cobblestones. His stomach churned; he ignored it.

James turned his lantern's spotlight toward the dead woman's face. She was young and had probably been pretty. Her eyes were still open, her mouth, too, as if it was frozen in a scream that no one seemed to have heard. Her throat was slashed wide open. *What sort of a monster…?* But he wasn't sure he wanted an answer to that question. Her skirts had been hiked up indecently around her waist, and she was wearing neither shoes nor stockings. Acid burned at the back of his throat. Where the woman's belly should have been, there was only a gaping red hole.

Only the gentle touch of the other man's hand on his back kept James from throwing up; he turned away from the woman's body toward his… it didn't seem fair to call the other man his attacker any more. He wasn't sure what to call him.

"Never seen a corpse close up, have you, then?" the stranger asked in a far kinder tone than James would have expected.

Unable to speak past the lump in his throat, the young constable shook his head. Nodded. Eventually found his voice. "I've seen plenty of corpses, just none… none like this. I… I was on patrol down here last year, but I never saw for myself what he did to them." He might as well say aloud what he was sure they were both thinking. The dead woman's injuries bore an eerie resemblance to those inflicted on half a dozen harlots last year by a man known only as Jack the Ripper.

Was it possible? Was the Ripper back?

"Got yer flask on you?"

James blinked up at the other man. "What?"

"Be a good time for a nip."

"I'm on duty."

"You're kidding."

James shook his head. He swallowed back another mouthful of bile and squared his shoulders. Like it or not, he had a job to do.

ALUN watched the young constable with interest, lingering at the scene only—he told himself—because he was sure a lycan had killed the dead woman. That meant sooner or later the leader of the London wolf pack was going to come down on him, just like he had last year. Not that Alun had had anything to do with those murders; he didn't think any lycan was responsible for the Ripper killings. *It was prolly just an ordinary man*, he thought bitterly. Humans were more capable of atrocities toward their own kind than any other species he'd ever encountered—but that hadn't stopped the pack leader from blaming him for killing those girls. After all, he was *diangen*, an outcast, exiled from his birth pack by his own father, and just like humans, wolves looked first to their outcasts when they needed somebody to blame for the evils of the world.

Alun fished the nearly empty packet of cigarettes out of his coat pocket and lit one up. The bittersweet tang of burning tobacco was a welcome relief from the stench of the city, of blood, and of death.

A few yards away, the bobby got out his notepad and began scribbling things down. He was so engrossed in his work that he almost forgot to blow his whistle to summon assistance.

Alun slunk further into the shadows when two more constables arrived several minutes later, on hurried feet. One of them—a boy who hardly looked old enough to shave—threw up as soon as he saw the body. The other, an older man who reeked of gin, told the boy to pull himself together and go fetch the coroner. The boy looked more than a little grateful to have an excuse to escape. He ran swiftly from the alley, pushing his way past a knot of gawkers that had begun assembling, alerted by the bobby's whistle, curious to see what was happening.

The older constable turned his attention—his ire—on the younger man. "What're you doing there?" he demanded, his tone scathing. "Making notes like you're some kinda inspector? Gorblimey, Heron! Best put that away b'fore the *real* inspector gets here!"

Color blossomed in the young bobby's face, and he stuffed his notebook back into his pocket. Alun heard his heart rate quicken as he started to stammer what might have been an apology to the older man.

The other constable ignored it. "Do something useful with yourself for a change, and get ridda that rabble." He waved his hand toward the entrance of the alleyway.

Alun felt his hackles rise as a low growl rumbled in the back of his throat. He didn't understand his agitation, but found himself gazing after his young bobby, following the young man's movements intently. *Heron.* His name was Heron. It suited him.

Heron was slim and graceful, not tall, but hardly short, either. Although he couldn't see his bobby's eyes from this distance, Alun remembered them; they were the color of a storm-gripped sea, and he smelled of sweet musk and damp earth… green grass. It reminded Alun of his home—the home of his birth, in Wales. He closed his eyes, and for a moment, he could almost see the farm where he'd grown up, almost hear his mother's laugh, almost taste the fresh air.

He opened his eyes. There was little point in dwelling on a place he could never return to. He pitched his half-spent cigarette to the ground. Like it or not, London was his home now.

The sound of an approaching single-horse carriage drew Alun's attention back to the alleyway's entrance. Gawkers were still milling about, despite the constable's best efforts.

Heron.

Alun was barely aware of the smile tugging at the corners of his mouth.

The carriage came clattering to a halt, and both passengers hopped out. One was the young constable who had been sent to fetch the coroner;

the second, Alun presumed, must be the surgeon himself. He was a portly little man, much shorter than average, with full, white mutton-chop side burns—and he seemed in a foul mood. "I don't know why you boys were in such an all-fired hurry to get me out of bed! There's not a goddamn thing I can do in the dark!" he shouted, by way of greeting.

"But look at her, Doc," pleaded the older constable, the one who had ordered the surly little man to be summoned. "She's just like those girls from last year. The Ripper—"

The little man snorted. "Never assume anything, Waverly."

"But—"

"Listen to the doctor's advice, Waverly," said a new voice.

Alun's hackles rose again, and he turned. The speaker was easily as tall as he and had a strong build; he smelled of cigars and bourbon. A huge handlebar mustache dominated his hard face, and humorless dark eyes peered out from underneath the brim of his derby.

He strode toward the dead woman's body without reservation. "Gentlemen, let's get a little more light over here, shall we?" he said over his shoulder. He frowned when his gaze settled on Heron and his broken lantern. "What the hell happened to your torch?"

Shite! Alun suddenly regretted his decision to stick around. Assaulting a constable was indeed a crime, and as soon as Heron told them what had happened…. Alun surveyed the alley, hoping for a way out, but there was no easy escape. He edged further into the shadows.

"I… erm… I guess must've dropped it, Inspector Lamont," Heron stammered in reply to the angry question.

The inspector's eyes narrowed. "Either you dropped your torch or you didn't! There's no *guesswork* involved."

Heat rose in the young blond's face. "I dropped it, Sir," he answered meekly.

The other two constables snickered.

Alun's lip curled back, but he held himself in check, kept his silence in the shadows. Police Constable Heron should be the *last* of his concerns. So Alun just watched as Lamont spent the next ten minutes berating the blond for his negligence. "I hope you realize the cost of replacing it will come out of your wages!" he finished with a snarl. Then he turned on the other two constables, who were clearly enjoying the show. "Stop twittering about like a pair of ruddy schoolgirls and give me some light over here!"

With frustration burning in his cheeks, Heron sagged against the wall near Alun, bringing with him the scent of sweet musk and green earth. He peeled his helmet off his head and ran one hand through sweat-sopped ash-blond hair, not seeming to notice how close he was to the other man.

"He's a real arse," Alun murmured quietly, not wanting to startle him. He held out his pack of cigarettes.

"No, thank you. And yes, he is, isn't he?"

Alun shook his head. "You don't smoke, either?"

Heron chuckled wryly. "Yup, pinnacle of virtue, that's me."

The sarcasm in his tone made Alun smile. "Thanks, by the way. I owe you."

"For what?"

"Not mentioning the circumstances under what you come to drop your torch."

The constable shrugged. "He'd still tell me I had to pay for it. No point in making trouble for you too." He settled the heavy helmet back onto his head and pushed himself off the wall.

"Why don't you let me buy you a drink—or a cuppa tea?" Alun suggested impulsively. It seemed the least he could offer; Heron could have caused him a lot of trouble if he'd wanted to. Alun wasn't sure why he hadn't. "There's prolly a couple of early houses opening up. You must be entitled to a tea break, 'specially after something like this." He nodded toward where the inspector was still trying to get more light on the dead woman's body.

Heron regarded him a moment. "If I say 'yes', will you tell me your name?"

Alun gave over a wry smile. "Alun Blayney." He held out his hand. "You?"

"James Heron." Heron accepted it—and hissed loudly in pain when Alun's fingers clenched tightly over the raw skin on the back of his hand.

The lycan winced too; it was his fault. If he hadn't been so rough... he shook himself. Why should he care about a human, even one with eyes like those, one who smelled of green grass and sweet earth? "Sorry," he apologized anyway.

Heron shrugged it off, but the little coroner had spotted them and made his way over. He examined Heron's injuries with a critical eye and informed the inspector that he was sending James home for the night—and no, he wasn't going to listen to any of the inspector's protests, the boy's health came first. He wasn't listening to Heron's protests, either.

"It's been a harrowing morning," the surgeon said to James. "Why don't you save yourself the walk and take my carriage? I'll send Mr. Collier out this afternoon to fetch it—heaven knows he could use the exercise. I can catch a lift to the mortuary with our poor, unfortunate lady over there. I'm sure she won't mind sharing," he added with a smile.

"That's really all right, Dr. Stodderley," said Heron, still trying to argue.

"You're quite right, my boy, it is." He turned to Alun. "You'll see he gets home safe and sound, won't you?"

The lycan balked. But how far could Heron live from Whitechapel? Besides, it was already too late to get to a doss house, so he might as well see the younger man home before he went to find a place to curl up and sleep for a while. He could always rent a room tomorrow.

Chapter 2

THE drive was taken mostly in silence, but for Alun's part, he found the quiet between them comfortable. He was fairly certain Heron did too. The younger man didn't press him for personal information or, worse yet, try to make small talk.

Alun only began to feel uneasy as the constable drove them further and further west; the streets grew wider, straighter. They even seemed to be cleaner. At length, Heron halted the borrowed carriage in front of one of the red brick townhouses that lined a wide, straight road. "You rent a room *here*?" Alun wondered aloud. Heron hadn't driven them clear into the West End, but they were a long way from the narrow streets and overcrowded slums of Whitechapel.

Instead of answering his question, the constable asked Alun if he'd care to come inside. "We could have that cup of tea," he offered hopefully.

"I'd hardly want to intrude on your landlord," Alun told him. All of the houses on the block were surrounded by tidy, fenced-in front yards and had flowerpots and window boxes making them look cheerful and inviting—unless of course one didn't belong there. Alun didn't have any business in a place like this.

Heron shot him a wry smile. "No worries there, Mr. Blayney. It's the landlord that's invited you. If he had a problem with your being here, I'm sure he would've said so by now."

Alun blinked. "You... *own*...?" He looked at the house again. He didn't know how much a constable earned in a year, but it surely wasn't enough to keep a place this size in coke and firewood. There must be at least three bedrooms, maybe four.... He cleared his throat. "I'd hardly like to barge in on your family, then," he said sensibly.

The constable's face clouded over, his smile faltering. "No worries there, either. I have little family of which to speak, and none of them live in London."

The sadness of his tone tugged at Alun's heart. He knew all too well what it felt like not to have a family—not to have anyone. "I... I s'pose a cuppa tea wouldn't hurt nobody," he said slowly. Cautiously. "As long as you're sure it ain't no inconvenience."

"None at all." The constable's smile turned to pure sunshine again. Without waiting for further discussion, James hopped out of the carriage and secured the reins to the post at the curb. He patted the horse's cheek and promised her that someone called Davida would be along shortly with a bucket of water and some carrots. "And I'm sure Mr. Collier won't be long to come and fetch you home," he crooned. "Then Mrs. Stodderley can spoil you properly."

In response, the horse bobbed her head, snorting as if in agreement. Both men laughed.

"You've quite a way with animals," Alun observed.

"It's not hard to get on with Nell, here." James gave the mare's ears a final scratch and turned toward the house. He opened the low iron gate and gestured for his guest to precede him up the walk.

Alun noticed at once that there were no weeds growing in between the stepping stones, and it looked as if the porch steps had been recently scrubbed clean. He fidgeted with his dirty shirt cuffs and adjusted his collar, buttoning up the top two buttons to make himself look more presentable. Before they got even halfway up the walk, the front door swung open, and a thin elderly woman stepped out onto the porch. She wore a long, white, starched apron and a black high-collared dress; a dark scowl was etched across her unforgiving face, making Alun wonder if Heron had led them to the wrong house.

Undeterred, the younger man stepped in front of his guest and removed his helmet before addressing the tiny woman. "Good morning, Mrs. Dunberry."

"You're home early." It sounded more like an admonishment than an observation. "And not alone, I see." Her gaze raked over Alun, making him feel more out of place than ever.

"Good morrow, Missus," he said in his best imitation of courtesy.

The lady continued to scowl—then her gaze settled on James's bandaged hands. "What've you done to yourself?" she wanted to know.

"Hm? Oh, nothing. Just a bit of a scrape," he lied easily.

Mrs. Dunberry's expression gave Alun the impression she knew she was being lied to, but she didn't press the issue. "Come along inside, and I'll fix your breakfast."

Alun hesitated; it didn't sound as if the invitation included him, never mind that it was James's home, which could only mean that Mrs. Dunberry worked for him. But how did a lowly police constable afford a housekeeper?

"You don't have to go through any special trouble," said James.

Her scowl deepened. "Nonsense. Get cleaned up, and I'll see you get a proper meal, the pair of you. There's hot water on the stove for washing," she added, casting an equally disapproving look at both of them.

"You really don't have to—" James began to protest.

Alun laid a hand on the smaller man's arm to still his tongue. It wasn't an argument he was going to win. James seemed to realize it too.

He flashed a bright smile up at Alun. "Well, Mr. Blayney, after you, then." He gestured for his guest to go inside.

For just a moment, Alun smiled too.

He made his way up the porch steps and entered the front hall. He imagined it was supposed to be welcoming, brightly lit by the morning sun, with polished wood and gleaming brass everywhere—there was even a bouquet of fresh gladiola sitting on a small marble table, next to a wide, curving staircase. But it wasn't welcoming to someone like Alun. He belonged *there* even less than he belonged in the foul, overcrowded streets of London's East End. More than ever, he missed the mossy green smell of the woods, the damp earth under his paws. His whole body ached with deep longing for the home he knew he would never see again, and he didn't understand it. He hardly ever thought of home, his birth pack. There was just no sense in pining for what was lost.

Alun gave himself a good mental shake and turned to face his host. "You... you have a lovely home, Heron. *Mr.* Heron," he corrected himself, red-faced.

"Thank you, Mr. Blayney. I... it's comfortable." James's smile seemed tight. Forced. "Why don't we go to the kitchen and wash up?" He nodded toward a door at the end of the long, wide hall.

Mrs. Dunberry was already halfway there, so Alun followed after her, uneasiness tightening in his gut. He wasn't a charity case; he had money in his purse. Hell, he'd offered to buy Heron a drink—at least a cup of tea! He glanced over his shoulder at the blond, intending to find some polite way to excuse himself from the man's home, but the half-formed words died in his throat when he met Heron's mossy-green eyes. He didn't belong there, but he wanted to stay. Besides, only a fool turned down a free meal.

When they got to the end of the hall, James reached around his guest and opened the door for him; the room beyond was warm and bright, done up in cheerful shades of yellow and cream. Sunlight filtered in through a bank of tall windows along one wall, and on another, there stood a small black cooking range and a worn wooden table with two chairs. A narrow stairway led up to the second story—it was probably meant for the servants. Through the windows, Alun spied a small garden with late vegetables still on the vine, though he didn't know if it was unusual or not for upper-class folk to have gardens. The few West Enders he'd had the misfortune of meeting certainly didn't like getting their hands dirty. Maybe Heron had a gardener.

"I'm afraid the house is pretty old." James's voice cut through the lycan's thoughts. "We lack a good many modern amenities, hot running water being one of them." His apologetic tone seemed to vex Mrs. Dunberry. James ignored her scowl. Alun got the feeling she scowled a lot.

Alun wondered if the age of the house was the reason the kitchen was on the main floor; in most homes, proper houses like this, the kitchen and scullery were in the basement, though Alun didn't know why. The cottage he'd grown up in certainly hadn't needed a basement to hide the place where meals were prepared. Of course, his family hadn't employed servants. The well-to-do seemed to like to keep their "menials" out of sight and out of mind.

Heron used a towel to pluck the bowl of steaming hot water off the back of the range and set it on the table. "Here we go," he said over his shoulder to his guest.

Alun smiled his thanks and rolled up his sleeves. He was aware of how unkempt he must look to these people. Rich people, people who lived in nice houses and had servants, looked down on people like him—poor men, East Enders—thinking they were stupid, slovenly. Thought they didn't care enough to keep themselves clean. But how could anyone keep themselves clean when even the drinking water was filthy?

Alun accepted the slip of soap from his host's outstretched hand without looking at him, and dipped his hands into the hot water. Regardless of what anyone thought, he hated being coated in grime from the streets and soot from the chimneypots and was glad of the opportunity to rid himself of some of it.

Suddenly, a heated, primal scent hit Alun hard, making him feel like he'd been punched in his gut. He steadied himself. The scent was... it was like sweet grass that had caught fire. It was heat and smoke and... James Heron? He sniffed again, recognizing the constable's scent, only... stronger.

Alun turned to see that the younger man had removed the heavy blue coat of his uniform and was standing next to him, wearing only his trousers, braces, and a thin cotton shirt. The top three buttons were undone, revealing a patch of soft blond curls. Alun averted his gaze quickly. Just as quickly, he looked up again, carefully hiding his wanton stare behind long bangs. Heron's chest was lean and muscular, tapering into a trim waist.

Alun's tongue darted to his lips as James unbuttoned his shirt further, revealing hardened, dark pink nipples. The patch of fine golden hair on his chest became a thin trail leading down his stomach and vanishing into the top of his trousers. Alun's cock twitched as he imagined it ending in a soft nest of curls surrounding the younger man's sex—as he wondered what it would feel like to bury his nose into those soft curls and inhale the scent of heat and smoke at its source. He watched with growing hunger as Heron sluiced water over his chest, his pink nipples becoming harder—

"Oh for pity's sake!" Mrs. Dunberry shrieked. She'd just come from the larder, and her arms were loaded down with food.

Alun jumped at the sound of her voice, his mind racing as fast as his heart, scrambling to come up with an explanation for the huge bulge in his trousers.

"Master James!" she continued, not looking at their guest at all. "Dress yourself this instant!"

To Alun's surprise, James laughed—he had a fearless laugh, the kind the lycan envied. "It's only you and Mr. Blayney," he protested, assisting Mrs. Dunberry with her burden—she had enough food to feed a small army. "I'm sure *he* knows what a man looks like, and you," he cupped her cheek with one hand and pulled her forward, pressing an irreverently familiar kiss to her forehead. "*You* helped me in and out of the bath a thousand times when I was a boy, or so you're wont to remind me at every turn. Mrs. Dunberry practically raised me," he explained to his guest.

Alun felt certain his face was as red as the peppers James was setting down on the countertop. "Then perhaps you'd best button up your shirt in due consideration of the good lady's sensibilities," the lycan heard himself saying, although the last thing he wanted was for James to cover himself back up; he could look at his chest all day and never get tired of it. *Then again, maybe it'd be for the best he does cover up*, he decided. If the other man remained in his current state of undress, Alun was sure he would have to sit with a pillow over his lap throughout breakfast, and how in the world would he explain that?

"For you then, Mr. Blayney, not her," James quipped over his shoulder.

"Not out of a sense of propriety?" Mrs. Dunberry challenged him.

"Never that." He pressed another kiss to her forehead before making his exit up the back stairs, promising he wouldn't be long.

"I swear, that boy's going to be the death of me," Mrs. Dunberry muttered after him. Her expression was soft. Affectionate. It hardened again the instant she turned back to Alun. "He's a good man, you know," she said sharply.

"Yes, Missus," he agreed in a subdued tone, hoping she hadn't noticed the way his trousers were stretched taut between his legs. The smile that had formed on his lips over the playful exchange between James and Mrs. Dunberry was gone.

"Good men are easily taken advantage of," she went on, her tone still brusque. She began chopping vegetables with a long, sharp knife from the cutting board. "I'll be keeping my eyes on you, Mr. Blayney, and this house while you're in it."

Alun didn't respond; he doubted he was going to be there long enough for it to matter.

JAMES surveyed the crisp cotton shirts hanging in his wardrobe. It wasn't that he had so many to choose from that he didn't know what to wear—though he did have an extensive wardrobe—but rather, a rare streak of vanity was rearing its ugly head, making him indecisive. Something casual, certainly, to keep his guest at ease, because he'd seen the discomfort that had come over Mr. Blayney when they got inside the house. He knew he might be making a grave mistake in offering a man like Blayney hospitality in his home; for all he knew, the man really had killed that girl…. *But if he had, I would be dead too.* It was a sobering thought. He'd never been so close to death before, not like that, not his own. Or what *would* have been his death, if Blayney were really a killer. But something in James told him he wasn't.

At length, he selected a light blue shirt out of his wardrobe. His mother had always liked him in blue, particularly that shade of it; she said it brought out the green in his eyes. He smiled, remembering her; her eyes had been the same color as his. Or maybe it was fairer to say his eyes were the same color as hers. He doubted it mattered.

James paired the shirt with plaid wool trousers and a dark blue waistcoat. He would forgo a jacket, however, no matter how much his housekeeper was sure to object. It seemed silly to dress so formally knowing he would be going to bed within the hour.

His stomach growled loudly, as if to inform him he wasn't doing anything before he ate something.

That came as a sobering thought, too, as James wondered how long it had been since Mr. Blayney enjoyed a proper meal—a proper bed. The dark East Ender had offered to buy him a cup of tea earlier, but he hardly looked like a man of comfortable means. Maybe, James thought, he should invite his guest to stay the day, get some sleep. He must be exhausted, and he had been kind enough to see him safely home.

His mind made up, James dressed quickly and headed back downstairs, hoping Mrs. Dunberry hadn't run the poor man off.

Chapter 3

ALUN was relieved when his host insisted that, as it was only the two of
them, it would be silly to eat in the formal dining room. A meal taken in
the kitchen was informal, comfortable—relaxed. When the lycan thought
of formal dining rooms, his imagination conjured images of crystal goblets
and dozens of forks lined up alongside delicate china. Thankfully, Mrs.
Dunberry set the kitchen table with very ordinary-looking silver—only
one fork at each place setting—and simple earthenware plates and cups.

"Don't pay Mrs. Dunberry any mind," James said to him, after she'd
served their breakfast and taken her leave. "She's really not as awful as
I'm sure she must seem."

"I…." A rush of heat overtook Alun's cheeks.

Heron merely chuckled. "She puts everybody off, Mr. Blayney,
including the late Mr. Dunberry—while he was alive, I mean. Here." He
passed over the platter of fat venison sausages laid out on a bed of red
peppers and sweet onions. Alun couldn't remember the last time he'd been
presented with anything that smelled or looked so sumptuous. In his
childhood, perhaps. His mother's table had never been so lavish as all this,
but there had always been meat. Mutton, beef, pork—sometimes venison.
In the city, meat was an expensive commodity, yet it was something every
fully grown lycanthrope needed a steady diet of. But the only meat he
could hunt for himself were rats, and while they weren't in short supply,
they were hardly appetizing. The occasional meat-filled pastry he bought
from street vendors didn't provide nearly enough sustenance for a lycan—
and they weren't much more appealing than rodents he could catch for
himself.

"Help yourself," said James, pulling his guest up from his thoughts
with a heartening smile. "Please," he encouraged, when Alun continued to
hesitate.

Alun cleared his throat and took the platter from his host's hands. Usually when a person was nice to someone like him, it came with a price—but what could Heron want from him? He had... damn, he had everything a man could want. "Thank you." He managed to at least remember his manners as he slid the two smallest sausages onto his plate, along with a few slices of pepper. He wasn't particularly fond of peppers, but he didn't want to seem rude.

"You have to take more than that," James told him. "Mrs. Dunberry is going to expect all of this gone by the time she comes back, and I can't eat the rest of it all by myself. Please, have some more."

"I—"

Heron's smile broadened. "It really is your duty as a good guest to help me empty these plates, Mr. Blayney. I swear, there'll be bloody hell to pay if every platter isn't empty when she returns. And don't think for a moment that she'll go easier on me just because I pay her wage."

Alun couldn't help but chuckle at his tone; Heron almost sounded frightened. Then again, he had no trouble envisioning Mrs. Dunberry having a go at James—and probably him as well, as if they were little more than a pair of errant children—if the plates weren't emptied to her satisfaction. "I suppose I owe it to you to at least try," he agreed sheepishly, taking two more sausages from the platter.

James handed him the eggs and then the bread, insisting that he take as much as he liked.

"So... where in Wales are you from?" James asked, as they dug into the meal.

Alun blinked. How had Heron known—?

"Your accent," he explained.

Of course. "It ain't nowhere you ever heard of, I'm sure," he retorted gruffly. As if being an urchin from the slums of the East End wasn't bad enough, he was Welsh too. The English looked down on... well, they looked down on everybody, but no one more so than their closest neighbors.

James swallowed hard, looking uncomfortable. "I'm sorry, I just... was curious. We don't have to talk about anything you don't wish to." His tone was nothing but sincere, apologetic.

It made Alun regret snapping at him. "I grew up on a farm in southern Wales," he said, less gruffly. "It weren't no place special—no place you'd wanna hear 'bout."

"Everyplace is special to the people who live there," countered James.

Alun shot him a quizzical look. It wasn't the sort of answer he'd have expected from a man like Heron, but there was nothing patronizing in the constable's tone. There was nothing patronizing in his expression either. Alun's expression softened. "It weren't much, jus' this tiny little parcel of land, but it was ours, so I guess... I guess that made it special," he admitted.

"What kind of farm was it? I mean... did you raise or grow anything in particular?"

"Sheep, mostly. An' we had a cow of course, an' a small garden, just enough for us—though there were a lot of us." His smile became genuine. He hadn't spoken of his family in longer than he could remember. "It was me an' six brothers. One sister. And my *taid*—my grandfather, my mam's tad——lived up the road a ways. He was always at our place, though." More than anyone else, he missed his grandfather.

"I was close to my grandfather too," said James, seeming to pick up on a measure of his guest's thoughts. "I miss him. When he retired from medicine, he went back to Northumberland. That's where I grew up, mostly, but I came back to London when I was fifteen. This was his house."

"Do you get to see him much?"

"Not as often as I should. He doesn't like to travel, his arthritis is pretty bad, and I... I guess I keep making excuses not to visit. I'm not on the best of terms with the rest of my family."

"You shouldn't let that stop you." Alun cleared his throat. It wasn't his place to give advice to a man like Heron. "I... I'm sorry, I shouldn't presume...."

James waved it off. "I miss being out in the country. The city is so... stifling. You must hate it. Having grown up on a farm, I mean." He seemed a little uncomfortable too. "I suppose you're not the only one being presumptuous," he apologized.

Alun's chuckle broke the tension. "I think more than anything else, I miss having fresh fruit in summer. Nothing beats the taste of plums straight off the branches of the tree. I used to spend hours up in those trees, seeing how high I could climb, eating plums as I went. Mind, I was only a wee lad, so the trees prolly seemed higher up than they really were."

James laughed with him. "My weakness was strawberries. My brother and I used to stuff ourselves silly every June... but that was a long time ago." His smile tightened. Alun didn't press him as to why; he just teased Heron about strawberries being safer than plums, seeing as they grew so close to the ground.

"We had this old oak tree, though," said James. "I used to think that if I could just climb high enough, I could touch the moon. One time, I got so high up in the stupid thing, my grandfather had to fetch the ladder and get me down. I was terrified. I never did touch the moon." He sighed wistfully at the childhood memory. "It's silly, the things we believe as children."

"My mam used to tell me it weren't never silly to believe in anything, no matter how impossible it seemed." He doubted, however, that his mother had suspected what he would grow up to be when she said that. She hadn't even *tried* to intervene on his behalf when his father threw him out of the house, their pack. He'd only been thirteen.

"She sounds like my mother," said James.

Alun hoped not. He was saved from having to respond by Mrs. Dunberry, as she came down the back stairs. She had changed into a handsome wool suit, making her look less like a servant, and more like the lady of the house. It didn't surprise Alun; he was certain she was more to her employer than a simple menial.

James rose politely to his feet as she descended into the kitchen. Alun stood up only a heartbeat after him, but he knew it must show that he wasn't much of a gentleman.

Whatever her thoughts were on the matter, Mrs. Dunberry kept them to herself. "You could take a lesson from him," she said to her employer, scrutinizing Alun's empty plate.

Heat flooded his cheeks, staining them deep red. He wasn't certain Mrs. Dunberry was actually paying him a compliment. Perhaps it was time to take his leave.

But James only laughed. "It's hardly my fault you cook like you're feeding the Royal Army, Mrs. Dunberry."

She wrinkled her nose, which only caused him to laugh harder.

James reached over and clapped a friendly hand on his guest's shoulder. "Mr. Blayney and I have made a valiant effort, good lady, but I fear we are stuffed to the gills. We surrender. We can eat no more."

She ignored his carrying on. "You mean *he* made a valiant effort. What *you* eat would hardly sustain a sparrow."

"Should I remind you that birds eat several times their body weight in seed each day?" James quipped back.

"Only if you wish me to 'forget' to purchase those dreadful sweets you like so much from the market."

"You're a cruel woman," James informed her, still grinning.

"So you say."

Some of the impishness faded from James's expression, then. "Why don't you let me get my coat and accompany you, Mrs. Dunberry—you wouldn't mind, would you, Mr. Blayney?" he asked of his guest. "You're welcome to remain here, take your rest."

Alun blinked, shocked by the invitation.

"Oh for pity's sake," Mrs. Dunberry protested. "I went to the market by myself yesterday morning, and the morning before that, and the morning before that as well. I'm perfectly able to do so again today. Sit yourself back down and finish your eggs. *Both* of you." She eyed James sharply.

Alun sat back down, though James remained standing. Alun reckoned he knew the real reason Mrs. Dunberry didn't want to leave him alone in the house, and he didn't blame her for fearing he would rob them—or worse. What did she know of him? *And if she did....* he nearly shuddered. Wolves and men were, by their very natures, enemies. The fact that James Heron didn't know what kind of monster he was didn't change anything.

Feeling less jocular, Alun waited in the kitchen while James walked Mrs. Dunberry to the front door. He didn't belong there. *But as long as I am here, I s'pose I can at least make myself useful*, he decided. He got back up and began clearing the table, removing the dishes to the sink in the scullery to be washed, though he figured there must be a maid somewhere in the house whose job it was to pick up after Heron.

He was surprised when the constable joined him a few minutes later, carrying a pot of hot water from the stove. Without a word, the younger man rolled up his sleeves and began scrubbing the heavy iron skillet that was already soaking in the sink. Alun made no attempt to keep his amazement from showing on his face. Well-to-do people didn't scrub pots and pans!

Heron flashed over a bright smile. "I've always thought it was rather silly for a grown man not to do his part in his own home."

"Wouldn't most folks say you going to work every day *is* doing your part? A constable's job ain't exactly easy."

James laughed, but it wasn't a cheerful sound. "I think we both know it isn't a constable's wage that keeps this place going."

"I wasn't gonna pry."

"My family is… comfortable," James told him anyway.

Unable to think of anything else to say, Alun rolled up his sleeves and sidled in next to him at the sink. Within minutes, the two men fell into easy rhythm with James washing and Alun drying, then setting the clean plates aside to be put away in the pantry when they were done.

"May… would you mind me asking you a personal question, Mr. Heron?" Alun began tentatively, after they'd finished.

"Only if you'll call me James."

"I'll be expecting you to call me Alun, then," he answered without thinking.

James flashed that sunshine smile again. "Fair enough. And by all means, ask whatever you like." He led the way back to the kitchen where he put the kettle onto the stove for more tea. James sat back down at the table; Alun sat next to him.

"It's hardly any of my business, but I was wondering how long it's been just you an' Mrs. Dunberry."

"My parents died when I was seven. My brother, Thomas, was twelve. Officially, we went to our grandfather's care, but he didn't think London was a healthy environment for a pair of growing boys, so he sent us to Northumberland and our Uncle John and Aunt Dora. Uncle John hired Mrs. Dunberry to look after Tom and I."

"How long's your brother been gone, then?" Alun asked quietly.

James looked away. "Fever took him nine months ago."

Alun reached out and laid his hand on the other man's arm; the pain of loss and death was something he knew all too well. "I'm sorry."

James shrugged but accepted the comfort, settling his hand on top of Alun's. The constable's hands were strong. Calloused. Warm.

"It's been harder on Anna, Tom's widow," James told him. "She was with child when he died. She gave birth to my nephew only a few weeks after we buried her husband. William Thomas. William was my father's name." A ghost of a smile teased at his lips again, and he tightened his grip on Alun's hand, lacing their fingers together. "Little William looks just like Tom."

"I…." He didn't know what to say, so he gave James's hand a gentle squeeze. His mouth was filled with cotton, his stomach crawling with ants. James met his gaze dead on, and the lycan's gut twisted with desire. "Where are they now—your sister-in-law and nephew?" he asked, trying to think about anything but the kiss he wanted so desperately to press to the younger man's mouth.

"Northumberland. My grandfather looks after them. I suppose my Uncle John does, too, after a fashion." His expression soured. "My Uncle and I have… differences," he explained. "It's better for everyone that I'm not there. They have everything they need."

Alun heard the words he didn't say: *They don't need me.* The unspoken statement struck a chord in the lycan's soul. *Diangen* meant unneeded—unwanted. He understood why *he* was unwanted, but how could anyone not want James?

Alun shook himself. Even if he could forget for the moment that James was a constable, and that all forms of contra-sexual pleasure were punishable by law—and never mind that the chances of James being inclined toward men were slim—James Heron was human. No human would ever be able to understand or reciprocate the bond lycans shared with each other. Humans and lycanthropes could couple, produce children… *be lovers*, Alun thought bitterly. He knew how humans treated their lovers.

"Are you all right?" The soft sound of James's voice drew him gently up from his unhappy thoughts. James was still holding his hand. He was sitting so close, Alun could feel his breath on his face.

"Yeah," he lied. He didn't feel James's trembling or see the look in his mossy-green eyes, a mirror of the wantonness in his own dark gaze. He was only aware of the ache in his soul and how badly he wanted to bury his nose against the younger man's neck and inhale his scent. He wanted to taste his skin, his mouth... his seed.

"Alun?"

"Sorry, I... I'm just tired, I reckon," he lied again. He pulled away before he did something they would both regret. Alun got to his feet, increasing the distance between himself and temptation, and took the boiling kettle from the stove, using a thick towel to shield his hand from the heat.

James got up too. He walked across the room to fetch a pair of clean cups from the pantry, then brought them and a little tin of assorted teabags over to the stove. Alun poured the water, falling once more into an easy rhythm with the younger man—James only hesitated a moment before choosing for both of them, dropping a small, white, hand-tied teabag into each cup.

The sweet-smelling stream filled Alun's nose. Rose... lavender... something green and mossy, just like the young blond standing next to him. He didn't realize that a smile had crept back onto his lips as he cradled the cup in his hands, gazing over the top of it at James.

"It's an old recipe of my mum's," James told him. "She always gave me a cup before bed. Said it would help me sleep." He leaned up again the counter, his own cup clasped in both hands. He shifted to rest his shoulder against Alun's.

Through the place where their arms were touching, the lycan swore he could feel both their hearts beating. He closed his eyes a moment and enjoyed the soft rhythm hammering between them. It was so easy standing next to James... too easy. "Do you think you'll catch whoever killed that woman?" he asked, needing something else to think about.

James shrugged, his shoulder rubbing against Alun's arm. "Maybe. Sometimes it feels like police work's nothing but hit and miss—and at that, mostly miss. The only way we ever seem to catch anybody is in the act." He sounded bitter. Angry.

"You been with the Yard long?"

"A little over a year."

Alun said nothing for a long while. He drank his tea. "Why'd you bring me back here, James?" he asked at last. "You don't know me from Adam."

"I suppose not."

"I could've killed that woman."

"But you didn't. I know you didn't."

"How? Because I *said* so?"

"Because you were right. If you were a killer, we wouldn't be standing here talking. Dr. Stodderley would be cleaning up my body too."

Alun didn't answer. He *was* a killer. He hadn't killed that woman, he'd had no cause to, but he knew death and pain from both sides. "You shouldn't be so trusting," he heard himself say. His tone was harsher than he meant it to be.

James didn't seem bothered by it. "I can't help it. I think it's my mum's fault." He blew across the top of his cup, cooling the hot tea, filling the air with more of the brew's sweet scent. "I don't remember her as much as I'd like, but she always found a way to see the best in everybody. I remember my father saying more than once that a less charitable woman wouldn't have given him the time of day, let alone married him. They were very much in love...." His voice trailed off. "Sometimes I'm not sure I'm remembering that right. They had every reason not to love each other, but I'm *sure* I've never seen any other couple so devoted to each other as I remember my parents being. I just don't understand it. They were so *different* from one another," he explained. "Father was a surgeon, and very rational man. My mum she... she was an artist, a poet, a musician. Anything *but* a rational thinker." He chuckled softly, seemingly half lost in his memories as he drank his tea. "She believed in fairies and dragons. Father didn't believe in anything he couldn't put under a microscope and examine. But they loved each other. I just don't know how."

"Love don't need explanations, it just... it is." Pain lanced across Alun's heart, but he ignored it. "It's as real as... as both fairies and things what you can put under a microscope." He laughed, just a little.

He was surprised when James didn't laugh. He looked him square in the eye instead. "Do you really believe that?"

"Aye. It's just not everybody gets to know what it feels like to love like that." His voice was barely a whisper. He cleared his throat. "I... I oughta be going. Thanks. For... for breakfast an'... an' the company. It ain't real often somebody like you takes half a minute with somebody... somebody so different." He shrugged, hoping the heat he felt in his cheeks wasn't visible to the other man.

"I meant my invitation, Alun. You're more than welcome to stay the day, get some sleep. You must be exhausted."

"I've intruded on your generosity more than enough already."

"You've not intruded at all."

Alun hesitated. He didn't feel as dead on his feet as the handsome young constable looked, but he *was* tired and he had promised himself a real bed... but....

"Please," James entreated. "It's hardly as if I lack the space. Finish your tea, and let me show you to one of the guestrooms."

Reluctantly, Alun agreed. It was a bed, nothing more. A chance to get some much-needed sleep.

WHEN James awoke at dusk, Mrs. Dunberry told him that Mr. Blayney had left already. She hadn't seen him go, and nothing appeared to be missing from the house. James decided not to tell her differently, even though something *was* missing.

Alun wasn't there.

Chapter 4

A SHAGGY black dire wolf sat, hidden from view, under an overhang next to the Thames River, watching the sun setting behind the Tower Bridge, thinking. Trying not to think. The last rays of the blazing sun cast an orange glow over the river, making the water look like it was on fire. Toward the eastern horizon, the sky was darkening, and the first stars were coming out. A cool breeze blew across the water, bringing with it the familiar stench of the city. Alun closed his eyes. His whole body trembled with the need to howl, to cry out in frustration and pain, to tell the night how lonely he was.

But he didn't dare.

He was *diangen*. He was forbidden to sing out to the night, to the moon—it was one of the many prohibitions the London pack's leader had imposed on him. As a full-blooded lycan, a dire wolf some three or four times larger than any timber wolf, Alun's howl was louder and deeper than an ordinary wolf's—an ordinary lycan's. Even city folk would know at once that there was something unnatural in their midst if they heard his cry.

But that wasn't the reason for the injunction.

Singing to the night was how wolves communicated with one another, not that any wolf wanted to sing with him. He hadn't shared his song with other wolves since he was a boy, a cub running and hunting on his birth pack's land. Land he would never see again. Land he thought he'd stopped missing decades ago. Then he met James Heron, and suddenly his soul was inflamed with need, with desire… with loneliness. He would never have James, not as a lover—not even as a friend. How could he? He was a cardsharper from the East End, and James was a wealthy man, handsome, and no doubt well educated.

Alun shook himself. It didn't matter.

His stomach rumbled, reminding him he would need to find food before he did anything else. He supposed he had enough money to buy himself a proper dinner—then he would rent a room for the rest of the week and try to forget having ever met James Heron.

ANY hospital mortuary could be used for police autopsies—or any number of other buildings, for that matter, including the deceased's own parlor—but James knew Andrew Stodderley preferred the facilities at St. Luke's, even over those at the modern and prestigious hospitals, like St. Thomas's. St. Luke's was smaller and served a less affluent community, but was near to where Dr. and Mrs. Stodderley lived—it was also where both James's father and grandfather had worked, so it was a place the young constable knew well.

James cleared his throat to announce his arrival in the large, well-lit room. Although the windows were open to let in the late summer breeze, the smell of putrefying flesh was strong, and James was content to linger at the doorway a moment longer, waiting to be invited in. He wore the same clothing he'd put on earlier that morning, with the addition of a dark blue jacket, white necktie and gloves, and a black bowler hat. Mrs. Dunberry never would have let him out of the house, otherwise.

On the other side of the room, Dr. Stodderley stood on a low stepstool beside the cold metal table. He appeared to have just begun his examination of the man lain out before him; even from the doorway, James could see that the dead man had found his way into the coroner's care after having drowned. He was bloated, and his skin was a disheartening shade of yellow-gray. It looked as if fish—or maybe rats—had been nibbling at the dead man's extremities. It made James glad he didn't work near the river. Too many bodies turned up there.

When it became obvious that Dr. Stodderley hadn't heard him the first time, James cleared his throat again, more loudly.

The little surgeon's head snapped up, but as soon as he saw who it was, his irritated scowl gave way to a broad, welcoming smile. "James! What a pleasant surprise, do come in!" he beckoned, a bloody scalpel still in his bare hand. "You're out and about early this evening," he observed. "Off the graveyard shift, I take it?"

James nodded. "I hope I'm not interrupting anything."

"Not at all, not at all. Although… if you could do me the kindness of taking notes while I work, I would much appreciate it. I fear Mr. Collier is still at his supper. Ever since taking up with that young lady of his, he's been dawdling more and more over his meals," he grumbled.

James bit back a snicker. He couldn't help envying Mr. Collier and his young lady. It had been a long time since he'd had someone to "dawdle with" over long suppers… breakfasts. Everything in between. His stomach fluttered, and color bloomed in his cheeks; he could scarcely wait to get back to Whitechapel. He was certain he'd never seen Alun Blayney before last night, but surely he wouldn't be that difficult to find again. James didn't know what he was going to say to him when he did… an invitation to supper, perhaps. He hoped that wouldn't seem too forward. Presumptuous. But he was quite certain he'd seen a telling bulge in Alun's trousers while they were washing up, and he doubted it had anything to do with Mrs. Dunberry. He'd so hoped Alun would still be there when he woke. If he had been…. James found himself staring at the cold gray floor between his shoes. He was blushing.

And Dr. Stodderley was still waiting patiently for an answer to his question. "It would be my pleasure to take notes for you," James told him.

Whatever the surgeon thought of his long lapse, he kept it to himself. "How are the hands, by the way?" was all he wanted to know.

"Healed over almost completely," James reported. When he'd taken the bandages off this evening, he'd been surprised to find his hands hadn't been injured nearly as badly as he'd thought, but it had been pretty dark in that alleyway. He found the doctor's assistant's notepad and took up a position on the other side of the body, where he would be out of the way but still able to see what Dr. Stodderley was doing. "Would you object if I ask you a few questions about the lady from last night?" he said.

"Not at all, my boy. I rather imagined that was the reason you were here. I just reckoned I'd get a bit of work out of you." He shot over a wink.

James snickered—he didn't really mind being put to work. As Dr. Stodderley spoke, he took notes; in between the doctor's dictations about the dead man, James asked his questions. He wanted to know how the woman had died. He wanted to know if the Ripper was really back, though he didn't say as much aloud.

"Perhaps you'd like to have a look for yourself," the older man suggested, stepping down from the stool. "I think I'm about ready for a cup of tea. Would you care to join me? After you've had a look at that girl from last night, of course."

"Would you mind?"

"What, buying you tea, or rewarding your patience by letting you see the poor girl for yourself?"

James flushed a deep shade of pink. He knew it wasn't his job to be poking around the mortuary looking at bodies, but he couldn't help his curiosity.

"Help yourself… ah, thank you," he said when James came around and handed him a towel for his hands. "Careful," he warned, as the younger man assisted him in removing the heavy leather apron he wore over his suit, to protect it from blood and other hazards of the job. "Your Mrs. Dunberry will have my hide if you come home a mess."

James chuckled. There was no arguing with that. He hung the apron up on its hook and turned back to the doctor.

"Go have your look." Stodderley nodded to the door leading to the storage room, where blocks of ice helped preserve the dead until the living were ready to bury them. "She's to your left, second shelf from the bottom. Poor dear, she'll probably appreciate the company."

"Hasn't anybody come to claim her?" James asked in surprise. He didn't remember much besides the blood, the slashed throat… the mutilation… but he seemed to recall that she was pretty. Young. Somebody should be missing her by now, surely.

"Not as yet. Though I can tell you she was no pauper."

"What do you mean?"

"She was in good health and had eaten a rather decent meal just before her unfortunate demise. Some sort of meat and a good helping of potatoes and bread. Not exactly the last supper of a common whore. That and her liver seemed in good shape. I can't say she'd never touched a drop, but she wasn't hitting the bottle on a regular basis, like Bob there." He nodded to the dead man on the table in the middle of the room.

"Bob?"

"What does one do when one is neither swimming nor sinking?"

James groaned.

The doctor grinned. "Without a bit of gallows humor, my boy, I fear I might go mad."

James left him to his washing up and stepped inside the chilly little room to examine the woman from last night. What he really found himself thinking about was the way Alun Blayney had so effortlessly pushed him up against the wall, pinning him there. The way the taller, stronger man had buried his nose in his hair, inhaling his scent, the way he'd growled into his ear and brushed his lips up against his neck. If he'd had the courage to, James could have turned his head and sealed his lips to Alun's then and there.

Heat overtook his cheeks—the morgue was hardly a place to be thinking about the kiss he wanted to give a total stranger.

James jumped when the door opened; it was Dr. Stodderley. If the surgeon noticed the pink tinge of his cheeks, he didn't comment. "Did you know, my boy, that Mr. Cook speculates there's a murder committed in London nearly every six minutes, most of them in this God forsaken hellhole?" he said.

James let out a low whistle. "I had no idea." He turned his attention to the young woman he was supposed to be here to see. The sight of her lying dead on the rack was more than enough to kill any lingering daydreams about kisses he wished he'd stolen in the dark. "She looks hardly twenty," he murmured, sobered by the thought.

"We won't know with any certainty how old she was until we can confirm her identity, and heaven knows how long *that* will take—but you're right, she seems too young to have ended up here," he agreed, his tone softening some.

James bent over for a closer look at the dead girl's wounds. Her throat was slashed, practically from ear to ear; the wound looked like a ragged, laughing mouth. James shivered. He turned to his friend. "Was she strangled?" he asked. The Ripper had strangled his victims, but this girl's neck was too badly mangled for him to really see whether or not it was bruised.

"You tell me. Look at her eyes."

Gently, and making every effort not to look at her throat, James lifted one of the girl's eyelids, then the other. Her eyes were hazel. They must have been stunning, when she was alive. Now they were just dull. However, "No spots," was all he said aloud. The whites of her eyes were clear, not bloodshot.

"And that means?"

"No broken blood vessels. She wasn't strangled."

"Excellent! Now, let's see about getting that tea, shall we?"

James agreed, although he was tempted to say he needed something stronger than tea. Even if the girl's murder wasn't the work of Jack the Ripper, there was still a madman loose on the streets, because surely this wasn't the work of any sane human being.

"Feeling better then, are you, Heron?" Inspector Franklin Lamont's voice rang out across the mortuary; his tone was scathing.

James didn't meet his gaze. "Some, Sir, thank you," he answered sheepishly. He folded his hands behind his back, not wanting the inspector to see that his hands were practically healed.

Lamont's gaze raked over him anyway. James shifted his weight from one foot to the other; the inspector's eyes narrowed as he took in the cut of James's suit.

"What can I do for you, Inspector Lamont?" Dr. Stodderley inquired sharply, coming in between the two men.

Lamont's lips twitched downward in a frown. "Have you finished with that bangtail, yet?" he wanted to know.

James opened his mouth—then shut it again. No matter how much he hated the term bangtail, there was no point in arguing with a man like Lamont.

"Enough to tell you her throat was slashed," said Dr. Stodderley, "and that her... how to put this delicately...?"

"Tools of the trade?" Lamont suggested.

The surgeon shrugged. "Her uterus was removed, presumably by someone who knew his way around the human body."

"So it's true. The Ripper—"

"I wouldn't go leaping to conclusions, Inspector," Stodderley cut him off. "There are a number of facts about the girl's murder which don't support that supposition. It's all in my report. I don't suppose you and your boys have had any luck discovering the poor girl's identity?" he asked, effectively changing the subject.

Lamont's expression softened, and James saw genuine frustration burning in his eyes. "Nobody knows nothing. Nobody's even seen her before. It's like she just appeared in that alley outa the same thin air her killer disappeared into."

"SHE weren't from around here, luv," said Emily Harris, the older of the two women Alun stopped to ask about the dead girl from last night. Emily was handsome for her age—she was nearly fifty, Alun reckoned, with silver pin-curled hair and crow's feet around her nearly violet eyes. Had she lived some other life, she would have been a beautiful woman.

She'd told him once that she used to have a proper job, leastwise until the bottle got the best of her; it was like that with a lot of the women who ended up on the streets. Even now, as early in the evening as it was, Emily's eyes were glazed over, and she swayed a little from side to side.

"You're *sure* you didn't know her?" Alun pressed the matter of the dead woman's identity gently, but insistently. He liked Emily, but he didn't trust her to remember her own name half the time.

"Why d'you care?" snapped the other woman, Betty... something. Alun didn't know her well. Betty always shied away from him, stiffened in his presence. She rarely said more than a few words to him, though to the best of his knowledge, he'd never given her any reason to be wary. Then again, some humans just had more sense than others and naturally shied away from predators. Even now, she fidgeted nervously with the lace cuff of her soiled blue dress; on the hem, Alun smelled mud and dung from the street and the seed of her last three customers.

In response to Betty's question, he merely shrugged. "Curious, I s'pose, just asking after local gossip." He shoved his hands into his pockets. "The papers're saying she's one of you girls," Alun lied. Well, he reckoned the papers *were* saying that, but he didn't know. Wolves, his father had always insisted, didn't need to read or write. Books and newspapers were for humans.

"She might've been," Emily answered him. "You know how it goes, luv. So many young ones come an' go. Ain't no keeping track o' all of 'em."

"What do you care if she were a bangtail, anyway?" Betty wanted to know. She wasn't a pretty woman, but pretty wasn't a job requisite for a whore. "You don't got no use for girls."

Emily laid a hand on her arm, stilling her angry tongue. "If she were a working girl, she's in a better place now," she advised, tilting back her flask. It was nearly empty.

"Come on an' I'll buy you a drink," Alun offered kindly.

Betty tried to stop her from going with him, but Emily accepted his crooked elbow with a warm smile and a genteel nod, sliding her arm through his as if he was some kind of gentleman escorting her on a Sunday picnic. "I wish more men was like you, Mr. Blayney."

He returned her smile and thought to himself, *No you don't.*

JAMES wasn't entirely surprised when he found himself on Regent Street, late in the evening many weeks later. Somehow, Regent Street was where he always ended up when he was unhappy; it was the one place where he was sure he would run into Robin Perris. James still felt guilty when he thought about Rob—about what he'd done to Rob—but tonight it was worse, not that that stopped him from being there. Almost a month had passed since the first—and last—time he'd seen Alun Blayney. He'd looked everywhere he could think of for the lanky Welshman; people seemed to know Alun, but no one knew where he was. Which could only mean that Alun didn't want to be found. *At least not by me.*

"You're looking dapper t'night, Constable." Robin greeted James with a broad grin and a tip of his scarlet beret.

James jumped at the sound of his voice; he hadn't heard Rob come up behind him. He never heard Rob come up behind him.

Robin chuckled. "One o' these days, James…." He shook his head.

Despite his weariness, James returned Rob's broad smile. "Not half so dapper as yourself," he replied earnestly. Underneath his brocade waistcoat, Rob was wearing a blouse that had probably been made for a woman, but it suited him. So did the trousers that were so snug, they left absolutely nothing to the imagination.

"Feeling like company, are you?" queried the younger man.

James's face clouded over, and his smile faded. "Not… not like that, Rob."

Carefully, covertly, Robin brushed his fingertips across the back of the constable's hand.

James didn't pull away. He never pulled away from Robin's touch.

"How about just… just a friend, then?" the Irishman offered tentatively.

"I'd like that," said James, his smile returning.

Robin smiled too; James didn't realize he'd never offered his friendship to the younger man before, not aloud, not plainly. He had no idea how much something so simple meant to Rob.

Robin gave his hand a little squeeze and then let it go before anyone on the street noticed. "Come on then. I've something I've wanted to show ya for a while, now, an' ya look like ya could use some cheering up."

"Rob…," James warned, though the glint in his eyes betrayed little more than good humor. He doubted Robin had meant that quite the way it sounded.

Rob swatted his arm. "You're a right rascal, you are. I've a mind to not take ya now."

"Take me where?"

"The theater. Not yer posh kinda theater, mind," he cautioned. Then, more thoughtfully, he added, "you might not like it. It's a bit… ribald if ya ken me meaning. It's jus' some friends o' mine, nothing fancy like. An' it's all in fun, no one means nothing by it." He sounded apologetic.

"That sounds utterly perfect," James assured him. He needed something to take his mind off Alun Blayney. But then a new thought occurred. "As… as long as you're sure I'll fit in?" asked James, more than a little self-conscious of the fact that he didn't fit in on the East End—and ironically, he didn't feel as if he fit in on the West End, either. No matter where he went, he was like an outsider looking in, looking for a place to call home.

"None o' that, now," Rob told him firmly. "You're with me t'night. If I says you're welcome, you'll be made welcome, you'll see."

"All right. And… thank you," he said, meaning it.

"Isn't this what friends're for?"

James smiled; he didn't miss the sincerity in Robin's tone. "Absolutely."

Chapter 5

THE morning after a second woman's mutilated body was found in Whitechapel, Alun was yanked from his doss house bed and deposited on the hard wooden floor with a painful thump. He yelped, but didn't fight back. His assailants could only be described as a pair of common ruffians—except there wasn't anything common about them. They weren't even human, they were lycanthropes, not that any human looking at the two huge burly men would ever know it.

As soon as they let go of him, Alun rolled over, belly up, and tilted his chin, bearing his throat in submission.

Another lycan, a female called Rhianna, crouched in the shadows, in her wolf form. She was a full-blooded lycan, like Alun, but where he was lean and hard muscled, she was emaciated. Her shaggy black coat was gnarled and matted, her dark eyes were dull and sunken in. Alun's heart ached as he counted her ribs from across the room. Females should be cherished, protected, not left to starve. His heart ached all the more because this female was Dark Moon-born, a Spirit Dancer like him, someone who could pierce the veil and transverse between this world and the next—though *unlike* him, Rhianna was fully trained and initiated and should have been held in highest regard by her pack. When Alun met her gaze, Rhianna's lip curled back in a snarl. She had never made any secret of her distain for him. None of them did.

The fourth and final member of the party stood by the door, calmly watching the scene unfold, a smug, self-satisfied grin on his face. His name was Percival Shilton, and he was the London pack's leader, a muscular, tawny-skinned man with too-long red hair and humorless silver eyes. He strode over to Alun and knelt next to his head, placing one large calloused hand casually on his throat. Alun tilted his head back further and returned his gaze submissively to the floor.

"There's a good *cwn*," crooned the pack leader, his tone patronizing. Speaking Welsh—*cwn* was the word for "dog"—when he himself was English, only added insult to injury. Or perhaps injury to insult. Alun wasn't a dog, he was a full-blooded lycanthrope, and they both knew it. Even so, he kept his tongue still. Speaking out of turn would only make things worse than they already were. "You are *my* little doggie, aren't you, lad?" Rather than waiting for a reply, he released his hold on the Welshman's throat and lifted his hand to Alun's lips.

Though it sickened Alun to the very marrow of his bones, he rubbed his face against the pack leader's outstretched fingers, nuzzling them, kissing his knuckles and covering himself in the other's repugnant scent as if he were little more than a lap dog showing obeisance to his master. He kept it up until Percival finally patted his cheek in mock-affection. "Such a good boy," he soothed, stroking Alun's face and hair. "Such an *obedient* little doggie. Aren't you?"

Alun swallowed back the bile burning in his throat and closed his eyes. "Yes, my Lord." He had to force the words out.

Percival settled his hand on Alun's throat again, just lightly, and turned to the two big sneering lycans standing near the door. "See, what did I say, boys? He's a good doggie." But when he looked back down at Alun, his face grew cold. "Or has ye been a naughty little doggie?" he queried, tightening his grip on Alun's neck. "Been sniffing up whores' skirts, *cwn*?"

Trembling, Alun shook his head. "I swear, m'Lord, I had nothing to do with those women."

Percival snorted. "I'm sure you didn't." It was no secret that Alun fancied men. Percival grabbed hold of his hair, pulling it so tight Alun's eyes watered—but he didn't dare move.

The pack leader smirked and pulled Alun's face up right next to his own, so that when he spoke, Alun felt the heat of his breath and smelled his last meal rotting in his teeth. "I'll make ya a deal, ya wretched *cwn*, 'cause I know ya don't want to be seeing my face again any more than I want to be seeing yours. You'll find the mongrel who's killing whores before the Yard comes sniffing round the wrong doors an' finds things we don't want 'em to find."

Alun swallowed hard and would have nodded if he could have, but instead, he was forced to speak. "Yes, m'Lord," he agreed, knowing as well as the rest of them that lycans would only survive as long as humans didn't believe in monsters any more. If that perception changed, it would be the Spanish Inquisition all over again.

Percival opened his fist, dropping Alun unceremoniously to the floor. "I don't know why your father disowned you; you're such a good little lap dog. But just so's we understand each other," he stood up and motioned to the two big lycans who had roused Alun from his bed, "I want ya to know what'll happen the next time ya see me...."

JAMES took an involuntary step back when he saw the body wrapped in dirty, blood-soaked clothes—but then the man lying in the middle of the floor moaned, proving he wasn't dead after all, although he might be better off if he were. The man moaned again and shifted, rolling over, and James's gut wrenched. *Alun.* James's knees almost buckled under him. The Welshman's whole face was bruised and bloodied—broken. His lip was split wide open, seeping yellow pus; his eyes seemed swollen shut.

And the landlord who had flagged James down near the end of his shift, to complain about the tenant who refused to vacate the premises, was still carrying on about the mess, wanting to know who was going to pay for damages. Nearly everything in the room was broken, though all James cared about was the bloody wreck of a man curled up on the floor, moaning in pain.

It took all of James's strength not to strike the landlord for his callousness, but that wouldn't help matters any. It wouldn't help Alun. He wasn't sure if anything would. It would be a miracle if Alun survived.

James didn't believe in miracles.

Alun managed to open one eye, just a crack, and peer up at James's face. He tried to speak, but he seemed too weak. James was sure Alun recognized him. He wanted to sink to his knees, to wrap his arms around the injured man—to run for a doctor—to kill whoever had beaten him. Bruised, bloodied fingers reached for James's pant leg.

"Oi, you!" the landlord shouted, moving as if to kick Alun's hand away.

James had his truncheon out before he could think; he used it only to block the other man, laying it (perhaps harder than he ought to have) across the landlord's chest to stay him where he was. The obnoxious little man glared in outrage, but James ignored him; at his feet, Alun sobbed, cringing away from him, making James wonder whether it was the landlord he was afraid of, or him. James's gut churned—did Alun think he could *ever* hurt him?

Turning a baleful glower on the landlord, he said, "I need you to go write down everything that's been damaged. Send the list to the precinct house, care of Police Constable James Heron—that's me. I'll see to it *personally* that this matter gets resolved amicably. While you're doing that, I'll get him out of here." It broke his heart to sound so cold. He doubted the landlord had any idea what "amicably" meant, but he seemed to understand he would get paid, and that was all he cared about. James wondered fleetingly how much of the damage to the room had been by Alun's attackers and how much of it was a part of the doss house's natural "charm"—but it didn't matter. The landlord was gone.

James sank to his knees. "Alun," he breathed, afraid to touch the other man, afraid to hurt him.

Alun didn't respond.

Swallowing back a lump of fear, James laid a hand gently his shoulder. *Please....* Still nothing. "Alun," he whispered. "Please...." *Please don't be dead.* "Alun, wake up, it's me, it's James. James Heron. *Please.*" Tears stung at his eyes as he reached for Alun's neck to see if he could find a pulse. Before his fingers touched Alun's skin, the East Ender drew in a ragged breath. James wanted to shout for joy! But his elation was short lived. Alun's breath was ragged. Labored. Shallow. James could only begin to imagine how much internal damage he'd suffered. "Can you move? We have to get you out of here."

No answer.

"Alun? *Please.* You can't stay here."

With another low, agonized groan, Alun rolled over to face him; his eyes were barely slits, surrounded by purple, swollen tissue. "W-wha' e'er y'say, Cons'able," he croaked, his harsh words running together through swollen lips. His arms shook as he tried to get himself upright. James moved to help, but Alun pushed him away, toppling himself back over in the process.

"Alun, please," James entreated, not understanding why his efforts were being met with such resistance—unless Alun honestly thought he'd meant to strike him when he pulled out his truncheon. "Please let me help you."

"I don' need yer help."

James heard the pain—and the anger—in his voice. "Alun… just… just let me get you out of here. Dr. Stodderley lives nearby. Let me get you to him—"

"No!" Alun spat blood; James couldn't tell if it was coming from his lips, cuts inside his mouth, or his lungs.

"You need a doctor."

"What's it matter t'you?"

"It matters. Alun. Please. Just let me help. Alun… *you* matter." He swallowed hard, but the lump in his throat refused to go away. "Everybody matters," he added, softly. "Now, please just let me get you to Dr. Stodderley."

"*No.*"

"Alun—"

"No doctor," the East Ender rasped.

"I'll pay for it—"

"*No!*" He coughed, spitting up more blood.

"This is no time to be ruddy proud!"

"'T's not th' money. I c'n pay. No doctors. *Please*. James. Please." He reached out again; this time James clasped his hand. "No doctor, James."

"All right," he gave in, but only because he didn't want to waste more time arguing. There was no telling when the landlord would return. "But you still have to get out of here. If I hail a cab, do you think you can make it as far as the street? I'll help you," he added.

"I think I can walk, but I-I've… I've nowhere to go."

"Yes you do. I'm taking you home."

"Y'can't... can't jus' walk off yer job...!"

James snorted. "You've seen for yourself where I live, Alun. I won't starve if they give me the sack for leaving my post. Now no more quarreling. Leastwise not until you're well enough to do it properly," he added with a forced grin. His comment had the desired effect: Alun smiled, at least as much as he was able. More importantly, he stopped arguing.

EVERY gully the cab rattled over jarred Alun's bruised and battered body, making him moan. Whimper. Making him relive every horrible blow Percival's goons had delivered. One of the big lycans had held him while the other used his fists like sledgehammers to pummel Alun's ribs, his gut. His face. Alun hated himself for his own weakness, for taking it, for not fighting back. He was a full-blooded lycan, stronger than any of the rest of them. But he was *diangen*. He had no right to fight back. He had no right to anything.

Another bump in the road made him wince—whine. Burn with shame.

James held him tighter, buried his face against his hair, whispered soft, soothing words into his ear. After getting them both into the cab, the younger man had unabashedly pulled Alun into his lap and draped his heavy wool coat around him, surrounding the lycan in his sweet, earthy scent. That, more than anything, brought Alun comfort—at least until another sharp jolt of the cab sent an explosion of pain through his already-tortured body.

"It's just a few more miles," James promised. "Hang on. You're going to be all right."

Alun heard the desperation in his voice and knew James didn't believe his own words. He wanted to tell him that he *would* be all right, that lycans were heartier than humans. If Percival had wanted him dead, he would be dead. If the landlord hadn't tried to eject him into the streets so soon after the beating, he would have slept and his body would have mended. By nightfall, he would have been able to shift into his wolf form and limp off to find someplace quiet where he could finish healing in peace. In a week's time, no one would ever know he'd been injured.

But he couldn't say any of those things; he could never tell James what he was. He whimpered again, and again James soothed him as best as he knew how. "We're almost there, I promise."

Alun tried to respond, but he was too tired; he closed his eyes and let his head sag against the younger man's chest. James's heart thumped softly in his ear. Warmth overtook him, and for a moment Alun felt... safe. He knew that as a *diangen* wolf, he would never know what it felt like to rest in the arms of a mate, but James Heron's kindness was close, it had to be.

Chapter 6

EVEN before he opened his eyes, Alun knew where he was. A feeling of warmth came over him, and he lay there a long moment, savoring it. It wasn't the softness of the mattress or the sheets that didn't scratch his skin; it wasn't the smell of fresh linens. It was the sweet, earthy scent of James Heron and the soft sound of the younger man's breathing, the beating of his heart, that made Alun feel at ease. The rational part of his brain told him he should be anything *but* at ease, comfortable, but... he was.

He barely remembered their arrival: Mrs. Dunberry's unexpected concern, James telling his housekeeper that no, she didn't need to send for Dr. Stodderley, he could care for Alun himself, he just needed her to bring hot water and clean towels, some bandages. Then James took Alun upstairs, stripped him down, and washed him so very carefully, telling him over and over how he didn't want to hurt him. Apologizing every time Alun winced.

After James got him into bed, things went blank for a while.

The first time he woke up, he hadn't known where he was. He'd panicked, aching muscles straining, ready to fight. To flee. But then James was there, telling him he was safe... *home.* When Alun looked into those mossy-green eyes he almost felt like it was true. Only no human could be his home, even one who plied him with tea and broth and laid fresh compresses on his bruises and cuts. Even one who sat with him until he slept again.

The second time he woke, Alun found James sitting in the bed next to him, reading aloud from a book. It wasn't one Alun knew—not that he knew many—but it wasn't the words that mattered, it was the sound of James's voice that told him he was safe. He was where he wanted to be.

He'd lain still for many long moments, not wanting James to know he was awake, not wanting him to stop reading. He didn't know that James had already been reading to him for almost an hour, occasionally reaching down to stroke his hair or his cheek, relieved that the swelling finally seemed to be going down.

When James finally noticed he was awake, he smiled and coaxed Alun into drinking more tea, eating a bit of bread and some cold beef—the leftovers of his own, barely touched, supper. Then James picked the book back up and started reading again. Alun shifted as close as he dared and closed his eyes.

Waking for the third time, Alun saw through an opening in the heavy brown drapes that night had fallen over the city. Next to him, James was asleep. He was still in his day clothes, and lay, most propitiously, on top of the blankets. Alun smiled; their noses were so close together that if he'd dared, he could have leaned in and stolen a kiss. He imagined the constable's pink lips would feel as soft as they looked, that his mouth would taste savory and earthy. He ached to find out, to touch him… *to make you mine…* but instead, he only reached out and brushed a strand of hair off James's forehead.

"Why'd you bring me back home?" The word stuck in Alun's throat. "If you were…." *Lycan.* If James were a lycan, Alun would bury his nose in his hair, inhale his scent, tell him what he wanted. A mate. Or at least someone he could curl up with at night, wake up with in the morning. Someone to face the day with. Maybe a pair of male lycans could never form a proper mating bond, but at least a lycan would have understood what he wanted. Needed. Another lycan would want the same things from him. A human never would. Never could. Humans didn't mate. They married. Divorced. Hurt one another.

As if in response to his thoughts, James shifted closer, bringing his head to rest on Alun's shoulder, and Alun gave in to temptation. He wrapped his arms around the younger man; James was the perfect fit against him. *If you were mine….*

In his sleep, James let out a soft, contented-sounding sigh.

Alun closed his eyes. Even if James was different, if he didn't lie and wouldn't cheat, he was *still* human. Humans feared what they didn't understand and hated what they feared. He didn't know why James had brought him home, why he'd risked so much to help him. He only knew that if James ever discovered what he was, he would turn on him the way men always turned on wolves. It was, as his *taid*, his grandfather, would say, a fact of life.

"I should be going," Alun whispered, not wanting to wake the sleeping man—not wanting to leave, but knowing he had to. It would be better for both of them if he wasn't there when James woke up. But first, he leaned in and rubbed his cheek gently against James's soft hair, covering his face in the younger man's scent. It would only last a few hours, but he wanted—

"Alun?"

He froze, panic fluttering in his chest. "I…." How could he explain what he was doing?

James didn't give him the chance to try. He tilted his head and sealed his mouth to Alun's, taking the kiss the lycan had been too afraid to steal. James's kiss was fervid, almost brutal, and he tasted of green earth and honey. Of fire. When Alun felt James's tongue playing at his lips, he opened them, granting the younger man full access to his mouth. James's tongue slid over his, exploring every bit of his mouth as he deepened the kiss—as he slid his arms around Alun's neck and drew him closer still.

Yes! Mine! The lycan's soul howled with wild joy as his cock surged to life. He rolled them over, startling the young man who was now lying under him—but James didn't protest. He only smiled, that big, bright, sunshine smile of his and tilted his head to one side submissively as Alun leaned in and pressed his lips—his teeth—to James's throat so James would know he was being claimed.

Alun froze. James *wasn't* his. He wasn't even lycan! Shaking with the effort, Alun pulled away. Goddess, what was he thinking! He turned away from the younger man, not wanting to look at him. Not able to look at him.

The softness of James's touch, when he laid his hand on Alun's back, startled the lycan.

"You didn't have to stop," said James. "I liked that. A little rough can be fun."

Alun shivered. It wasn't the cool air on his bare skin; it was that he'd never been ridden so hard and fast by his beast before, and never… never like this. His beast only took him in moments of anger. Pain. Bloodlust. Fear.

"Alun?"

"I have to go." His voice was little more than a raspy whisper.

"Please don't." James pressed a soft kiss to the middle of Alun's back. "Lie back down with me. We—we don't have to do anything you don't want to." He sounded so hopeful, it broke the lycan's heart. "But I can promise you that I'll make it worth your while, Alun. I'll do whatever you want me to."

"I… I can't." Alun pulled away. Behind him, he heard James moving; it sounded like he'd pulled his knees up to his chest, and Alun imagined he was hugging them. "James—"

"Please, at least stay the rest of the night. I'll go to another room. I won't bother you."

Alun turned then, glaring at him. "This is your room." James hadn't put him into one of the guestrooms, he'd put him in his own bed. *He shouldn't leave his room for me.*

"It doesn't matter. I just… you can't be well enough to go back out there. It's only a few hours 'til dawn. Please at least stay until it's light out. Nights… nights aren't safe, Alun."

Alun snorted. If James only knew. "I'm fine," he said. Then he blinked. And he *was* fine. Wounds that should have taken a week to heal didn't hurt at all. It was impossible, unless… *when a wolf lies in the shelter of his mate's love, he becomes whole, the body heals fast, his spirit is invincible…* or so Alun had always been told. But James was human, male; he couldn't be the other half of a lycan's soul. "I'm fine," he said again, well aware that James was scrutinizing him in the dark. "It weren't as bad as it looked," he insisted. He doubted James believed him, but what else could he say?

When James reached out to run his hand gently over Alun's cheek, he didn't pull back. He closed his eyes and allowed the touch, even though it went against all reason. When he felt James's fingertips brushing over his lips, he kissed them. His heart ached as he nuzzled James's hand; it felt so good to be touched like this by someone he wanted touching him.

"Lie back down with me," James said again, his tone pleading. "We'll do whatever you want."

Alun swallowed hard; fear and desire waged a tug of war inside him. "You don't know what you're asking."

"Yes I do."

He started to shake his head to tell him that no, he didn't, he couldn't, but the words died in his throat when he felt James's lips on his again. The kiss was soft. Sweet. Almost chaste. When James pulled back, they both opened their eyes. "I know what goes on in the back alleys," James said softly. Alun's spine went rigid, but before he could speak, James pressed another soft kiss to his lips. "All I'm trying to tell you is that that isn't what I want. I don't expect... you can have me *however* you want me, Alun." As if to emphasize the point, James reached between the lycan's thighs and began stroking his already-rigid cock. He smiled. "I think you want it too."

Alun swallowed again. "I... I don't want to hurt you. I'm stronger than I look, James."

James's smile became an impish grin. "I remember the way you pinned me in that alley. But I'm not afraid of a little rough and tumble. Try me." His tone was playful, challenging. Seductive. He gave Alun's shaft a gentle squeeze, causing the lycan to groan.

Desire tightened in Alun's gut; James was right. He wanted this, wanted it more than he'd wanted anything in a very long time. But he was still afraid. "James—"

"Shhhh. I'm not afraid of anything."

"You should be."

"Well, I'm not," James countered, leaning in again.

Alun stopped fighting. Was it so wrong to take what James was willing to give, to take what little pleasure came into his life? He'd had human partners before—a human lover—he just had to be careful not to overpower James. He just had to hold his beast in check, something he'd been doing his entire adult life.

James nipped at his lower lip, demanding access to his mouth once more. Alun gave into him gladly. He closed his eyes and let James take control of the kiss. It wasn't hard to give in when James was stroking him the way he was, running his hand up and down his cock, the sensation sending wave after wave of pleasure through the lycan's body.

When James's soft lips migrated to his neck, Alun lifted his chin, giving the human access to that, too; he only bristled when James came too near his throat—but James backed away without seeming the least bit troubled by the low warning growl. He simply returned his attention to Alun's jaw... his lips. He leaned into Alun, pressing him back until he was lying prone underneath James on the soft mattress, and suddenly, the lycan realized James wasn't merely seducing him, he was *claiming* him. Softly. Sensually, with little more than his lips and tongue—and the slow steady stroking of the hand still wrapped around his sex—James was making him his. The wild, untamed part of Alun's soul howled with glee... it *should* be fighting, trying to wrestle for control. But Alun didn't *want* to fight. He didn't want to dominate. He only wanted to please the younger man, and at the moment, it seemed to please James very much to be lying on top of him, making him unbearably hard.

"You're wearing too many clothes," Alun complained.

James shifted so he could meet his gaze. "What are you going to do about it?" he inquired, a glint of mischief in his eye.

"Maybe I should take 'em offa you," he suggested, his tone gruff.

James's smile was wicked. "Maybe you should."

Alun rolled them over, switching their positions so he was straddling the younger man, pinning his hands on either side of his head. He saw the startled look on James's face, heard the acceleration of his heart, and for a moment.... But James wasn't frightened. Heat smoldered in those mossy-green eyes, lust. With a puckish grin, Alun pulled James's arms over his head, securing both wrists in one hand, freeing the other to deal with buttons.

JAMES watched Alun's face through half-lidded eyes as the dark Welshman undid the fastenings of his waistcoat and shirt. Alun peeled back the fabric slowly, a smile playing at his lips—he obviously liked what he saw. Pride swelled in James—he'd never been excessively vain, but he loved the look of appreciation on Alun's face as he slowly undressed him. Strong fingers caressed James's chest in little circles, raising gooseflesh on his skin. Alun grasped his nipple between his thumb and forefinger and gave an experimental squeeze; James moaned. It hurt. It felt good. It made him want more.

"Like that, do you?" Alun inquired.

"I told you. I'm not afraid of a little rough and tumble."

"This ain't nothin'," came the husky reply.

James's response died in a gasp as Alun took his nipple into his mouth. He teased it, holding it firmly between his teeth, flicking his tongue over the tight, sensitive nub, making James squirm helplessly against the stronger man. "I'm still wearing too many clothes," he reminded Alun.

Alun's grin sent a chill up his spine. "Maybe next time you'll wear less clothes to bed."

Next time. James liked the sound of "next time." He tilted his head, and Alun gave him the kiss he'd hoped for. "Take me any way you want, just please take me soon," he begged when Alun let him speak again.

"First tell me what else you want me to do," he said, in a low throaty growl that made James shiver.

He swallowed hard at the order. Invitation. It was hard to tell which it really was—but it didn't matter. When he'd woken up to find himself nestled in Alun's strong arms, it was so good. So perfect. So utterly unbelievable. But here they were. Alun was on top of him, holding him. About to make love to him. "I'd like it if you sucked something else," James admitted.

Without a word, Alun sat up. Then he dipped his head down—and sucked on James's earlobe.

Startled, the younger man gasped. Then he laughed. "I had something else in mind, sweetheart," he informed his lover.

Alun cocked his head, one brow arched inquisitively. "You've a foot fetish, do ya?"

He laughed harder. "Not hardly. How about closer to the middle?"

Alun smirked. "I might be able to oblige you that." But before he did, he captured James's mouth in another soul-burning—soul-satisfying—kiss. "Lie still," he hissed, when James reached up to encircle him with his arms. "I want you to lie there, and take what I give you."

James dropped his hands obediently back down to the mattress without complaint.

"I'm going make you forget what any other man's ever felt like," Alun rumbled into his ear, his tone and hot breath causing gooseflesh to rise on James's neck and arms. He kissed James's neck, bit his throat.

"If you leave a mark there," James warned softly, "we're going to have an awful lot of explaining to do in the morning."

"Guess I'll have to leave it where your housekeeper won't see."

"I guess you will," James told him.

He felt Alun's smile against his neck.

Alun kissed and nipped at James's shoulders and chest—leaving several bruises in his wake, the younger man was sure—and James sucked in air as Alun bit down hard again on his already purple-bruised nipple. His cock strained against the fabric of his trousers; he was desperate to have it free. He wanted, *needed*, to feel Alun with his bare skin.

As if realizing that his mind had wandered, Alun flicked the tip of his tongue hard against James's aching nipple, causing him to cry out pain. "What were you thinking about?" he demanded gruffly.

"You. Inside me."

The answer made Alun smile. He licked his lips, hunger danced in his eyes, and James's cock strained in response. The East Ender's dark gaze never left James's face as he kissed and nipped his way back down the younger man's body, finally settling between James's legs. Alun nuzzled and lightly nipped his groin through his trousers until James was aching. "Please. Please, Alun, I'm going to come in my shorts if you keep that up!" More than ever he needed to feel Alun's skin on his sex. His hand, his mouth, he didn't care; he just wanted to be touched.

Finally, slowly, Alun undid the buttons of his fly. One… two… three… four… James's erection sprang free of its confinement, and he could breathe again. His trousers had never seemed so tight as they'd been the last half hour! When Alun tugged at his waistband, James lifted his legs, making it easier for Alun to remove both his trousers and drawers. Alun deposited them by the side of the bed and leaned back in, going straight for James's aching shaft.

James groaned as warm, soft lips engulfed him. Alun took him all the way to the back of his throat, causing James's eyes to roll back in his head. He was sure he was going to come, but he fought not to. He wanted to enjoy this—Alun's mouth felt so good. "I'd like to touch you, Alun," he whispered. "Please?" He glanced down hopefully.

Alun nodded his permission.

James reached down and ran his fingers through Alun's coarse, dark hair. *Next time.* He wanted there to be a next time, and a time after that and on after that. Alun looked up then, and James met his gaze, held it. There seemed to be so much hidden behind those black eyes. James wanted to know it all—he wanted to share every part of himself, as well. Happy at the thought—and quickly losing the ability to think—James closed his eyes, losing himself in how good Alun's tongue felt as it snaked the length of his shaft, laving every inch of him. Alun lavished the same attention on his balls, first caressing them with gentle fingers, then with his mouth and tongue. He was sure he'd never been with anyone so thorough.

James gasped when he felt his ass cheeks being spread wide, just before Alun pressed the flat of his tongue against his entrance. "That... that's incredible," James murmured.

"No one ever done this to you before?" Alun sounded surprised.

James shook his head, though he had no idea whether or not Alun could see him. It didn't matter, nothing mattered, not as long as Alun kept working his tongue against his hole like that.

Alun stopped just long enough to say, "You're in for a treat, then." He gripped James's ass tighter and thrust his tongue forcefully past the ring of muscles and into him.

The invasion was so sudden, James swore aloud. But then he melted as Alun's tongue began to dart in and out of him, slowly at first, then faster, deeper. "More... please... Alun." The other man didn't answer, but James's breath hitched in his throat when he felt one of Alun's fingers joining his tongue inside him. James fisted his hands into Alun's hair and arched his back, thrusting himself toward the warmth of Alun's mouth, forcing Alun's finger deeper inside. It burned, but it felt so good!

"Easy," Alun warned. "I don't want to be hurting you, remember?"

"Lotion—there's lotion on the bureau."

Without a word, Alun withdrew; the sudden emptiness made James groan, missing the contact.

"I'll be right back, promise," Alun assured him.

James couldn't help but appreciate the view as Alun padded toward the dresser on the other side of the room. His ass was round, muscular, and his legs… God, his legs! Long. Lean. Strong.

Alun turned around and smirked when he saw James's intent expression. "Enjoying yourself, are you?"

Heat overtook James's face, and Alun chuckled.

"Maybe I should just stay over here, then," Alun teased, leaning against the bureau, posing for him, his cock sticking straight out, taunting James. "Let you just watch me all night."

"You're a cruel man, Alun," James observed, grinning.

Alun chuckled. "Just now figuring that out, are you?" He made a show of slicking up his cock.

James's mouth watered. "I could do that for you," he offered.

"You could. But watching you squirm is too much fun."

At last, Alun sauntered back over to the bed, seemingly in no hurry at all. He knelt down between James's legs and used his lotion-slick fingers to open James's hole wider, stretching him gently, first with one finger, then two, reaching deeper inside until he was hitting James's prostate with every smooth, *slow* stroke. James whimpered. "Please, please, Alun!" He was near tears, he was so frustrated, so desperate.

"Shhh," Alun crooned softly. With his free hand he lightly caressed James's cock, making him cry out. "Tell me that you're mine, and I'll make you come so hard you'll be seeing stars."

"I'm yours, Alun. All yours."

Alun plunged three fingers into him, hitting his prostate again, sending lightning shooting through James's veins—at the same time he leaned in and took James's cock all the way to the back of his throat, sucking, swirling his tongue around it. Within seconds, James exploded, crying out, emptying himself… it was like he was emptying his whole self into Alun, not just his seed.

Sweating, panting, twitching with aftershocks, he looked up to see Alun smiling down at him. James shivered when he felt the touch of the other man's lips on his hipbone. It was a soft, sweet kiss. Alun trailed more soft kisses all the way up his body, each one making James quiver, until at last he came to James's mouth again. He hesitated, but James leaned up, greeting the kiss—wanting it. He savored the feel of Alun's lips on his and loved the taste of himself in Alun's mouth, salty, sweet. Just a little bit sour. He wrapped his arms around his lover's neck, and Alun held him tight, seeming to enjoy the moment of tenderness just as much as he did.

"Ready for more?" Alun asked, at last.

"*Yes.*"

Chapter 7

JAMES lay curled up tight against his lover's chest, listening to the other man's heart beating soft and steady under his ear. He'd never come twice in such quick succession before last night, but with Alun buried deep inside him, filling him, hitting his prostate with every thrust... he smiled. "I am yours, Alun. All yours. For just as long as you want me."

Alun sighed in his sleep and pulled James closer; James pressed a soft kiss to his chest. He was sure he'd never felt so happy. He didn't know what was going to happen when Alun woke up, when they were forced to face their lives, but... but he didn't want the other man going back to Whitechapel. He didn't want Alun going anywhere.

Only, how could he want a virtual stranger so much he was willing to sacrifice...? James sighed. Chances were he didn't have as much to sacrifice as he had twenty-four hours ago. Inspector Lamont wasn't the only person at Scotland Yard who didn't like him, and when he'd walked off the job yesterday, he'd given them everything they needed to let him go. James didn't care. He didn't need his job, and without it he would have so much more time to spend with Alun. Time to get to know him. Time to show Alun he wasn't the only one who knew how to go down on a man.

A light rapping at the bedroom door snapped James out of his reverie.

"Master James?" came Mrs. Dunberry's soft voice.

James slid out from under the covers. Alun stirred and reached toward the place where he had been lying, but he didn't wake. Instead, he pulled James's pillow to him, burying his nose in it. James smiled. Maybe Alun wouldn't want to go back to Whitechapel. Maybe he wouldn't want to go anywhere.

Mrs. Dunberry tapped on the door again.

James grabbed his shirt from the floor and pulled it quickly over his arms—over the bruises Alun had left on his shoulders and chest. He opened the door only a crack, so he could hide the rest of himself behind it. He was rock hard again. "Good morning, Mrs. Dunberry," he greeted his housekeeper softly. He knew was grinning far too broadly, but he couldn't help his good mood.

She gave him a sour look. "Hardly morning any longer, Sir. Sergeant Buchanan is here to see you. I've already informed the sergeant that you weren't receiving visitors," Mrs. Dunberry added before James could ask her to convey as much to his unexpected guest. "He says the matter is urgent and he'll wait until you *are* ready to receive company."

James groaned. Buchanan was just stubborn enough to wait around all day if he had to. "Very well. Please tell him I'll be down in a few moments."

She nodded. Hesitated. "How is Mr. Blayney this morning?" There was a measure of genuine concern in her tone.

James couldn't help his randy smirk. "Oh… better, I think. I suspect he'll make a full recovery quite soon."

Mrs. Dunberry raised one slender eyebrow but kept her thoughts to herself.

"Would you bring some hot water up to another room so I can wash before seeing the sergeant?" James asked her.

"Of course, Sir."

He shut the door and leaned against it a moment. He wasn't ready to face Sergeant Buchanan, but it didn't seem as if he had any other option. Before heading across the hall, James pulled clean clothes out of his wardrobe. Then he tiptoed over to the bed and pressed a tender kiss to the sleeping man's temple. "I won't be long," he promised in a soft whisper. And when he came back, he was going to wake Alun in a *very* pleasant way.

Grinning, he shimmied into his trousers and darted across the hall to the other bedroom to make himself presentable for the sergeant. The sooner he got rid of him, the sooner he could be back to his lover's bed.

CLEANED, shaved, and wearing a fresh suit of clothes, James joined his guest in the front parlor. It was a large room decorated in rose and cream, with polished sheesham wood end tables from India and delicate papier-mâché chairs that had been James's grandmother's. The lace curtains were pulled back, letting in bright, warm sunshine that made everything in the room gleam with golden light.

Sergeant Alexander Buchanan sat, looking very uncomfortable, in one of the sturdier high-backed chairs near the window, his helmet resting in his lap. He was a stout man of thirty some years, with thick mutton-chop sideburns and a broad handlebar mustache. He stood up so abruptly when James came into the room that his helmet nearly tumbled to the floor. "I'd thought certain somebody was having one over on me," he declared.

James frowned. "Sergeant?"

"This house. I thought for sure there was no way one of my boys lived *here*. But here you are."

"Yes, and welcome," James said sincerely, extending his hand. As irritated as he was by the sergeant's unexpected arrival, he couldn't deny that he liked the man. Buchanan was nothing like Lamont—in other words, he wasn't a pompous ass.

Buchanan accepted his hand. "If you'll pardon my bluntness, Heron, I'd like to know just what the deuce you're playing at here."

"I'm not playing at anything, Sir, on that you have my word," James assured him. "I'm just... that is, I *was* a police constable, the same as every other man on my relief."

"So you don't want your job, then?"

James blinked. "I'm sorry? I didn't expect I had a choice, Sir."

The sergeant opened his mouth and then closed it again. He looked around the parlor, as if he was making his mind up about something. "Tell me something, lad—an' forgive me if I'm speaking outa turn—but have you fall on hard times or something?"

"What? No. Of course not."

"Then why—?" He stopped abruptly when Mrs. Dunberry came into the room carrying a silver serving tray.

"I thought you gentlemen might like some tea," she told them in an even tone.

James's smile was genuine. "Thank you, Mrs. Dunberry. That was very thoughtful of you."

She wrinkled her nose. "Will the sergeant be staying for lunch?"

"Oh, no, Ma'am," Sergeant Buchanan was quick to say. "I'd hardly want to impose."

James was just as glad.

"Will there be anything else, then?" she inquired of her employer.

"Thank you, Mrs. Dunberry, but I think we're fine."

With a curt nod and the barest dip of a curtsey, she took her leave.

James turned back to the sergeant and nodded for him to resume his seat. He did, though he didn't look any more comfortable than he had before.

"Tea?" the younger man offered, as he poured his own much-needed cup.

"No. No. Just an answer."

"Sir?"

"What's a man who lives in a house like this doing working as a police constable in Whitechapel, of all places?"

James stirred his tea. He took a seat across from the sergeant's chair. "My grandfather was a police surgeon, Sir, leastwise until his eyesight started to fail him. This was his house, although to be fair, it was his father's house before he inherited it. He was a surgeon too. Not for the Yard, of course." There had been no Scotland Yard back when his great-grandfather was practicing medicine. James paused a moment to drink his tea and collect his thoughts. He didn't use his family name for a reason, although the grandfather of whom he was speaking was the one called Heron. He had money, but no real fame. His father's family, conversely, had fame—or at least a title—but no money. "My grandfather doesn't like to think of himself as 'wealthy', Sergeant. He says the measure of a man's riches has nothing to do with the size of his purse, although I understand that most people would look at this house and disagree. I happen to think my grandfather *is* a very wealthy man, Sir, by his own standards as well as by other people's. I know he's proud of the choices I've made."

"Even the choice you made when you abandoned your post yesterday?"

James swallowed hard, but forced himself to meet the other's brown gaze. "Yes, Sir. There were extraordinary circumstances. I don't expect that to excuse my actions, but I would do the same again, if faced with the same situation, Sir."

Thankfully, the sergeant didn't inquire as to the exact nature of those "extraordinary circumstances." "Well, whoever you are, Heron, you're right well connected. Word has it, it come down from the commissioner himself that you're still with the department, assuming you want yer job. But I'm warning you," he said, wagging his finger at James's face, "you'd best not be making no habit of this sort of thing. You can come back tomorrow. *Night*."

"Night?" He wasn't due back on the overnight shift for another month.

"You'll be on night relief 'til further notice." He sounded genuinely apologetic. "It was Inspector Lamont's idea. I'm sure 'e's hoping you'll quit."

James sipped his quickly cooling tea. He'd expected to be told he was no longer in the employ of the Metropolitan Police—he was prepared for that. He was even looking forward to it; constables worked long hours and got very few days off. He didn't mind, but it left him with little free time to pursue personal interests. When he'd joined the constabulary, he hadn't had any personal interests beyond his garden, but now…. His stomach fluttered. Now there was Alun.

But there was also the matter of his own pride, which wouldn't let him quit. He drained his teacup. "I suppose I'll see you tomorrow night then, Sir," he told the sergeant, as their paths would no doubt cross when he was starting his shift and the older man was ending his. "And thank you, Sir."

"Don't thank me, lad, thank whoever's looking out for you."

ALUN lay motionless for many long moments after James left the room. He'd only woken up in time to hear the last part of his conversation with the housekeeper. He assumed this Buchanan James was dreading seeing so much must be James's superior officer. A part of him wanted to rush downstairs to stand by James's side while he faced down the unwelcome man… but that was foolish. James wasn't in any danger, and he doubted Buchanan had any amorous designs on him—his temper flared at the possibility, though. James was *his*.

He shook himself. How could James be his? James was human. What was more, he was some kind of gentleman; one look around his house proved that. James had money. Privilege.

What would he ever want with a man like me?

But last night… *I'm yours, all yours…* James's own words.

Hollow platitudes, Alun told himself. What else could it be?

He pushed off the covers; they smelled too much like the younger man. Everything there did. It overwhelmed Alun, and he couldn't think! He got out of bed and began pacing unhappily back and forth in front of the window, trying to sort himself out, trying to make sense of what had happened last night. James Heron was hardly the first toff to crawl down to the East End looking for a three-penny fuck. Just last summer, down on Cleveland Street, all kinds of well-to-do gentlemen had visited a brothel that specialized in young men. Leastwise they had been until the authorities caught on, and the whole place was shut down. And who was it that got in trouble? Not the wealthy patrons. No, it was the boys who paid the price. *The people like me, the ones with nothing.*

Alun's pacing became faster and more furious. The room was too small! He needed to run, to clear his head, to burn off the energy threatening to eat him up alive. He needed to feel grass beneath his paws and bathe in cool, clear water, not in the stinking, rotting filth of the Thames. He wanted… he *needed*… to be home.

Before he realized what he was doing, Alun flopped back down onto the bed and pulled James's pillow up to his nose. He closed his eyes and inhaled deeply of the other man's scent. Every instinct in him screamed the same thing: he already *was* home.

But how could James Heron be his heart's home?

He couldn't be. He was human.

With his whole heart aching, Alun got back up and crept to the bedroom door. Stretching his senses to their very limits, he listened. He heard muffled voices coming from downstairs, James and another man… he shifted his attention away from them quickly, before rage and jealousy got the better of him. It took almost more control than he possessed, but he hadn't survived as long as he had as a *diangen* wolf by giving in to rash impulses. Presently, he heard Mrs. Dunberry join the men—cups clinked against saucers. She must be serving tea.

Alun knew he had only a few precious seconds to make his escape, so he bolted out of the bedroom and down the back stairs as fast as he could—even as a man, he was possessed of preternatural speed. As soon as he was out the back door, he shifted shape. As a fully grown, full-blooded lycan, the transformation took less than a single heartbeat. He felt a shiver of pleasure, and four feet touched the ground where only a moment before two had been.

The pleasure was short-lived. Alun's wolf form, unlike those of Percival and most of the rest of the London pack, would never be mistaken for a large dog or even a timber wolf—not that a wolf, even an ordinary one, was something anyone expected to see roaming the city streets. But at least an ordinary wolf wouldn't cause the same panic as a dire wolf, a creature easily three times larger than any timber wolf.

Alun cleared the back wall of the garden in a single, easy leap and made for the shelter of the nearest alleyway, using what little Spirit Dancer magic he knew to pull the meager shadows to him like a shroud, praying he could find a way back to the East End without being seen by the humans. The Dark Mother taught her children to manipulate shadows, to conceal themselves and even cloud the minds of others—but those were the gifts of a fully initiated Spirit Dancer. Alun wasn't initiated; what he could do amounted to a few parlor tricks, but at that moment, it was all he had to escape unnoticed.

AFTER seeing Sergeant Buchanan to the door, James retrieved the serving tray from the parlor and took it back to the kitchen. Mrs. Dunberry was fixing sandwiches at the counter. She looked up at him and frowned. "I could have gotten that."

James shrugged. "I know." He took the tray into the scullery and rinsed both cups, even though only one had been used. (Mrs. Dunberry insisted that every cup be washed before it was put away). He set them next to the sink to air-dry, and then washed the tray, drying it carefully so as to avoid water spots. He could well imagine what any of his neighbors would say if they saw the master of the house doing dishes. He chuckled at the scandal it would surely cause, and rolled down his sleeves. Today, at least, he had ulterior motives for washing up after himself. He was certain Mrs. Dunberry intended to take lunch up to Alun, but if he dawdled long enough in the kitchen, he'd be able to take the sandwiches upstairs in her stead. James didn't want what he had planned for his lanky Welshman to be interrupted by lunch—or much of anything else, though he imagined Alun was probably hungry.

James returned to the kitchen and surveyed the tray Mrs. Dunberry had arranged. Tea, sandwiches and fresh cobbler with cream. Oh, *that* gave him ideas…. Wearing a smile that was entirely too randy, he offered to save her a trip and take the meal upstairs to their guest. His housekeeper gave him a shrewd look, but didn't argue.

James ascended the back stair feeling giddy. He still had his job and as long as the hours were, he did take a great deal of pride in the uniform. *And*, he wasn't expected back in until tomorrow night. That gave him and Alun a day and a half to indulge themselves in whatever pursuits they could dream up for each other.

James balanced the tray carefully in one hand and opened the bedroom door as quietly as he could, not wanting to wake his lover—or at least not wanting to wake him with clattering china.

The room, however, was empty.

Chapter 8

DARKNESS fell over the city, allowing Alun to come out of the shadows at last.

Still in wolf form, he found the place where the second woman had been murdered. It was a narrow alleyway between two smaller lanes—a good place to kill someone. There was only a single soot-darkened streetlamp standing sentry at one end of the alley; its light barely penetrated the inky passage. The cobblestones had been washed clean of all physical evidence of the crime, most likely by residents of the tenements on either side of the alley, people who, thankfully, were either asleep or out for the night. Even so, Alun smelled the dead woman's blood; an anxious whine escaped his throat. He could smell her fear. Her pain. Death hadn't come easily. Alun doubted it had come quickly. Her scent was familiar, but only barely—she could be any one of a dozen whores he knew from the streets. He sniffed for the lycan's scent too; it was the same scent he'd smelled before, but it didn't belong to any wolf he knew. He wished he could follow it, track the rogue werewolf—stop him before he killed again—but the smells of the street beyond the alley would cover up the strange lycan's trail in no time, especially once Alun shifted back to his human form.

Frustrated, Alun turned back to the shadows. Rooting around in the dirt and garbage that lined either side of the lane, he found a small gold crucifix. Alun closed his eyes. Claire Walker wore one just like it. He supposed it wasn't proof positive that she was the one who had been killed there—the pendant hardly unique—but his gut told him it was hers. This alley would make for a good place for Claire to bring a client; she had remarked to him once how it was easier for her when she didn't have to look at their faces.

Gingerly, Alun picked the crucifix up by its chain and crept deeper into the shadows. There was only one person who might be able to help him identify the killer: the woman who had died here. Claire hadn't been dead long, so she *should* still be lingering just on the other side of the veil. If she'd drifted further, he wouldn't be able to track her. A fully trained Spirit Dancer could... but Alun would never be initiated into the deeper mysteries of the Dark Moon. His training had ended when he was banished from his birth pack.

Alun settled himself on the hard, uneven cobblestones and closed his eyes. Even if he wasn't fully initiated, he was still a child of the Dark Moon. Slipping between the worlds was as natural to him as breathing—or so his *taid*, his grandfather, used to say. He had been their pack's Lore Keeper and Alun's mentor; Alun would have been his successor if he hadn't been banished. A cold knot tied itself in his gut. He didn't want to be *diangen*. He wanted to know the joy of the mating bond. He wanted to love someone. To be loved in return. He wanted... he wanted something he knew he could never have.

Another soft whine escaped his throat. Ever since meeting James Heron, Alun had felt so hollow inside, so raw. Last night only made it worse, because somehow, for just a few hours he'd thought.... Alun shook himself. James didn't want him. How could he? James didn't even know what he was.

Alun rested one large paw on top of the crucifix to give himself something solid to hang onto while he crossed between the worlds to try and find Claire's spirit. He didn't worship the same God the humans did, but he sent a call toward heaven anyway, asking for whatever aid the alien being might be willing to give him in finding Claire. Alun's grandfather had said—very quietly, when no one else was around—to never ignore foreign gods when working for the benefit of one of their followers. One never knew where they would find help when they needed it most—and at the moment, Alun would take whatever help anyone was willing to give him.

He listened to the steady rhythm of his own heart beating, the sound of his breath moving in and out of his lungs. The noise of the street faded, seeming further and further away with each breath he took. He felt dizzy, lightheaded. He flexed his paws against the ground as a wave of icy cold surged through his prone body. Suddenly, he couldn't move—couldn't breathe! Panic rose in his chest as he drowned under the rush of viscosity… but then the moment passed. He could breathe again. He'd passed through the veil.

Alun only hoped that back in the solid world he was still breathing, his heart still beating, because even under the best of circumstances, it was dangerous to cross over to the spirit side of the veil—and his present circumstances were far from ideal. He had no guardians, no spirit helpers to protect him, to watch over both his soul and his body while they were separated. After he was declared *diangen* by the elders, his pack's spirit allies and helpers turned their backs on him, just like the rest of the pack did, and Alun didn't know how to make allies of his own. In his experience, the kinds of spirits willing to deal with an outcast were better off left alone.

Alun opened his eyes and rose to his feet. The spirit world looked much like the physical world, though the colors were off, and there was a sense of "wrongness" that Alun could never quite put a name to. Overhead, the sky was tinted red, yet the shadows had a purple cast. The streetlamps were iridescent and bright, yet their rainbow light didn't reach very far into the darkness—darkness that prevailed, day or night. Noises were muffled, but scents were sharper. Buildings towered over him, looming like dark daemons, living entities, ensouled by the lives and deaths of the people who dwelled within them. They made Alun shiver, but he refused to let himself be unnerved by the way the tenements seemed to stare at him unwelcomingly. As long as he didn't stray too far from the places he knew, he should be safe enough.

Alun shifted back to his human form and picked the cross up off the ground. He didn't need his wolf's nose and ears in the spirit world; here his senses worked the same no matter how he clothed himself.

A soft feminine gasp drew Alun's attention, and he turned to see Claire Walker staring at him, mouth agape. She looked much the same as she had the last time he saw her, her long blond hair coiled into a braid on top of her head, and she wore a faded blue dress that had once been the color of the summer sky. Around her shoulders, a dirty yellow shawl was draped. She only had one shoe on and was standing rather awkwardly because of it.

"Hallo, Miss Walker," he greeted her politely. Sometimes shades appeared as they had looked at the moment of death, other times they looked as they had in life. Neither state was a sure indication that the person knew they were dead, so Alun didn't make any presumptions.

Claire merely continued to stare.

Alun understood why. Since he hadn't been wearing clothing in the physical world, he was buck naked now. It was entirely indecent of him, though Claire of all people knew what a man looked like under his clothes. "Perhaps you'd allow me to borrow your shawl?" he asked her anyway. Lycans weren't especially body conscious, but humans were a different matter.

She gave a jerky nod and unknotted the shawl from around her shoulders, tossing it to him, not seeming to want to get too close.

Alun caught it deftly. "Much obliged," he said with what he hoped was a friendly smile. He tied the shawl around his waist. "Better?" he asked, even though he was sure he must look ridiculous. "Miss Walker?"

"It don't really matter, do it?" She spoke at last, her voice trembling.

Alun watched as her gaze continued to drift over his body. Beyond the obvious impropriety, now covered absurdly by a long, pale yellow shawl, Claire could see markings of a Spirit Dancer on his chest, not that she would understand what it meant. The dark, downward-turned crescent was invisible in the physical world, but here, the Goddess made her claim known to all. Alun had been surprised to find the mark still there, after he was banished from his pack. He had expected the Goddess to abandon him the same way his family had—after all, according to the elders, it was her laws he was breaking by being the way he was. But she hadn't left him. He'd never been sure what that might mean, if it meant anything at all.

"You have nothing to fear from me," Alun told Claire, as gently as he could, keeping his distance so as not to spook her. "I'm here to help, if I can. Do you know what's happened?"

"I've died." Her tone was as hollow as the look in her watery blue eyes.

"Do you know how?"

She wrapped her arms around her body tightly. Protectively. "I... I don't.... Why? Why would anybody want to hurt *me*?" she sobbed.

"I don't know," Alun told her the truth.

"Why can't I remember what happened?"

Alun took a slow step forward; when Claire didn't balk, he crossed the rest of the distance between them. He gathered the unresisting girl gently into his arms. "Shhh, it's better you don't recall," he lied. Well, it probably was better for her that she didn't remember having her throat slashed, but for him it wasn't good at all. "Do you remember *anything*?" he asked, pressing her gently. "Did you see his face?"

"I... I don't think so. It all happened so fast." She looked up at him. "Where are we? What is this place?"

"It's all right, nothing can hurt you now," Alun assured her, even though he wasn't sure it was true. He didn't know what lay beyond the first layer of the spirit world, but it had to be better than the world Claire had left behind her. "You won't ever have to spread your legs for another man. You won't go hungry or cold ever again."

She nodded, wiping away her tears. "How is it you can touch me, and why are you naked? Are... are you...?" She didn't seem to be able to ask the question.

"I'm not dead."

"Then how are you here?"

"It don't matter. But I need you to tell me as much as you can about last night." Even if she didn't remember her attacker, she might be able to give him a direction, some clue, anything to keep Percival from coming down on him again. "Please, it's important."

"I... I spent the night with my friend, Martha—Martha Smith. She lives up on Woodseer Street. She's got a room there. She lets me stay with her sometimes, when I've nowhere else to go."

"What else do you remember?"

"Martha shared her bread with me, and... and she made us tea." She smiled—but then it faltered and more tears came. "I'm never gonna see her again, am I?"

"No. I'm sorry."

She swallowed hard; Alun doubted he'd told her anything she didn't already know. Sometimes a spirit just needed to hear it from someone else. "What am I?" Claire wanted to know.

"A spirit."

"You mean a ghost?"

"Yes. A ghost."

"What kind of man are you then, Mr. Blayney, that you're here but you're not dead too?"

"I'm not a man. I ain't human."

She blinked at him, as if seeing him for the first time—then her eyes grew wide and she scrambled away from his grasp, still hobbling with only one shoe on. "What… what are you?" she gasped.

Alun knew that as soon as he admitted he wasn't human, some part of Claire's mind would allow her to see him as he really was, a being with two bodies, but only one soul. "I'm a lycanthrope," he answered her honestly. Calmly. She was dead now; there was no harm in telling her the truth. "A werewolf."

"You… you murdered me…!"

"If I'd killed you, why would I be here askin' you 'bout it?" he snapped, though he remained where he was, not wanting to frighten her further. Claire might not realize it, but if she chose, she could flee to places in the spirit realm where he couldn't follow, and he needed whatever information she could give him, no matter how meager it was. "Claire, listen to me. I'm the one person who might be able to catch the ruddy bastard what done this to you." He tried to sound sensible. "Please. Let me help."

She paused, studying him a long moment. "It was… it was something like you what killed me, wasn't it?"

Alun nodded.

"Why?"

"I don't know."

"How do I know I can trust you?"

Alun held in an exasperated sigh. "I can't hurt you."

"You could still lie to me."

"Why would I want to?"

"I… I'm not sure," she admitted, still hesitant, still keeping her distance.

"Just tell me the last thing you remember. Please, Claire. It's important."

She swallowed hard, her gaze breaking away from his. "I'd already seen one gentleman," she began, looking embarrassed. Contrary to what rich people thought, women like Claire seldom enjoyed having to sell their bodies for money. Most had had decent jobs once, but got turned out, either when there was no more work or when they refused the advances of their employers. Alun didn't know what had brought Claire Walker to the streets, but maybe now that she was dead, she would find some peace. He liked to think that death was more peaceful than life. Claire cleared her throat and went on, still looking uncomfortable. "It was early yet, so I took the money and went for a drink to make the rest of the night go better. I went to the Frying Pan, an' I guess maybe I had more than one drink. Coming out, I… some bloke called me over, nobody I ever seen before."

"What did he look like?"

"I… not as tall as you. A little younger… maybe a lot younger." She frowned. "He weren't dressed… he weren't no toff, but he weren't from the streets, neither. His hair was dark, almost black, and his eyes…." She shuddered. "His eyes were silver. That's all I remember." She bit her lip. "I… I can't remember what happened next—but it was him, wasn't it? That was the bastard what sent me here."

Alun nodded. Silver eyes and black hair. It wasn't much to go on, but it was something.

"What happens now?" Claire wanted to know.

"I s'pose it's time for you to move on."

"Move… where?"

He shrugged. "You're a Catholic, ain't ya?"

"Whores don't go to heaven, Mr. Blayney."

"All I know is you can't stay here."

"Why not?"

"Because if you do, you'll never be able to leave. You'll stay tied to the physical world, but not able to touch anyone or anything in it. You'll be trapped here, Claire, stuck in between the living and the dead. It's no way to be."

She swallowed, fear dancing in her eyes. "Will you do something for me, 'fore I go?"

"If I can," he answered carefully. It wasn't wise to make promises to the dead.

"I… I've a daughter, her name's Alice. Alice Miller. She lives with my parents in Hathersage. My mum's named Alice too. My father's called

George. I know it's a distance, I wouldn't expect you to be able to get it to her right away…." She bit her lower lip. "But my cross…?"

"I'll see she gets it."

"Thank you, Mr. Blayney. What—what do I do to move on?"

"Whatever feels natural, I guess."

Claire stood for a long moment, just looking around, not seeming to know what to do—Alun wished he could tell her, but he didn't know, either.

Finally, Claire kicked off her one shoe and walked toward the end of the alleyway. She wasn't even halfway to it before she began to fade….

Alun opened his eyes. He was lying as a wolf in the cold, dark alleyway. Overhead, the moon hung low in the sky. He stood slowly and stretched his sore muscles, unsure of how long he'd been there. Time passed differently in the spirit realm. An hour could seem to last all night, or a day could pass in the blink of an eye.

Fabric rustled behind him; Alun crouched low, growling out a warning, his hackles raised as he turned to face down the interloper.

"It's only me, *diangen*," Rhianna spat with naked contempt. She was as gaunt as a human as she was a wolf, and her long black hair was matted and gnarled. The tattered dress she wore hung around her too-thin body, looking like little more than rags. Her feet were bare. Her eyes blazed with hatred at the sight of him. "You're a fool for going to the spirit side without someone to watch over your body." She told Alun what he already knew.

He shifted back into his human form; unlike Claire, Rhianna didn't respond with shock at the sight of him standing there naked—she didn't react at all. Alun didn't bother reminding her that he didn't have the luxury of having someone to watch over him when he crossed the veil. "What are you doing here, Rhianna?" he asked instead. "If Percival finds out—"

"Who do you think sent me? What have you found?"

"Tell your damned pack leader I don't answer to him!" he snarled angrily—impulsively. "I'm not a member of your pack, remember?" They wouldn't have him. No one would.

Rhianna balked, obviously startled by his tone. She studied him a moment before stepping closer. When she reached out her hand to touch his chest, Alun remained still, allowing the contact without protest. He could hardly remember the last time another lycan had touched him, except to hit him—except for Percival demanding obeisance.

Rhianna's touch wasn't tender, however; it wasn't kind or gentle. Her eyes narrowed as she met his gaze. "You're healed."

He shrugged. When she took her hand away, he shuddered at the loss of the warmth, hating himself for not being able to conceal how much it hurt to be so alone. "Have you eaten?" he asked. He didn't have money, but they could hunt, he would gladly share whatever he caught with her.

Only Rhianna's face twisted in anger. "I'll share no meal with you, nor take meat from your hand, *diangen*!" She spat at his feet. Without another word, she shifted into a tall, skinny dire wolf, her rags falling around her feet, a pool of filthy cloth. She gave him one last disdainful look before escaping into the darkness.

Alun ignored the pang of loneliness, but then his mind went immediately to James. He wondered for the thousandth time what James had thought when he found his bed empty. *Prolly just as glad he didn't have to tell me to get out*, he told himself. He didn't believe his own bitter words, but it didn't matter now. It was too late to go back and make amends. Besides, what would he say?

"MASTER JAMES," Mrs. Dunberry called from the backdoor. "It's getting dark; you should come in. I've made hot chocolate," she added, by way of extra enticement.

James had been toiling in the back garden all day, turning under the earth, laying down straw, readying the beds for winter. Anything he could think of to occupy his mind and hands—anything to keep from hurting. He'd said fewer than half a dozen words to his housekeeper since discovering Alun gone. He didn't know how the other man had gotten out of the house without being seen—or where he'd gone with neither money nor clothing—but James believed Mrs. Dunberry when she claimed not to have seen him go.

James supposed it was naïve to think that Alun would ever be interested in pursuing something more substantive than… than whatever last night had been. It was just that every time he thought about the way Alun had looked at him, the way he'd touched him, held him afterward, all those soft touches and tender kisses… it seemed so much more than just sex. *Which I guess is what makes me naïve,* he thought bitterly, blinking away more tears. He was a fool to think someone like Alun would want a man like him, a toff, a rich man... but didn't Alun know he wasn't like that?

"Master James?" Mrs. Dunberry called again, drawing his attention back to the garden and the world around him.

"I'll be in shortly," James promised his housekeeper. He just had to put up the tools first. They had been his mother's—his father used to joke that he had a black thumb, while both of his wife's were green as emeralds. She would laugh and say she loved him anyway. James missed them both so much.

He ran his fingers over the worn wood handle of one of the shovels. He could almost feel his mother's hands. Fresh tears stung at his eyes. "I really thought...." His throat seized up, choking off his words. It was stupid anyway; she couldn't hear him. She was dead, and he didn't believe in heaven and hell or angels... God. One was born, lived, and died; it was as simple as that. But that didn't stop him from talking to his mother now and then, pretending just for a moment that she could hear him, that she could answer and tell him it would be all right.

"I thought I could love him," he whispered past the lump in his throat. "I still could," he admitted, squeezing the shovel's handle tight, as if it was his mother's hand. "I just... I want what you and Father had. I want someone I can come home to, someone to lie down next to at night. Someone to wake up with. Someone to love, someone who will love me in return. Why is that so difficult? Just because the someone I want is a man? I don't want to hurt anybody or change anybody else." He wiped the moisture from his cheeks. He didn't know what either of his parents would have said about his loving a man.

"But I have to believe you'd understand," he whispered to them in the dark. He had to believe that his mother, who had accepted everybody, Jew or Black, Asian or Indian, man or woman, would tell him that it was all right to be different.

"Look at the flowers in the meadow," she used to tell him. *"Do they all look the same? Wouldn't it be boring if they were all alike? Nature has made us all different, Jamie, but we're all Nature's children. Never forget that."*

He had to believe that his father, who had no use for the rhetoric of either the Church or the Crown, who believed that all things had a reason and an explanation, would have accepted him as he was. He had to believe that both of his parents would love him no matter who he loved.

James had come to terms with his sexuality nine years ago, when he was just fifteen—although he reckoned he'd always known he was different from his brother, Thomas, and their friends. He still remembered his first tantalizing kiss with another boy, a young man who worked on the estate. Uncle John had been furious when he discovered them. Peter was dismissed at once, sent away, told if he ever came around again, he would have to face the authorities.

Thomas tried to tell James it was for the best, that all he needed was to find a nice young lady, someone like Tom's Anna, and then everything would be all right. Tom reminded him that there were certain things a young man did in proper society—and certain things he *didn't* do.

"What you want simply doesn't enter into it, Jamie... not that what you seem to want is entirely natural," he'd added, his face pinched up in disgust. James didn't believe he said it to be cruel; Tom just didn't understand. He didn't want to. So James moved to London to be away from them.

If it wasn't for his grandfather, James was sure he would have believed his brother and uncle, would have believed there was something wrong with him. But his grandfather, like his father, was a rational, reasonable man. "Homosexual," he had said some psychologist called it, when a man favored other men. He said it was perfectly normal, just different. *"Different like all those flowers your mother used to talk about,"* he'd added with the kind of smile that told James everything would be all right. He wished his grandfather were with him now. Maybe *he* could help James understand what he'd done wrong, why Alun had left without a word.

James put the gardening tools into the shed and trudged back up to the house. He didn't notice the soreness of his muscles. All he felt was unbearable emptiness as he walked into his house knowing Alun wasn't there.

JAMES knocked on Robin Perris's door the next afternoon—and he felt like a cad for being there. It seemed the only time he went looking for Rob was when he was hurting. He knew they were supposed to be friends— they *were* friends—but he wasn't blind. Rob never pressed him, teased him, maybe, but he never made an issue of how much he wanted more than James's friendship. Wanted more than to simply be bedded by him again. Perhaps it was Robin he should be courting, not someone who had twice fled his home without so much as "goody-bye." And James enjoyed Rob's company; Robin made him laugh, made him feel comfortable. James certainly couldn't complain about his bedroom skills, either. It didn't bother him, what Robin did for a living. He wished Rob didn't have to spread himself for strangers, but there were few places a man like Robin, someone soft and sensitive—uneducated—could find honest work.

Finally, the door cracked open and a pair of inquisitive, bright green eyes peered cautiously out at him. "James!" he cried at once, throwing the door open wide as a broad, welcoming smile bloomed on his beautiful face. The elation in Robin's tone would have made James feel even more awful—guilty—if he hadn't found himself suddenly reeling. He'd never seen Robin in the full light of day before, and standing there in the afternoon sun, Robin looked *so* young. Shame needled at the constable's soul, making him sick to his stomach. Had he really slept with a *boy*?

Still grinning, Robin held out his hand. "What a pleasant surprise! Please, come in."

Dumbly, James clasped Rob's outstretched hand and allowed himself to be drawn into the tidy little room. Was Robin even old enough to be living on his own?

"Won't you please have a seat?" the young man invited him in the perfect imitation of courtesy.

James swallowed. Nodded. In addition to the simple bed and its lavender duvet, there were a pair of plain wooden chairs set up by a small table in front of a window; the window was hung with lace curtains. No doubt the duvet and curtains were Rob's addition to the room.

James sat down with a soft thud and turned his attention to the lithe Irishman whose bed he'd occupied, if only for a single night. It had been a different bed in a different rented room, one without lace and lavender. James felt nauseous. Rob was just a boy!

Robin sat down in the other chair, still beaming. "It's good to see you, James. I'm only sorry I've nothing to offer."

"I… you seem to be doing all right for yourself," he managed, his tone subdued. Robin's lodging was just one step above a doss house, but it looked comfortable, like Rob had been there awhile.

Robin flashed a sly smile. "What can I say? Business has been good."

James's gut twisted. "I… should go." He started to stand, but the young man's hand on his stayed him.

"It ain't what ya think, James."

James blinked. "What?"

"Business. It ain't what ya think."

"I—it's none of my concern," James told him flatly. Regardless of how old—or young—Robin was, he'd been spreading himself for other men long before James met him. James pulled himself to his feet. "I'm sorry to have intruded on you. I'm sure you must be busy. Good day—"

"James, wait! Please. You just got here an' there's something I've been dying to tell ya."

James met his gaze, those brilliant green eyes that had held him captive the night they'd…. He looked away. Robin had found him drunk in a pub a few nights after Tom died and, deciding he was in no state to go home—to go anywhere alone—Rob brought him back to his room, just so he he'd have a safe place to stay until he was sober enough to get home. *And I fucked him.* "How old are you, Robin?"

Rob bristled.

"Please. I need to know."

"I ain't no babe, if that's what ya wanna know."

"That's not an answer."

"I… it's the best you're gonna get. Please let it lie."

"I can't. Not after…." He swallowed hard. "How can I let it lie, Robin?"

"Because we're friends an' I'm asking you to. *Please.* I ain't no babe, and I ain't never lied to you about nothing. I won't ever, either, which is why I'm begging you to let it go."

James opened his mouth, then shut it again. He believed that Robin would never lie to him, though he didn't know why. If he pressed him, right now, Robin would tell him exactly how old he was—and James was certain he would regret knowing.

He met Robin's gaze—held it a long moment. There were times, like now, when he looked into those almost unearthly green eyes and thought he was looking into the eyes of an old, old man, someone who had seen so much. *And all of it bad.* "I'm sorry, Robin," he whispered, not even sure what he was apologizing for.

Robin nodded. "Apology accepted. Now, please, stay... just for a bit," he entreated.

Reluctantly, James sat back down. Partially reluctantly. He didn't want to leave, he just wasn't sure he should stay. "You... you said you had something to tell me?"

Impish joy flickered back into Robin's eyes. "I... ya remember... ya remember that theater I took ya to?"

"What of it?" James asked. The performance hadn't been quite as risqué as he'd expected, though Adelphi it wasn't.

"I've been doin'... that is, there was an opening an'... an' I got meself a little part an' then one thing led to 'nother an' now I'm acting regular like, an' I've wanted to tell you, only...." His cheeks were as red as his waistcoat—James was sure it was the first time he'd ever seen Robin blush. "It ain't like it's real theater or nothing, an' I'm sure you won't think it was no better than spreading meself for a few pennies, but I... I love it."

"I think that's fantastic news, Rob," James told him in earnest.

His enthusiasm wasn't contagious. "I know most people don't think acting's much above being a whore."

"I'm not most people."

Robin hesitated. Then, "No. No ya ain't," he agreed softly. "You... you're the reason I'm doing it, James."

"Me?"

He nodded. "I *am* old enough to know what I been doin', what I was doing, because I... I know what ya think of it. What most folks think, anyway. Acting don't pay much, but it's steady money. Honest money. I've regular hours too. An' if ya wanted, I—I could... that is... ya could come in. As me guest, ya know, for free," he said hopefully, even though they both knew money wasn't an issue for James.

"I can't."

Robin's expression fell. "O' course," he said simply.

"It's not that I don't want to, Robin. It's that I *can't*. Inspector Lamont has me on nights, 'until further notice'."

"What? Why?"

"It's a long story. And it doesn't matter," he decided, forcing a smile. "I've got a few hours before I have to be in. Maybe I could buy you supper?"

"I—I'd like that, but—"

"Good." James cut him off before he could come up with any excuses not to accept.

Robin stood up and got his too-big purple coat down from the hook next to his bed. He beamed with pleasure when James offered to help him into it, but when he turned, there still seemed to be uncertainty playing across his face. "Ya know me better than *anyone*, James," he said quietly.

"What?" James blinked; he hardly knew Rob at all. Was the other man—boy?—really *that* guarded?

"You… you're one of the very few people I've ever really trusted. One of the few I've called me friend an' really meant it. Thank you for being me friend, James. It… your friendship means… I just wanted ya to know how special you are to me."

James swallowed hard; there seemed to be so much that Robin wasn't saying… so much he didn't think he wanted the younger man *to* say. "Come on, let's get some supper. I want to hear all about your new profession," he told Rob, his tone forcibly light.

Robin smiled too. "All right. But I get to pick the place we eat."

ALUN leaned back against the trunk of the twisted old tree he'd climbed. Its bark was rough, but he reveled in the feel of it under his hands. There were few places he could find peace amongst the trees—few places he could find trees at all. He knew better than to venture into the pack's territory outside the city, just as he knew better than to venture into the

West End, although he'd seen Hyde Park once, and eyed its green, tree-filled expanse with longing. But he didn't belong in a place like that. He belonged here, amongst the gnarled old trees that grew in the sheltered confines of a centuries-old graveyard. It was hardly the kind of woods a lycanthrope's heart craved, but it was the best a *diangen* could hope for.

Above him, the silver moon shone full and bright in the night sky. The full moon meant he was likely to be safe from Percival, at least for the next few nights—the London pack's leader was Full Moon-born and would no doubt be spending the next few nights in revelry, hunting with the other Full Moon wolves of his pack. Deer and other game ran through the pack's lands, south and east of the city proper, near St. Paul's Cray and Scadbury. Alun had been there a few times, but he'd never been permitted to hunt there.

Over a week had passed since Claire Walker was murdered—since Percival's visit. Since he'd left James's posh home.... Alun swallowed hard. He was sure he would never see his beautiful young blond again. He told himself it was for the best. James couldn't be his mate, and he didn't want to be James's lover—not that he thought a man like James would actually want him as a lover. He didn't know what that night had been about, but it wasn't meant as a prelude to anything, it was just... it was what it was. James's heated platitudes didn't mean anything. How could they? No one meant the things they said in the throes of passion.

Instead of pining over what would never be, Alun tried to concentrate on the larger issue.

If there was a strange wolf prowling the streets of the East End, he was doing a good job of keeping himself hidden. But why? Was it another *diangen*? If so, what had he done to make himself an outcast? There were all sorts of reasons a lycan would be banished from his pack—certainly the propensity for killing humans was cause enough. Lycanthropes survived by remaining hidden—wolves amongst the sheep, his father used to say. His father had little use for humankind.

But why would a wolf go cutting up girls? It didn't make any sense. He'd heard of rogue lycans killing for sport, for the sheer enjoyment of watching a human bleed, but a wolf wouldn't use a *knife*, he would use his teeth, his claws. Why would a wolf intentionally act like a man?

Alun sighed and closed his eyes. Thinking about it only made his head hurt. How could Percival expect him to track down the rogue wolf, anyway? He was *diangen*…. Alun let his head fall back against the tree trunk. He doubted Percival actually meant for him to stop the rogue; this was just one more way for the pack leader to torment him. Maybe it was time to leave London. What he'd said to Rhianna was true, he didn't owe Percival anything, certainly not any loyalty. The man made his life a living hell, every chance he got.

Except that if the humans found the killer first, if they discovered he was a werewolf, every lycan would pay the price, even him. That was the rationale he used to justify why he didn't run. His heart and soul knew there was another reason: London was where James Heron lived.

Chapter 9

ALUN leaned against the wall outside the Ten Bells pub watching people go by, sucking on the end of a thin black cigarette, and wondering if there was a rogue wolf hiding in the crowd somewhere, his scent masked by the smells of the street. It wasn't inconceivable. London was a big place, full of all sorts of Otherkind: daemons, vampires, other shape shifters—even the odd wizard or two. It wasn't difficult to hide in a city so big and so diverse, even if one didn't actually mean to. Alun had been in London for almost six months before Rhianna became aware of his presence—made Percival aware of it. Alun stubbed out his cigarette and pitched it to the ground. Tobacco was a luxury he rarely afforded himself, but his purse was full of other men's money and the hour was still early—it was hardly midnight. He was no closer to solving his problems than he had been a week ago, but at least he wouldn't be sleeping on the cobblestones tonight. He was turning to leave, to find a room to rent, when a familiar scent hit his nose: sweet musk, spice. Warmth.

Home. The word hammered through his aching soul, filling it with longing. With need. Before he knew what he was doing, Alun was searching the faces on the street, fervently seeking out the source of the scent. He knew he wouldn't dare approach James, not after the way he'd left him, but to see him, to know he was well… finally he found what he was searching for, but… it wasn't James. It couldn't be. The man standing on the street corner chatting with Emily Harris had his back to Alun, but he was wearing a constable's blue uniform. James wasn't a constable any more. He couldn't be, not after walking off his post.

Guilt plagued at the lycan's heart; James had lost his job because of him. He knew the younger man didn't need a job, but that was all the more reason to suppose he *wanted* to be a copper. Alun cursed James for his sentimentality—he should have just left him there, it was what anyone else would have done!

But James Heron wasn't like anyone else Alun had ever known.

He snorted contemptuously. He didn't *know* James Heron! Heron didn't know him! If he did, James wouldn't have taken him home, wouldn't have taken him to his bed. *He wouldn't have told me he was mine.* If James had any idea what he really was, he would have done to Alun what humans always did to lycans. Alun lit another cigarette and returned his gaze to the man standing across the street, wanting to know why he smelled so much like James. It needled at him—James was special. Unique.

Mine.

He shook himself again. James would never be his.

The street was too noisy for even sharp lycanthropic ears to pick up any of the conversation, but Alun saw Emily's smile and knew the constable wasn't giving her any trouble. Most of the boys were all right, but there were one or two who harassed the girls, forcing them into giving out a free suck or knee trembler up against a wall if they didn't want to get hauled in.

A new scent caught Alun's attention: sharp, sulfuric. Daemonic. A low growl rumbled in the lycan's throat in response—and the he saw him. *It.* Alun's hackles rose as Robin Perris sidled up to the man in the constable's uniform and laid a hand gently on his back—the constable leaned into it, just a little (or so Alun imagined), and Alun nearly launched himself across the street, fully intending to remove Perris's hand from the rest of his body. But it *wasn't* James, and even if it were, he had no claim on Heron. He had no right to feel protective, possessive. Hurt. He'd left the young blond's bed without so much as a good-bye. He doubted James ever wanted to see him again, let alone become the object of his heated desire.

Then he berated himself for thinking he was important enough for James to care about at all. By now, Heron had no doubt forgotten the entire incident.

The man in the constable's uniform turned, casting his profile into the light, and Alun's heart caught in his throat. *James!* Alun ached to cross the street, to say… something. Anything. Just to be near the other man. But he knew what James must feel toward him. Contempt. Anger. Resentment. It would kill Alun to know James hated him.

And Robin.... Alun bristled again. James couldn't possibly know what Perris was, what he *really* was... *but he must know what Rob does for money.* Jealousy burned in Alun's veins. Rob was a Mary-Anne, a male harlot, the sort who serviced other men. Alun would know. Ten years ago, he'd been a regular client of Perris's. He wondered if that was how James knew Perris—as a client. But he had no claim on Heron, no right to say who he associated himself with. He might have had that right once, but he'd relinquished the privilege when he'd left James's house the way he did.

James turned his head a little more, and Alun knew he'd been spotted. He couldn't read the younger man's expression, but it didn't matter. It was too late to run; James had already excused himself from his companions and was crossing the street, heading straight for where Alun was standing.

Alun's palms grew moist as his mouth grew dry. His heart thundered in his chest. His gut tightened unbearably. He forced a smile that was only partially contrived—he was happy to see the other man, happier still that he had his job—but the smile died on his lips when he saw the storm brewing in James's mossy-green eyes. It was every emotion he was afraid of.

"Evening, Constable." Alun pushed the words past the lump in his throat.

JAMES swallowed hard. *Constable.* The return to formality was like a knife digging in his gut. His knees had gone to jelly when he turned and saw Alun standing there, those black eyes smoldering, watching him... or at least he'd thought he saw heat in Alun's gaze. Maybe he'd only seen what he wanted to see. "Mr. Blayney." He returned the Welshman's greeting in a cool tone. "You seem well," he added. No one who saw Alun today would realize that just a week ago, he'd been a bruised, bloodied mess.

A ghost of a smile flicked across Alun's face—and then it was gone. "You too." He shifted his weight from one foot to the other. "Nice night. Not too cold."

"Nice enough, I suppose," James agreed. And then he was out of things to say.

They both were. But neither walked away.

"You still got your job," Alun finally said into the awkward silence.

James nodded.

"I'm glad," Alun told him.

"Me too."

"I—" both started to say at once—and suddenly the tension broke. James laughed; Alun smiled. James still couldn't be sure what he saw in Alun's black eyes—eyes the lanky East Ender seemed more determined than ever to hide behind his long bangs—but James knew what he wanted; it was standing right in front of him. He just had to figure out how to get it. "My shift ends at nine," he said. "Would you consent to meeting me for breakfast?"

Alun blinked. Behind thick bangs, his brows knitted together and he shook his head.

"*Please*. Just one meal. What could it hurt?"

Alun hesitated. Then relented. "There's a early house on Commercial Street—" he began.

"I know the place. I'll meet you there at ten."

"Ten o'clock," Alun confirmed, still sounding reluctant. "I… I gotta go."

James nodded, his heart pounding so loudly in his ears he could barely hear his own voice. "I'll see you at ten," he said, and Alun took his leave. When James turned back around, Emily was chatting with a fellow who looked like a prospective client.

Robin was gone.

James swallowed, guilt pricking at his conscience. He didn't see Robin for the rest of the night, even when he went looking.

THE last few hours of James's shift dragged on into eternity. He hadn't honestly expected Alun to agree to breakfast so easily. But he had, and that had to mean something, didn't it? If James had believed in God, he might have prayed that it did. He knew he was likely being a fool—and he realized that Inspector Lamont was watching him intently, as he carded his fingers through his sweat-dampened hair, trying to get it to look presentable.

James shot the inspector a tight-lipped smile and wished him a good morning, before taking his leave from the precinct house. Lamont had been watching him more closely than ever since he'd come back to work. James didn't care, not right now. Right now, all he could think about was seeing Alun again, and what he was going to say to the lanky Welshman. What Alun might want to say to him. The nearer James got to the pub where they were to meet, the tighter the knots in his stomach became. What if Alun didn't show? Or what if he was there, but he told him that he had a wife, children—or just that he wasn't interested? Or what if he *was* interested, but didn't want the complications? It wasn't like two men could court, get married, set up a household together....

Preparing himself for the worst, James opened the pub door—and saw Alun sitting at a corner table, watching the entrance over the top of a mug. James's heart hammered in his chest, and he made his way over, trying not to hurry his steps, trying not to seem too eager to cross the distance between them. Trying not to get his hopes up too high. Just because Alun was there didn't mean things would go the way James wanted them to. "I hope I haven't kept you waiting long," he said by way of greeting. The pub was quiet at that hour of the day, but it was hardly the intimate setting James would have preferred. The place smelled of food, both fresh and stale, whisky, rum, ale, cider, and human sweat.

As to his comment, Alun merely shrugged. "Just got 'ere."

James nodded, awkwardly. "Do you want another?" he asked, nodding at the half-empty mug in Alun's hand.

"I'm fine." He hesitated a moment, then set down his mug. "They've still got some fresh pastries left, the kind with venison sausage. I asked 'em to save us a couple. If you're interested."

James's heart raced faster. Had Alun really remembered that venison sausage was his favorite? He must have! James took a shaky breath and let it out. "Why don't I go get us a couple?" he suggested, trying desperately not to sound too over-eager.

Alun nodded his agreement, and presently both men were eating, sustaining conversation that was only a little bit strained.

"I hope you don't get into too much trouble with your Mrs. Dunberry, for being so late in getting home, I mean," Alun managed to tease, as they were finishing up their meal.

"I'm sure she'd be furious if she found out where I'd had my breakfast. She doesn't approve of the way 'city people' eat." He rolled his eyes.

Alun snickered. "She'll not hear a word from me, I promise."

James's smile faltered. "Does... does that mean you'll be coming back to my house again?" he asked, forcing the words out before he lost his nerve. His shifted his gaze away from Alun's face, not wanting to see the "no" in his eyes before the other man said the word aloud.

"I wasn't sure you'd be wanting me back," Alun told him.

James looked at him, not believing Alun actually thought that. But apparently, he did. "I'd have invited you home with me last night, if I'd thought you would accept," he said softly. "I still would. Will. Am. I mean... assuming you don't have a wife to go home to."

Alun blinked again, but then his gaze dropped. "No," he said softly. "Never had a wife, no children, neither. It's like I said before, I don't got no one, least not anymore."

His tone broke James's heart; Alun had had someone once, he was sure of it. Maybe a lover, maybe just his family—his parents and those six brothers and his sister... his grandfather. Whoever it was, he'd loved them, he missed them. James didn't know how Alun had lost his family, but he did know what it felt like to be alone in the world. He wanted to hold Alun, to kiss him. Make love to him. But the best he could do was to slide his boot up against Alun's under the table and give his foot a little nudge. "Come home with me, Alun."

JAMES was so close, his scent so strong, that Alun could almost taste him—and it was pulling his beast up from the depths, up too close to his skin. If they were anywhere else, he would take James on the spot. "You don't know what you're asking." The words came out a husky growl.

They made James smile. "I think I proved to you once before that I know *exactly* what I'm asking, Alun." His tone was dangerously seductive.

Alun jumped when he felt the light touch of James's hand against his crotch under the table.

James ran his fingers up the length of his swelling shaft. He stopped at the head, circling it with his fingertips, licking his lips. "I know what it's like to feel like you're all alone, Alun. But you're not alone. I'm right here, and I want you."

Alun's gaze darted around the pub; no one could see what was going on under the table. No one seemed to even be looking at them. "You're gonna get us arrested," he hissed anyway.

James chuckled, but shifted so he was sitting a more respectable distance from his companion. "There's a story for the papers. Constable sullies…." He hesitated, a flush of pink overtaking his cheeks.

"I *ain't* no criminal," Alun growled.

"I didn't mean—"

"Yes you did. It's all right," he added to the apologetic look on James's face. "I s'pose I can't exactly claim to be an upright citizen, neither. An' you're right, it would be funny. But just the same, I can think of better ways to spend the day," he said, wondering how much he was going to regret the decision to go home with James. Or maybe it wasn't a decision, not exactly anyway, because a *decision* was something a person elected to do, something they had a choice in. He had no choice.

One more time, he told himself as they left the pub together. He would give into lust and temptation one more time and then he was through with James Heron.

Chapter 10

ALUN waited behind James on the porch while the constable opened his front door and called "hallo" to Mrs. Dunberry. "I think we're in luck," he said over his shoulder. "She must've already gone to the market. No one else should be in either," he added. He was grinning like a school-boy who knew he was getting away with something he shouldn't be doing—the expression made Alun laugh. There was something incredibly impish about the younger man. He liked it. He liked James. He tried to tell himself it didn't matter, they'd never be more than… whatever they were at that very moment. It hurt. Alun decided not to think about it, he didn't want anything to spoil what little time he had with James.

By the time Alun was through the front door, James was already peeling out of his blue wool coat. Alun grabbed him by its collar and pulled him into a rough, hungry kiss. If he was only going to allow himself this one last time with James Heron, he wasn't to waste a moment of it on small talk or polite conversation.

James yielded to him at once, parting his lips, letting Alun have his mouth. He slid his hands down Alun's body and groped his crotch like he had in the pub. Swift, nimble fingers undid the buttons, and within seconds, James was on his knees, taking the head of Alun's already half-hard cock into his mouth. Alun groaned—James's mouth felt so sweet, and his tongue… Goddess! Alun moaned out the younger man's name as James snaked his tongue skillfully over the entire length of his shaft.

He gripped James's shoulders and rocked forward, inviting James to take him deeper, wanting to touch the back of his throat, wanting to watch his cock vanish in between those gorgeous pink lips. James seemed only too happy to oblige.

"Shite, James, I think I'm gonna come just from this," he warned.

James smiled up at him. He pulled back just long enough to invite Alun to come anywhere he wanted. Any way he wanted. "I'm yours, remember?"

Alun pulled James to his feet and into another savage kiss—he yielded without hesitation. James tasted of him, of salt and sex, of excitement. *Mine*, Alun's soul wanted to howl—but he held himself in check. James wasn't his. He was… he was a distraction. A dalliance. Just the same, he pressed his nose to James's neck and inhaled deeply—there wasn't even a trace of Robin's scent on him. Alun growled his approval and bent the compliant young man over a low coffee table, growling his intentions into his ear. First, he was going to take James here, now, fast and hard, and then they were going to go up to the bedroom and he was going to take him again. James quivered.

"Complaints?" Alun asked.

"No." He barely got the word out before Alun was on him again, yanking his trousers down to his knees.

James gasped in surprise when Alun pressed the flat of his tongue to his opening. The gasp quickly became a moan, and James wriggled his ass back against Alun's mouth, begging for more.

Alun used both hands to spread the younger man's ass cheeks wide, giving himself better access to the little pink rosette. He smiled and kissed James lightly, causing him to shiver. He nipped, teasing him—bit harder, marking James's ass with a deep purple bruise, making him moan. By the time Alun pressed his tongue past the tight ring of muscles and into his entrance, James was white-knuckled and whimpering, begging to be fucked.

"Don't move," Alun told him. James nodded. He seemed both relieved and disappointed at being given a moment to catch his breath.

Alun padded to the kitchen, and was pleased see that the oil he'd seen before was still sitting near the stove. He brought the entire bottle back to the parlor with him—James was right where he'd left him. Alun smiled appreciatively at the sight of his bobby's firm, round ass sticking up into the air, just waiting for him. "Goddess, you're somethin' t' see," he murmured.

"I only hope you plan to do more than just look at me," James told him over his shoulder; his eyes burned with unmasked lust.

Alun's smile deepened. Turned wicked. "I don't know. You're mighty fine just like that." He toed off his shoes and stripped completely out of his trousers, before coating his erect cock with oil. He ran his hands up and down his own erection, making a show of slicking himself until he glistened. "I could come just standing here looking at you."

"Oh, God—please, Alun!"

"Tell me what you want."

"Fuck me. Fuck me hard. Right here. Then take me upstairs and do it again. Do it anywhere you want. I'm yours, Alun. All yours. Please. No more teasing."

Alun knelt behind James and slid an oil-slicked finger gently into him. James groaned and arched his back. "Yes. God, yes," he moaned.

"Easy, *cariad*," Alun whispered. "I might wanna fuck you senseless, but I don't want to hurt you."

James nodded. He sat still while Alun worked his opening, stretching him. Alun wrapped his free arm around James's chest and found his nipples, teasing and tormenting them as he inserted a second finger to join the first. James hissed with pleasure as Alun's fingers found his sweet spot, his prostate, and raked against it over and over and over, until he had his young lover panting again, begging, desperate for more.

Alun pressed his nose against James's neck. He rubbed his cheeks over his skin, covering himself in James's scent. "Whose are you?" he whispered in James's ear.

"Yours. I'm yours, Alun," he answered without hesitation. "Please...."

"Please what?"

"I want more of you... all of you... *please*...." He was nearly incoherent.

Alun slid his fingers out of the tight passage. James shuddered at the loss, but held himself still while Alun positioned his cock against the sweet, tight little hole. "Remember my promise," he growled softly, the only warning he gave before thrusting himself into James. He was rewarded by a deeply satisfied moan from the younger man's throat.

"Don't stop," James whispered urgently. "I want you. I want all of you. Please don't stop." It was like a litany as Alun hammered relentlessly into him. James met every thrust with one of his own, forcing Alun's cock balls deep into him, until it was the lycan who was shuddering, crying out his lover's name, feeling helpless as he realized James had turned the tables and was fucking *him* senseless!

Alun lost himself in the frenzy of sensations, the ripple of muscles squeezing against his shaft, the rhythmic pounding of flesh against flesh, the scent of the other's desire mingling with his own. The sweet warmth of James's body, and the whimpers of pleasure coming from his lips as he told Alun how good his cock felt, how much he wanted him.

When he finally released his seed, it was like his whole body was emptying out into James, filling him.

Mine! His soul howled defiantly. *Home! My mate.*

Alun nearly collapsed onto James, but managed to wrap both arms around his blond's slender waist instead, holding him tightly—tenderly—as aftershocks rocked through him.

"Alun?"

"Sorry," he gasped; he must have been crushing James under his weight. Alun released his hold and felt James wince as pulled out of him. "I didn't hurt you, did I?"

James rolled over to face him. "Maybe a little. I'm not complaining, sweetheart," he assured him quickly, cupping Alun's face in both hands. He drew him in, brushing his lips with a soft, reassuring kiss. He startled Alun when he held him there for several long moments before flashing a puckish grin. "But I will complain if you don't do something about *that*," he nodded toward his still-hard cock.

The lycan returned his smirk with one of his own, and before James could react, he hauled the younger man over his shoulder and bolted up the stairs, straight into the bedroom. Alun deposited him onto his bed and made short work of his clothing, tossing it unceremoniously onto the floor beside the bed along with what was left of his own. Then he crawled on top of James and kissed him. His lips. His throat. His chest. He tasted every inch of James Heron, covered every inch of him with his scent before drinking his seed. Before making love to him again.

JAMES lay, feeling boneless and sated, curled up against the warmth of Alun's body. He could hear Alun's heart beating softly under his ear. Strong arms encircled him, making him feel safe, warm. Alun looked down at him and smiled, pulling him tighter.

James closed his eyes for a long moment, just enjoying the closeness, the contact. He didn't want to spoil it, but there was something he had to ask. "Will you be here when I wake up, Alun?"

Black brows furrowed at the uncertainty in his tone. "Is that a question or a request?"

"Both?"

"What d'you mean, 'both'?"

James took a deep breath and let it out. He didn't know how to say all the things he wanted to say, even though the words were simple. He was falling in love with Alun and wanted to know if Alun thought he would ever feel the same way about him. But that was too much to risk. "I'd like you to be here when I wake up. But... if you're not planning on staying, if you're going to leave again, I... I'd just... please tell me now, so I won't be disappointed when I wake to find you gone."

Alun swallowed hard and hesitated for long enough that James wondered if even that was too much to ask for. "I'll be here," he promised, but his tone was impossible to interpret.

Having no other choice, James accepted the answer and closed his eyes, letting sleep wash over him.

ALUN woke in the early evening to find James still curled up against him, though somehow, the younger man had managed to cocoon himself up into the blankets, leaving him bare. "Good thing I don't get cold as easy as that." Alun chuckled, feathering a soft kiss to the top of James's head. He closed his eyes and inhaled the younger man's scent before rubbing his cheek gently against his hair. His heart sang with joy. It ached. He was falling for the human, and no matter how hard he fought it, he couldn't stop himself. He wanted James, his soul had already claimed him... but James was human. Humans didn't mate, they married, divorced... hurt each other. Not that wolves were perfect, far from it, in fact, but another wolf would understand what it meant to claim a mate. Another wolf wouldn't betray him the way a human would. The way a human had.

Feeling too restless to stay in bed, Alun untangled himself from his lover's arms and slid out of the bed. James grumbled unhappily in his sleep.

"I'm not going any further than to answer nature's callin'," he promised softly, though he wondered what Mrs. Dunberry was going to make of him being in the house. He fumbled for his shirt and realized with cold dread that his trousers were still downstairs in the parlor. There was no way to explain why he was upstairs without them; there would be no denying what they'd done. He was tempted to stay in the bedroom until James awoke, but what difference would that make? Coming down together might even make them look twice as guilty.

With a resigned sigh, he reached for James's pants. They were hardly an ideal fit. Had he been in better humor, he might have laughed at the irony of *him* wearing a constable's uniform trousers.

He buttoned up his shirt and slid into his waistcoat, trying desperately to make himself look presentable. It wasn't working; he didn't look the least bit respectable. It didn't help that his shoes were still downstairs as well.

Barefooted, in James's trousers and his own shirt and waistcoat, Alun exited the bedroom; even before he got to the top of the stairs, he could hear James's housekeeper puttering about in the kitchen.

"Good evening, Mrs. Dunberry," Alun announced his presence quietly, when he was halfway down the back steps. Mrs. Dunberry was standing at the stove, her back to the stairs, and he didn't want to scare her. No doubt it would be James she was expecting.

She paused a moment before looking over her shoulder, a carefully neutral expression etched across her face. "Mr. Blayney. Will you be joining Master James for supper?"

"I...." He hesitated. But he had a hard time imagining James not inviting him stay for supper after having asked him to stay the day in his bed. Still, he didn't want to presume. "As long I'm welcome." He shrugged, slipping his hands into his pockets. James's pockets.

She gave over a curt little nod. "Well. I suppose there's enough for two. If I'd been told we would be having company, there would be more."

"It smells lovely," he said, trying to mollify her.

She refused to be pacified. "I'll get you some warm water to wash up with," she told him in a brusque tone. Her gaze raked over him. "Unless you'd prefer a bath...?"

"No, water for a basin's fine," he told her quickly, not wanting to take advantage of the lady's good graces.

"You look ridiculous, by the way," she added tartly. "Yours are there." She nodded to the trousers he hadn't noticed. His trousers. They were draped over one of the chairs by the table. "I put your shoes by the front door," she went on. "Which is where shoes belong when they aren't on one's feet."

Heat stained Alun's cheeks. Without a word, he grabbed up his trousers and beat a hasty retreat to attend to nature's calling. He wondered exactly how much trouble the elderly lady was going to make for James. For him. She probably needed her job—who didn't?—but that didn't mean she would take her employers indiscretions easily. Besides, James had money; he could pay for her silence. It wasn't the rich who paid the price in situations like these; it was the poor who ended up doing hard time in prison.

People like me.

ALUN returned to the kitchen on lead legs; he'd changed out of James's trousers and was carrying them.

"You can lay those over the chair," said Mrs. Dunberry, not looking at him when he came in. "I'm sure you'll want to clean up, upstairs," she added, as if she knew it was more than just his hands and face that needed washing. "By the time you're done, there should be hot water for tea. Unless of course you'd prefer coffee?"

"Tea's fine, thank you."

She nodded and turned back to the stove without another word.

Recognizing the dismissal for what it was, Alun picked up the pitcher of hot water and mounted the stairs. With each step he felt more pensive, more anxious. More filled with dread. He stopped outside James's bedroom door—James's breathing was slow and easy, he was still asleep. Not wanting to wake him, Alun slipped into the room across the hall, the bedroom he'd slept in the first time he was there. He stripped down and applied a liberal amount of soap to the cloth. Soap and hot water were rare luxuries. Usually the best he got for washing was icy water from a public fountain. He scoffed at himself. How many times had he bathed as a wolf in the ice-encrusted lake back home? Home. *James.* He knew this house would never be his home, but its master was the home his heart craved, the home it had claimed against all reason.

But just because he wanted something didn't mean he was going to get it. Even if James was different from other men, there was the matter of his housekeeper. What would she want for her silence, he wondered.

Chapter 11

A FISSION of joy danced through James's heart when he got halfway down the back stairs and saw Alun sitting at the kitchen table, drinking a cup of tea. James took the remaining steps two at a time and bounded over to him. He had to clasp his hands behind his back to keep from throwing his arms around Alun's neck in greeting.

When he'd first opened his eyes, James knew at once that he was alone in the cold bed and was certain Alun had run away again. He'd been angry at himself for trusting the man who had twice left him without so much as a good-bye. Now he was angry at himself for not trusting him more. He should have known that Alun wouldn't go back on his word.

"Did you sleep well?" James inquired of his guest, flashing him an impetuous grin.

Alun flushed a deep shade of pink; James noticed he was wearing his own trousers and that his uniform pants were draped over the back of the chair. James had to fight back his chuckle; there was certainly no hiding what had happened from Mrs. Dunberry now, not if Alun had come downstairs wearing his clothes. James helped himself to a cup of tea and sat down next to the other man, sliding his bare foot against Alun's under the table.

Alun gave him a wide-eyed look.

James simply grinned and drank his tea as he rubbed his feet against Alun's—his tall, lanky Welshman had remarkably warm skin. "What's for supper?" James asked Mrs. Dunberry casually.

"Nothing special, though it might have been if you'd bothered to mention we'd be having company," came her sour reply.

"I'm sure Mr. Blayney and I will be pleased with whatever you've made—especially if that's one of your apple pies I'm smelling."

"It is." She remained impassive. "Supper should be ready presently." She hesitated a moment, then turned to face James fully. "I've promised Mrs. Sullivan I'd give her a hand with the twins tonight, if you've no objection. Poor dear, they've both got colic. I wouldn't have agreed to help if I'd known you were having... *company*." She cast a baleful glower at Alun.

Alun fidgeted in his seat. James merely shrugged. "No worries, Mrs. Dunberry. Mr. Blayney and I can see to our own supper. Do please extend my regards to Mrs. Sullivan."

Mrs. Dunberry gave him a wary look, but didn't argue. She dried her hands off on a dishtowel and removed her apron. "I'll be just next door if you need me for anything."

"We'll be perfectly fine," promised James, unable to hide his grin. Mrs. Dunberry was hardly into her bonnet and out the door when he leaned over and pressed a warm kiss to Alun's mouth.

Alun didn't respond.

James settled back into his chair, trying not to feel too hurt. "What's the matter?" he asked.

"Are you *trying* to get us caught?" Alun hissed, his gaze darting after the housekeeper. "It's bad enough...." But his sentence trailed off. "I came downstairs wearing your trousers!"

"I figured."

"How can you...?" He shook himself. "You don't know what it's like, James, for people like me."

"Alun—"

"It ain't men like you who end up in prison!"

"Alun, she won't care. Mrs. Dunberry already knows about me, sweetheart."

Alun blinked at him, his expression incredulous.

"I figured out a long time ago that I like men. She knows. It's safe." He met Alun's dark gaze, but the other man's eyes were impossible to read. "And anyway, she won't be back until midnight at the earliest. We can do whatever we like and not have to worry about interruptions." Cautiously, steeling himself for another rejection, James laid his hand over Alun's.

Alun twined his fingers into his immediately, and James could breathe again. He rubbed his thumb over the calloused hand he was holding, wondering exactly what kind of heartache he was setting himself up for with the dark East Ender. Alun was mercurial in his moods, one moment all over him, the next cold. Distant. *Unless it's really just what he says*, he thought. The so-called "Blackmail Charter" of 1885 had made all acts of sexual behavior between men illegal, even when it was behind closed doors, between consenting adults. "Mrs. Dunberry wouldn't do anything to hurt me. She won't do anything to hurt you, either, I promise," he added. He lifted Alun's hand to his lips and brushed it with a kiss. "I know she can seem a little surly, but she's just overprotective of me. We've been through a lot together. Do you want me to talk to her?"

"And say what?"

He shrugged. He knew what he wanted to say, that he was falling in love with the handsome Welshman, but had no idea what Alun felt, what *he* wanted. "Whatever you want me to."

"Let it be."

Reluctantly, James nodded, telling himself he shouldn't read too much into the statement. Alun had no reason to trust Mrs. Dunberry. No reason to trust him. "Will… would you like to stay the night?" he asked hesitantly—hopefully. "I have to go to work in a few hours, but I'll be home in the morning." Maybe if they just spent some time together....

"There are things I need to be doing tonight." Alun's tone left no room to argue.

James nodded. "I… will… will I see you again?" he asked.

Alun's brows knitted together. "How could you not? Whitechapel is where I live, remember?"

James heard the bitterness in his tone; he hated it. "I don't mean out there, Alun." He feathered another soft kiss to Alun's hand. "I mean… will I… will we… will you visit me again? Here. Will you come back?"

"What *exactly* are you asking me for?"

James took a breath and let it out. It was now or never. "People say all kinds of things that they don't mean, Alun, especially during… when things get heated. But… if… if you really want… *me*… I want you too. However… whatever you want it to be. I'll take whatever you're willing to give me and give you anything you want in return."

Alun hesitated so long, James was sure he'd made a mistake, said too much or maybe too little—but then the other man pulled him into a kiss that went all the way down to his toes. James gave into it, parting his lips, allowing Alun full access to his mouth. Alun fisted his hand into James's hair and drew his head back—James didn't fight it. He let Alun kiss his neck—his throat. He didn't balk when he felt Alun's teeth scraping against his skin. "Anything you want," he murmured.

Alun pulled James into his lap. "Right now, I just want you," he growled. He was rock hard against James's thighs.

James canted his hips, showing Alun that he was hard, too, that his erection was straining against the fabric of his trousers. "I want you, too, Alun," he whispered as he pushed one hand between them and unbuttoned Alun's fly so he could stroke the other man's cock. Alun groaned. He thrust himself into James's hand.

"Not like this," James told him. He wanted to watch Alun come, but not against his palm. He undid the buttons of his own fly and released the aching erection from his damp trousers, then he slid its length across Alun's shaft slowly, up and down, pleasuring them both—frustrating them both. Coating them both in combined pre-ejaculate fluid until they were slick with it, until they were both panting, desperate, wanting more.

James unbuttoned Alun's waistcoat and shirt first, then his own. Neither of them needed to be naked for what he was planning, but he wanted to see Alun's chest. Tentatively, he pressed his mouth to his lover's skin. Alun moaned softly, giving him the go-ahead to kiss, lick, suck… nip. Alun, it seemed, liked it just as rough as he did. James beamed with pleasure at the discovery. While he explored Alun's body, Alun somehow got him out of his trousers.

"Get the oil," Alun said into James's ear.

Without a word, James got up and got it off the counter. He took a generous amount of oil into his hand and slicked Alun's cock. Then he lowered himself over his lover's lap, forcing Alun's erection into his entrance, certain that he could take anything.… His breath caught in his throat, and for a second, he thought he was being rived in two.

"James—"

"I can take it. I want to," he breathed. "It hurts, but it's a good kind of hurt."

"All right. Just relax yourself and take it slow," Alun told him. "I don't want you hurting yourself for me." He captured James's mouth in another kiss, giving him something to think about besides the burning, the mingled pain and pleasure going on in his ass.

James loved the way Alun's mouth tasted, salt and earth and rich black tea. He loved the way he kissed him. "You make me feel so full," he said, when Alun finally released his mouth. "It feels so good, Alun. *You* feel so good."

"You feel good, too, *cariad*," Alun whispered. "Hot. Tight. I could do this all day with you."

James chuckled. "I'm not sure my ass could take it—but I'd love to try."

"Me too."

James gripped his shoulders for support and rode Alun, slowly at first, then building up speed, taking him faster, harder. Deeper. Then suddenly Alun shifted under him, so that every thrust hit James's prostate, sending waves of fire and ice shooting through his body. James lost himself in a haze of pleasure as he rode Alun harder still, as his own shaft slid up and down against Alun's stomach. James's breath became ragged, his calves and thighs burned, throbbed. His sweat-coated forehead fell forward and rested against Alun's neck. "Come for me," James begged. "Let me feel you spill inside me."

Alun shuddered at the sound of his voice, and James felt the familiar rush of warmth deep inside. His toes curled, and he clung to Alun tighter.

Still quivering with aftershocks, Alun reached between them and took hold of James's erection. "Your turn," he said—and it didn't take long. James emptied himself into Alun's hand—all over his shirt—then sagged against him, spent. Dazed.

Happy.

Alun encircled him in the safety of his strong arms and feathered soft kisses onto James's temple, making him shiver—making Alun hold him tighter, seeking to warm his goose-pimply flesh. "You should get dressed," Alun whispered into his ear.

James nodded, but wasn't in any hurry to move, it felt too good just lying against Alun, being supported by him. Feeling the rise and fall of his chest as he breathed—listening to his heartbeat. James closed his eyes, feeling like he could lie there forever.

Home. The word drifted through James's thoughts unbidden and from out of nowhere, but he knew at once it was exactly the right word to describe the way he felt with Alun. He looked up and met the other man's gaze. "I've never done that with anyone else," James confessed, softly. Shyly.

"I don't reckon too many people have." Alun couldn't help but grin.

"No, I mean, I've never done *this* with another man."

His brows furrowed. "You said—"

"I've known other men, Alun, but they've never known me, not like this, not inside me. I've always been the one on top."

ALUN was left speechless by the revelation. While wolves placed no special value on virginity of any sort, there was something appealing about James giving him something he'd never given anyone else. He cupped his blond's face gently and pulled James into another kiss.

When James finally slid away from him, Alun felt the pang of loss immediately. Lycans were tactile beings by nature, craving physical contact—touching. Being touched. Alun had had few opportunities for intimacy over the last twenty years, but he knew from experience that humans weren't clingy creatures.

"I've got a shirt you can wear," said James, casting an apologetic look at the mess he'd made of Alun's shirt.

"I don't think I'll fit in one of yours, leastwise, not comfortably."

"It's not one of mine."

Alun's head snapped up. He was *not* going to wear another man's shirt.

"It's Tom's," said James, cutting off his angry thoughts at their proverbial knees. His expression was difficult to read, but Alun knew that he must have seen his jealous ire for what it was.

Shame washed over the lycan. "You don't... you shouldn't... it'll be fine," he lied. His shirt was covered in James's seed, but he didn't want to take his dead brother's shirt, though it was for very different reasons than he would have refused another man's. Thomas Heron had died nine months ago. By now, most humans would have disposed of their dead loved one's effects, all but a few important mementos, perhaps. Whether Tom's shirts were somehow special to James, or he had simply been unable to bring himself to get rid of his brother's belongings, didn't matter. James still had them. That meant they were important to him.

Alun, however, was the only one who seemed to think it was an issue. "Go ahead and get cleaned up," James told him. "I'll be back down in a minute."

He turned to leave, but Alun caught his arm. "James." He didn't even know what he wanted to say or how he could apologize for acting like such a git over a shirt.

James's smile surprised him. "You don't have to apologize for acting like an ass. But you don't have to be jealous, either, Alun. I'm not seeing anybody else. I haven't in a long time." He leaned up and pressed a soft kiss to Alun's lips, then hurried up the back stair.

JAMES'S heart fluttered wildly in his chest as he pawed through Tom's old wardrobe in the attic. He was sure it had been jealousy he'd seen in those black eyes, and if Alun was jealous… he shook himself. He didn't know what it meant, but he had to hope it meant Alun felt a measure of… of something… for him. "I know you wouldn't approve," he said to his brother as he extracted a clean, white cotton shirt from the back of the wardrobe. He knew speaking to Tom was pointless, his older brother was long gone, but somehow talking to him made James feel better about filching one of his old shirts. "I'm not hurting anyone. I just want to be happy. That *can't* be wrong." It only took him a few more minutes to find the rest of what he was looking for.

When James returned to the kitchen, carrying fresh clothing for both himself and Alun, he found his lover stark naked, washing himself off with a clean cloth. "Now there's a sight a man could get used to." James couldn't stop the words that sprang to his mind from coming out of his mouth. To his immense delight, Alun turned and grinned at him.

James smiled too. He hurried over to Alun and pressed a kiss to his Welshman's lips before he lost his nerve. Sex was one thing, but a little tenderness, a stolen kiss, that meant so much more.

Alun wrapped his arms around James's waist. "I'm not sure your Mrs. Dunberry would approve of having a strange man naked in her kitchen," he teased when their lips parted. "I think she'd approve even less of the way he can't keep his hands offa you." He reached down and cupped James's ass in both hands.

"Just for the record, the man who pays the good lady's wages doesn't object to having your hands all over him."

Alun chuckled. He drew him into another kiss before going back to washing off.

Still smiling, James grabbed a clean cloth from the drawer next to the stove and started to wash up as well. He didn't miss the heated looks Alun kept shooting his way. What he wouldn't give for another few hours…. He sighed. He didn't have a few more hours. "I brought down a pair of trousers, too, and a jacket, in case you wanted them," he said, nodding to the clothing he'd dropped onto the table when he came into the room.

"Are you sure that's all right with you, me wearing your brother's clothes?"

"Thomas certainly doesn't have any use for them, and they don't fit me," he said sensibly.

Reluctantly, Alun nodded. James knew Tom's old clothes were of considerably better quality than anything Alun could ever have afforded on his own, even though they were nothing fancy; he hoped Alun wouldn't be uncomfortable accepting the gift. He knew what Mrs. Dunberry thought of the Welshman, that he was little more than a gold-digger taking advantage of a kind man's generosity, but James knew better. Alun had accepted his hospitality, and he'd let him buy their breakfast this morning, but James was sure the other man wasn't looking for charity, for handouts. James wasn't entirely certain what Alun was looking for. *I only hope it's the same thing I want.*

"I meant what I said about seeing you again," James ventured as they got dressed. "Maybe… tomorrow?"

Alun hesitated. "James, I… you don't know me."

"You don't know me, either," the younger man countered. "We can rectify that easily enough. I'd welcome it, in fact." Heat bloomed in his cheeks as he wondered if it was possible to sound any more idiotic. But he pressed on anyway. "I *want* to know you, Alun. I'd like for you to know me too. I want… I want more than a few stolen afternoons, sweetheart. I hope… I hope that once you get to know me, you'll want more too." James made no attempt to keep the hopefulness from his voice. He leaned forward and pressed his lips to Alun's mouth. It was a soft, closed-mouth kiss, but Alun returned it, and warmth washed over James once more.

Then he felt Alun's hands on his shoulders, only instead of pulling him further into the kiss, Alun pushed him away, holding him firmly at arm's length. "James, listen to me a minute. Please. We're different, you and me. I don't live in a nice house or have a proper job. I'm not *like* you. I'm a bloody cardsharper!"

"Do you honestly think that matters?"

"It matters to most people."

"Not to me. I'm… I accept you exactly as you are, Alun. All I'm asking is that you do the same of me. All I'm asking is for you to give this a chance. Is that really too much to ask?"

Alun looked away, almost closing his eyes, lost in thought—but then he ran his hands down James's arms, his fingers grazing the young man's flesh lightly, tenderly, raising goose bumps—raising his hope once more. "I don't know," was the answer he gave.

James's heart raced; it wasn't the answer that he wanted, but it wasn't the worst thing Alun could have said. "I like being with you, Alun. I enjoy your company. I like talking to you. You make me feel comfortable, in a way few people do. Yes, the sex is amazing," he added. "But I want you to know that that isn't all I'm looking for. I want something… real."

"I like being with you too," Alun admitted softly, though it sounded like he was afraid to say the words aloud. "But I'm not what you think, James. *Who* you think. Getting to know me, you… you're gonna end up finding out things 'bout me that'll break both our hearts."

The anguish in his tone was crushing. James freed one hand and brushed the long fringe away from Alun's eyes. "I *don't* believe that," he told him. He cupped Alun's face, and Alun leaned into his touch. He kissed James's fingers and nuzzled his hand. "There are things that just don't matter, Alun," James told him.

"And there are things that *do*."

The hall clock chimed seven. James knew he would have to leave for work within the hour if he intended to be on time for his shift.

"Meet me in the morning. Come back home with me," James entreated. "We can talk more—or not at all," he added to the fearful look that crossed Alun's face. "You can tell me as much or as little as you like, I don't care. I just want to see you again, to hold you. To touch you. To kiss you." He leaned in and feathered another soft kiss to his lips. "Please? At least give me tomorrow to prove to you that I don't care who you are or where you're from."

"I'll meet you at ten, same place as we met this morning." The words, barely a whisper, seemed to slip out of their own accord.

"Thank you." James pressed yet another kiss to his lover's mouth. "We should eat something," he said when he drew back from him. His insides were too much of a jumble for him to be able to eat anything himself, but he didn't want to send Alun out onto the streets without a decent meal.

Chapter 12

UNEASINESS tightened in Alun's gut as he walked the cold, dark streets. The streetlamps were sputtering again, barely illuminating the night around him. He regretted his promise to meet James in the morning—but how could he deny him? How could he deny his own heart, his own desire to be near the young blond every chance he got?

Alun swore at himself. He could *never* let James get to know him. He was a lycan. James was human. That was the end of it. If the only things separating them were what James thought: money, prestige, education, then maybe it would be possible, but James didn't know what he was—and he could never find out.

The wind shifted, and Alun caught the scent of blood on the night air. Human blood. He considered shifting—he was faster on four legs than two—but he couldn't risk being seen in wolf form running through the streets, even the streets of Whitechapel, where people tended not to notice the monstrous. Besides, just because he smelled human blood didn't mean it was the killer he was charged with stopping. People died at the hands of other people, ordinary people, all the time.

Alun stayed to the back alleys, clinging to the shadows, pulling the darkness in close around him, because even on two legs he was faster than a human and didn't wish to be seen. His heart thundered in his ears, and the night air burned in his lungs. The smell of blood and death drew him forward, guiding his way through the fetid streets until at last he rounded a corner and found himself in a small, enclosed courtyard. He skittered to a halt near the entrance. He smelled bile and urine—the excretions of death. The scent of stale sex lingered in the air as well, cheap ale and even cheaper perfume—the smells of a woman who sold her body for money. With his senses straining, muscles tense, Alun edged cautiously forward, his breath still coming in ragged gulps, his heart thundering in his chest.

He didn't smell anything but the woman. Cold dread filled him as he recognized her scent, and he prayed he was mistaken, that it wasn't really Emily. It was a selfish prayer; everyone had friends, people who cared about them, who would miss them when they died.

Swallowing back a cold lump, Alun inched toward the dying woman. As his own heartbeat slowed, quieted, he became aware of hers. It was a faint sound, ticking out her last few minutes of life.

Alun stopped short again when he got close enough to see past the shadows, past the bloodied rags of her dress—when he could finally see what they'd done to her. Her throat was cut, her body bleeding, seeping a pool of red from between her legs. His fists clenched. Emily was still conscious, though only barely. Waves of panic rolled off her—she must be able to hear his approach, but she couldn't possibly see who it was.

"It's all right," Alun whispered, so she would know it was him and not her attackers come to finish the job. "Emily…." Alun knelt at her side. Tears bit at his eyes as she stared up at him, recognizing him at last. Her lips moved, but no coherent sound came out. "Shhh, don't try to speak, darlin'," he soothed, wiping a few strands of blood-soaked hair from her forehead. She twitched, crying, hardly able to move. "I'm here, I promise, Em," Alun told her. "I won't leave ya to die in the dark… shhh." He used the cuff of his jacket to wipe away the blood from her face, keeping his eyes locked on hers. She was so afraid. He took hold of her hand and held it tight. Her fingers were as cold as ice.

Emily had been one of the first people he met when he arrived in London; she'd been good to him, to everyone. She didn't deserve to be butchered in the street like an animal, left to die on the cold cobblestones. Anger boiled in his veins—Alun pushed it back. Later. He would be angry later. He would hunt down whoever had done this to her and…. He swallowed hard, but the lump in his throat refused to go down.

"Listen to me, Em, it's not scary," said Alun. "The other side, there's nothing there to be scared of. I promise you. It looks just like here—no, no, it's all right," he said quickly, when she tried to speak again. "It's only just like here right on the other side of the veil. After that… after that it's *beautiful*," he lied. He'd never ventured any further than the world's "spirit mirror"—the place that looked almost exactly like the physical world. But his grandfather had always told him that the spirit world was a strange and wonderful place. "It's beautiful, Emmie—you'll see. An' you

can go anywhere you like, just by wishing it. You could go back home...."
His throat closed and tears fell, making it hard to see, but he refused to let
go of her hand to wipe them away. "You'll be safe and warm, Emmie.
Safe and warm, I promise."

A ghost of a smile tugged at the corners of her mouth... and then she
was gone. He felt her spirit slip out of her body a second before it
shuddered with its last breath.

Still clinging to Emily's cold, bloody hand, Alun howled his rage
and his pain into the night.

"Oi! You there!"

A light shone directly in Alun's eyes, blinding him so he couldn't
clearly see the man holding it, though he heard his ragged breaths and
smelled the stench of his fear and the sweat-damp wool of his uniform.
With rage still burning in his blood, Alun rose to his feet, his beast riding
close to the surface of his skin. A second light joined the first as another
constable arrived on the scene. Alun's lip curled back in a feral snarl. Two
humans were no match for a full-grown lycan—even as a cub, he could
have taken a couple of bobbies.

Then a third man rounded the corner. His scent hit Alun like a fist to
the gut, stopping him dead before he started, cooling the blood in his veins
to frozen ice.

James.

JAMES watched helplessly as the two men who had arrived on the scene
before him charged at Alun, bringing him down like he was some kind of
wild animal. He swallowed hard, unable to move. When he'd first turned
the corner, he hadn't recognized the man standing over the woman's
blood-soaked body as the same man he'd made love to, just nine hours
ago. He'd looked... crazed. Savage.

James had been walking his beat when he heard the whistle and
came running. The dead of the night had almost past, men were starting to
get up for work, get out onto the streets. Bakers' ovens were being filled
with loaves of fresh dough to be baked into bread for the onslaught of

early morning customers; produce sellers were arriving at their stands. In a few hours the sun would be up.

With each hour that had ticked past, James felt growing anticipation, lightness; his gut and heart trembling. He'd made up his mind that he was going to tell Alun how he felt—maybe he wouldn't use the word "love," it seemed a bit premature to commit to something so strong, never mind that he was *sure* it was what he felt, but James could tell Alun that he felt a deep and growing affection for him. He could express his desire to spend more time together. There were no rules of courtship for a man who liked men, but it didn't seem unreasonable to declare his feelings plainly and give Alun the opportunity to either accept or reject his affection. Perhaps, if things went well, by Christmas it wouldn't seem improprietous to offer Alun a room at the house. (Of course, it was his own room that James had in mind....)

But then he rounded the corner, stepped into the courtyard, and saw Alun standing over the dead woman's mangled body, his face twisted, contorted in a feral mask. If he hadn't recognized the clothing Alun was wearing, James might not have known it was him at all.

The awful sound of wooden truncheons striking human flesh pulled him from his stupor. The other two constables were raining blows down on Alun and he was just.... James froze again. Alun was curled up on the ground, protecting his head and belly, but he wasn't fighting back, he wasn't even trying to crawl away. He was just lying there, letting them beat him senseless.

James felt sure he was going to be sick. Alun had said there were things he would find out that would break his heart—was *this* what he meant? That he was a cold-blooded murderer? He *couldn't* be.

Could he?

"Oi!" James shouted, running toward them as fast as he could. "You—Mills!" He grabbed the first man by the coat, pulling him away from his lover's prone body so hard that the tall, lanky constable nearly lost his balance and toppled to the blood-sodden ground.

"Fucking—whose side're you on, Heron!" Mills seethed, looking for an instant like he was getting ready to take a swing at him.

NO ONE heard Alun's low growl, or saw the rage glinting in his black eyes. Years of enduring Percival's abuse may have allowed him to take a beating, but James was his home, his shelter, whether the human would ever understand that or not. But James didn't need his protection. He wasn't afraid of the man he was facing down, even though the other constable was younger, taller, and probably stronger.

"IS *THIS* how you want to represent the uniform?" James demanded angrily, gesturing toward the crowd that was beginning to assemble in the courtyard's entrance.

Shamefaced, Mills lowered his baton.

"You always was a bleeding little girl, Heron," sneered the older constable, a man called Stanwix. He was a stout, thick-armed fellow, known to have a disagreeable temper and aspirations of grandeur. He'd taken the sergeant's exam twice—and failed it twice. "You ain't much better," he snapped at Mills, his tone full of contempt.

James barely heard him, hardly smelled the whiskey on his breath. He looked down at Alun—his stomach churned, and bile rose in his throat. Alun wasn't moving. *Please....* But then he saw Alun's back expand and contract with a shallow breath. He was alive. It took all of James's strength not to reach for him, cradle him in his arms. Beg him to say it wasn't him who had killed the woman lying behind him. But he didn't dare.

James wrenched his gaze away from his lover's bruised, battered body and forced himself to look at the dead woman. It made his heart and soul sick to think that the same man who had kissed him, held him, might have murdered her. James couldn't make out much in the dark—and he was too afraid to let himself raise his lantern and look at her properly— but even in the shadows, he saw the pool of blood. She was ripped up, just like the others.

Just like the first woman.

I'm no killer. Alun's harsh words echoed through James's memory... but Alun had been kneeling over that woman's lifeless body in that alley.

James closed his eyes. He remembered the first time they made love. It had been savage. Tender. Incredible. And when they were through, Alun curled up behind him. Held him. Buried his nose in James's hair. Kissed him. How could that man…. Pain lanced through the constable's heart. That same beautiful Welshman had hardly looked human when James saw him standing over the woman's body here tonight.

He opened his eyes again. Alun was on his feet, his face an impassive mask, his eyes turned toward the ground. Stanwix handcuffed his wrists behind his back, gruffly telling him to behave himself if he didn't want another beating. Alun said nothing. Did nothing.

"Get that rabble outa here," Stanwix told James, waving his truncheon toward the onlookers—and James had no choice but to turn his back on the man he'd been planning to ask to live with him and trot over to the growing crowd to try and disperse them.

Every step away from Alun hurt.

ALUN could see the emotions playing on his… on James's face as the young constable turned away from him. Fear. Hate. Hurt. It was James's pain that was the hardest to endure—not that he blamed the younger man for any of the things he was feeling. Alun's rage had been so close to the surface that he would have torn the other two constables apart if James hadn't rounded the corner when he did. The only thing that had stopped him was not wanting James to see him do it—not that it mattered. James had seen the monster rise to the surface. A lycan didn't have to fully shift his shape for the beast inside to become visible.

He stood still while the burly constable searched him, found the small knife he carried in his pocket. There wasn't any blood on it, he hadn't used it for anything nefarious, but that didn't stop them from declaring it the murder weapon. Next, they found his purse full of coins. It wasn't the money that got the constables' attention, however, it was Claire's crucifix. Clearly, it was a woman's, though they didn't know whose, not yet anyway. Alun had no doubt they'd figure it out eventually. He had no doubt that they were right when they sneered at him that he would hang by Christmas.

Alun cast a surreptitious glance toward the crowd. He could see on their faces that they believed him guilty of Emily's murder. There would be no arguing his innocence, not here—not anywhere. It didn't matter, there was only one person he wanted to believe him. *No*, he decided. The further he could keep James away from all this, the better it would be for the younger man. Alun didn't want anyone thinking James had anything to do with this—with him. His heart ached, but he knew it was the right thing to do. The only thing to do.

The burly constable turned his attention toward the other one, the boy James had called Mills, and told him to go fetch the wagon so they could haul in their prisoner. "And see somebody gets Inspector Lamont and the police surgeon too!" he hollered as Mills began to lope away.

Alun returned his gaze to the ground when James started walking toward him again.

James called the burly constable aside and said there was a man from the newspaper in the crowd who wanted to talk to the police. He said he figured the other constable should handle it, him being a senior officer and all. Alun didn't miss the insincerity in James's tone, although it didn't seem as if the other constable noticed it. Under other circumstances, he might have smiled at James's cleverness, the other man's idiocy. As it was, all he felt was cold and empty. Afraid. Not for himself—he could face the gallows—but didn't want to drag James there with him.

As soon as the other constable was occupied, James sidled up to Alun. He stood close enough that Alun could hear his words, but not so close as to arouse suspicion, should the other constable look their way— not that it seemed likely. The burly man was too busy pandering to the press, trying to get his name into print as the hero who had arrested a brutal murderer. He was smart enough not to claim that the man in custody was actually Jack the Ripper, but he intimated that the people of Whitechapel could rest easy now.

"Alun." James's tone was ragged, thick with too many emotions. It ripped through the lycan's heart, slicing into his soul. "Alun, *please*," he begged. "Tell me what happened here."

Alun didn't dare look at James when he answered him. "I told you," his voice was cold. "You don't know me. You don't know what I am." He glanced briefly in Emily's direction. "Leastwise you didn't know 'fore now."

James shuddered—nearly sobbed. He turned away.

Alun closed his eyes. Last night felt like a lifetime ago.

When he heard James walking toward Emily's body, Alun steeled himself against what he knew the younger man's reaction would be. A moment later, he heard James gasp. James knew her the same as he did. He'd been talking to her just last night.

JAMES knelt by Emily Harris's side. Her skin was still pink. It was warm to the touch. Soft. She couldn't have been dead even half an hour. He turned to look at Alun's back. Alun was slumped over, head still down, wrists secured behind his back. *Defeated.* But was it the defeat of a killer who knew he'd been caught or that of an innocent man knowing he couldn't defend himself against overwhelming evidence? Knowing that even his lover had abandoned him?

I'm no killer.

You don't know me.

Which was the real Alun, the man who had held him, made him feel safe, loved, or the madman he'd seen standing over Emily Harris's body, the man whose rage-filled howling he'd heard before he even rounded the corner?

"Oi there!" Inspector Lamont thundered at him as he rounded the corner. "What d'you think you're doin'? Get away from there afore you contaminate the scene! Heron," he said when James turned to face him. "Shoulda bloody well known it'd be you snooping above your damned pay grade. Do something useful for a change and get that mucksnape loaded into the wagon." He hooked his thumb at Alun.

Behind Lamont, a big black police wagon had come as far as it could, stopping at the narrow courtyard entrance.

James shuddered. There was nothing he could do but obey the order. Before dawn, Alun's hair would be shorn off—lice were a major problem in prison. Then Alun would be locked in a tiny, filthy cell. There would be fleas, bedbugs. Rats. He might have to wait for a week or more, before the magistrate saw him to determine whether or not the Crown had enough evidence to commit him over for trial. Chances are the magistrate would decide it did. And men on trial for murder were rarely granted bail—not that Alun could afford it. He'd be rotting in prison until his trial began. But Stanwix was right, he'd hang by Christmas. Tears bit at James's eyes; in his daydreams, Alun was supposed to be moving in with him by Christmas.

"Heron!" Lamont snapped.

"Yes, Sir, sorry, Sir." He bobbed his head in apology and hurried toward the prisoner. Bracing himself against the tumult of emotions, he took Alun by the arm; he didn't speak. Blessedly, the other man returned the favor.

Behind them, James heard Lamont questioning Stanwix about what he'd found when he arrived on the scene. Mills would be next, then him; the inspector might not like him but he wouldn't ignore procedure. What James didn't know was what he was going to say, especially if Lamont happened to ask him about the first woman. He knew he wouldn't have long to make up his mind.

When they got to the police wagon, James rounded his compliant prisoner hard and fast, slamming his back up against the wagon with a thud, forcing Alun to meet his gaze. Startled, Alun seemed to hardly be breathing as their eyes locked. James saw fear there, the kind of fear he never would have expected out of the other man.

"Why'd you do it?" he demanded furiously. He was sure the driver could hear him, but it didn't matter. It was the kind of thing anybody would ask after seeing poor Emily Harris slashed up like she was. "Why kill that woman? She wasn't anything to you, just another unfortunate," he growled, anger unabated.

Pain flickered through Alun's dark eyes—hopelessness filled them. He turned his head away, eyelids sliding shut. "I ain't got no more to say to you than I had to say to the other one." James felt him shivering. It wasn't the cold.

From the driver's seat, the other constable gave a cold laugh. "Fancy that." He smirked at Alun's statement. "You need help getting 'is sorry carcass loaded?"

"I've got it," James answered him. He pulled open the wagon door and shoved Alun inside. Alun fell to the hard floor and stayed there, moving only enough to curl his knees up against his chest. James hesitated. Then he shut the door and walked away.

ONCE the wagon door closed, Alun let out the sobs he'd been fighting so desperately to hold at bay. He told himself that this was what he'd wanted, what he'd calculated for when he suggested his guilt to James—and he *did* want to protect him—but nothing could have prepared him for how much losing the other man's friendship was going to hurt.

Chapter **13**

"MASTER JAMES—" Mrs. Dunberry stopped midsentence. She stepped back and regarded him for only a brief moment more before asking what was the matter.

James knew why she was asking, what he looked like; his eyes were red-rimmed. Bloodshot. He'd spent the last hours of his shift thinking about Emily Harris—about Alun. He hadn't seen Emily's friend Betty, but that wasn't unusual. By 2:00 a.m., most of the girls who earned their money on the streets had found a place to sleep for the night, be it a doss house or someplace less friendly. *So what was Emily doing out at four o'clock in the morning?*

He wondered if Emily's friends knew yet that she was dead—but surely they must by now. He wondered if they would believe Alun had killed her. He closed his eyes to steady himself. He saw Alun's face in his mind's eye, those beautiful black eyes, his smile... the stricken expression Alun had worn when James asked him why he killed Emily.

"James?" Mrs. Dunberry said softly, abandoning the thin veneer of formality as she pressed her hand to his shoulder. Normally, he would have appreciated a reprieve from the usual tediousness of it, but not today.

"I'm all right," James lied. Inspector Lamont had caught him after his shift ended at nine to question him about Emily's murder. He'd recounted everything exactly as it had happened. Twice. The only thing he omitted was the beating Mills and Stanwix delivered to Alun. Reporting it would only mean he'd have to stay longer while Lamont looked into the matter. As it was, it seemed as if the inspector was keeping him later than he needed to. James had lost nearly half the day as a result.

He handed his helmet to Mrs. Dunberry, and peeled out of his coat. "I need you to get my gray suit out of the attic and air it. I'll leave the choice of shirt and necktie to your discretion," he added. She had always done a better job of dressing him than he'd done himself. "And ask Rose or Davida to bring up a pitcher of hot water to my room." Either of the women Mrs. Dunberry had hired to help her run the house could handle hot water, but she was the only person he trusted to assemble an outfit for him.

"I take it you're planning on going out this afternoon?" It was only barely a question.

"I'd like to be gone within the hour... two at the most."

"And your breakfast?"

"Bring something up to me, would you? Nothing too heavy," he added. "Maybe just some tea and toast." Bile filled his throat. He wasn't going to be able to eat, but if he didn't at least ask for a tray, Mrs. Dunberry would argue with him.

She hesitated, seeming to sense that he wasn't going to eat anything she brought—but then she nodded. "As you wish, Sir. Do you need anything else?"

"No. Thank you, Mrs. Dunberry." He headed up the stairs, taking them two at a time. The only thing he needed was the one thing Mrs. Dunberry couldn't give him. He needed Alun.

ALUN didn't look up when the cell door opened. It was a tiny chamber, cramped—too cramped for a lycanthrope. Lycans needed space to roam, fresh air... there was no fresh air anywhere in London. A small, barred window near the top of the whitewashed brick walls was the room's only source of light. The window was both too high up to reach and too small to escape through—not that he had the fortitude to think about escape.

Two young guards stepped nervously inside. One carried the tray with Alun's lunch, the other was there to make sure the prisoner didn't do them any mischief. Alun scoffed. He could rip them both to shreds without even shifting shape—but what good would it do? Where would he go that he wouldn't be hunted down, either by the humans or his own kind? He was *diangen* in both worlds now. His only "escape" would come at the end of the hangman's noose.

"I don't see the point of giving 'im any lunch if he ain't gonna eat it," one of the guards commented to the other. Alun hadn't touched his breakfast.

The other shrugged. Alun was certain that left to their own devices, the guards would let him starve. There was no doubt in anyone's mind that he'd killed Emily and Claire and all those women from last year too.

He didn't care. He didn't raise his head up off his knees to look in his jailers' direction as they spoke, or even after the door was shut and locked behind them. He didn't move to touch his food or to turn his face to the thin shaft of sunlight coming through the grime-covered windowpane. He knew in his heart he'd made the right decision when he shut James out, pushed him away, but it felt like his soul had been ripped in half. Who could live with half a soul?

"MY LORD MOWBRAY," the elderly gentleman greeted James with a warm smile and an outstretched hand.

"Sir Walter." He accepted his hand and returned his smile. It had been over a year since James had set foot in the old man's office. It was a comfortable, well-appointed room, filled with books and furnished with thickly padded chairs. Sir Walter's desk stood opposite the door; like the man who sat behind it, it was large and imposing. "As I recall, you used to call me Jamie."

The other man chuckled. He gestured for his guest to have a seat in one of chairs by the window. "You were a boy when I called you that. Besides, as *I* recall, you used to call me 'Uncle Walt'," he countered.

James nodded, conceding the point; only the slightest smile played at the corners of his mouth. Sir Walter Gill wasn't his uncle by blood, but rather a close friend of his grandfather's, his mother's father. Both men had not so quietly expressed their hopes that James and Walter's granddaughter, Lucille, would take a fancy to one another. Such was never the case. Just the same, James asked after her as he sat down in one of the green velvet chairs. He hadn't seen Lucy since he'd moved back to London.

"Doing as well as a headstrong girl can, I suppose. She's twenty-three and still not engaged. Not even any prospects from what I understand, though heaven knows, her mother and I have both tried." He shook his head. "Scotch? Or brandy?"

"Brandy, please."

Walter stepped over to the sideboard where several crystal decanters sat glittering in the sunlight. He selected the one he wanted and poured a healthy portion of the dark amber liquid into a pair of cut crystal glasses. "Shall I presume this isn't a social call, my Lord?"

"No. And… if it's all the same to you, I prefer to use my mother's name, Sir Walter," James told him.

Bushy white eyebrows arched up on the old man's face. "Oh?"

"It's easier for me."

"Well then, allow me to propose the following." Walter passed one of the glasses over to James. "If you will do me the great courtesy of calling me 'Uncle', at least when we are behind closed doors, I shall gladly call you Heron."

James smiled in earnest and raised his glass; Walt touched his to its lip, sealing their bargain with a soft *clink* of crystal. Walter sat down in the chair next to James's. "So. What can I do for you, Jamie?" he wanted to know.

James bought himself another moment more to think by sipping at the brandy. It burned his tongue and throat, but did little to bolster his courage. "I've come to retain your services."

Walt frowned. "You require an attorney?"

"Not for myself. For a… a friend." Guilt plagued him. He hadn't treated Alun as a friend this morning, and he hated himself for it. Alun *was* right, he didn't know him. He didn't know what he was—but he knew what he *wasn't*. He *wasn't* a killer. "Have you read today's paper?" His gaze flickered toward the morning paper still sitting on the other man's big mahogany desk. The story of Alun's arrest had run front and center on the first page. He wasn't named by name, which most likely meant Alun had refused to identify himself to the inspector. Lamont, on the other hand, was not only named, but there was a photograph of him to go with the article, as well as an artist's sketch of Emily Harris's body.

"I read it every morning with my tea," Walt answered his question.

"I know the man they arrested last night in connection with the recent string of murders in the Whitechapel district." He waited for a reaction, but Walt merely nodded, so he went on. "I know the evidence seems conclusive, but I also know in my heart that he didn't kill those women."

"The Crown will appoint a competent attorney to help the man defend himself. This is a capital case, Jamie."

James took another sip of brandy, but the lump of cold fear in his throat refused to go down. "I know that. But please. He'll go to the gallows without proper representation. Uncle Walt, a court appointed barrister isn't going to fight for him. They're already convinced of his guilt, you read that yourself in the article."

Walt waved his hand dismissively. "They say those things to sell papers."

"What makes you think people won't believe it? Magistrates, judges, barristers, and jury members read the papers too. *Please*, I'm not asking you to take Alun's case as a charity. I'm more than prepared to pay you."

The older man took a breath and let it out, his hesitation making James feel like he was sitting on razor blades. "Perhaps," Walt said at last, "you'd better start at the beginning."

James nodded. He took another sip of his brandy; the glass was nearly empty. He'd known that if Walt agreed to help, he would have to explain his connection to Alun. At the same time, he didn't dare divulge the... intimacy of their relationship. He had no idea what Walt believed about people like him, men who loved other men, and he couldn't risk telling him the truth, not if he wanted Walt to help Alun. But how else could he explain why he was so desperate to help someone like Alun?

"Jamie, if you want me to represent your friend, I need to understand the facts of the case against him."

"I know, Sir. But... please, isn't there anything you can do to get him out of prison on bail? Today, I mean," he explained.

The older man couldn't contain his chortled scoff. "Even if I *could* get in to see a magistrate on your friend's behalf today—which isn't likely—the chances of anyone being released on bail in a capital case are slender under the best of circumstances, Jamie. If I'm to believe what the newspaper is saying, these are hardly the best of circumstances."

James nodded. He studied the remains of the brandy in the bottom of his glass for a long moment. "What... what if he had references?" he asked, almost afraid to hope. "What if someone was willing to guarantee that he would appear at his trial? Someone willing to post whatever bail the magistrate set? Would they let him out, then?"

"Jamie, I know you're your mother's son, but are you certain you're willing to stick your neck on the line for this fellow?"

"Yes," he answered without hesitation. He drained the last of his glass. Even to his own ears, he'd spoken too quickly.

Walt let out a long, low sigh. He reached over and pressed his hand to the younger man's shoulder. "I doubt it matters, my boy. No magistrate is going to grant a man facing the gallows bail, not even if the Queen herself came down and offered her word on his behalf. The best we can do is work for a speedy trial."

Unable to lift his gaze from his glass, James nodded. He hadn't expected to be able to get Alun out of prison tonight, but if he could have... he closed his eyes. When he asked Alun why he'd killed Emily Harris, it was because he wanted to see his reaction, to know whether or not Alun was guilty. The pain he'd seen in the other man's face wasn't that of a guilty man who had been caught, but rather of an innocent man who had been abandoned. "How long will he be stuck there?" he wanted to know, his voice a hollow whisper. He hated himself for doubting Alun, if only for a moment. He hated himself even more for allowing Alun to think he still did.

"That depends on what you tell me," said Walt. "If I have enough to work with, I can get the case dismissed before it even goes to a grand jury—but you say the evidence against him is strong?"

James nodded. "Two constables saw him standing over the body of Emily Harris, the woman who was murdered last night. A third arrived on the scene shortly thereafter."

"All right." Walt rose to get a notepad and pencil from his desk. "Tell me as much as you know, in as much detail as you can. I'll need the names of these constables, as well."

"Spencer Mills, George Stanwix. And James Heron."

Walt stopped midstride. He turned back around and regarded James for a long moment. "The beginning, Jamie," he told him. Before he returned to his chair, Walter reached for the decanter and, without asking, refilled James's glass.

James downed half of it in one gulp. "There... there are details of our... acquaintanceship... that it might be... prudent to leave out," he told him, stumbling over his words, unable to meet the other's icy-blue gaze.

"What *sorts* of details?"

"It's not relevant to the case being brought against him. I doubt anyone besides Dr. Stodderley, that's the police surgeon, knows we're at all close. I mean, that isn't to say that we *are*... close, that is...."

"Stick to the facts, James," Walt advised him.

He nodded. "Dr. Stodderley offered Alun... Alun Blayney, he's from Wales... anyway, Dr. Stodderley offered us—me—the use of his carriage one night. The night the first woman was killed." He gulped down another mouthful of brandy. It burned all the way down to his stomach.

"Did anyone else see the two of you together?" Walter's remained blessedly calm. Professional.

"There were other constables on the scene. I suppose they saw."

"Let's assume that they did and that the prosecution either has or will piece together that their murder suspect has a friend in the constabulary. I'm going to advise you to do some things that you're not going to like—"

James's head snapped up, but the sour response died on his tongue. "I've already done things I regret, Uncle Walt," he admitted instead.

"Of that I have no doubt. But unless it seems of relevance, you've my word that I won't pry into your private affairs. Nevertheless, you need to insulate yourself from this situation—no arguments. I'll take your friend's case, but *only* on the condition that you do exactly as I say. Starting with telling me whom you trust."

"What do you mean?"

"This Dr. Stodderley, for instance. If we ask him about those dead girls, will he go running to the inspector in charge, this...." He reached for the newspaper sitting on the corner of his desk.

"Franklin Lamont," James supplied. "No. No, I'm sure he wouldn't."

"Good. Then let us start there and see exactly how compelling the case against your friend actually is."

"Let *us*?" he asked hopefully.

"I said I wanted you to insulate yourself, not sit on your thumbs, boy. But you must proceed with caution, do we understand one another?"

"Yes, Sir. Thank you."

"Don't thank me yet. You haven't seen my bill." He grinned.

James managed to laugh; he suspected that that had been Walt's intention. He told him as much as he could about Alun and the murders, then he took his leave to let the other man work. For the first time since he'd seen Alun standing over Emily Harris's body last night, James felt a measure of hope. Sir Walter Gill was one of the best attorneys in London, if not all of Britain. He had been a judge for many years, and both before and after that had tried cases on behalf of the Crown as well as representing men and women accused of all sorts of crimes against it. If anyone could to help Alun, it was him.

"JAMES, good to see you, lad," Dr. Stodderley welcomed him with a friendly smile. It was early enough that the doctor's assistant, Owen Collier, was still on hand to take notes while Stodderley worked. Collier was taller than James by at least a foot, and lankier too, with large hands and feet, though his countenance wasn't unpleasant to the eye. He and James exchanged polite but silent nods, while Dr. Stodderley kept talking.

"What can I do for you, James?" he asked. The body he was working on wasn't Emily Harris; secretly, James was grateful. He would have to see her before he left, but he was just as glad to not have to see her any more cut up than she'd been last night.

James didn't answer the little man's question. He wasn't sure what he was looking for, but he would take whatever he could get, anything to prove Alun's innocence. Only despite what he'd said to Walt, he wasn't sure he could say that to Dr. Stodderley. He considered the old surgeon his friend, but....

"Grisly business last night, eh?" the doctor said then, almost absently. Then he paused and looked up at his visitor in earnest. "How are you holding up, lad?"

"Well enough, I suppose, Sir."

Dr. Stodderley put down his scalpel and scrutinized him a long moment. "Hmmm. Yes. Well." He turned to his assistant. "Mr. Collier, be a good lad and go fetch some tea for us?"

Collier blinked at him. "What about Mrs. Harcore?"

"I don't suspect she'll be needing a cup, will you, Madam?" Dr. Stodderley directed his question to the body on the slab. "No, it doesn't seem so. Run along—the dead will wait, Mr. Collier. The living are parched." He shooed the reluctant young man out of the room. After he'd gone, the doctor turned once more to James. "Now. What can I do for you, lad?" he asked again.

James swallowed hard. "May I see Emily Harris's body?"

"You know you're always welcome to have a look around, James. You would have made a fine surgeon, should you have chosen to follow in your father's and grandfather's footsteps." When James said nothing, he went on. "I finished her up about an hour ago. Would you like to see my report, or form your own opinions?"

James chewed on his lower lip, uncertain.

"Why don't you form your own opinion first," Dr. Stodderley suggested; his tone seemed to have softened.

"Thank you." He followed the surgeon to the storage room where Emily was laid out. James had never noticed how pretty she was before. If he just looked at her face, not her injuries—she must have been a truly beautiful woman when she was younger. Bile burned in the back of his throat. It was different looking at someone he knew.

"What do you notice first?" Dr. Stodderley asked, his voice jarring James from his thoughts.

James cleared his throat and tried to reassert a professional demeanor. Now that Emily had been cleaned up, he could see that there were deep bruises on her wrists, but no bruising on her neck. She'd been tied—no, held down—but not strangled. "This isn't the same as the other two," he said, casting a sidelong glance in Dr. Stodderley's direction.

"Go on," the surgeon encouraged. "How was this poor girl's death different from those of her fellow unfortunates, so recently murdered?"

James took a moment to collect his thoughts. To look at Emily's wounds. "The other two had their necks slashed straight across," he began. "Emily Harris's throat is slashed off-center, her jugular vein wasn't cut. Her throat doesn't appear to be bruised." He reached down and opened one of her eyelids and then the other. "Her eyes aren't bloodshot, confirming that she wasn't strangled."

Dr. Stodderley nodded. "What else do you see?"

"The wound across her throat seems more shallow than the other victims'. I'm not sure it would have been fatal, at least not instantly so." He leaned in to get a better look, parting the slit carefully so he could see more deeply into the wound. "Her carotid artery is cut... but it's not severed. It wasn't a quick death." His stomach churned. What if he was wrong? What if Alun... he shook himself. The man he'd made love to in his kitchen less than twenty-four hours ago *wasn't* the same man who had inflicted this kind of brutality on Emily Harris. *But what were you doing there?* he wondered, perhaps for the thousandth time since leaving Walt's office.

Walt had made him swear he would stay away from Alun, no matter how much he wanted to do otherwise. James knew he could get in to see Alun if he lied, said it was official business—no one would question him if he was in uniform. He just wanted Alun to know he hadn't abandoned him, that he... that he loved him. A day ago he wouldn't have dared say the words aloud, but now they were burning in his throat and on his tongue, desperate to get out.

The gentle touch of the doctor's hand on his back made James jump.

"I know the man they took into custody's some kinda friend of yours," he said quietly.

James's eyes widened.

"I've not said anything. Not that anyone's asked the question directly, mind," he added, not really making it clear what he would say, if someone did ask him.

James only nodded. "He didn't do it."

Dr. Stodderley didn't look convinced. "One thing Lamont *did* ask about was a necklace. He wanted to know if Claire Walker had come in wearing a crucifix."

"Why?" James asked, though he knew the answer, at least in part. Stanwix and Mills had found a gold cross in Alun's purse.

"Some of the other girls told Lamont the crucifix they found on your friend had belonged to Miss Walker—all I could say for sure was that she wasn't wearing it when she came to me," he said before the other could ask.

James's knees went weak.

"Having the woman's necklace doesn't prove guilt, my boy," Dr. Stodderley told him.

"But it makes it look like he did it."

TWO days after Alun's arrest, and the whole of Scotland Yard was still celebrating—all but James. It had been all he could do not to hit someone—anyone. Everyone.

He'd hardly slept; every time he tried, he was haunted by nightmares. In some of them Alun really was the killer, a wild-eyed monster dripping in blood. In others the East Ender was sent to the gallows as an innocent man, and all James could do was watch while the noose was placed around his neck, while the lever was pulled. He couldn't stop them. He couldn't even tell Alun that he loved him.

More than ever he wanted to go to Alun—but he kept his word. He went to work. He did his job. He told himself that everything would work out.

Out of the corner of his eye, James caught a swirl of purple. For once, he saw Robin coming before Rob even crossed the street. The hour was late, and the streets were dark, nearly deserted, and the last thing James wanted was company, but he waited for Robin to catch up to him anyway, doing his best to force a smile.

"I'm sorry," the redhead greeted James simply. "I wanted to come find ya yesterday, but…."

James waved it off. He didn't even know why Rob was apologizing.

Glittering emerald eyes regarded him a long moment. "I know he's a friend of yours, James. Blayney, the man they arrested," he stated. There was none of the usual puckishness in Robin's demeanor. "An' I know he ain't guilty. Man might have his faults, but he ain't no killer, not like that."

James blinked, taken aback. "You…?" He knew Alun? He swallowed hard; the lump in his throat remained. It made sense. Alun liked men. Rob was a Mary-Anne, or he had been one until recently. It shouldn't bother James that their paths had crossed. But it *did* bother him. It bothered him a lot. He cleared his throat. "What makes you think he's anything to me?" James wanted to know.

"The other night. The way ya… ya know him, James. Ya cares about him."

He heard the hurt in Robin's voice, heard what the younger man didn't say aloud: *please don't lie to me.*

James nodded. "I know him," he confessed. The other night, when he'd had stopped to say "hallo" to Emily on the corner… he closed his eyes. That was the last time he'd seen Emily alive, the last time he ever would see her. Robin had joined them, to tell him about a small part he'd landed in a "right proper theater," and James had been so happy for him— but then he saw Alun across the street, leaning up against the wall outside the Ten Bells, and it was like the rest of the world ceased to exist.

Robin's soft hand curled around James's; he accepted the comfort of the young man's touch. "I don' know Blayney, not really, but I know he didn't kill those girls, James. He ain't like that."

"Thank you." It seemed like a weak response, but James didn't know how else to express his gratitude. He wasn't even sure Mrs. Dunberry believed in Alun's innocence.

"You don't have to thank me. But I…." Robin hesitated. "I want ya to know I… I'm happy to be your friend, James. An I… I know there ain't nothing I can do about what's happened to Blayney, but if ya ever need anything, all ya have to do is ask. There is *nothing* I wouldna' do for ya, James, or… or for someone who was important to ya. *Nothing.*" When Rob met his gaze, James didn't see a teenage boy looking up at him. He didn't even see a man. Robin seemed… ageless. Eternal.

James shivered. "Thank you," he breathed, unable to think of anything else he could say.

In answer, Rob gave his hand a gentle squeeze—and then he let go.

Chapter 14

ALUN looked up when he heard three sets of footsteps stop in the corridor, just outside his cell door. Keys rattled. It was too soon after his untouched lunch tray had been collected for the guards to be bringing his supper. Alun snorted. Maybe Inspector Lamont had come back to ask him more questions, questions Alun would refuse to answer, just like the last two times Lamont came to see him.

He hadn't eaten his breakfast, or his meals from yesterday or the day before or the day before that, either. He'd declined his right—obligation more like—to attend Sunday church services with his fellow inmates. (Who would walk down to the chapel in chains.) Alun wondered idly—contemptuously—if rather than Lamont, maybe it was the priest coming to call, offering him redemption and a chance to unburden his conscience by confessing his misdeeds. If so, he wasn't interested in talking to him, either. No Christian priest could absolve him of his sins.

But the tall, imposing-looking man the guards opened the door for wasn't a priest, not unless priests smelled of expensive cigars and scotch. Even Alun knew the cut of an expensive suit when he saw it. He closed his eyes as the knots tightened and twisted in his gut. He was still wearing Tom Heron's clothes, the finest clothing he'd ever worn in his life, though it hardly looked fine anymore.

Alun shuddered as he remembered the impulsive hug James gave him, just before they left the shelter of his house four days ago. They'd been standing at the front door, about to leave, when suddenly the younger man wrapped around Alun's neck. He was startled at first, but then Alun returned the embrace. He loved being touched, and when James held him, it felt so… so natural. So *right*. Alun had lowered his nose to his lover's neck, taking a last—he hadn't expected it to be his last!—deep breath before they pulled away from each other and headed out into the London night. Fear and joy had warred inside him then. Now there was only fear.

"Show a little respect," one of the guards snapped, harsh words pulling Alun from the bittersweet memory.

The stranger placed one large hand on the guard's chest, stopping him from hauling Alun to his feet. "That'll be all, gentleman," he told them. His tone was authoritative. Alun suspected that in his youth, his visitor had been a man to be reckoned with; he still had the air of an alpha male.

Nevertheless, the guards wavered, hesitating at the doorway. Clearly, they were nervous about disobeying, but were no doubt just as unhappy about the idea of leaving the well-dressed gentleman alone in a cramped cell with a "madman." A cold hand closed around Alun's heart and squeezed tight. There was only one person he wanted to convince of his innocence, one person he wanted to know that he wasn't a killer—not a butcher, at least. But that one person was the man he'd all but confessed his guilt to in the effort to keep him away, keep him safe. And it had worked.

Maybe tonight, Alun thought, he would find the courage to step over to the spirit side permanently. All he had to do was step out of his body and not come back. It should be easy....

He hardly heard the guards slip out of the room.

"When I asked after your general state of health, the guards told me you'd not eaten since your arrest."

Alun looked up at his well-dressed visitor. The man had taken a seat across from him. "What's it to you?" Alun wanted to know.

The man took a breath and let it out again, as if reconsidering his tactics. "My name is Walter Gill." He didn't bother extending his hand. "I've been retained to assist you in your defense."

The lycan's frown deepened. "Since when do barristers work on Sunday?" *Or visit prisoners in their cells.* He'd never been pinched before, he knew enough to keep his nose clean, keep out of Percival's sights, but he knew how it went. The Crown would feel obliged to assign him a barrister, seeing as murder was a hanging offense, and those in power didn't want to appear cruel. But he didn't expect to see an attorney before the real thing, his actual trial. Tomorrow's court appearance was just a formality—a show for the public. The magistrate would ask him a few questions—questions he wasn't going to answer—he'd hear the constables read their statements... *James.* Pain lanced through his soul, crushing him, forcing him to double over, to show weakness in front of the stranger. Never in his life had Alun felt so hollow, so helpless to stop the cold from overwhelming him.

Tonight, he decided. Tonight he would step over to the other side and never come back. He would rather die than have to look into James's beautiful moss-green eyes and see how much he'd hurt him. Alun only wished he had some way to tell James good-bye. *Maybe after*, he thought. Maybe once he was in the spirit realm he could find James and at least say the words, even if James would never hear them.

Alun shrugged off the strong hand that gripped his shoulder. Walter Gill was only trying to steady him so he didn't fall over, but Alun didn't want his help. "Save yourself some trouble and go home," he growled, allowing a measure of his beast to come to the surface.

"Tell me you're guilty, and I promise you, you'll never see me again," Gill snarled right back.

Alun met his gaze, intending to lie and tell him *exactly* how he'd butchered Emily. Anything to be left alone.

"Before you do," Gill cut him off before he could start, "I want you to know that there is one person in this city who believes you're innocent of the crime of which you've been accused. He's the only reason I'm here. If you tell me he's wrong, I will—quite gladly—go back and repeat to him *every* detail that you tell to me."

Alun blinked, hope blooming in his chest… fear. Dread. *James.* It had to be James. But it couldn't be! He'd all but told James he killed Emily Harris… only if it *was* him and Gill made good on his promise to James what he said now… his stomach churned. "Who… who hired you?" he asked at last, almost afraid to hear the answer.

Gill hesitated. Then, "Lord James Mowbray," he said.

The lycan froze. *Lord… Mowbray?*

"I suppose the name wouldn't mean anything to you. You know him as Heron. It was his mother's name, God rest her soul. Jamie is every bit her child. Lily was a kind, too compassionate woman, easily taken advantage of." His eyes narrowed sharply, his meaning clear.

Alun nodded. "James is too generous for his own good too," he agreed.

Walter Gill almost smiled. Almost. "Jamie is entirely convinced of your innocence, Mr. Blayney. Personally, I have no opinion one way or the other. So whatever you have to say for yourself...?" He left it open for the other to speak.

Alun swallowed hard. A part of him wanted to lie, to tell this man he'd done everything they said he had and more. He wanted to protect James, to keep him from being dragged into his problems any further than he had already—but he knew what it would do to James if he lied. He leaned his shaved head back against the cold, hard wall and stared at the water-stained ceiling of his cell. *Goddess, why does he still believe in me?*

He's your home, your mate, came the answer, unbidden, startling Alun. But James was human. He could never be a mate, never love Alun. If he saw him for what he really was…. He swallowed hard, knowing that if he ever wanted more than a few stolen hours with James, he had no choice, he had to trust him. Tell him. Risk… everything.

Assuming he didn't end up swinging from the gallows for something he didn't do.

"Mr. Blayney?"

"I found Emily Harris's body, but I didn't kill her," he said, his voice little more than a ragged whisper.

"All right."

Alun looked up. "You believe me?"

"James believes you. I do trust his judgment, at least in some things."

Which wasn't exactly the same thing as saying he believed him… but maybe it didn't matter. "What… what do I do now?" Alun asked him.

"I understand you've not said anything to the police?" It wasn't quite a question.

"I ain't said nothing to no one."

"Good, lad. You keep it that way. The only time I want you talking to anybody but me is in front of the magistrate tomorrow—there you'll have to answer whatever questions the Crown prosecutor puts to you. Not to answer will only make you look guilty," he advised. "The magistrate can ask questions, too, though he usually doesn't. Regardless, you'll have to answer."

"What difference does it make what I say? Those constables got me dead to rights, an' they know it."

"As I understand it, no one saw you actually committing a crime."

Alun blinked at the man.

"*Did* they see you kill Miss Harris?"

"How could they have? I *didn't* kill her!" he insisted. "I liked Emily, she were a friend, a good an' decent lady. I know what she done for money, but that didn't make her deserving of being cut up like that!"

Gill nodded. "If you say that to the magistrate exactly as you've just said it to me, *and* if the constables' stories bear out that they didn't actually see you murder Miss Harris, there is the slenderest of chances that the magistrate will decline to commit you over for trial for lack evidence, Mr. Blayney."

"What does that mean?"

"It means you could be out of this place by tomorrow night."

Alun felt a sob rising up in his throat. Tomorrow? He could be out *tomorrow*?

"Don't get your hopes up," Gill cautioned him. "They need to pin this grisly business on somebody, and right now you're the only person who looks good for killing those girls. Even if they're only charging you with the one murder, the other two will be on everybody's mind. No doubt that awful business from last year, as well."

"I didn't kill them, either, *any* of them," he insisted.

Gill nodded again, but didn't comment. Without further ado, he rose to his feet and called for the guards to let him out, leaving Alun alone in the tiny cell once more, this time with entirely too much to think about. When his supper arrived a few hours later, Alun managed to eat half of it; he ignored the jeers from the guards about finally getting hungry enough to lower himself to eat their food. He didn't care what they thought.

He curled up on the hard, narrow cot and desperately sought out the last of James's scent on the clothes he was wearing. He closed his bloodshot eyes and tried to sleep. Tomorrow. There was the slenderest of chances that he could be out of here tomorrow.

JAMES felt sicker and sicker with each step he took toward the Old Bailey building, where the Crown would present its case against Alun. Because James had been called by the prosecutor to give his accounting of Emily Harris's murder, he'd been begrudgingly permitted to leave his post early today. He didn't want to testify against his friend. His lover. He told himself he wasn't really speaking against Alun, he was simply telling the truth about what happened that night. The truth, Walt promised him, was all they needed. James wasn't sure he believed him.

"Oi, Heron!" Mills clapped James good-naturedly on the shoulder when he caught up with him on the courthouse steps. "Ready to see that animal gets what he deserves?" He beamed.

The knots in James's stomach tightened, but he managed a noncommittal sort of nod. In his heart, he knew Alun hadn't killed Emily Harris, he hadn't killed anybody. He deserved to be set free today, so yes, he very much wanted Alun get what he deserved today.

James caught sight of Rob in the crowd, a swirl of purple wool, a bright red cap. The young Irishman shot him a tight-lipped grin, but didn't approach. Just the same, James was grateful for his presence, grateful there was one person in the crowd who believed in Alun's innocence. It seemed like everyone else in London—in all of Britain—thought he was guilty.

A huge black wagon, drawn by four horses, rattled its way around the corner—the prison transport. Rob vanished in the sea of faces as the crowd surged forward; everyone was vying for a better look. They jeered and hissed as the wagon drove past. James's knees gave way. It was Alun they were jeering at.

Mills gripped James's shoulder, steadying him. "Don't be nervous, mate," the younger constable said, misunderstanding James's reaction. "You just say what you saw, and the court does the rest. Bloody bastard'll be swinging by Christmas."

Bile burned the back James's throat, and his knees were so weak he was sure he'd never make it up the rest of the steps. He'd almost summoned the courage to try, when he spied Emily's friend Betty in the crowd; there where half a dozen other ladies, harlots, standing with her. Hatred burned in their eyes; there was no doubt in James's mind that if the prison wagon's driver stopped and dumped Alun on the street in front of them, those women would tear him apart with their bare hands.

"Come to watch the show, I 'spect," said Mills. He sounded like he approved, like if it was up to him, he'd let the girls have a go at Alun.

James turned away from the street, but looking at the large, imposing courthouse doors was even harder than looking at the crowd. By noon, Alun's fate would be sealed. He tried to tell himself this was just the first phase of the trial process, but if the magistrate held Alun over, there would be no saving him from the gallows. No jury would acquit him.

"Shite, Heron, you all right, man?" Mills hissed. "What's gotten into you?"

"Never been to one of these before," James told him feebly. It was the truth, but only half of it. He'd never been called to testify in a capital case, but that wasn't the reason he was so wobbly on his feet. He'd hardly slept since Alun's arrest. Exhaustion had managed to claim him at the end of his shift yesterday morning, causing him to fall asleep on the tram on his way home; if not for the driver, he would have missed his stop. Once in his own bed, however, sleep refused to return, so he'd spent the rest of the day in his garden. There wasn't much to be done so late in the season, but having his hands in the rich, damp earth, the sun warming his back, made James feel close to his mother and that brought him a small measure of comfort. Maybe he was deluding himself, believing she would understand about him, that she would like Alun, but he had to keep telling himself that if she were alive, she'd be standing right next to him, helping him find the strength to get through this.

James trudged up the steps, following dutifully along behind Mills as they entered the courtroom. It was smaller than he'd been expecting—or maybe it just seemed smaller because the gallery was already crammed to capacity with whispering onlookers. *All come to see Alun*, he thought miserably.

The room was simply arranged. A long table sat at its head with chairs for up to three magistrates; there was a desk for the court clerk in front of the magistrate's table; more desks and chairs were set up for attorneys behind it. The witness box sat on one side of the room; opposite it sat the dock for the accused. James swallowed hard. He didn't believe in God, but at that moment, he needed to pray to something—someone—that at the end of the day Alun would be free to come home with him. *Please*, he begged silently.

"Come on." Mills tugged at his sleeve, pointing to a knot of uniformed constables sitting in the gallery. "Stanwix is already here, let's go sit with him." He waved aside the usher, almost politely, when the man offered to assist them in getting to their place. It looked to James like every constable not on duty had shown up. Inspector Lamont wasn't sitting with them, however. James spotted him sitting front and center, a look of smug satisfaction on his face.

Dutifully—sullenly—James followed Mills over to where Stanwix was holding a couple of spots for them. Mills breathed a contented sigh as his ass touched the hard bench. "I don't know how you do it," he commented to James.

"Do what?"

"Never complain. My feet're killing me."

Next to him, Stanwix snorted. "I gots the answer to that." He pulled a flask out of his pocket. "A little nip now and then helps with all sorts of pain."

Several of the other constables snickered—they stopped laughing when Lamont turned to glare in their direction. James was sure the inspector's cold, hard eyes settled on him especially, even though he hadn't been laughing.

He wasn't given much time to consider it. The clerk came in and called the room to order. A moment later, a single red-robed magistrate took his place behind a long table—he sat in the center chair. The magistrate was younger than James had expected, though he looked imposing enough in his long scarlet robe and white powdered wig. As soon as he was seated, the clerk announced the first case of the day.

There were six hearings before Alun's. Each man was brought in the same, and settled into the dock before the clerk read the charges against him. Then the magistrate asked the accused if he had anything to add. Two of the men had witnesses to speak on their behalf, but none had legal counsel, although that wasn't unusual.

Only one out of the six was discharged and sent home; the rest were committed over for trial. With each commitment, James lost a little more of the scant hope he'd been trying so desperately to hang onto, so that by the time Alun's case was called, he was sure it was over before it had even begun. The papers were right: Alun would hang before Christmas, and James would be the only person who would mourn.

Just five days ago, James had been painting pictures in his head of a very different sort of Christmas. He'd not had the heart for any of the frivolities of the holiday season last year. It had been so soon after his brother's death. Anna invited him to the estate, of course, but he'd declined, though he told Mrs. Dunberry she was welcome to go if she liked. She had friends and family in Northumberland. Dutifully, she'd stayed in London with him, despite the fact that he was determined not to partake in the usual Christmas cheer. There was no tree, no garland, no mistletoe, not even a wreath on the door.

This year was going to be *so* different.... He closed his eyes against the sting of tears and cursed his own naiveté. For all he knew, Alun wouldn't have accepted his invitation to move in, anyway. Alun was right, they barely knew each other.

His heart sank further when Alun was brought in, shackled and chained like an animal or a madman. His hair was shorn off, and he still wore the clothing he'd been arrested in; there was dried blood caked on his sleeves and his trousers. In the gallery, men and a few women hissed and jeered at him, yelling "murderer," and "butcher," until the magistrate demanded order.

James laid his damp palms flat against his knees, willing himself to remain stoic despite the tumult of emotions roiling inside him at the sight of his lover in chains. Alun looked so much thinner than he remembered. There were cuts and bruises on his face; some of them were older, brown, but most were fresh and dark purple. His lip had been recently split; it was red and swollen. Alun didn't look up to seek him out in the crowd; he didn't look at anything but the floor in front of him as he was led to the dock.

Even though James knew already what the charge was, it was all he could do to suppress the sob rising in his throat when the clerk read the words aloud: the defendant stood accused of the murder of Miss Emily Harris, the penalty for which was death.

ALUN kept his head down, his eyes on the floor as the charge was read. He could *feel* James's presence in the courtroom; his heart pounded against his chest. Every instinct told him to look up, to search for James's face in the gallery, to claim whatever hope seeing him offered... but he was too afraid. He didn't want to see the look on James's face when the younger man saw him beaten and shackled. No true lycan would ever allow himself to be reduced to the state he was in by mere humans. But then again, he wasn't a true lycan. He was *diangen*.

He closed his eyes as hisses and jeers rang out through the courtroom. He heard Betty's soft sob, caught a whiff of her cheap perfume…. He clutched at the rail while the magistrate called for order yet again. Was there no one in London who didn't believe he'd murdered Emily Harris?

James. He believed in him. Alun started to turn, to open his eyes, to seek out James's face in the room so he could to convince himself that the one person he wanted to believe in his innocence really did. As long as James believed in him, nothing else mattered.

But before he could find his lover's face in the crowd, Alun caught another scent. Earthy. Musky. Lycan.

Percival.

And he'd brought Rhianna with him.

The smug pack leader gave a nod when their eyes met. Acid burned in the back of Alun's throat; his hackles rose. Percival smirked. He was enjoying the show. Next to him, Rhianna remained impassive, as usual.

Then the sound of the magistrate's voice drew Alun's attention to the front of the room once more. "Does the defendant… Mr.…?" The red-robed man shot over a questioning look.

"Alun Blayney, my Lord," he answered demurely, his voice little more than a hoarse whisper. He could almost hear Percival's snicker.

"Right, then," said the magistrate. "Have you anything to add, or say in your defense, Mr. Blayney?"

Alun swallowed hard. Until yesterday, his plan had been to say nothing and let them do whatever they wanted to him—assuming he wasn't able to simply step over to the spirit side and never return. But now….

"Mr. Blayney?" the magistrate questioned him again.

"I didn't do no harm to Emily Harris, Sir, or Claire Walker, or that other woman neither."

It took the magistrate ten minutes to quiet the room back down again.

Chapter 15

JAMES felt his heartbeat quicken when George Stanwix was called to the witness box to give his accounting of Thursday morning's events. Inspector Lamont had already given his deposition: he'd arrived on the scene after the arrest was made and had witnessed little—not that that stopped him from taking as much of the credit as he was able.

Stanwix was sworn in and asked to tell the court, in his own words, what had happened on the morning in question. He licked his lips, looking nervous. His gaze darted from Lamont, to Alun, to the magistrate, and back again.

"Constable?" the Crown prosecutor prompted him. The prosecutor was an older man who had introduced himself as Silas Chandler when he took his place at one of the desks in front of the magistrate's table. Like every other attorney in the room, Chandler wore a long black robe and powdered white wig. Like over half of them, he had a ruddy face, a sure sign that he drank too much. He didn't seem drunk now, however; he was keen-eyed and sharp.

Stanwix glanced at Alun again, but Alun wasn't looking at him or anyone else. He just stood there, head down, giving no indication that he was even listening to the testimony being given against him. It broke James's heart all over again to see him looking so defeated.

In the witness box, Stanwix cleared his throat. "I was on me regular route," he began, his words only slightly slurred by whatever he'd been sipping from his flask during proceedings. "It was… about half past three, a quarter of four in the morning, maybe. Just past the 'in between' time, the time when most folks is done for the night but not yet starting for the day—'cept bakers and the like, but there ain't too many of those in that part of the city. Anyhow, like I said, I was walking m' regular route when I heard this… well, there ain't no way to describe it, m'Lord." He turned to the magistrate. "I swear on me life, I didn't know what I was gonna find when I rounded that corner, but sure as hell... erm...." His face flushed pink. "That is to say, I didn't 'spect to see no man, I thought maybe a wild animal had got outa the zoo or something, but there he was—*him*." He pointed to Alun, who stood passively in the dock. "He was sitting practically on top of that bang—erm, that *unfortunate*," he corrected hastily. "He was sitting over her, an' he was covered in her blood."

"What happened next?" Chandler inquired, casting a dark look in Alun's direction.

"I blew me whistle," Stanwix told him. "I... I wasn't sure I'd be able to take him down meself—'sides, it's regulation, you see. Anyhow, it was Mills what come running, Sir. Constable Mills, there." He pointed. "Me an' him took down the man what killed that woman, that man there." He pointed again to the defendant. "Constable Heron arrived shortly afterward. I told him to see about getting the crowd to disperse—a lotta folk had shown up to see what the ruckus was all about," he explained. "Then I sent Mills to fetch the Inspector and police surgeon. An... I guess that's about it, m' Lord."

"Thank you, Constable," Chandler sat back down, seeming satisfied by Stanwix's story.

Walter Gill stirred for the first time since the proceedings had begun, standing up before Stanwix could escape from the witness box, something the constable appeared desperate to do.

"Excuse me, my Lord. Constable." He nodded at each in turn, his tone betraying nothing but cordial civility. "Constable Stanwix, if you wouldn't mind, I've just a couple of questions for you."

Stanwix fidgeted nervously with the cuffs of his coat. "Yes, Sir?"

"You said you and your colleagues took down the man you believed had killed Emily Harris, is that correct?"

"Well, we didn't know who she was at the time," said Stanwix, eyeing him suspiciously. "Why?"

"I was just wondering if you saw Mr. Blayney *actually* kill Miss Harris."

"Well... no... I mean... we didn't *see* him do it, but he was kneeling over her like he had done. 'Is face was all twisted up, like... like he was some kind of madman!"

"Was he holding a knife or any other weapon?" Gill's tone remained mild.

"No. But… but we found one on him when we searched his pockets," the constable informed him.

"What sort of knife?"

"A pocketknife."

"Large… small…?"

Stanwix frowned, giving over an incredulous look. "It were a bloody pocketknife… excusing me language, m'Lord." He glanced at the magistrate again. The man nodded and Stanwix went on. "It were a pocketknife, small like, so as fit into a bloke's pocket."

Walt gave a satisfied nod. "Was it clean or bloodied?"

"It were clean, but that don't mean—it were in 'is pocket already!"

"Yes, you said, thank you. Oh… did you find any other knives or other weapons on the scene, Constable?"

"No, Sir." He sounded angry and his face was reddened.

"Did you find anything else on the defendant's person?"

"Yes! There was a cross—a crucifix—in his purse. It belonged to that girl what got killed a few weeks ago, Claire Walker," Stanwix declared triumphantly.

Water Gill remained unperturbed. "Are you certain?"

"What d'you mean?"

"I mean, are you certain the crucifix was Miss Walker's? Did you give it to her personally?"

"What? Me? No! She were a… you know, one of those *unfortunates*," he lowered his voice when he said the word. "I ain't never fraternized with those girls."

In the gallery, several of the ladies snickered, but no one said anything.

"I'm a married man," Stanwix insisted.

"Then how do you know it was Miss Walker's necklace?" Gill asked him.

"Well… I… that is…," he stammered helplessly.

"Thank you, Constable," said Gill. "I've no more questions for this man, my Lord," he told the magistrate.

As soon as Stanwix was back in his seat in the gallery, he took out his flask and downed a huge mouthful of its contents, muttering angrily, not quite under his breath, about how damned barristers were what was wrong with the legal system. James ignored him. His heart raced faster. He was sure no court-appointed counsel would have thought to ask questions like that!

Mills was called up next; he gave the same story and had the same questions put to him by Walter Gill. His answers, though equally reluctant, were the same. He hadn't seen the suspect actually kill, or in any way cause harm, to the dead woman, nor had there been a knife or any other weapon in Alun's hand when they first came upon the scene. The small pocketknife they found on his person was clean when they found it.

The Crown prosecutor called next for Police Constable James Heron.

ALUN tried to face James when he was called to the witness box, but he couldn't seem to lift his head. He couldn't make himself look into those moss-green eyes for fear of what he would see there. Hearing James's voice was going to be agony enough, especially after listening to the inspector and the other two constables give their depositions. Surely they'd done a thorough enough job of condemning him. Why did the magistrate really need one more man to tell the exact same story?

James was sworn in and asked to tell the court about the night Emily Harris was murdered.

"I heard the whistle and ran toward the sound of it. When I rounded the corner and came into the courtyard, I saw the accused standing near the body of Miss Emily Harris. Constables Mills and Stanwix were already there when I arrived on the scene."

Alun closed his eyes against the tears threatening to overtake him. James's voice sounded impossibly cold.

"What happened then?" inquired the Crown prosecutor.

"Nothing, Sir. I mean… that is to say, Constable Stanwix and Constable Mills arrested Mr. Blayney exactly as they said they did and searched his pockets. They already described the items they found, Sir."

"Did you see the items yourself, Constable?"

"Only at a distance."

"Thank you, Constable. Sir Walter?" Chandler turned to the defendant's counsel.

Alun kept his eyes closed; he was sure James had changed his mind. Why else would he sound so cold?

A new scent hit his nostrils... musky... copper tinged... lycan... familiar. He scanned the gallery... *there*. At the very back of the courtroom, near the door, in case he had to make a quick exit, stood a lycan not more than twenty-five years old. He had dark hair. Silver eyes. Just like Claire described. He was big... not like Percival's two goons, but he looked like he could be a dock worker or a rough tradesman. *Exactly the kind of man who could walk up to a whore with a few shillings and not make her suspicious....* The silver-eyed lycan met Alun's gaze and flashed a toothy grin. He was about to get away with murder.

"CONSTABLE HERON," Sir Walter began by asking the same questions he'd already put to Mills and Stanwix, "when you arrived on the scene, was Mr. Blayney holding a knife or any other weapon that you could see?"

"No, Sir."

"Did you see Mr. Blayney harm Miss Harris in any way?"

"No, Sir."

"Did you find a knife anywhere in the courtyard, *other* than the small pocketknife Mr. Blayney had on his person?"

"No, Sir."

"Was there any blood on that knife?"

"None that I saw, Sir," James answered helplessly, wondering what Walt was trying to prove. So far he hadn't done anything but confirm the Crown's case.

But then Walt smiled. "One last thing, Constable. You heard both Constables Stanwix and Mills tell us that Mr. Blayney's face was 'twisted up', like that of a madman. Did Mr. Blayney look mad to you?"

James's heart jumped. He forced his expression to remain neutral, however. "I don't presume to know what goes on in the minds of other men, Sir."

"Well, did Mr. Blayney *look* like a madman? Or did he perhaps look like a man who had come upon Miss Harris in the courtyard—a man who was overtaken by shock and grief at what had been done to someone he knew?"

"I... I suppose it could be the latter, Sir. I would certainly be overcome, if it were me finding the lady like that."

Angry rumblings rippled throughout the room as James was excused from the witness box. His legs—his whole body—felt weak, and his stomach churned violently. It took all of his concentration to keep his face a neutral mask, to put one foot in front of the other and walk back to his seat in the gallery without stumbling. Without betraying any hint of the hope surging in his chest.

Lamont glowered at him with unmasked fury—Stanwix too. Even Mills was regarding James as if he was some sort of traitor. James didn't care. He took his seat calmly, and focused all his attention on Dr. Stodderley, who was being called up to the witness stand next.

The surgeon took his oath and testified as to what he had found when he examined Emily Harris's body. "Her neck was cut off to the side." He demonstrated by making a slicing motion with his fingers against his own neck. "The carotid artery was cut, but not severed."

"Could you explain what that means?" asked Chandler.

"That she didn't die immediately of the wound, but most likely exsanguinated—bled to death—some while later."

"Were there other injuries to Miss Harris's body?" the prosecutor wanted to know.

"Yes. There was bruising on her wrists, the pattern of which is consistent with human hands—that is to say, she was held down, rather than tied up," he explained. "This suggests that more than one person is responsible for Miss Harris's death."

The prosecutor blinked in surprise. "I beg your pardon?"

"It would be rather difficult to both hold down a flailing victim *and* cut her throat. I stated as much in my report, which I gave to Inspector Lamont."

Chandler cleared his throat; he looked uncomfortable. "I see. Were there any *other* injuries to the victim, Doctor?" he pressed on as murmurs spread throughout the gallery, forcing the magistrate to once more call for order.

Dr. Stodderley hesitated a moment, sparing a glance toward the ladies in the room, before continuing in a professional tone. "There were multiple lacerations to her vaginal opening—deep cuts. Again, the wounds weren't such so as to provide an immediate end to her suffering."

"You make it sound as if you believe Miss Harris suffered a great deal before she died. Is this correct—did she suffer?" asked Chandler. He shot another baleful look in Alun's direction.

"Most certainly she suffered," Dr. Stodderley snapped. "Miss Harris bled to death on the cold ground after she was brutally attacked! There is no doubt in my mind that beyond her physical injuries, she was terrified. Who wouldn't be?"

"Thank you, Doctor. I have no more questions for you. Sir Walter?"

Walter stood up. "Dr. Stodderley, how long would you estimate the knife was that cut Miss Harris's... forgive me, I'm not a medical man... I believed you called it her 'vaginal opening'?"

Dr. Stodderley nodded. "The blade would have had to have been at least seven or eight inches long."

"Longer than a pocketknife, I take it?"

"*Considerably* longer than a pocketknife."

Rather than trying to silence the uproar, the magistrate ordered the courtroom cleared; James didn't want to leave, but he didn't have a choice.

And Alun still refused to look his way.

Chapter 16

ALUN stood mute, barely able to breathe while the magistrate took his time deliberating his fate. The only people left in the courtroom besides he and the magistrate were the two barristers, a few bailiffs, and the clerk.

At last the young, red-robed magistrate looked up from his silent musing. He regarded only the two attorneys, not sparing even half a glance for the man whose life he held in his hands. "I must admit that I am presented here with a difficult decision, gentlemen," he said, his tone somber. "And I regret deeply the decision I feel I have no choice but to make."

Alun had to grasp the rail in front of him to keep from falling. *No choice.* The magistrate had no choice. He would send Alun to trial. The jury would be made up of the same people who had been ejected from the courtroom, people who assumed he was guilty because they wanted him to be guilty, because they needed somebody to blame. He would be convicted... hanged.... He closed his eyes. His whole heart ached. He would give anything to see James one more time, just to tell him he hadn't killed Emily. He didn't care what anyone else thought, but he needed James to know he hadn't done it. He needed James to believe in him.

The magistrate continued, "Mr. Chandler, I have no choice but to discharge the suspect."

"My Lord!" Chandler objected.

Alun's head snapped up. Discharged? Free? He couldn't have heard that right!

"Through no fault of yours, Mr. Chandler," said the magistrate, "the Crown has not presented this court with sufficient evidence to warrant holding the prisoner over for trial." His voice was thick with remorse. Anger. "Though I have no doubt that a grand jury would grant the Crown a bill of indictment, I do not believe it would be based in fact, but rather emotion and supposition. Therefore, I cannot in good conscience permit the Crown's case against the accused to go forward—as much as I would like to. The prisoner is hereby discharged and free to go."

Alun was still shaking, drawing in ragged breaths. Free? *James.* Goddess... James.

A moment later, one of the bailiffs was removing his shackles; the man looked sickened. Alun barely noticed. He was free... *James.* His heart hammered in his chest. *Goddess, thank you.* He cast a quick glance at the ceiling, the sky beyond.

"Mr. Blayney," said the magistrate in a heavy tone, drawing his attention. "You should count yourself lucky today. Not many men in your position would have been fortunate enough to... come by such esteemed representation. Sir Walter." Anger and outrage seemed to dance in the magistrate's eyes. Alun suspected that Gill was going to pay for this, somehow.

Gill, however, seemed unconcerned. "My Lord." He bowed, then turned to the prosecutor. "Mr. Chandler." He extended his hand.

"Sir Walter. Good show—well played. I only hope... well...." He cast a dark look in Alun's direction. "Let us hope for the best, shall we?"

Gill agreed and turned to Alun. "Mr. Blayney, I think perhaps you and I ought to leave by a less public exit." He nodded toward a side entrance.

Alun gulped in air. "Yes, Sir. I... thank you, Sir... my Lord," he added with a hesitant look at the magistrate, the man who had literally handed him his life back, even though clearly he wasn't happy about doing so.

On jelly-kneed legs, Alun followed Gill out of the courtroom and into the narrow back hall. He stopped as soon as the door was shut behind them; his legs simply refused to work. He ran both hands over his face, unable to believe it was over. *James....* Goddess, would James want to see him? Did he believe in Alun's guilt—or his innocence? Alun sagged against the wall, fighting back a sob.

"Breathe, lad." Gill patted his arm; it was an unexpected show of sympathy, but Alun appreciated it.

"Just tell me I ain't dreaming," he begged.

"This is very real, Mr. Blayney, but it's far from over. You heard that rabble back there. There's not a soul in London who thinks you're innocent of butchering those women."

Sobered, he nodded, his mind spinning with new fears. All he had were the few coins in his purse—and that was assuming he got it back. The police had taken it from him the night he was arrested. They'd taken Claire's necklace too. He had to find some way to get that back; promises to the dead were never lightly made, never lightly broken. "What... what happens now?"

"James has asked me—should things turn out favorably—to convey you back to his home."

James. Alun shuddered again. James wanted to see him.

"Of course," Gill went on, his tone brisk, "whether you chose to accept his hospitality is up to you."

Alun blinked, pausing a moment... but then he understood the other man's meaning exactly. Gill didn't want him going to James. He didn't know if it was because he suspected the nature of their... friendship, or if he just didn't want the younger man dragged into the mess that was Alun's life. And Gill didn't even know the half of it. Alun still had to deal with the rogue wolf. The silver-eyed werewolf was sure to be even less pleased than the rest of London's citizens to see Alun discharged. He was likely to feel threatened, since Alun knew his face now, as well as his scent. There was still the pack leader to deal with too; knowing the rogue's face wouldn't be enough for him. Besides, Alun was sure Percival would have been just as happy to see Alun go to the gallows. Why else would he have shown up like that? It certainly hadn't been to lend his support.

Gill cleared his throat. "I realize you're in a difficult position, Mr. Blayney. I wouldn't be opposed to lending you enough money to get you back on your feet. However much you think it will take. You could consider it a long-term loan, if you like. No rush to pay me back."

Alun's eyes narrowed. "In exchange for leaving London, you mean?" It really wasn't a question. He knew that was exactly what Gill wanted him to do.

"It would seem prudent, don't you think?"

Alun opened his mouth to say "yes." Leaving was the most sensible thing he could do, and for more reasons than Gill had any way of knowing. But if he left now, he could never expect James to forgive him. "I owe James better than to run away." He forced the words out before he lost his nerve. James had believed in him when no one else did, not even the people he'd known, done no harm to, the last ten years. Alun couldn't be sure if James still believed in him, but James deserved better than for him to up and leave without a word.

Walter Gill regarded the tall East Ender for a long moment, his thoughts carefully hidden behind the same mask of impassiveness he'd displayed in the courtroom. "I presume you're aware that Jamie isn't quite what he appears."

"I know he ain't no common man, Mr. Gill, if that's what you're saying. I knew it before you said so."

He nodded. "A man of his caliber is expected to do certain things with his life, Mr. Blayney. Marry. Produce children. Live in a certain way. He's well past the age where a man may 'dabble' simply to please his own fancy."

"I guess that's his business, ain't it?" He felt his hackles rising and leashed his temper. It would do no good to lash out here. Besides, Gill wasn't telling him anything he didn't already know.

"I suppose perhaps you're correct," he surprised the lycan by saying. "But these sorts of things have a way of becoming other people's business, Mr. Blayney. James will have to answer to the Mowbray name eventually, even if he doesn't want to."

Alun nodded. Whatever James felt for him, even if it was everything Alun wanted it to be, wouldn't matter in the end. James had obligations and his family who would see to it that he lived up to them. "I only want to tell him 'thank you' for believing I didn't kill those women. Nobody else… they all thought I done it." He owed James better than just running away. Again.

Gill made no comment. "My carriage is out back." He inclined his head to a door at the end of the long, narrow hall. "My driver will take you wherever you decide you want to go. I'll go out the front and see if I can't keep the mob occupied."

"Thank you."

He gave a curt nod and left Alun alone.

Alun stood in the hall for many long moments before finally gathering up the courage to go through the door; he had no real way of knowing what he would find on the other side. It wasn't any particular comfort that he recognized the same door he'd been brought in through— the one he would have exited by if things hadn't gone well. Alun couldn't help the irrational fear that he was going to find his jailers on the other side... but he stepped into the bright sunshine, anyway.

"Alun?" called a familiar, uncertain sounding voice.

Alun's heart pounded in his ears. *James*. He was waiting by the curb, standing in front of a plain blue carriage, looking anxious. Afraid.

James had removed his uniform coat, probably so he looked less like a copper and more like an ordinary citizen. He was shivering in the chilly autumn air, and even at a distance, Alun could see the dark circles under those beautiful gray-green eyes and the deep-set lines that seemed permanently etched around them. He was sure those lines hadn't been there a few days ago. Alun was sure it was his fault James looked like he did; it made him want to wrap the younger man up in his arms and bury his nose against his hair, beg his forgiveness. It made him want to hold him and never let go. It made him want to tell James how much he loved him.

But remembering Gill's words about family and obligations, Alun shoved his hands into his pockets and ambled over slowly, wondering how long would it be before James's obligations caught up with him and he was forced to marry. Produce an heir. What if encouraging James to "dabble" only hurt him more? Alun didn't know anything about the Mowbray name, but Gill had made it sound like they might be pretty important, that James wouldn't have a choice but to cave in to his family's wishes. He didn't want James to end up like him, *diangen*, an outcast.

But he still owed James better than to just run away again. "We should get you out of the cold," he suggested.

James laughed; it sounded strained.

Alun regarded him; he hadn't intended to say anything funny.

"It's nothing," said James to the questioning look on his face. "Come on." He gestured toward the waiting carriage.

Silently, Alun followed him inside, settling himself onto one of the velvet-covered benches while James pulled the dark curtains across the carriage's windows, to shield them from onlookers. James rapped loudly on the carriage roof to signal the driver that they were ready to leave. Then he hesitated, seemingly unable to decide whether he should sit next to Alun or across from him.

Alun just waited.

Finally James sat down across from him. He didn't meet the lycan's gaze.

"James...."

James cut him off: "I know you didn't kill Emily Harris, Alun. I am so sorry I let you think I did. Please... can you ever forgive me?"

Alun blinked, startled.

"Please," James begged, when he didn't respond right away. "I'm sorry. I'm so sorry. I never should have doubted you, even for a moment."

Alun shifted in his seat. "I did a good job of making you think I'd done it, James. There ain't nothing to be sorry for. Nothing to forgive."

"I let you think I'd abandoned you. After everything I'd said about wanting to get to know you, to be with you, to...." He closed his eyes. "All I can say is how sorry I am, Alun. I behaved dishonorably. I could swear it will never happen again, but I wouldn't expect you to believe me. All I can do is beg you to take me at my word."

"I wanted you to doubt me. I wanted you to stay out of it."

"*Never.*"

The fierceness in his tone made Alun smile. It made him afraid.

"Will you ever be able to trust me again?" James asked softly.

"I think you hiring some fancy barrister more than makes up for... for whatever you believed when you saw me in that courtyard."

"I saw just what Walt said. A man who had come across the body of somebody he knew. It was grief. Shock."

"I was ready to tear into those other two," Alun admitted.

"I don't believe that."

"You should, James. I *didn't* hurt Emily, but I would have hurt those two constables if you hadn't been there. I would have killed them."

James nodded. He was quiet a long while, making Alun wonder what he was thinking. He got his answer when James reached across the gap between them and ran his fingers gingerly over Alun's bruised face. "I can't believe what they did to you."

"It's nothing." Alun captured James's hand in his own and kissed it. *Nothing* had ever felt so good, so *right*, as being near James Heron. He held James's hand to his cheek; he was sure he could feel James's heart beating through his fingertips.

"Alun... I... there's something I want to say to you. Something I need to say. And I know it's going to sound quite mad, but... but I was *so* frightened the last few days. I thought I'd never see you again, and I just want you to know that I... I believe I'm in love with you."

THE instant the words were out of his mouth, James knew he'd made a mistake. Alun looked... shocked. Uncomfortable. But the way Alun had been looking at him only a moment before, the way he'd taken his hand, kissed it, held it to his face, James had felt so sure... *but just because maybe*—maybe—*he returns my affection that doesn't mean he wants to hear it*. Alun might not have a wife and children waiting for him, but that didn't mean he wanted a man. A suitor. A... husband. "You don't have to say anything," said James, pulling away. "Maybe it's better you don't." He turned his head to stare at the black curtain over the window.

"James, I—"

"I just wanted you to know, that's all," James cut him off. "I don't expect anything in return," he lied. It wasn't quite a lie. He hadn't expected anything, but he'd hoped Alun would tell him that he loved him too. James wondered if there had ever been a bigger idiot born than he, himself.

"You don't know me, James. You don't know... you don't know how badly I could hurt you. I ain't no killer, not like everybody believes, but I ain't... I'm not who you think. *What* you think."

James made no reply for a very long time. What was there to say?

"James, please."

"Please, what? You're right, Alun. I don't know you. I want to—so very badly, I want to. But how can I, when you won't tell me who you are? You keep saying that you're not what you seem, yet you refuse to give even the slightest clue as to what you mean by that! I do love you, and would willingly give you whatever time you needed to decide you can trust me, but—"

"What about your family?"

"What?"

"You ain't like me, James. You *got* family. People who care about you. Obligations. You... you don't wanna end up like me. An outcast. I can't ever go back to my home, James." Tears glistened in Alun's dark eyes. "They can't abide my choices. Me being with men. You don't wanna lose everything you got."

"Walter." The man's name fell out of James's mouth like a stone. "What did he say to you?"

"Nothing I didn't already know."

James met Alun's gaze dead on. "I want you to listen to me, Alun. Me, not Walt. Not anybody. I don't care what he told you, I decided a long time ago that I would never marry. I would never have children. I would never live my life to suit other people's ideas of what I should and should not do. This is my life. It's my choice."

"It ain't as easy as that."

"Like hell it isn't! Alun, I will tell you *everything* you want to know about who I am, my family—my family name. But you have to tell me your secrets too. I promise you, no matter what you say, it won't change how I feel. Nothing will ever make me look at you any differently than I'm looking at you right now."

"You can't know that."

"Let me be the judge of that, Alun. *Please.* I want so much with you, but there can't be *anything* between us if you won't trust me. I am begging you, won't you at least give me a chance to prove myself? I love you. And I really believe you love me too."

Alun swallowed hard and looked away. He nodded. "When we get to your house, I... we'll talk. I'll tell you what you want to know, an' then if... if you still want me... then we can talk about love."

Chapter 17

"ALL right, we're here," James stated the obvious as they walked in the front door. He threw his coat over the banister and turned to face the lanky East Ender. "Talk to me."

"Your room," Alun told him, even though it seemed as if they were alone in the house.

James opened his mouth to say something, but then changed his mind. He nodded and led the way upstairs. Alun followed; each step filled him with dread. There were no words to tell James the truth—no words he would believe anyway. He had to show him.

He shut the bedroom door behind them, and without a word, he crossed the room and drew the drapes tight. But then he just stood there, frozen, unable to face James, unable to go through with showing the younger man the kind of monster he'd fallen in love with.

James laid a hand gingerly on his back. "Alun, whatever it is, just tell me. I'll listen. I won't judge you. I know we come from different worlds and... and maybe you've done things I wouldn't have done. Couldn't have done. But... I trust you. I know that whatever it is—"

"It ain't like none of that." He turned around, forced himself to face the younger man.

"Then what?"

Alun swallowed hard, but the cold lump remained in his throat. He took James's hands in his again and caressed them; he pressed a kiss to each palm. "No matter what you see, I... I would *never* hurt you, James. I... I couldn't." He met his gaze, and in those moss-green eyes Alun saw everything he'd ever wanted, everything he was sure he would never have. *Home.* Love. Hope. *A mate.* "I love you. I love you so much that I ache with it. No, don't say nothing," he entreated, when James started to speak. "Just... just remember that I wouldn't ever hurt you, even if it were to defend myself. You… you could kill me, an' I wouldn't lift a finger to stop you."

"*Alun*—!"

"Just remember, James." Then Alun let go of his hands and stepped back. He closed his eyes, not wanting see the look on the younger man's face when he shifted shape. It took only the span of a single breath. His clothes dropped away. There was a tingle, a shiver of pleasure as he changed. Four feet stood where two had previously.

James's sharp intake of breath sliced through Alun's soul. He smelled his lover's terror, heard the mad racing of his heart—he knew what James must be thinking, what he saw. *A monster.* A devil. A nightmare given form.

A soft whine escaped Alun's throat. He opened his eyes, hoping, *praying*, he would find some small measure of understanding, of acceptance, on James's face. Anything to give him hope…. But all he saw was shock and fear. Disbelief. Revulsion. Everything he'd expected to see. Alun wished he hadn't closed the bedroom door against interlopers, because all he wanted was to run away, run until his lungs burned and his muscles seized up from exhaustion—he wanted to run until the pads of his feet bled, like he had after he'd been exiled from his father's pack.

Defeated, Alun slumped to the floor, closing his eyes again, unable to bear the horrified look on James's face any longer.

SHOCK and—he was ashamed to admit it—terror kept James rooted to the spot for too many heartbeats. The wolf, if one could call it that, was easily three times the size of any wolf James had seen before. Its fur was thick and black—silken. Beautiful. Long sharp teeth protruded from its… *his*… jaw. *Alun's* jaw. James shuddered. He had no doubt that a beast like that could overpower him and rip out his throat with very little effort.

But then it whimpered again, and James's heart broke to hear such a sorrowful sound. "Alun?"

The creature didn't move.

"Alun… is that… *how*…?" How was such a thing possible?

The wolf flinched as if he'd hit it. *You could kill me, and I wouldn't stop you….* Alun's last words to him before…. James took a hesitant, frightened step forward, but the beast didn't move. He took another step and then another until finally he sat down on the floor next to it. Him. "Alun, if that's really you, if you really… if you understand me, *please*, look at me," he beseeched. James's heart raced faster in his chest as it lifted its head—it could kill him so easily, but when James looked into the creature's eyes, beautiful, blacker-than-night eyes, he saw how terrified it was. *He* was. "I know you would never hurt me, sweetheart," James whispered. He fought down the last of his fear and laid his hand on the beast's head. Its fur felt like Alun's hair, coarse and thick.

It was trembling.

"I love you," James told him. He wrapped his arms around the wolf's neck and buried his face in its fur. He inhaled deeply. The wolf smelled like the man… or maybe the man smelled like the wolf. Or maybe it didn't matter. James rubbed his face against Alun's fur, covering himself in the rich, earthy scent. "Alun," James whispered his lover's name. "Alun," he repeated, over and over, sensing deep in his heart how important it was for Alun to understand he knew it was him. James rested his head against the wolf's broad, muscular back. Under his ear, James heard Alun's massive heart beating. Its rhythm seemed to be in sync with his own beating heart. "I must be mad," he murmured, "but… when I'm with you, I feel complete. It doesn't matter that you're… well, whatever you are. All that matters is that there's been a piece of me that was missing for so long, I never even knew it wasn't there until I met you. You're that piece, Alun, you're what's missing from my life. I know that sounds presumptuous, perhaps even a little insane—"

In one breath he was leaning against a giant black wolf and in the next the wolf was a man. A naked man. "Bloody hell," James swore at the suddenness of it.

Alun sat up. "I'm sorry, I didn't mean to startle you."

James barely heard the repentant words. "Alun, your face," he breathed. Even the worst of Alun's injuries were gone! The bruises had vanished, and the cuts were reduced to faint red lines. "How… is it… what… what you are…? What are you?"

Alun's gaze dropped. "You know what I am."

The unspoken word hung between them: *werewolf.*

James refused to acknowledge it. "I don't believe in myths and wives' tales."

"Even when you have one sitting in front of you?"

"You're not a myth. You're quite real."

Alun nodded. "I'm real. But it ain't a curse, I wasn't bitten by a wolf, an' I ain't no murderer." His tone was bitter. Defensive.

James understood. One of the superstitions about men who turned into wolves at night was that they got to be that way by murdering children, eating their flesh. Drinking their blood. "I know you're not a murderer, sweetheart, and I believe the rest of it, I believe that it's not a curse. I have a thousand and one questions for you, but right now that doesn't matter. I don't care *what* you are. I love *who* you are."

Alun swallowed hard; he didn't seem to be able to believe that, but when he pulled away from James, it was only find a more comfortable position, to lean his back up against the bed. James sat in front of him, letting his knees press up against Alun's.

"I didn't heal like this because I'm a lycanthrope," Alun told him, his voice shaky, soft, as if he expected James to reject the term. When James didn't say anything one way or the other, he went on. "I... I healed like this because of you."

"Me?"

Alun nodded. He looked away. When he spoke, his voice was so soft, James could barely hear him. "They say that when a wolf lies in the shelter of... of his heart's true home, his... his mate." He hesitated, but James didn't interrupt him. "When a wolf finds his mate, he becomes invincible. Werewolves need... love makes us whole, James. *You* make me whole."

James couldn't help the smile spreading over his lips—his heart— even though he could tell by Alun's voice that something was very wrong. "I feel the same," he assured him. "That's what I was trying to tell you."

"You don't understand! I'm not *human*."

His smile deepened. "I believe I've grasped *that* fact, thank you."

"James, please. This ain't something to laugh about!"

"Alun.... " James reached for his chin, tilted it so Alun was looking at him, at last. "Tell, me," he invited, softly. "Explain to me what's so wrong here."

"Wolves... mate." He hesitated over the word again, but James still didn't flinch. "It's a life bond, James. When a wolf chooses a mate, when his soul chooses it for him 'cause it's not some decision we just make, it... it's *forever*."

"You say that as if it's an unfavorable condition."

"Ain't it? You're not like me. You got family—"

"Alun, I would *gladly* have you for the rest of my life. I don't care what Walt told you. I have no intention of marrying someone I don't love simply because social custom dictates that that is what a man of my breeding and background is expected to do. I will be with whom I want—so long as that person wants me too. I want you. The only question remaining is whether or not you want me too."

"It ain't a choice."

"But whether or not you stay *is*."

"You really want me to?"

"More than anything I've wanted before in my life."

"What... what exactly are you proposing?" Alun pressed him for clarification.

"Move in with me. Share my bed. Be my lover. My partner in all things."

ALUN sat alone on the bedroom floor, resting his back against the bed. He was still naked. He didn't want to get anywhere near the blood-stained, filthy clothing he'd been forced to wear for the last four days. He had no doubt he'd been left in those clothes so he would look guiltier in the magistrate's eyes.

If it weren't for Walter Gill, it would've worked. If it weren't for James... he closed his eyes. James. How could his soul have chosen a human mate? Humans hurt each other. Lied. Cheated. Alun knew all about humans. He pulled his knees up to his chest and wrapped his arms around his calves, resting his chin on his knees. He should be happy. He *was* happy. The man he wanted as his mate had accepted him—more than accepted him. James wasn't afraid of him. He loved him.

But Alun had heard those words before. Ten years ago, when he first came to London, he'd trusted his heart to a human. Daniel Baker, Danny to most of his friends. Danny wasn't like James, he didn't talk about love or finding the missing piece of himself, but they'd lived together. Shared a bed. Been lovers. Partners. Alun never told him what he was, he hadn't dared—hadn't felt he needed to. In the end, he was just as glad; Danny betrayed his trust and broke his heart.

The sound of James's footsteps nearing the bedroom door brought Alun to his feet. In addition to footsteps, he heard water sloshing and china clattering against the metal serving tray. He smelled meat… cheese… bread. Tea. He opened the door just as James got to it.

A smile of relief spread across the blond's face when Alun took the overburdened tray from his arms. In addition to food, James had brought up two pitchers full of hot water for washing.

"What'd you do, empty out the larder?" Alun found himself teasing, despite the nervous flutter in his stomach.

"I figured you must be at least as hungry as I am," James answered with a grin. He poured the water in the basin while Alun set the tray down on the bureau.

Alun caught the scent of heat rising on the younger man's skin, but it wasn't desire. It was… nervousness? Alun turned to look at him—James looked away, quickly.

"Go ahead and eat," James said. "I need to clean up."

Sharp lycan ears heard the quickening beat of the younger man's heart, and anyone could see the pink coming into James's cheeks as he disrobed—but surely he wasn't suddenly body conscious. It made Alun wonder why the other man was suddenly so uneasy. *Maybe 'cause he's only just now starting to realize what kind of monster he's asked to move in with him.*

Doing his best to ignore the tightening in his gut, Alun sliced off a thick slab of cheese and took it over to James, who had already soaped up the washcloth and was sponging himself off. James shot him a quizzical look when he held it up to the younger man's mouth.

"You said yourself you were hungry," Alun told him, keeping his tone carefully neutral. James accepted the offering from his fingers with an appreciative grin—without seeming to hesitate, either. He nipped playfully at Alun's fingertips, kissing them as he devoured the cheese.

"A food fetish, too, I see," Alun joked, mostly to cover his own anxiety and confusion. James wasn't *acting* like he wanted him to leave. "Maybe I need to start making a list."

"Just hungry," James assured him, his tone difficult to interpret.

Alun turned away. Then he turned back again. He couldn't stand the feeling that he was dangling on the end of a string. If James had changed his mind, if he'd reconsidered....

"What's the matter?" James asked, before he got the chance.

"If... if there's something you'd like to say to me, please just say it, an' get it over with."

James looked as if he'd been caught in a bear trap. "I'm having a hard time believing this is real," he admitted.

"What part? That I'm a...." He bit his tongue on the word "monster." "A lycanthrope, a werewolf," he said instead. Even he heard the bitter anger in his tone.

James put down the washcloth and came over to him. He laid his hand on Alun's chest and closed his eyes, as if he was just... listening. Alun stood utterly still, waiting. Wondering. Hoping. Hardly breathing.

"No," James answered him at length. He opened his eyes and met the lycan's gaze dead on. "It *is* hard to believe that something as extraordinary as what you are could exist at all, Alun, but that isn't it. I'm having a hard time believing that you're here. That you're safe. That you love me. I'm afraid to believe.... You didn't really answer me when I asked you to stay. I know how impetuous it was to ask, and I know the risks," he added quickly, "but I'm willing to take them if you are."

Alun brushed his fingers lightly across James's cheek. He cradled his face in both hands. "There's things besides your family an' the neighbors to be worrying about, *cariad*," he warned.

"What does that mean? That word, '*cariad*'. You keep calling me that."

Heat overtook Alun's cheeks. "I... I hadn't realized. It's Welsh. It means 'beloved'," he admitted sheepishly.

James smiled. "Will you stay with, me, Alun? In this room? This bed?"

"Yes."

James sagged against him. "Thank you." He pressed a warm kiss up to Alun's lips. "I suppose I owe you some explanation, as well. I promised you that if you told me your secrets, I would tell you mine."

"It don't matter to me who you really are, James."

"It matters to me; I want you to know. I've seen too many people torn apart by secrets, Alun. I will *never* lie to you. I'll never hold anything from you, either. My name is James Mowbray. Heron was my mother's name. My father is—was—the Earl of Northumberland. I suppose that makes me the Earl of Northumberland since Tom's dead, but it's a minor title, I assure you. The estate was in shambles before my parents married. All of the money I have comes from my mother's family—mostly from her father and grandfather. My father had the title, but hardly had a penny to his name when he and mother met—but that isn't why they married. They truly loved each other. That's all I've ever wanted for myself, someone to love me the way they loved each other. They were as different as night and day, Alun, but that never stopped them.

"Uncle John is my father's younger brother. When my parents died, he took custody of Tom and me. He knows I'm a homosexual—he discovered it quite by accident. I may be bold, but I wasn't foolish enough to tell him. He knows I will never marry, Alun. He knows I will never produce an heir, that I've arranged for my nephew to inherit the estate after I'm gone. It's his home, not mine—and that infuriates my uncle. He always thought that *he* should be the next Earl of Northumberland. I think he was hoping Anna would either miscarry or at the very least give birth to a daughter."

"He sounds like a spiteful man."

"He is. But don't for a moment think he's a pauper. He's made his own fortune. He'll not interfere in my life, Alun. We endeavor to leave each other alone."

"Then maybe we should talk about something else," he suggested softly.

James leaned up and pressed another soft kiss to his lips. "I can think of a few things…."

Chapter 18

AFTER they both cleaned up—Alun was in even more need of hot soapy water than was James—they ate. Then Alun laid his mate down on the bed and very slowly reacquainted himself with every part of James's body. When he finally got to his opening, he took his time stretching James, using his tongue and his fingers until James was shaking, begging to be taken. Alun kissed him long and hard before obliging him; nothing had ever felt so right or so good as when he emptied his seed into his mate's body.

They washed up again, sponging each other off with water that had long gone cold. Neither cared. They curled up together under the covers.

James slept. Alun couldn't. Now more than ever, he needed to settle matters with Percival, with the silver-eyed werewolf. The *other* silver-eyed werewolf. Percival had silver eyes, too... he shook himself. Lots of wolves had silver eyes. But it did seem odd that Rhianna hadn't noticed the rogue wolf in the courthouse. Even if Percival had been oblivious—Full Moons sometimes were—*she* should have smelled the interloper. Of course, just because Percival hadn't attacked the other wolf on the spot didn't mean anything. Percival might be a king in lycan territory, but in a London courthouse, he was nothing, no one.

Just like me.

Alun pulled James closer, burying his nose into his mate's soft hair. James smelled of fire, of green grass. Of *him*, his seed, his sweat. And that was exactly as it should be. James's scent, his nearness, calmed Alun's nerves.

Downstairs, the clock in the parlor chimed six times.

"James, it's six o'clock." Alun shook him gently. He didn't want to wake him, he didn't want James going in to work, not tonight, but they both knew he had no choice. Alun only prayed that he'd be safe out there. "*Cariad*—"

"Fifteen more minutes," came the younger man's sleepy reply.

Alun chuckled. "Fifteen minutes. I'll bring you up some tea."

"Love you."

The words—the ease with which James said them—made Alun's heart surge. Just the same, he teased him, "You only love me 'cause I promised you tea in bed."

James rolled over and gave him a sleepy, mischievous, smile. "I love you for other things, too, sweetheart. I might even prove it to you after I've had my tea."

Alun chuckled some more. "Go back to sleep. I'll bring the tea. Then we can talk about you showing me your 'preciation."

Smiling, James closed his eyes and rolled back over without another word.

Alun smiled too. He still had a dozen worries plaguing at his mind, Percival and the pack at the top of that list, but they could wait, at least until after he and James had had their tea.

Having no desire to ever get near the clothes he'd worn for the last four days again, Alun filched a pair of trousers from James's wardrobe; Mrs. Dunberry was right, he looked ridiculous in his lover's clothes. At the moment, however, they would have to do. He had worse luck getting into one of the younger man's shirts, but was saved from certain humiliation when he found the oversized bathrobe hanging up near the back of James's wardrobe. It wasn't what he would call proper attire, but it was better than facing James's housekeeper half-naked.

This time, Mrs. Dunberry turned to look at him, before he was even halfway down the back stairs; her expression was difficult to read.

Alun forced a congenial smile. "Good morning."

"Mr. Blayney," she acknowledged his greeting in a tone that was as neutral as her expression.

"I…erm… I've offered to bring the tea up to James. Mr. Heron, I mean," he told her, feeling suddenly awkward. James insisted she was all right with their… involvement… but how much did she know about James's role in his release? What would she think of him moving in?

Her only response to his statement about the tea was a curt nod.

Alun fidgeted. "I... could we speak plainly with each other a minute?"

"Are you certain you wish my candor, Mr. Blayney?"

Shite. No, he wasn't sure at all. "Yes, Ma'am," he said, anyway.

"Very well." She nodded toward the table, inviting him to sit.

Alun waited until Mrs. Dunberry sat down before settling into the other chair; he noticed the special edition of the paper sitting on the table. His discharge from prison was front and center on the first page—he couldn't read the headline, but there was an artist's rendering of not only him, but Emily Harris too. Bile burned in Alun's gut, his throat. The artist had depicted him as a half-crazed madman. "I had nothing to do with what happened to her." He sounded defensive, and he knew it.

"For what it's worth, I believe you, Mr. Blayney."

Alun blinked.

"I won't pretend to trust your motives entirely," she warned in a stern tone of warning. "But I do believe that you're not a murderer."

"Thank you for that, Missus. I... I'm sure James'll be telling you himself when he gets up that he's... he's offered me a room here," he hedged around the truth. He wasn't sure it was his place to tell her anything, but if he was really going to live here, he was going to have to come to some sort of peace with his mate's housekeeper.

"Since you've asked for my candor, I'll do you the courtesy of giving it to you, Mr. Blayney. I loved both James and his brother as if they were my own, but James...he was such a sensitive child, it was hard for me not to feel especially protective of him, particularly as he grew older and discovered certain... uncomfortable truths about himself. I know he's taken a certain sort of liking to you, Mr. Blayney. The sort that most people wouldn't understand." Her eyes narrowed. "What I don't know is whether this... display of yours is genuine, or merely a ruse to take advantage of a good, decent man. A generous man. Someone who would give you his heart and more, without your having to ask for it."

Alun squirmed uncomfortably under her gaze; it wasn't just her bluntness, it was what she *didn't* say that gave him pause—and made him admire her all the more. If he was playing James for a fool, he'd best leave now, and find someone else to swindle or risk her wrath. He had no doubt that she would protect James with her last breath. "I... I know what it's gotta look like to you, Missus. Hell, to anyone. I don't half understand myself what a man like James could see in me. I know I don't got to tell you that I've got nothing, that I ain't exactly led my life on the straight an' narrow, neither. I ain't never broke the law, not really." Heat stained his cheeks. Sex with James was breaking the law—kissing him, holding him. Loving him. All of those things were illegal.

"There are laws that protect people, and then there are laws that make no sense," Mrs. Dunberry surprised him by saying.

He nodded. "I can't say I never hurt nobody, but I ain't a thief or a charlatan."

Mrs. Dunberry studied him for a long, thoughtful moment. Then she nodded. "You look about Tom's size. I'll get some of his things down from the attic for you. You really *do* look ridiculous in James's clothes, and I won't have you walking around half-dressed," she informed him, changing the subject so abruptly, the lycan's head spun. Then she got up from the table and started putting a tray together for him to take up to James.

"May... may I ask a personal question?" Alun inquired.

"You may ask."

But she wouldn't necessarily answer. It was fair enough. "Most people would prefer to turn a blind eye to certain 'uncomfortable truths' as you put it—"

"You'll find that I don't turn a blind eye to much of anything, Mr. Blayney," she retorted. She busied herself with the tea for long enough that Alun didn't think she was going to say anything more, but then she turned and faced him again. Her expression was difficult to read. "I had a brother like you, Mr. Blayney. Like James. Contra-sexual. Homosexual, Master Horatio once told me it was called. Horatio Heron, James's grandfather," she explained. "Call it what you will. My brother died in an asylum while the doctors were trying to 'cure' him. As near as I was ever able to tell, he wasn't ill until our parents sent him to that dreadful place."

"I... I'm very sorry...."

She waved it aside. "It was years ago, long before I even came to work for the... for Master John—James and Thomas's uncle." The slight wrinkle of her nose was the only indication she gave of her dislike for

James's uncle. "Here you go." She handed him the tray. "I'll thank you to bring it down when you're through."

"Yes, Missus. An'… thank you."

"I'm just doing my job, Mr. Blayney. Now—best get moving. Supper will be ready soon."

Alun smirked; the lady was far more than a common menial, and he knew it. So did she.

JAMES woke to the very pleasant sensation of soft kisses being feathered across his bare shoulder. He didn't typically sleep in the nude, but if this was the way Alun intended to wake him, maybe it was time to start. At that moment, however, there were other things on the constable's mind. "Is that tea I smell?" he asked.

Alun laughed; he leaned back and poured them each a cup. "Do you even remember me waking you up at six an' promising to bring some up?" he asked

"Vaguely." James pulled himself into a sitting position. He'd gotten barely four hours sleep, but he didn't care. Alun was here. He was staying. He was handing over a much-needed cup of strong black tea. James smiled his gratitude and didn't realize how intently Alun was staring at him until his cup was nearly half empty. He gave his lover a quizzical look.

"How… how're you able to so easily… accept…?" Alun began haltingly, as if he wasn't sure how to phrase his question.

"If you'd prefer I rally the villagers to get their pitchforks—I'm sorry, Alun." As soon as the words were out of his mouth, James regretted them. He'd meant it as a joke, but he could see by Alun's expression that it wasn't a joke at all. He set his cup down on the bedside table and reached for his lover's hand. "It really did happen like that, didn't it?"

Alun nodded. He twined his fingers into James's. "Whole packs— whole families—were slaughtered," he explained softly. "The only way for us to survive was for packs to split up, live apart. Wolves need other wolves, James. We need contact. *Physical* contact."

James gave his hand a squeeze and moved closer, so that their legs were touching. Some of the tension seemed to ease from Alun's body, and he continued to speak:

"When the Church started hunting us down, killing us—it weren't just us, lotsa folks suffered too, most of 'em ordinary humans. But when they started in on us, the only way to survive was to scatter to the four winds. A lycan might go his whole life not meeting another lycan, not knowing if he was all that was left.

"Not everything what happened to us was the humans' fault though," Alun went on. "Forced to live apart, we started living with humans. With regular wolves. We mated with... with both humans and wolves." He cast a questioning, frightened look in James's direction.

James only nodded, not judging. Alun was a lycanthrope, not a human. How could James judge werewolves by human mores?

"Not all mixed-blood children are born able to shift shape, James. There was a time when it weren't uncommon for lycan parents to kill those that could, just so they wouldn't have to live in fear."

James couldn't help but balk at that.

"I know it seems barbaric. Hell, it *was* barbaric. But there was those what thought it were better for their children to die as babes at the hands of people who loved 'em than it was for 'em to be hunted down, tortured... burned alive. I ain't sure I disagree. It weren't in my lifetime, but my parents, their parents, they remember what it was like to have to live with humans, to have to pretend to *be* human. To raise sheep instead of hunting. To never shift shape, never sing to the Moon. To be so afraid...." He closed his eyes, looking like a heavy weight had settled on his soul. "It's just the last fifty years we've started to live like wolves again."

James sat for a long moment, just holding on to Alun's hands. He'd always felt as if he didn't fit in with the rest of the world, but he couldn't imagine what it must be like for Alun, to be something as extraordinary as a lycanthrope, yet to be forced to live the life of an ordinary man—it must be an unbearable existence. "I suppose it's not going to be easy for you to explain me to the rest of your pack," he said softly. "I don't reckon they'll understand why you'd want a human for a mate." After everything Alun had just told him, James didn't understand it himself.

"I don't belong to a pack, James."

"But… you said wolves needed each other."

"I'm what wolves call *diangen*. Unwanted. *Unnecessary*. No pack'll ever have me."

"What? Why?"

"For the same reasons humans send good men to be locked away in Bedlam. Lycanthropes don't got no use for men who love other men, neither. I was banished from my pack, from the land I grew up on, when I was thirteen, an' I've been on my own ever since. My family won't have nothing to do with me. No lycan will. I… I ain't got no one."

"You have me," James told him fiercely. "Alun, you asked me how I was able to accept what you showed me yesterday. The answer's easy. When I looked into your eyes, I didn't see a wolf, I only saw *you*. I may not understand what you are, but I don't believe in demons or witches or any other superstitious nonsense. Lycanthropes are just as much a part of natural evolution as humans."

"It's not all superstitious nonsense, James. There are things in this world humans *don't* understand."

"Of that I have no doubt. Only a few hundred years ago we didn't understand that the Earth was round and that it revolved around the sun. There's no telling how many other marvels we have yet to discover."

"It ain't all marvels, James. An' not everything can be explained the way they figured out about the shape of the earth or what goes around what. There are things even I don't understand, even though I seen 'em with my own eyes."

James paused. He didn't want to argue, not about this. "The point is that if my choice is to accept you as you are, no matter how fantastical that seems, or to walk away, then it simply isn't a choice. I meant what I said before; I don't care what you are, it's *who* you are that I love. I started falling for you the day we met, and I have been daydreaming about having you here with me since then."

Alan blinked—and James blushed.

"I know how it sounds, Alun. But I wanted to get to know you, to touch you. To kiss you." He leaned in and pressed his lips to his lover's mouth. Alun returned his kiss eagerly. Ardently.

"I wanted to do that, too, that first day," Alun confessed. "It's why I left like I did, before you woke up. I was afraid… I didn't want to do something we'd both regret. Something I was sure I'd regret 'cause I couldn't imagine someone like you wanting the likes of me."

James smiled and started to speak, but his reply was cut off by a sharp rap on the bedroom door. "Supper's ready," Mrs. Dunberry announced from the other side.

"Thank you, we'll be down shortly," James called to her.

"I've taken the liberty of getting some of Master Thomas's clothing down from the attic and hanging it in the wardrobe," Mrs. Dunberry went on, "in Mr. Blayney's room. *Across the hall.*"

James bit back a snicker. "Thank you, Mrs. Dunberry." He listened to her retreating footsteps, then climbed into Alun's lap. "I hope you realize that as far as I'm concerned *this* is your room, sweetheart. Your bed." He leaned in closer. "I will do whatever I have to, to keep you here, too." James nuzzled Alun's neck, carefully avoiding his throat, understanding now why Alun had reacted the way he had the first time he tried to kiss his lover there.

He reached between them and undid the buttons of Alun's fly, freeing his engorged cock. "I believe I owe someone a 'thank you' for bringing up the tea," he purred, running his thumb lovingly over Alun's leaking slit.

"I believe you do," Alun agreed.

ALUN moaned at his mate's expert touch. Goddess, he'd never known anyone who seemed to enjoy touching a man's cock so much. James feathered tender kisses down the side of his neck, and Alun tilted his head, allowing the younger man full access, granting him silent permission to kiss—bite—his throat. To claim him fully. "I'm as much yours as you are mine, *cariad*," he whispered, hoping James would understand. "Mate. Lover. Don't matter what you call it."

James kissed his neck, nipped lightly at his skin; he continued to stroke his cock with one hand and lifted the other to Alun's dark nipple. Alun groaned when James took it between his thumb and forefinger to give a gentle pinch—then he pressed his palm flat against it, rubbing. Alun returned the favor; he couldn't get to his mate's cock, but both of his nipples were in easy reach. He'd never played with a man's body like this—never been played with. He growled happily.

"Why don't you get undressed?" James suggested.

Alun shed his borrowed clothing quickly and leaned back against the headboard; James straddled him. His gaze was hungry. Wanton.

It made fire run through Alun's veins. "I want you, James."

"I'm all yours."

"No. Inside me."

James gave him a startled look.

"I'm yours like you're mine, James. I want you to take me—" Alun was silenced by the fierce, possessive kiss James pressed to his mouth. When he felt James's tongue against his lips, he yielded at once. James deepened the kiss, dominated it, just like he had the first night they coupled.

James kissed his neck—his throat. Alun tilted his head further back, growling with pleasure—joy—as his mate claimed him, as James scraped his teeth against Alun's skin.

"Yours," Alun whispered. "I'm yours, James." He canted his hips, rubbing his cock against his mate's. They were both slick. James rubbed against him. "Shite, I could come just from this."

"You could," James agreed. "But you won't." It wasn't a request.

Alun shivered at the unexpected authority in James's voice. He liked it. He liked it even more when James kissed him again. His neck. His chest. His stomach. He nuzzled the nest of dark hair surrounding Alun's cock and looked up at the lycan, meeting his gaze as he encircled his cockhead with soft, pink lips. Alun groaned softly as James lowered his whole mouth over his shaft, taking in every inch of him. He bobbed his head up and down, flicking his tongue against the tender skin of Alun's shaft, sucking him harder still, making him writhe in ecstasy. Agony. "Goddess, please," he begged. "James…."

James cupped Alun's balls in one hand, caressing them. Teasing them. He pressed a finger lightly to Alun's hole. "I want to make you feel as fantastic as you make me feel," he whispered. He kissed him there, circling the tight entrance with his tongue until Alun felt himself relaxing under the warmth of his mate's gentle persistence.

Alun lost himself in the wash of new sensations, the slight burn, the intrusion of a finger... the pressure... the feeling of fullness... emptiness.... Alun arched his back, pressing himself toward James's finger, wanting to be filled again.

"Stay put," James whispered, pressing a soft kiss to Alun's skin. He got up from the bed, but only to fetch the lotion off of the bureau. When he returned, James settled himself between Alun's legs and rubbed his own cock with a generous amount of the lubricant. The sight of James touching himself made Alun's gut clench with desire. Goddess, but he was beautiful.

James pressed a lotion-slick finger to Alun's hole. He was already a little stretched, so it went in easily. James added a second digit, scissored his fingers open and shut, stretching Alun further, making him groan.

"Is that all right?" James asked.

"Yes... it's... Goddess, that feels good."

James grinned. He changed the angle of his hand, and fire shot through Alun's shaft, causing the lycan to swear. He'd always known it must feel good to be on the receiving end—why else would anybody do it?—but he never imagined.... Another wave of fire shot through him. James pressed his thumb to the soft spot between Alun's testicles and entrance and began to fuck his hole in earnest, first with two fingers, then with three. When the younger man lowered his mouth to Alun's shaft once more, it was over. Alun came hard and fast into the back of his mate's throat with a loud growl.

Seemingly satisfied with his performance, James slid his hand out of Alun's body and settled himself between his legs, his chin resting on the tuft of dark curls above his lover's shaft. Alun was still twitching with aftershocks; having James touch him like that, however innocently, wasn't helping. He realized belatedly that it probably wasn't an accident; James was nothing if not utterly wicked. But it was the best sort of wicked.

"Is that what it always feels like?" Alun asked him. "Like... lightning an'... an' sleet?"

James chuckled, sending vibrations through the lycan's cock, where his throat rested against it. "There's a reason I let you keep doing it."

"Shite," was all Alun could seem to say.

"I hope you realize I'm not half done with you," James told him with another mischievous grin.

"I'm not sure I can take more."

James only smirked. He feathered soft kisses over Alun's stomach and then his chest, his neck, his throat... his lips. "You said you were mine, remember?" he whispered huskily into his ear.

The lycan swallowed hard. He had indeed.

"Well then, I'm not half done with you."

JAMES curled up next to Alun, his head resting on the lycanthrope's strong chest. Alun had come a second time, with James inside him, leaving the younger man feeling more than a little pleased with himself for being able to coax a second climax from his lover so soon after the first one.

Alun feathered a soft kiss to his forehead. Downstairs, the clock chimed seven.

James groaned. "What I wouldn't give to spend the whole night in bed with you."

"So why don't you?"

"I have a job to go to, remember?"

"You could quit—"

"I'm not ready to give up being a constable, Alun."

"Why? You don't need the money. Police work ain't exactly a occupation for a rich man. A Lord."

James scoffed. "It's a minor title, sweetheart. I'm not rich, just comfortable."

"You're educated, James—you don't got to tell me, I can look at you and know it. There must be other things you could do, a proper job, like. A profession."

James shook his head. "I dropped out of university. I am educated but... but being a constable means not having to rely on my family name."

"Why do you hate your name so much?"

"I don't hate it. I'd just rather make my own way in the world." He shifted. "It's getting late. I have to get up."

Reluctantly, Alun nodded, opening his arms so James could sit up. "*Cariad*, there's something I need you to know before you go out there tonight. I ain't the only werewolf in London. There's others. A whole pack."

"You said you didn't belong to a pack."

"I don't. But that don't mean there ain't others like me around. They know… they know all about me, James, about why I'm *diangen*. Nothing happens in London that the pack leader *don't* know. And the minute you get upwind of *any* of 'em, they'll smell me on you. They'll know we've been together."

"If you don't belong to their pack, what difference does it make with whom you've had congress? Besides, you said they know you're a homosexual. It should hardly come as a surprise that your scent would be on a man."

"It ain't that simple, James. Lycans ain't like humans. They'll decide to make it their business."

James snorted; lycanthropes sounded *exactly* like humans. "I'm not going to hide in my house like a coward. That's no way to live."

"It ain't just the pack I'm worried about. The man who's been killing those girls… he weren't no man, James, he was a lycan. I smelled him on the body of that first woman. And… I saw him in the courthouse during my trial."

"We have to go to the authorities." If they arrested the real killer, Alun would finally be free from suspicion.

"And say what? Tell 'em the killer is a werewolf, tell 'em I know 'cause I'm one too? What would I testify to? Smelling him on the body of that first woman? They'd lock me up in Bedlam!"

"All right. But we still have to do *something*."

"No. *I* have to do something."

Alun's tone made James shiver. "What does that mean?"

"It means this is lycan business, James. It ain't something for Scotland Yard. James, even if there was some way to let that inspector know who the killer is, even if he'd believe me, and even without me telling him the killer isn't human… James, think about what would happen once the killer got arrested. Do you think he'd go quiet like I did?"

James swallowed hard. "No. I don't suppose he would." People would die, and then the world would know werewolves existed. It would be the bloody Inquisition all over again. "Why is a lycanthrope killing prostitutes?"

"I don't know. But the pack leader's made it my job to figure it out, an' even though I ain't part of his pack, I still gotta answer to him. That day you found me in that doss house—that'll happen again, if I don't do like he says."

"Surely if you're *here*…."

"It won't matter. Neither of us is safe until I figure some way to settle this once and for all."

"You're going back to Whitechapel, aren't you?" It wasn't a question; James knew the answer already.

"I have to. You said it yourself, James. Hiding here ain't no way to live. It won't help, no how. I wasn't kidding when I said Percival knows everything what happens in this city."

"What are you going to do?"

"I have to go back to where Emily died."

"What? Why? You heard Dr. Stodderley, it wasn't the same killer."

"I know. That's what scares me, because when she died… everything happened so fast that night, James, and when it was all over… all I could think about was how much it hurt to lose you. I never felt so empty."

James brushed his hand against Alun's cheek. "It's over."

Alun nodded. "And now I know that something ain't right about the night Emily died. I need to go back there and suss out what really happened. I need to know why she died the way she did."

"Let me go with you."

"No. *Cariad*, we can't let people see us together."

Chapter 19

ALUN thought back to the night Emily died, reliving as much of the detail as he was able to remember—much more than he was able to stomach. So much about finding her like that had felt wrong, but he'd barely had time to think about it. In hindsight, he was sure he didn't recall smelling *anyone* besides Emily in that courtyard, not until James arrived. But that didn't make any sense. When the beast rode close to the surface, lycanthropic sense became sharper, not duller.

Alun crept into the kitchen, silent. Unseen. Night had fallen fully and the house was dark, but he didn't need a candle to see where he was going. He felt like a thief, even though all he intended to take was a handful of table salt and a few cooking herbs. Finding the larder unlocked only made him feel worse—but it didn't stop him. He only hoped Mrs. Dunberry wouldn't miss what he'd nicked.

His pilfering complete, Alun went out into the back garden. He hadn't allowed himself much of an opportunity to look around the yard before—he'd either been making a hasty escape or coming out to use the water closet. Like most older homes, James's house had had a lavatory added long after it was initially constructed. Though the little room was attached to the house on one wall, there wasn't a connecting door; the only way to get to it was by going outside. Still, it was preferable to urinating on the streets—but the poor did what they had to. Giving himself the time to look the yard over properly, Alun couldn't help but be impressed. Neatly raised beds of dark soil were separated by a winding, narrow gravel path; the yard was small, but every bit of usable ground was being fully utilized. Though it was late in the season for most of the plants, many still had green, tattered leaves clinging desperately to their stems; a few even had drooping flowers that refused to give up their hold.

Alun closed his eyes and felt the softly humming life force flowing through the garden. He felt the love with which it was tended—*James*. He knew at once it was James who loved the garden, not his housekeeper or some hired caretaker. Alun could see the younger man in his mind's eye, losing himself in the dirt, sunlight glinting off his blond hair.... Alun's smile deepened. James loved the earth as much as he did. He supposed it shouldn't surprise him; James smelled of the richness of the soil, of sweet grass. His scent was as green and mossy as his sea-foam eyes.

A new image drifted into Alun's mind then, though he wasn't looking for anything more. He let the vision take him anyway. It was like a ripple, a memory, though not his own. A young woman sat hunched over one of the beds—but it wasn't a bed yet, she was just laying the shape of things. She was literally elbow deep in dirt. Wheat-colored hair hung in long braids, and her head was crowned with a floppy straw hat. Under its brim, Alun could just make out a pair of moss-green eyes....

"Mr. Blayney?" Mrs. Dunberry called sharply from the back stoop, shattering the vision. "What in heaven's name are you doing out here in the dark?"

Heat bloomed in Alun's cheeks at her tone; for the second time that night, he felt as if he'd been caught at something he shouldn't be doing. Maybe he was. He hadn't asked James's permission to explore his garden, but surely if he had, James would have told him it was all right. Wouldn't he? James spoke to him as if they were equals, but Alun knew the human world well enough to know that wasn't the case. James would always be his better.

"Mr. Blayney?" Mrs. Dunberry inquired, her tone sharper, still.

Alun shifted his weight from one foot to the other. He was wearing James's dead brother's clothes, his shoes. James had said, before leaving for the night, that he looked so much like a gentleman, no one would think twice about it if they saw him on the street. Alun wasn't convinced; he felt like a counterfeit. He didn't belong there. He didn't belong anywhere.

And Mrs. Dunberry was still waiting for an answer. He cleared his throat. "My *taid*—my grandfather," he clarified for the Englishwoman, "he used to... that is... we always had a garden an'... an' it's been years since I... since I come to London. Since I really been in anybody's garden. I don't mean no harm, I'm just looking around."

Mrs. Dunberry made a dismissive noise. "Just see you don't disturb anything. Master James is rather particular about the garden. His mother planted it. He won't let me change a thing, though goodness knows why. Most it's grown over with weeds."

He gave over a noncommittal sort of nod; he wasn't about to tell her the plants he'd found were anything *but* weeds. It made Alun wonder what kind of woman James's mother had been. Her garden had all of the usual things: mint, yarrow, lamb's ear, chamomile, and lavender—the things his own mother had grown. There were medicinal herbs as well, the sorts of things his grandfather had taught him to cultivate when he was still a boy, not that he'd had much use for such knowledge the last two decades. Alun was surprised—and pleased—that he could still recognize half of them: St. John's wort with its yellow flowers—celedine too. Prunella, calendula, Good King Henry, a patch of wild comfrey and elecampane against one wall. Lady's mantle and white-spotted lungwort were tucked up against the house where they wouldn't get much sunlight.

Also like his grandfather, the late Mrs. Heron—or maybe it was Mowbray, Alun supposed—had grown vervain, monkshood, belladonna, henbane, wormwood, and the overgrown mugwort bush that Mrs. Dunberry was currently wrinkling her nose at. Mugwort wouldn't do a person any real harm if they mistook it for something else and made it into a tea or a tincture, but monkshood, henbane, and belladonna were powerful hallucinogens, poisonous if used too liberally. Not all of those plants were perennials, but he remembered his grandfather telling him how plants reseeded themselves if left to their own devices—that certainly explained why James had henbane, though he was grateful for it at the moment. There were few places he could safely go where he could find it growing wild, and henbane was exactly what he needed for what he wanted to try tonight.

"Do you know... I mean, James hasn't said, but I didn't ask neither, an' I was wondering how his parents died," said Alun. He doubted the question sounded as casual as he'd hoped.

Mrs. Dunberry stiffened. "You'd have to ask James. Or better yet, don't. It's a sensitive subject, even all these years later, and hardly any of your concern, Mr. Blayney."

Alun nodded; maybe she was right. Even though James was his mate, that didn't give him the right to pry into his past. "Yes, Missus. I don't mean to put my nose where it don't belong. I... I appreciate knowing it's a tender subject for him."

"I'm sure you didn't mean any harm, any more than I meant to seem so ill-tempered. The last few days have been trying on this household— although I suppose you've suffered considerably worse."

"All that matters is that it's over."

"Let us hope so. I'm going to bed, unless you require anything more this evening…?"

"No, Ma'am. Thank you."

She turned back toward the house; then she turned around again. "Don't stay out in the cold too long. After all you've been through, I shouldn't think it's doing you any good. If you do need something and can't find it for yourself, my room is the last on the right. Please don't hesitate to knock on my door."

"Thank you. I don't think I'll be needing anything, though. Good night, Missus."

She nodded again and took her leave.

Alun gathered up a handful of henbane leaves, some mugwort, and few other herbs, tucking them into a spare handkerchief, and then quickly heaved himself over the back wall. Even on two legs, it wasn't difficult to clear the tall fence.

Knowing that there was hardly a soul in London who didn't believe him to be a murderer, Alun decided against taking the tram. He paused a moment in the shadows of the alley behind James's house and took the handkerchief of herbs out of his pocket. He took one of the henbane leaves and held it close to his chest, to the place where in the spirit world he was marked as a child of the New Moon. Alun whispered to the spirit of the henbane plant, knowing that henbane could, if the plant-spirit was inclined, make Spirit Dance magic more powerful. The henbane could guarantee that no one would see him as he made his way through the streets. Of course, spirits usually demanded something in return for their boons but Alun would deal with that when the time came. For now, he simply thanked the plant for the darkness he felt falling over him. No one would see him, or if they did, they would pay him no mind. That would be especially important once he reached Whitechapel.

JAMES walked slowly through the gray damp fog. It seemed thicker than usual; if he believed in fairy stories or wives' tales, he might be inclined to think it was more than just a heavy mist rolling in from the Thames. But even after learning that werewolves were real, James didn't believe in magic or boogeymen. Lycanthropes, in order to exist, *must* be a part of Charles Darwin's theory of evolution and natural selection. He wished he could puzzle out how something so extraordinary had come to exist— surely ancient man and wolves had never mated, their species were simply incompatible. So perhaps lycanthropes weren't wolves at all? Alun wasn't like any wolf James had ever seen before.

Werewolves, however, were the least of his worries. Rather, it was ordinary men who occupied James's thoughts, and not just killers and madmen. When he'd reported for duty at the start of his shift, half the men on his relief glowered at him, refusing to speak to him, even to acknowledge his tentative greeting. Some went so far as to say to each other—intentionally within James's earshot, he was sure—that *some blokes* weren't fit to wear a constable's uniform. Stanwix's voice was the loudest. The other half of the men on his shift—or maybe James was being optimistic, maybe it was only a handful—had expressed their sympathies to him for the way he'd been blindsided by "that killer's barrister." A few of the other constables wanted to string up Dr. Stodderley as well, for his role in Alun's release.

No one believed the court had appointed an attorney of Sir Walter Gill's caliber to assist Alun in his defense. They knew he must have had help from someone with money, and they were all out for that person's blood too. James knew it was only a matter of time before someone remembered seeing him and Alun together, either from when the first woman's body was found or after, when they'd spoken on the street and then had breakfast together. He hadn't been discreet; he hadn't thought he needed to be. He also knew it was a matter of time before Sergeant Buchanan told the rest of the men about James's house, that he was a man of means. What James *didn't* know was what was going to happen when someone—probably Inspector Lamont—put it all together and figured out that he had hired Walt to defend Alun.

The people of Whitechapel, ordinary folks James passed while walking his beat, were even angrier about Alun's release from prison than his colleagues in Scotland Yard—they were even more eager for revenge.

And they knew, too, that only someone with money could have hired Sir Walter Gill, and money was something Alun didn't have.

James decided that perhaps tomorrow he would write to his sister-in-law and tell her that he and a friend were coming to stay at the estate for a while. It would cost him his job, but that was a small sacrifice to keep Alun safe, and surely the werewolves of London wouldn't be able to track them all the way to Northumberland. Let *them* find the rogue werewolf and leave Alun out of it. Why should he be their lackey? It was bad enough the real killer would go unpunished, that he would never have to answer for his crimes in a human court of law.

James's thoughts returned to the murders themselves, and he wondered again why a lycanthrope would bother using a knife to kill someone. Nature and evolution had provided them with all the weapons they needed, sharp claws and teeth as long as one of James's fingers. Even when Alun wasn't a wolf, he was strong and agile—James didn't really doubt that he could have killed Stanwix and Mills single-handedly. It made no sense that a similar creature should be stalking Whitechapel's streets, butchering prostitutes in the shadows. He didn't doubt Alun's word, but he could make no sense of it. "Why would an otherwise rational thinking person, man *or* wolf, remove a woman's uterus?" Had he eaten it? Jack the Ripper had cut out Catherine Eddowes's kidney and uterus and eaten part of the former—though the thought of any human being eating part of another human sickened James to the core. "Which really only proves that the Ripper wasn't a rational, thinking man," he concluded.

James rubbed growing knots at the back of his neck.

"I could give ya a hand with that, if ya likes, Constable."

James swore aloud; Robin was walking right beside him, yet James hadn't heard his approach.

The slight redhead giggled—actually *giggled*! "You'll be giving yourself a heart attack b'fore you're thirty, you keep that up, James."

He sighed.

"Come here." Rob tugged at his sleeve, guiding him over toward a darkened stoop. "Sit," he ordered.

Helpless, James did as he was told; regardless of Mills's assessment of him, his feet were always tired, always ached. He just didn't see the point in complaining about it—but at that moment sitting felt good. So did having Robin's strong, skilled hands working out some of the kinks in his neck and shoulders. Rob seemed to know right where every knot was and how to get it to loosen up.

"Tell me if I press too hard," Rob told him.

"No. No, that's perfect," he assured the younger man, though Rob's hands were far stronger than he ever would have expected. "What are you doing out at this hour?"

"Couldn't sleep."

James didn't believe it was that simple, but he didn't want to call Robin a liar, either.

"You know," the young Irishman said thoughtfully—he reached around and slid James's helmet off his head, depositing it into his lap. "Talking to yourself ain't a good sign, James."

He froze. "How long… that is… how much…?" How much had he said aloud, and how much of that had Robin heard?

Robin placed his elbow on James's shoulder and dug down hard. "Lemme know if this hurts… an' to answer your question," he went on, without seeming to miss a beat, "I heard enough to know you're thinking 'bout those murders, not that I blames ya any, what with people're saying. I knows it was you who bought that barrister," he added.

"How…?" James had never told Rob he had money.

"James, I sees how ya dress when you're not on duty. You think I don't know a toff when I sees one?"

"I am *not* a toff."

Rob snickered at the indignation in his tone. "I don't mean no insult. You'll always be plain ol' James Heron t' me, so don't you get on no high horse," he teased.

James laughed—then groaned when the Irishman pressed down harder on the knot in his shoulder.

"Too much?"

"No. Shite."

Robin repeated the treatment on the other shoulder before rubbing his neck gently to ease out the last of the tension. He moved to sit on the stoop next to James. "Better?"

"Considerably, thank you."

"I could do more for ya, if ya let me," he purred lasciviously.

"Rob—"

"I know." His tone told James that he *did* know, with absolute certainty, that James's heart belonged to someone else—and it hurt Robin to the core. But Rob smiled anyway. "Still friends though, yeah?"

"Of course. *Always*, Rob. In fact, I want to take you somewhere." He couldn't keep the smile from tugging at the corners of his mouth.

Ginger brows shot up. "Oh?"

"Every year the Theatre Royal sends me an invitation to their Christmas production, but I never go. My grandfather was a patron," James explained. "This year I'd like to attend, and I'd like to take you with me." He'd gotten the idea some while ago, when Rob first told him about his passion for the stage, but everything had been so... difficult lately. "It would mean a lot to me, Robin," he said, when he saw a furrow across the younger man's brow. He'd expected Robin to be excited, happy. "I thought I could... you know, help you make some new acquaintances, business contacts, in the theater. I don't know everybody important, but there are a few directors and a couple of writers my grandfather has connections to. I'm sure I could use that to help you."

"I'm not sure that's a good idea, James. Your ma—your Mr. Blayney... I don't think he'd take too kindly to you an' me going anywhere together." His gaze dropped away from James's face. "It ain't no secret what I am."

"You said you were getting off the street! Rob—that's not what you're doing out here, is it?" James demanded angrily. He couldn't stand the thought of Robin whoring himself out for a few pennies a fuck. "Robin, you are worth so much more than that!"

Rob shrugged, keeping his lids down, hiding luminous green eyes, clearly not wanting to look at James—or not wanting James to look at him.

"Robin! *Answer* me. Is that what you're doing out here at this hour?"

"It weren't what I really meant, James," he told him, his tone still soft.

"If you need money...."

"No."

"Then what?" What was he so ashamed of?

"Forget it, James."

"Robin, *please*. Let me help you."

A thin smile cracked through the veneer of pain, and Robin turned to face him again. "Ya already have, James, more than ya know. Not many men've ever wanted to be my friend, even not knowing... not knowing the half of my life's story," he finished weakly.

"I'd like to know it, Rob. I'd like to know you better."

"No, you wouldn't, but thanks for saying so. I know you think you mean it, but trust me when I tells ya that there's things *no one* wants to be knowing. Now come on." He forced his smile wider. "Ya were talking to yourself b'fore, but maybe talking to another person'll help ya more with whatever it is you're trying to puzzle out."

"I...." James hesitated. He didn't want to share the grizzly details of those girls' murders with Robin.

"I know it's 'bout these killings. Don't worry, I got a stronger stomach than ya thinks. Let me help, James. Let me *really* be your friend, not jus' somebody ya *say* is your friend."

Reluctantly, James nodded. "But only if you'll let me be your friend, too, Rob. I won't pry into your past, but you have to promise me that if you ever need anything, you'll tell me."

"O'course."

"I mean it, Robin. Swear."

"I...." He hesitated, but then gave in. "All right."

"Say it."

"I swear, James. If there's ever anything ya can help me with, I'll tell ya. I'll let ya help."

Satisfied, James got to his feet; Rob fell easily into step with him and waited patiently for James to speak. It took several blocks for the constable to collect his thoughts enough to recount aloud the things he'd been mulling over in his head—he was careful to leave out the parts about werewolves, of course. To his surprise, Robin didn't flinch, even when he detailed how each of the women died. He supposed the young Irishman might already know, he probably had read the papers—he might even have been in the courtroom, though James hadn't seen him. Still, James wouldn't have expected someone like Rob, someone who had always seemed so soft and sensitive, to be able to hear such gory details without a single grimace. Robin's expression simply remained thoughtful, attentive. It made James wonder what kind of a life Rob had endured.

"I can think of one reason somebody might take out a woman's uterus, James. I mean assuming he's not just a lunatic," the younger man said when he was done talking.

James hardly registered that Rob hadn't needed to be told what a uterus was. In fact, Rob hadn't asked for clarification on any of the medical terms James found himself using, mostly because when he put it into clinical terms, it was easier for *him* to stomach the gory details.

Rob went on: "What if she was pregnant an' someone didna want anybody to find out? You know, if it were somebody's bastard? If she weren't real far along, nobody would know, would they?"

"Emily Harris was over fifty years old. I *doubt* she was pregnant."

"An' her parts weren't cut out, neither," Robin countered smoothly. "Only that first woman's was. An' ain't *she* the one nobody's been able to give a name to?"

"You can't possibly be suggesting that someone killed Emily Harris and Claire Walker *just* to cause public hysteria?" It was unthinkable! But if it was true, it had worked. With each subsequent murder, fewer people were concerned over the identity of the first woman.

Robin looked up at him with sad, ageless eyes. "I seen all kinds of awful things in me life, James. This would'na be the worst of it. I wish it were."

James didn't have the chance to respond. He hadn't heard the footsteps following him and Rob through the gray-blanketed streets. He only heard Robin's scream. A fraction of a second later, pain lanced through his skull and blackness cloaked his vision.

Chapter 20

COLD dread coiled in Alun's gut as he approached the place where Emily Harris had died. *Was butchered*, he corrected himself. Nobody deserved to die like that.

He'd retraced his steps as closely as he was able, starting at the place he first scented her blood, and ending up here, in a small, secluded courtyard that was tucked in between a couple of crumbling tenement buildings. In the light of day, it might be a pleasant enough place, but at night it was all inky shadows and hidden recesses. The air felt heavy; cold damp seeped into Alun's bones. He tried to tell himself it was just because it was late autumn, and he wasn't wearing an overcoat, but in his gut, he knew the cold gnawing at his skin had nothing to do with the temperature. He'd slept out on the cobblestones on nights worse than this and hardly felt it.

"You clean up rather well, Mr. Blayney. I must say, I'm impressed—and I don't impress easily," said a voice in the darkness.

Alun's hackles rose and he bit back a snarl. He knew the speaker's identity at once, what he didn't know was how an ordinary human had managed to sneak up on him. Not only hadn't heard Inspector Lamont's approaching footsteps, but he hadn't picked up the man's scent—stale tobacco and expensive bourbon. And how had Lamont even seen him? Alun hadn't released his cloak of shadows. There had to be some sort of enchantment at work over the courtyard, something that handicapped Alun's ability to hide—something that hampered his senses. Now, all he had to do was figure out what sort of magic it was, and why he'd still been able to smell Emily's blood from so far away. He only hoped that knowing would lead him to the killer, because whoever it was, it wasn't some mucksnape, some common human thug.

But first, Alun had a very different kind of problem to deal with. Lamont circled around to face him, looking very much like a predator sizing up its prey. *Only you got no idea that you're on the wrong side of that, Gov*, Alun mused darkly.

"You've come into quite a string of good luck, haven't you, then?" said Lamont. It was more of a challenge than a question.

Alun found himself standing to his full height, his head held high, as he met the inspector's gaze dead on. "I don't see how it's any of *your* business what kind of luck I've run into," he snapped. He wasn't breaking any laws, human or otherwise, and he *didn't* owe anybody an explanation for his clothing, least of all the man who regularly made his mate's life difficult.

Lamont took a step back, looking startled by the sudden change in Alun's demeanor. The last time they'd seen each other, Alun had been a beaten, defeated man. But that was before he learned that James still believed in him. Loved him. Wanted him. That changed everything.

"I should advise you to step lightly, Mr. Blayney," said the inspector. "I'll be watching you—me an' the rest of my boys. We'll be keeping our eyes on your friend Heron too."

A low growl rumbled in Alun's throat—he leashed his temper, quickly. Standing up to Lamont was one thing, but nothing would be gained by allowing himself to be provoked into a fight, especially if Lamont suspected there was a connection between him and James. "Don't rightly know who you're talking about, Inspector," he lied easily. He was good at lying. "But you just go an' watch whoever you want. I expect that's what they pay you for." He leaned back and crossed his arms over his chest.

Lamont remained, stubbornly rooted to the spot, for a several long minutes, fidgeting with visible discomfort under the lycan's steady gaze. Alun offered up a friendly seeming smile, and finally, Lamont turned and took his leave. Alun suspected he wasn't going far, but he couldn't be sure. Once Lamont got beyond the courtyard's high wall, Alun no longer heard the man's boot heels scraping on the cobblestones. He lifted his head and sniffed the air. He smelled the lingering scent of tobacco and bourbon, human sweat—fear—but nothing else, not even the ubiquitous stench of the Thames. *Except the night poor Emily died, I could smell her blood ten blocks away.* It was almost as if someone *wanted* him to find her. Anger twisted in Alun's gut. Emily had been bait—but why? Why lure him there, just to watch her die?

Unless someone wanted him to be accused of her murder, wanted to see him hang. Fresh bile rose in Alun's throat. Who could hate him that much? Surely it wasn't the real killer. Alun had no enemies, at least none capable of magic. The only people who disliked him were the men he played cards against, and he was very careful never to play against mages or vampires.

Alun shook himself. Useless speculation wouldn't help Emily—it wouldn't help him, either. Neither would the tears that seemed to have come out of nowhere. He wiped them angrily away from his face. "I'll find the ruddy bastard what done this to you, Emily, I swear I will. I'll bring him to justice. One kind of justice or another," he growled into the night air, heedless of how dangerous it was to make promises to the dead. This was one promise he intended to keep.

Alun fished the handkerchiefs out of his pocket, hoping he could remember everything his grandfather had taught him about Spirit Dancer magic. He'd never tried anything like this before—he could do little things, cloak himself in shadows, but he wasn't initiated, he had no spirit allies to protect him if something went wrong. But he'd sat by his grandfather's side hundreds of times while he worked and was pretty sure he remembered what to do… and really, it was a simple enchantment. He hoped.

Having already had some success with the spirit of the henbane plant in James's garden, he called out to it again, hoping it would help him. He couldn't tell whether it answered him or not, so he pressed on, starting by sprinkling a rough circle of salt on the ground where he planned to sit.

I'm sorry, taid. *I know how disappointed you were that I went all wrong, that I turned out like I did. I don't know what drives me to love men… a man. A human, no less. But I do love him. He ain't like other humans. Other toffs. You might even like him. He's a good and decent man. He's my mate….* He wiped the moisture from his cheeks. He would never forget the look on his *taid*'s face the day his father assembled the pack, told them of Alun's disgrace. Exiled him. He knew he was fooling himself to think his grandfather would give James half a chance. James was human. Male.

Alun closed his eyes, pushing the thought from his mind. He sat down in the center of his circle of salt. If this worked, he would see for himself what had happened here the night Emily Harris was murdered; he would see her killers' faces, and he would make good on his promise to bring the bastards to one sort of justice or another.

WHEN James's vision cleared, he was lying prone on the cobblestones, his whole body aching. His left arm was wet... blood. His blood.

"James!" Rob's voice drew his attention toward the younger man—a pair of behemoths were bearing down on him.

James hollered at them—it wasn't a coherent sound, just a guttural noise, but it was enough to get one of the brutes to look his way, enough to get them both to stop advancing on Robin.

"Run, James!" Rob screamed at him. "Get outa here!"

Dazed, James was sure he couldn't be understanding Robin correctly. He struggled to his feet and found his whistle.

"James, *please*! Go!" Rob yelled louder.

James blew his whistle and drew his truncheon. He knew it didn't significantly increase his chances, but he wasn't going to abandon Robin. He wasn't going to go down without a fight, either. He crouched low; the men were big, but probably not fast. If he could get in a couple of good hits... knee caps, ankles... testicles. He wasn't above fighting dirty. He licked his lips and swallowed back a mouthful of bile. Why hadn't anybody heard the commotion and come running? Surely, help must be on the way.

As one of the ruffians closed in on him, the other inched toward Robin. James swung his baton as hard as he could, hoping to incapacitate his assailant and get to Robin. His truncheon connected solidly with the big man's belly. The giant merely smirked down at him. "That all you got?"

The other behemoth shrieked and danced wildly back from Robin. Gooseflesh rose on James's arms. Before he could fully react, his attacker lunged forward, tackling him, sending him violently to the ground once more.

Robin screamed.

James struggled, but was easily overpowered.

And then it was over. When James looked up, he saw Robin lying in a pool of red. There was a huge gash carved in his stomach. Blood dripped from a long, curved knife in the giant's hand. Rob wasn't breathing. James sobbed out the younger man's name, but vice-like hands held him tight.

"You should thank us, copper," his attacker snarled. "We mighta just saved yer life."

The last thing James saw before he was dragged off to a waiting carriage were Robin's dull, lifeless eyes staring up at him from the cold cobblestones.

THE cold, heavy feeling began to lift from the courtyard as soon as Alun lit the rue and vervain leaves he'd brought from James's garden. He'd forgotten to bring something to burn them in, so he had to settle for an almost-dry patch of ground. It was less than ideal, but the dried, withered leaves caught quickly enough, filling the night air with pungent gray smoke. Rue, in particular, didn't have a very pleasant scent when it was burned. It didn't have an especially pleasant scent when it was just sitting around, either. It was little wonder most spirits disliked it.

Alun closed his eyes and focused on the soft, steady beating of his heart. As soon as he was sure the enchantment was lifted, he would work some magic of his own, shroud the courtyard in *his* shadows. Mostly, he wanted to keep out Inspector Lamont and any other humans who happened to be nearby, but hopefully he could weave a spell strong enough to keep Rhianna from sensing what he was attempting as well. He didn't need her telling Percival that he knew even a little Spirit Dancer magic.

Shite. Who was he kidding? She was fully trained, there was no way he could weave a spell strong enough to keep her out. But he had to try. He didn't need Percival knowing what he was doing, especially not if it actually worked.

Something flickered at the edge of Alun's mind, pressing heavily against the magical barrier he'd laid around him with his circle of salt.

When he opened his eyes, he knew at once that several things were very wrong. For starters, he was on the spirit side of the veil, even though he hadn't consciously crossed over. Secondly—and perhaps far more disconcertingly—the courtyard was alive with crackling black fire and the stench of burning sulfur. There was only one thing that could mean: a daemonic presence. But what could the Infernal have to do with Emily's murder? She might not have been a saint, but she hadn't been daemon-possessed. Alun was sure he would have smelled it if she was. Even when they possessed a human body, daemons never lost the pong of brimstone.

Summoning up his last shred of courage, Alun rose to his feet. He was painfully well aware that he wasn't *really* standing up, only his spirit was. Back in the physical world, his body was sitting on the hard ground with nothing but a circle of table salt to protect it, and there was little a daemon coveted more than mortal flesh. The salt might hold out the daemon—*if* he was lucky—but daemons often had human followers, and an ordinary man, even one who was daemon-beguiled, wouldn't be stopped by salt. If a mortal broke the circle, the daemon could claim Alun's unoccupied body as its own, stranding Alun forever in the spirit world. "Show yourself!" he demanded of the Infernal.

"I mean you no harm, Blayney," said the familiar lilting voice... well, mostly familiar. The cadence was the same, but the voice itself was deeper and richer now that it was coming out of the daemon's own throat, rather than that of young Irish body it usually occupied.

Alun had never seen Robin Perris in his—*its*—true form before. It was almost too beautiful to look at, as if one of the great master sculptors had carved its tall, lithe body from perfect, unblemished alabaster. Broad black wings were spread wide, as were Rob's arms, his palms turned toward Alun in empty-handed supplication. Each of his red-tipped fingers ended in a long, sharp talon. Hands like that could rip a man's soul to shreds in seconds. The only thing Alun recognized were the daemon's eyes, glittering like emeralds out of his sweet face. Alun turned away.

"Please, I ain't never done you no harm. You got no reason to fear me!" he pleaded.

Alun only grunted in response. He knew better than to give a daemon—or an angel—a straight answer. Celestials and Infernals were equally cunning and would twist and pervert mortal words to suit their own needs. It didn't escape his notice, however, that the daemon no longer seemed to be trying to break his protective barrier. "What do you want?" he asked it.

"To tell ya that two very big lycans took your... that they took James."

Alun's hackles rose. Percival's two thugs, it had to be! But... but daemons lied with the same ease with which he drew breath. Only what did this particular daemon have to gain from this particular lie? *Could be he's sending me to get myself killed*, he reckoned. If he went tearing onto pack lands on some fool's errand, he'd be ripped to shreds—Rob had to know that. "Where is he?" Alun asked the daemon, cautiously.

"I don't know. I swear I don't! He was alive when I left him, but I don't know how long that'll last. I... I'm sorry. I should've heard 'em... smelled 'em. But I didn't. I didn't hear *nothing* until it was too late an' then James...." He choked back a tearless sob. Daemons couldn't shed tears, or so Alun had once been told. "There was nothing I could do! I don't know what they wanted, but I know it weren't nothing good. *Please.* I know you've no reason to trust me, but please, I've never done you no harm! I know what James is to you—what you are to him. He's my friend, Blayney. I'm begging you, please get to him before it's too late!"

Alun studied the Infernal closely. He wanted to believe it wasn't lying, even if he didn't want to believe what it was telling him. He wanted to believe James's friendship actually meant something to the daemon— but daemons were lying, manipulative, self-centered... *and lycans can't mate with humans, and men can't mate with other men.* Lately, too many of the things Alun had held as hard and fast truths seemed to be unraveling before his eyes. Just like the cord that was supposed to connect Robin's daemonic soul to his human body.

Alun's gaze narrowed. The cord was frayed, thin, and looked like it might snap at any moment. If it broke, Rob wouldn't be able to get back into his body, he would be stuck on the spirit side of the veil until he could take another human husk and make it his own. Daemons and angels— djinn, fae—they were spirit creatures. They couldn't live in the physical world without possessing a mortal body. Alun didn't know why such creatures craved mortal existence so much, he only knew that they did. And while he didn't care what happened to Rob—or at least he told himself that he didn't—he didn't understand why the daemon was *here*, instead of back at his body, healing it. As long as the cord was still intact, Rob *should* be able to repair whatever Percival's thugs had done to him.

"*Please*," Rob implored. The thread continued to unravel. "For James's sake—"

Alun cut him off. "You're dying."

"Daemons *can't* die, you moron! When you're dust *I'll* still be here."

Rob was right. Infernals, like their Celestial kin, were immortal. But that wasn't the point. "Your *body's* dying."

"All that matters is James. I can help you find him, just please, trust me—"

"Idiot! Get back to your body while you still can! I'll find James on my own!"

"Please let me help."

"I don't *need* your help, I know where they took him."

Robin hesitated. Nodded. "If… if we never see each other again…."

"Don't be daft! You'll be turning tricks back on Regent Street before the end of the week!" Without waiting for the daemon to respond, Alun dropped himself back into his own body. It hurt—it hurt like hell—but it worked. He couldn't see or argue with Robin anymore, which hopefully meant Rob had gone back to his body. His *stolen* body, Alun reminded himself. It wasn't unusual for a daemon to kill a person in order to take possession of his mortal shell.

Alun shook himself. He didn't know if he believed the story Rob had once told him, about finding a boy's dead body by the side of road over a hundred years ago—healing it. Possessing it. He wanted to believe that Robin wasn't really a murderer, but what difference did it make if he was? He was a daemon and what was done was done. Alun gathered his supplies back up and bundled everything into his pockets. Then he stole into the shadows and stripped himself bare. He did his best to hide his clothes amid the boxes and refuse before he shifted shape. The last thing he wanted was for Lamont to come back to the courtyard and find nothing of him but his suit… although a perverse little corner of Alun's mind wondered what the inspector would make of it, if he did.

ALUN had been in London for less than six months when he first met Robin Perris. He'd come with the foolish notion that he would find work and be able to carve out some kind of honest life for himself in the city, maybe even find somebody to settle down with. Not a mate, that was out of reach for a *diangen* wolf, but surely in a city as big as London, he could find one honest man to love, someone who would care about him, love him in return. Someone who would be faithful to him. But honest men, Alun learned quickly enough, were few and far between. Humans didn't have the same ideas about fidelity as wolves; when someone better came along, they left. Alun knew he hadn't had much to offer back then, so it wasn't hard to do better than him. It still wasn't.

It never would be.

Knowing that didn't make it any easier on his heart when he found Danny kneeling in an alleyway in front of some toff. The other man's pants were down and Dan had his mouth wrapped around his prick. It had been all Alun could do to leash his temper, to not kill them both.

Later, Danny swore he'd only done it for the money. He said he loved Alun—said he'd done it for *them*. He still had the shilling. The sight of it made Alun sick. He took his few belongings and left without looking back. A few hours later he saw Robin on Regent Street for what would be the first of many times. Regent Street was one of the places where men found boys who didn't mind acting like girls in bed. Not all of them were contra-sexual; Alun didn't care. His intention that night was to get as drunk as his metabolism would allow and find something—*anything* male and willing—to screw up against the nearest wall.

Then the scent of hellfire and brimstone hit him.

He followed his nose, and despite knowing everything he did about daemons, he was still shocked by what he found: a sweet-faced, too-young boy with red hair and an easy smile.

Robin recognized him for what he was, too, Alun could see it in his fear-stricken expression. But Robin didn't ask for help from the other patrons of the pub when Alun hauled him up by the shirt collar and dragged him out into the street. He didn't fight Alun at all—he even told several concerned onlookers it was all part of a little rough and tumble. Daemons lied easily; no one doubted his word.

When he and Robin got into the seclusion of a darkened alley, the boy was quick to plead his case, to swear that he'd never hurt anybody, that all he wanted was to be left alone. He offered Alun whatever he wanted in exchange for a little compassion. Alun accepted his offer that first time, he told himself, only because he was already half drunk—after that, he reckoned it didn't matter. He was *diangen*. He was already damned, and Robin was so very sweet in bed. Why shouldn't he be? He'd had centuries to hone his skills.

Chapter 21

ALUN'S heart lurched when he found Robin's body crumpled in a pool of cold blood on the cobblestones, a long, wicked-looking gash in his belly. When he pressed his nose to Rob's cheek, it was like touching a block of ice. Under the scent of brimstone and floral perfume, Alun could smell the decay of dead tissue. A recently dead human wouldn't smell of putrefaction so soon. But if he had really been occupying that body for over a century, maybe it was already too late, maybe Rob had been away for too long and couldn't heal himself. Maybe it had been too late the moment he died. *An' maybe all he needs is time.*

Helpless to do anything else, Alun shifted shape and closed Robin's eyes. As gently as he could, he pulled his body off the street, tucking him out of view amongst the refuse—it seemed so unfair to put Rob in with the garbage. He held back his howl of frustration. Not knowing what else to do, he prayed to his Goddess that Rob would find some way to heal what Percival's goons had done to him. He didn't know if she would intervene—if she even could. Neither angels nor daemons were a part of the natural world, part of her world. *But he came to me when he didn't have no reason to. That counts for something, don't it?* He could only hope. Pray.

He shifted back into his wolf form, and a soft whine escaped his throat as he buried his nose into Robin's bright ginger curls again. It pained him to leave Robin in the alley surrounded by rats and garbage, but there was nothing more he could do. *If I never see you again, I'll remember you as a good person, little blodeuyn*, he promised. Blodeuyn—flower. Rob always smelled of some sort of flower, lavender or acacia, sometimes heather.

Alun turned back to the street to sniff out James's scent. He'd only tracked Robin's scent at all—he told himself—so he could pick up

James's trail, just to be sure Percival's goons really took him where Alun thought they would. He didn't want to waste half the night getting to St. Paul's Cray if James was somewhere else.

"YOU'LL live," the woman told James in a cold, scornful tone. She was an awful scarecrow of a creature, the kind James might feel have felt sorry for if he'd seen her on the streets. She cleaned his wounds with rough hands and a look of disgust etched across her face, like he wasn't worth her time—either that, or she didn't see the point in tending the injuries of a man her compatriots intended to kill. Neither was a comforting thought.

James had seen nothing of the harrowing journey, having been bundled into the back of a carriage with a dark cloth sack thrust over his head. His wrists were bound roughly behind his back, his ankles tied tight to prevent him from "hurting himself," his captors had sneered. The woman tending his wounds seemed to see no reason to untie him.

"Where am I?" he asked her.

He'd been hauled out of the carriage as unceremoniously as he'd been hoisted into it, carried a short distance, and dumped onto a bed of damp, musty straw before the sack was pulled off his head, giving him his first look at his new surroundings. The building was small, so perhaps it was a shed; it smelled of animal dung and half-rotten wood. There was only one small window too high up for him to see out of, and the door the woman had come in. Beyond the walls, James heard the muffled sounds of voices, mostly male, laughing. Singing. When the door had opened, he'd glimpsed an orange glow that might be coming from a campfire somewhere nearby. He hadn't smelled any of the usual smells, but rather burning wood mingled with roasted meat. The scent made his mouth water, and his stomach rumble loudly, reminding him that it had been several hours since he'd eaten. The woman didn't even offer him water.

She didn't answer his question, either. She didn't even look at him.

He hissed in pain, wincing away from her touch as she scraped his raw skin with the rough cloth, causing fresh blood to flow. "What're you trying to do! Make it *worse*?"

She only sneered. "Be glad enough for this. It's more than you deserve."

"Why are you doing this? Why did you bring me here?"

She went back to ignoring him.

It was impossible to guess her age, but James doubted she was more than forty. Her hair fell in loose, dirty curls around her hips. She might have been pretty if she weren't so gaunt—so cruel.

"What do you want with me?" he tried again. "I've never done anything to you, I don't even know you!" It was becoming increasingly difficult not to give in to fear. To guilt. Rob was lying dead in the street, and for no other reason than he'd been out with him tonight instead of at home where he belonged! "Please—what do you people *want*?" James begged.

She didn't answer, she just scraped the cold, wet cloth against his skin again, making him cry out. Dr. Stodderley treated the dead with more care than this woman showed him!

"That cut needs stitches—or I can bind it, your choice."

He swallowed hard. He didn't want her touching him—but he didn't want to bleed to death, either. "Stitches. Thank you," he added.

She snorted. "I'll be right back."

"I don't seem to be going anywhere," he retorted.

She gave over a cold, mirthless laugh, then left him sitting in the musty dark again, alone and terrified.

James slumped against the wall and closed his eyes.

He opened them again just as quickly; with his eyes closed, it was too easy to see Rob's face smiling in his memory. Their last conversation had been far from light, but being around Rob made him feel good. Happy. Tears stung at James's eyes. He wished more than anything that he'd insisted Rob go home instead of selfishly enjoying his company tonight. "I'm so sorry, Robin. Please forgive me."

At length, the door opened up again, letting in another gust of savory smells from the campfire beyond. His "nurse" however, had brought only the supplies she'd need to stitch up his arm. Apparently, his captors thought enough of him that they didn't want him bleeding to death, but not so much that they were willing to share their meal.

"What are you called?" James asked the woman. Maybe if he could garner some information, there might be a way out of this, a way to bring Rob's murderers to justice. A way not to end up dead himself.

The woman snorted. "Chances are you won't live long enough to even need stitches, so I don't see where knowing my name's gonna make any difference. D'you?"

James forced himself not to look away from her. "No. I suppose not," he agreed. He sat still and gritted his teeth while she stitched the gash in his arm—in the dark. Fuck, how could she see?

The needle hurt every time it pierced his skin, but not half as much as the possibility—the very real probability—that he was never going to see Alun again, never hear his voice, or taste his kiss. He tried to tell himself that the one day they'd had together was worth an entire lifetime—and it was, it was worth *everything*, but it wasn't fair! Perhaps it was stupid, selfish even, but he wanted a proper life with Alun, like the life his parents had had. Fresh tears filled his eyes, but he blinked them away. He wasn't dead, not yet. That meant there might still be a way out. "Would it really hurt to tell me why you brought me here?" James asked the woman again, as she finished stitching his arm.

She regarded him for a long, cold moment. "Percival wanted you."

"Who's Percival?"

"The last person whose face you're gonna see." Something about that fact seemed to make her very happy.

ALUN watched from his vantage point, high up in the branches of an old pine tree, as Rhianna exited the small shed for a second time. He could smell James's blood on her more acutely this time, and it was all he could do to stay where he was as his soul howled with rage, the beast rising close to his skin—but it would do neither of them any good if he was caught too. Soon. Soon there would be blood on the forest floor....

He'd slipped past the sentries almost too easily and made his way downwind of the gathering, before assuming his human form so he could scale the tree. From there, he could see both the shed where James was being held and the bonfire, around which the entire pack seemed to be assembled. Mostly male, mostly Full Moons, none full-blooded lycans except for Rhianna—it was little surprise that Percival surrounded himself with his own kind. *But how could a pack so unbalanced survive?* Alun remembered both his father and his *taid* speaking on the importance of balance in a pack, of having equal numbers of Full, New, and Half-Moon wolves. Equal numbers of warriors, Spirit Dancers, and peace makers. Equal numbers of males and females.

Alun had been watching the pack for some while, but he still had no idea what was going on. There were at least thirty lycans present, eating, drinking, laughing—even singing, while the minstrels and storytellers plucked out cheerful melodies on a variety of instruments. There was a bodhràn drum, a fiddle, a harp, a dulcimer. It was the sort of revelry Alun would expect to find at one of the high holy days, yet they were well past equinox, nowhere near to Nos Galan Gaeaf—Samhain, the local wolves called it, Summer's End. And at the center of it all sat Percival, with a stein in one hand, the other clutching his mate's knee. She was an attractive woman, healthy and well fed—nothing like the pack's Lore Keeper.

Alun watched Rhianna closely as she rejoined the rest of the pack, heading not for the warmth of bonfire, but rather into the shadows on the outskirts of the clearing. No one looked at her or offered her a place to sit by the fire. No one gave her a portion of the meat, even though there was food in abundance. Alun didn't understand it; his *taid* had been a Lore Keeper, like Rhianna, but he was accorded the greatest of respect by his pack. He was second only to the pack leader.... But Rhianna's plight wasn't Alun's problem. He'd offered her his friendship when they first met; she rejected it.

Alun didn't hear the sound of soft footfalls on the forest floor, he only felt a sharp pain slicing through his thigh—he barely had time to cry out before he crashed to the forest floor and the wind was knocked from his lungs. In the distance, the laughter ceased. Alun clutched at the source of the burning pain: a wooden shaft stuck out of his thigh, the arrow buried many inches into his flesh. The sentries were on him before the rest of the pack arrived; Alun realized then that he hadn't slipped past the sentries at all, but had been allowed to get as far as he had.

Percival leered down at him, a self-satisfied grin playing across his features. "Welcome, *cwn*, good of you to finally show up." He smirked. "I was beginning to doubt Rhianna's assessment of certain… things. I thought I might have to punish her for telling me lies. After all, even a *diangen* with your unnatural tastes wouldn't defile itself with a human—would you, *cwn*?"

Alun let out a low, threatening growl; one of the sentries silenced him with a vicious kick to the ribs. He yelped, curling in on himself, praying that nothing was broken.

Snickering, Percival knelt down at his side. "There, there, *cwn*," he crooned softly. He ran a large, calloused hand over Alun's stubbly scalp. "There's no need for that. We're all friends here."

Alun's stomach churned violently at Percival's touch. When he placed his hand up to Alun's his face, it was all Alun could do to keep from bringing down his teeth on it. Never again! He would no longer supplicate to Percival. He turned his head away instead, refusing to nuzzle his fingers. Alun braced himself to feel the back of Percival's hand or another kick from one of the sentries, but rather than showing outrage, the pack leader threw his head back and howled his laughter into the night. "You've grown balls, *diangen*. I'd like to say I respect that—but I *don't*." His tone turned cold. "Perhaps I should fix that little problem for you—what do you say?" He took the knife from his belt and raked its sharp tip painfully up Alun's already injured leg, leaving a trickle of blood in his wake. "Can you show me the respect you owe me?" He jabbed down hard, causing Alun to whimper and pressed his other hand to Alun's face again. "Or do I have to remove your balls? Just one little kiss, that's all I'm asking. One kiss to show you still know who's alpha. I'll even get Rhianna to look at your wounds, afterward."

Alun lowered his gaze and remained motionless.

JAMES heard the commotion and struggled to his feet, hoping he'd be able to see what was happening through the grime-streaked window. He leaned against the wall for support and balance, scraping his injured arm raw in his efforts—but at last he could see outside! A ring of men and a few women were huddled off to the side of the clearing, looking at something at the base of an old pine tree….

SEVERAL jeers rang out from the ring gathered around Percival and Alun, suggesting that if the *diangen* wasn't going to use his balls, then perhaps the pack ought to cut them off.

Alun's gut tightened.

"What do you say?" Percival asked lightly. "*Should* I castrate you? Or do you have a use for those?" He tapped the inside of Alun's thigh with the knife, coming so close to his testicles that Alun winced. "Or maybe," Percival's tone darkened, "I should just slit the throat of your pet human. Haul him to his feet!" he roared.

Alun jerked, slithering out of reach of the hands grabbing for him. He stood up and yanked the arrow from his leg, giving free voice to his pain and fury.

In the span of less than a heartbeat, he shifted shape—shocked gasps rang out around the circle. Some pack members shifted, hackles rising, growling; others just got out of the way, their tails between their legs. Alun guessed by their reactions that Percival had neglected to mention to his pack that the *diangen* living in Whitechapel was a full-blooded lycanthrope. The air was heavy with the scent of the pack's fear.

Alun lowered his head and snarled out a warning to the few Full Moons who were brave enough to come too near—he *would* kill any who came within his reach. They danced back away quickly. Even Percival's enforcers, who were as big as wolves as they were as men, weren't any match for an outraged dire wolf—at least not while the pack was in its current state of disarray. Alun knew that wouldn't last long, and there were few options open to him. He maneuvered himself so he was facing Percival once more, and met the alpha's panic-stricken gaze dead on. It wasn't what he wanted, but it was the only way. Alun curled back his lip and growled his challenge.

The rest of the werewolves froze at the sound. The *diangen* had just challenged Percival for leadership of the pack.

Chapter 22

JAMES felt sure he was going to throw up when he saw Alun standing there, covered in his own blood—then his scream—the sudden transformation into a wolf. James shuddered and slumped against the wall of the shed, closing his eyes tight. He'd never seen anything so terrifying as Alun crouched within the ring of werewolves, snapping, snarling, wickedly long teeth flashing white against his midnight coat. It made James understand where the stories about lycanthropes had come from. He was sure Alun was going to kill them all—or get himself killed trying.

Ignoring the pain shooting through his injured arm, James struggled against the coarse rope binding his wrists, desperate to get free—though what he would do with his freedom, he didn't know. He just knew he had to find some way to get to Alun, some way to get them both out of there alive.

He'd made only a little progress when the door opened, and the scrawny scarecrow of a woman stepped inside. She said nothing; she didn't have to. The eight-inch hunting knife in her hand told James everything he needed to know.

"Why are you doing this? What do you want?" he asked anyway. He tried to inch away, but only succeeded in toppling himself over into the damp straw. James was sure his life was over, and it wasn't fair! Alun was less than a hundred yards away and he wouldn't even get to say good-bye. "Please—" he sobbed.

But instead of stabbing him or slicing his throat, the woman grabbed hold of James's legs and cut through the ropes that bound his ankles. Then she hauled him to his feet; she was frighteningly strong. "If you behave yourself, you might just live long enough to see your 'mate' become pack leader," she growled into his ear. "Not that it's going to do *you* any good. Move!" She shoved him out the shed door.

WHEN Percival didn't answer his challenge immediately, Alun threw back his head and howled it to the Moon. The savage beauty of his song rang through the night and silenced every other sound in the clearing. He settled his gaze on the pack leader once more, his dark eyes easily conveying the question: would Percival meet the challenge or would he prove himself a coward in front of his entire pack?

Before he could answer, movement on the edge of the circle of orange firelight caught Alun's attention—it caught Percival's too. The pack leader cursed; Alun snarled. Rhianna was pushing James out of the shed; his hands were bound behind his back, and she held a knife to his throat. It was all Alun could do to hold himself back because he wanted nothing more—or less—than to knock James out of her grasp and tear the bitch's throat out, to feel her blood.... Alun pulled back his rage, directed it all at Percival. This was *his* pack. He was in control—or at least he was supposed to be—and once a challenge had been issued, *no one* had the right to interfere. *Or are you so bereft of honor that you'll use treachery to win a fight you're afraid you can't win?* Alun wondered. Given the whisperings of the other lycans gathered around them, Alun guessed he wasn't the only one asking that question.

Percival turned to Rhianna, a snarl on his lips. "Let the human be, he's got no part in this!" His tone left no room to argue, but Alun saw the nervous look on his face—the sneer on Rhianna's. The situation was boiling out of control. "Rhianna!" Percival bellowed. "You *will* obey me!"

She dropped the knife away from James's throat. Percival turned his attention back to Alun, his palms open, beseeching at least a momentary truce. Alun took a step back, raising his head a fraction of an inch, signaling his willingness to listen.

"There's room to negotiate, Blayney," said the pack leader. "This doesn't have to end in bloodshed. Rescind the challenge, and you and the human can both walk out of here unharmed. I give you my word, I swear it by the Moon herself! Neither you or your human will ever hear from me or mine again, if you just walk away now." He was afraid; Alun could hear it in his tone. Smell it in his sweat. The oath he was offering was the most sacred oath a lycan could give—but could he trust Percival to honor it?

Alun turned his eyes to James once more, and his mate met his gaze. Held it. But Alun couldn't read anything in those moss-green depths. James was hurt because of him—bleeding, frightened. Alun had gotten him mixed up in a world no human could hope to understand.

A world he might not even survive.

I'm so sorry, cariad. *I never meant for any of this to happen, I only wanted to love you.* Alun felt his heart breaking. James wouldn't be able to love him after this. How could he? *Unless we both walk out of here, now, with no more bloodshed...* was it too much to hope for? If he showed James that they weren't monsters, if he proved they were capable of civilized negotiations....

"Rescind the challenge," Percival whispered at him again, his tone more urgent. "You'll leave unharmed, *both* of you, I swear. I've no wish to fight you."

Alun started to nod. He had nothing to prove, all he wanted was James's safety, and if there was a way to secure it without a fight—

"*No!*" Rhianna shrieked in protest. "There is *no* room to negotiate here! A challenge was issued—you *can't* walk away from it, *either* of you!" As if to emphasize her point, she pressed the blade to James's neck again, making him wince as a slow trickle of blood leaked from the new wound.

Alun tensed, snarling, ready to lunge at either her or Percival. Ready to kill the entire pack if he had to. Ready to give up any hope of James ever loving him again as long as it meant James would be safe.

Rhianna continued: "The *diangen* called his challenge out to the Goddess with your whole pack as witness, Percival! You *must* answer it! Fight or abdicate. Those are your only choices. *Decide.*"

Percival glowered at her; Rhianna's declaration had tied his hands. "I will fight," he said heavily.

Alun understood what he didn't say: the pack leader would fight to the death. Challenges didn't have to end that way, but Percival's ego wouldn't allow him to yield any more than it would allow him to abdicate. Alun wouldn't yield because if he did, Percival would never allow him and James to walk out of there alive.

"Sit the human down by the fire and let him watch," Percival told Rhianna.

She flashed him an impudent smirk, but didn't disobey. Alun's gaze trailed after them as Rhianna pulled James roughly by the arm and sat him down as instructed, well away from the rest of the pack. He didn't want James to watch, but clearly, it wasn't his choice. It didn't matter. The expression on James's face told Alun he'd already lost his mate. When this was over, James would tell him, in some polite way, Alun was sure, that he didn't want a lycanthrope for a lover anymore. He didn't want him in his house... his life.

But James would be safe. That was all Alun cared about.

With one last desperate look in the young human's direction, Alun lifted his head to the night sky and howled loud and long, singing out years, *decades*, of pain. Anger. Loneliness. Loss. He'd had barely a single day with James.... Alun was shocked almost into silence when another voice joined his... then another... and another, until it sounded like nearly the entire pack had joined his song. Alun had heard that full-blooded lycans had the power to move mixed-blood wolves, to sway their emotions, even their loyalty—but he had never thought it was true. He didn't really care. He closed his eyes and howled out his love for his mate, his anguish at knowing that no matter what happened here tonight, he would lose him. He thanked the Goddess for the one day of true happiness she'd given him with James. It was more than he'd ever expected. More than a *diangen* wolf deserved.

JAMES listened in wonderment as one by one the other lycanthropes began to howl along with Alun's heart-wrenching song. Many of those still in human shape shifted so they could sing along. It was so beautiful— the most beautiful thing James had ever heard, Alun's deep, rich voice leading the chorus of ordinary wolves. He was so beautiful....

But then suddenly the pack leader shifted into a huge golden timber wolf and hurtled himself at Alun's injured hind leg. He knocked into Alun hard and fast, drawing blood from the wound and putting an end to the incredible song. James cringed when Alun yelped, but Alun rolled away and found his feet quickly enough, facing his opponent with his head lowered, his lips curled back in a fierce snarl. They circled each other slowly.

Next to James the woman Percival had called Rhianna growled. It was difficult to tell which of the two combatants she really wanted to emerge as the winner. James just held his breath. Alun had the advantage of size and strength, but he was badly injured, and regardless of what he'd said before about a mate's love being able to heal all wounds, there seemed to be an awful lot of blood trickling down his hind leg.

James winced again as Percival lunged forward—Alun danced out of the way, but only barely. The next time he made a dive for Alun, the pack leader sank his teeth into Alun's right shoulder. Alun cried out, hobbling, favoring his injured leg. He went down. James could hardly watch; there was so much blood, and all of it was Alun's.

It seemed to take forever, but finally, Alun shook Percival off him and got back to his feet—only now he was favoring his right front leg as well as his left hind one. James didn't have to ask to know that there was no room for either of them to yield, or even ask for a respite. He stole a glance at the other lycans. The rest of the pack had formed a wide circle around the two combatants, but it didn't seem as if they cared who won or lost, they were simply enraptured in the fight.

A yelp from the center of the circle drew James's attention back to his mate. But this time it was Percival who had cried out, as Alun sank long, sharp teeth into his flank. Percival squirmed, kicking, scratching, scrambling to get free. Alun held him fast.

"Will the rest of them really accept Alun as their leader if he wins?" James asked Rhianna in a quiet tone. "Even though he's *diangen*?"

She snorted. "They'll accept him—but not *you*. If he wants to lead, he'll need a proper mate, a lycan. A *female*. Of course, once he takes a real mate, he won't be *diangen* anymore, will he?"

James swallowed hard. If Alun wasn't *diangen* anymore, he might be able to go home and see his family again. Or maybe he could stay here, live with his pack, hunt like a wolf, have a proper life. *He could be happy....* He could live like a wolf was supposed to live.

PERCIVAL freed himself, but Alun didn't give him a chance to recover. He sprang forward, catching Percival's hind leg in long, sharp teeth—bone snapped between his jaws, sickening him. Wolves weren't supposed to fight like this.

The pack leader howled as he twisted free, stumbling out of Alun's reach. When Percival sprang at him again, Alun lunged forward; he sank his teeth into the back of Percival's neck. The pack leader screamed. Alun nearly choked on the other wolf's blood, on his own bile.

Yips and shouts rang out around the circle—it was impossible to tell if they were directed at him or their leader, but it didn't matter, it was done. Alun dropped Percival to the ground. The defeated lycan hit the dirt with a whimper, blood spilling out from his wounds onto the soil. He was still breathing, but he didn't move.

Alun looked around the circle and caught sight Percival's mate, her hands fisted up so tight that her knuckles had gone white. Tears streamed down her cheeks and icy hatred burned in her eyes. How could he blame her? He was killing the other half of her soul.

He was too afraid to seek out James's face in the circle; what must this look like to a human?

Movement at his feet brought Alun's gaze down to the fallen pack leader. Percival shifted back to his human body. He was too badly injured to roll over and expose his neck, to supplicate himself to Alun, so he just lowered his eyes. "Always... always knew it'd come t' this someday, Blayney," he breathed, his voice coming out a hoarse whisper.

Alun shifted to his human form too; he ignored the startled gasps from the rest of the pack. No doubt they'd expected him to kill Percival where he lay. Alun leaned in close and lowered his blood soaked lips to the dying lycan's ear. "I never wanted this," he told him. "I *never* would've challenged you. I just wanted to live my life in peace! I don't *want* to be pack leader."

"Yes you do. It's in your blood. You're a real lycan, we're jus'... just poor imitations. It's why... why we set you up."

"What?" he hissed.

"You figured it out, didn't you? That last one, that woman you got arrested for murdering, it was Alex and Nigel what killed her—on my orders, don't blame them. But... you should know... it was Rhianna's idea," he coughed, spitting up blood. "She said you'd found a... a mate," he spat out the word with distain. "It was *her* idea to bring that human here. I ain't so sure this wasn't what she wanted. Me dead. You as alpha. There's things you need t'know 'bout that bitch—" but his words were drowned out by a woman's scream.

Alun looked up just in time to see Percival's mate lunging at him; she shifted mid-stride, and sank sharp teeth into his shoulder, knocking him to the ground with a hard thud. He cried out in pain, she in victory.

JAMES watched helplessly as Alun struggled against the big silver wolf, grappling with her, trying to keep her from getting at his neck. One minute Alun was a man, and the next he was the wolf, rolling her onto her back, pinning her. She yelped and then lay silent, blood soaking the ground beneath her, coloring her fur crimson.

James closed his eyes and missed Alun looking up, seeking him out at last—he missed the pained look in his mate's black eyes when Alun saw him turning away.

"Squeamish?" Rhianna jeered.

James shook his head. He wasn't squeamish; he felt sorry for the woman who had attacked Alun. He could all too well imagine how he would feel if Percival had won, if he'd sat there helpless and watched the man he loved more than anything die in front of him. "What... what happens now?" he asked weakly. "Will... will anyone else challenge him?"

"They might. If they do, I'm sure he'll kill them too."

James swallowed hard—hadn't there been enough blood shed for one night?

"What did you *think* was going to happen?" Rhianna asked him, her tone snide.

James regarded her for a moment, before telling her the truth. "I thought you were going to kill me."

"I still may."

"No. You won't," said another woman—she was wearing trousers and a waistcoat, a man's shirt, and her short, shoulder-length hair was honey colored and tied back away from her face. She looked hardly twenty, but carried herself as if she was used to being obeyed. "Get up," she snapped at James.

He realized she was holding a pocketknife. It was open. He eyed the blade with suspicion and didn't move.

Growling her annoyance, the blonde grabbed him by his uninjured arm and hauled him to his feet. She turned him so that his back was to her and sliced through the rope around his wrists, freeing him.

By the time James got himself turned back around, Alun was coming toward them. Toward *him*. James's heart raced in his chest. Alun's shoulder was still bleeding, and he was favoring his injured leg, but otherwise he seemed all right. It was all James could do to keep himself from running to him and closing his arms around Alun's neck—from telling him how much he loved him. All he wanted was for them to go home.

The smile that had been forming on his lips faded, however, when he saw the cold look in his lover's black eyes. James's gaze flickered to Rhianna. If she was right, all Alun had to do was take a female lycan to be his mate and... *and he could live here.* Hadn't Alun said how much wolves needed each other? *If I truly love him...* if he loved Alun, he would stand aside, he would let him be happy. James had to shut his eyes to keep the pain of the inevitable from coming out as tears. It didn't seem fair... but life wasn't fair, James knew that already. If it were, Alun wouldn't have spent most of his life living on humanity's scraps.

He opened his eyes when he felt a pair of hands on his shoulders; it was the blonde woman. She shoved him forward. James stumbled and would have fallen flat on his face if Alun hadn't caught him.

"That's what you came for," said the blonde. "Take it and go. We don't need a *diangen* as a pack leader."

James looked up at Alun, his heart aching, hoping to see some glimmer of warmth in the other man's dark eyes, some bit of hope, anything he could latch onto—but there was nothing. As soon as he was steady on his feet again, Alun let him go.

"We'll choose another," the blonde went on. "You and your human can go back to London where you belong."

"*No!*" Rhianna snarled. "He challenged the pack leader, and he won." She eyed Alun sharply. "It's time for you to take your place. You're a full-blooded lycanthrope. Leadership is your *right*. Your obligation."

Alun merely nodded. His eyes were locked with Rhianna's.

Like I don't even exist anymore, James thought, sullenly. Standing aside was the right thing to do, but that didn't make it easy.

Rhianna called for someone to bring warm water so Alun could clean up, and in short order a bucket was carried over. The young man who brought it gave Alun a wary look, but Alun ignored it. He crouched down and washed his hands and arms, his face—he refused Rhianna's assistance when she offered it, and simply dumped the entire bucket against his chest to cleanse himself of the last of the blood, both the dead lycans' and his own. When someone handed him a blanket, he accepted it without a word and wrapped it around his shoulders, not seeming to be looking at anything at all. Seeming to want to look at *anything* but James. James slunk further and further into the shadows, wishing he could disappear into them completely and never come back out again.

"I should tend your wounds," Rhianna told Alun; she seemed content to ignore James, as well.

"There's nothing that needs your help," Alun told her.

She didn't press the issue.

Around the fire, the rest of the werewolf pack milled restlessly, half of them still naked. None of them seemed bothered by either the bone-numbing cold or the indecency of their own nudity.

"Are you all right?" Alun's gruff question made James jump.

He shook his head, but said that he was fine even though his arm hurt; it throbbed all the way from his shoulder to his fingertips and was probably infected. "Alun, I...." His voice caught; tears pricked at his eyes. There was so much he wanted to say, but a soft, plaintive, "please," was all he could force past the lump in his throat. *Please don't leave me. Please choose me over them. Please come home with me.* It was the most selfish thing he'd ever wanted in his life, but he wanted it with all his heart.

"Give me five minutes," said Alun. "Then... then you can say anything you want to, an' I'll listen."

Not knowing what else to do, James nodded. He was startled when he felt the soft touch of Alun's hand on his. He looked up again—there seemed to be a thousand emotions tangled up in the lycan's black eyes, but James couldn't make out any of them. He gave up trying after only a few seconds, and wrapped his fingers around Alun's instead. *I love you. I need you. I'll do anything to be with you*, he thought fiercely.

"Five minutes," Alun repeated; his voice quivered. "I just... please, give me five more minutes, James."

James nodded again. "You can have as much time as you want, *anything* you want," he promised, hoping Alun would understand what he really meant.

"What I want... it don't matter what I want."

Before James could tell him that it *did* matter, Alun let go of his hand. He stalked back to the center of the clearing, only instead of speaking to the pack, Alun raised his face to the sky and let out a long, keening howl. He cried out a second time and a third, and by the fourth cry, the rest of the pack—his pack now—began to join his song....

Chapter **23**

EVENTUALLY the song died away, and Alun spoke. "Burn the bodies of the dead," he declared, his voice carrying throughout the entire clearing. "Give them whatever honor you're moved to give. If you're moved to give none, give none, but neither cause grievance to those who mourn." He turned slowly, so that he met the eyes of every lycan there—nearly all dropped their gazes to the ground in subordination. Or at least fear. "By the time the sun sets again, I expect anyone who can't abide me as leader to be off pack lands."

THE last statement garnered shocked mutters from all around the circle— but as Alun's gaze raked over the assembled pack again, silence fell once more over the clearing, so that the only things James could hear were the thumping of his own heart and the gentle crackling of the dying bonfire.

"If anyone thinks they're strong enough, you're welcome to challenge me," Alun said defiantly to the silence. The few lycanthropes who were still glaring at him lowered their eyes, showing their new pack leader a modicum of begrudging respect—or at the very least conveying that nobody wanted to fight him.

James let out the breath he didn't even realize he was holding. When Alun started back toward him, he found he couldn't look at him; his stomach was fluttering too madly with hope. Fear. He hardly noticed that Rhianna was still next to him and that she was watching Alun too.

When Alun came back to him, James asked him what was going to happen next.

"Percival and his mate's bodies'll be burned." Alun's voice was full of remorse. Heartbreak. He turned to Rhianna. "I'd expect the *Lore Keeper* might have a hand in it," he told her sharply.

She swallowed back whatever comment was on the tip of her tongue and nodded. "Of course." She cast a dark look in James's direction before taking her leave.

"Lore Keeper?" James queried, ignoring the growing number of important questions he wanted to ask—questions he was afraid of the answers to.

"She's New Moon born," Alun explained. For a moment, his eyes sparkled back to life, making James glad he'd asked. "There's three kinds of werewolves, James. Full Moons—fighters, hunters—and Half Moons— they're peace makers and judges. Then there's the New Moons. I know you don't believe in magic, but we… we're the ones who speak to the spirits. It's why it's always a New Moon who gets appointed to be her pack's Lore Keeper, because it's the Lore Keeper who's responsible for making sure the pack never forgets its past. She's also supposed to make sure they don't get so stuck in it that they can't move forward, neither. At least that's what my *taid*—my grandfather—used to say. He was my birth pack's Lore Keeper. I would've been Lore Keeper after him if I… if I'd not turned out to be *diangen*," he added softly, the light fading from his eyes.

"What if you weren't *diangen* anymore?"

Alun gave him a startled look.

"You're the pack leader now, aren't you?" said James. "Doesn't that change your circumstance?"

"I'm *diangen* because I like men, James. That ain't never gonna change."

"But what if… what if you took a wife—a mate, I mean? A woman. A lycanthrope."

Alun's expression was impossible to read. "Wolves mate for life. I can't take a new mate just because it suits me." The heavy resignation in his tone broke James's heart all over again.

"*Does* it suit you?" he wanted to know.

"It doesn't matter."

"It does to me!"

Alun was quiet for too long. When he did speak, his voice was so soft, James almost didn't hear him. "I would never choose anyone over you, *cariad*, even if I could."

For a moment, hope soared in James's chest. It was short-lived.

"Mating is a lycan instinct, James. I might not be able to walk away, but *you* can. You *should*. Walking away comes natural to humans."

The last statement cut James to the quick. "Is that what you *want* me to do?"

"Look around you!" He gestured toward the clearing—the lycanthropes preparing to burn their dead. "This ain't no place for a human. I never wanted to be pack leader, James, but now I am, an' I just... there weren't no other way, I'm sorry. I don't expect you to understand. I'll make sure you get home, safe."

"Damn you, Alun," James swore angrily, finally losing his battle with the tears. "Do you honestly think so little of me? Do you believe that I could give you my heart one moment and then take it away again the next? Or do you just believe that only wolves—only lycanthropes—know what it means to love? Well, let me tell you something: you are full of shite! If anybody's walking away tonight, it's *you*. You and that sanctimonious attitude of yours. If you truly want me to, I will bow out of your life as gracefully as I know how, even though it breaks my heart. But you had better be certain that this is what you want, Alun."

"James—"

"You will never get a second chance with me, Alun. My heart couldn't endure it." He was shaking. "So if you have any doubt at all, any reservation about sending me away...."

"It ain't about you and me anymore!"

"Yes. It is."

"You saw the way I killed 'em, James. How can you even *look* at me?"

James pulled him into a rough, needy kiss—a desperate kiss. He slid his hands up to Alun's face and cupped the back of his head, holding him.

After a long moment's hesitation, Alun finally gave up. Gave in. His lips parted, and he encircled James in his arms; he slid his tongue past the younger man's lips and into his mouth, taking control of the kiss. At least until James wrestled it away from him again. The exchange left them both breathless, weak-kneed, and wanting to do a whole lot more than just kiss.

James stared him straight in the eye. "I love you. That hasn't changed. It never will. All I need to know is if you still love me—if you still want me."

"I love you. I want you. I just don't know how—"

"We'll figure it out," James promised him. "But don't you *ever* tell me to walk away from you again, because next time I *will* leave you, Alun."

Alun nodded. James was serious.

RELUCTANTLY, Alun let go of his mate and looked back to the rest of the clearing. To his pack. They didn't feel like "his," but at least in name, he was the alpha male. Every single lycan had stopped what they were doing to watch him and James kiss. Some were visibly disgusted by what they'd witnessed and turned away quickly when they noticed Alun looking at them—others simply turned back to whatever they'd been doing before, not seeming especially disturbed by the kiss. Lycans weren't shy when it came displays of affection, especially between mates... *but we're both men, he's human....* They could never accept that James was Alun's mate—could they?

Alun brushed his fingers against the back of James's hand and was more than a little relieved when James accepted his touch, took his hand. By rights, James should be making him work a whole lot harder to regain what he'd nearly thrown away. *But I will work hard*, Alun promised him silently. *You'll see. I'll earn this.* He gave his mate's hand a gentle squeeze and leaned in to feather a soft kiss to his forehead. James was shivering. "*Cariad?*"

"I'm all right. I just...." He hesitated. "I'm not really all right. So much has happened tonight. Can we talk later? Please? In private?"

"Of course." He wrapped James back up in his arms and held the younger man until he stopped trembling. He closed his eyes and rubbed his cheeks against James's hair, covering himself with his mate's sweet, earthy scent; covering James with his musky, lycan scent. "Mine," he murmured softly; no one could hear but him and James. No one else mattered. "There's still stuff I need to do here, *cariad*."

"Do what you need to, Alun."

Alun feathered a soft kiss to the top of James's head and stepped back from him, surveying the clearing. Rhianna was standing on the other side of the campfire. She glared at him—at James—her hands balled into white-knuckled fists. Was Percival right, *had* she manipulated him into challenging the pack leader? She'd certainly pressed the challenge forward, even when Alun was ready to let it go. She knew Alun was full-blooded, knew Percival didn't stand a chance against him, especially not with James's life at stake—and that was her doing too. That put Emily's blood on her hands as much as it was on Percival's—Alun wondered if she realized that. Or maybe she thought he didn't know, or wouldn't care. After all, to Rhianna, Emily was just a human whore...

Alun looked around for Nigel and Alex, Percival's two big goons—they were nowhere to be seen. Probably, they'd already fled, fearful of Alun's wrath.

He returned his gaze to James. "Can... *will* you still trust me?"

"I never stopped trusting you, sweetheart. I still do. I always will."

"Thank you." He didn't deserve James's trust any more than he deserved his love. *But I will make it up to you*, he swore again. "I... there's things about a pack... things I need to sort out. I...." He faltered, unsure how to explain to James what he was about to do—unsure how much James understood about wolves.

"If I have questions, I'll ask you later."

"All right." Alun slid the blanket from his shoulders and wrapped it around James, who was still shivering in the cold pre-dawn air. More than the blanket's warmth, Alun needed the rest of his pack to see that his wounds—even the deep arrow wound in his thigh—had completely healed. That was his proof to them that there was a mating bond between him and James; it was the kind of proof even Rhianna couldn't ignore. He felt all eyes on him as he stalked to the center of the circle. He didn't have to call for silence when he was ready to speak; there had been little talking to begin with, and it died away quickly.

"My mate is a man called James Heron," he said in the steadiest voice he could muster. "An' he's human. You don't got to like 'im, you just have to accept that he's *mine*." He couldn't help the possessiveness of his tone. He glanced at James, but if the young blond objected to the declaration, it didn't show on his face. If anything, he seemed to stand a little taller, his shoulders a little more squared. He met Alun's gaze and held it, and what Alun saw in those moss-green eyes gave him the courage to look at the faces of the rest of the assemblage. No one else met his gaze. No one challenged his authority. He reckoned that meant they were all planning on leaving come the next sundown, but that didn't stop him from continuing. "The pack needs a alpha female," he said. He ignored the murmurs, the low, angry rumblings, around him.

Alun doubted they'd expected him to declare an alpha female tonight. He was equally certain, however, that if he didn't, Rhianna would step in sooner, rather than later, to remind him that the heart and soul of any pack were its two alphas. Of course, it was almost always the pack leader's mate who was the alpha female. Alun wondered if Rhianna had expected him choose a female over James—or had she intended for James to be dead before he arrived?

Even now, there seemed to be a look of expectancy in her dark eyes. She was the only other full-blooded lycan in the pack; it must make perfect sense to her that Alun would name her as alpha female, even if he had no intention of sharing his bed with her.

Alun shifted his gaze to the other females gathered around the fire. There weren't many, and they fidgeted nervously under his scrutiny. The males didn't look happy either—but none of them seemed ready to challenge him, at least not yet.

With only the barest of nods, Alun summoned Rhianna to him. She strode forward with her chin held high, though she kept her gaze respectfully focused on the ground. She stopped a few feet from where he stood and knelt, pulling her long, matted hair away from her neck, offering up it in obeisance. Alun let her stay there like that. He turned his gaze to each of the other unmated females—four in all, including the girl dressed like a man—summoning each to him with a look. None came to him as quickly as Rhianna had. Eventually the four other women knelt in front of him, offering up their throats. Around the circle their fathers and brothers growled, looking uneasy.

Alun turned his gaze to the five women in front of him. Rhianna sat quietly, waiting. The woman in men's clothes raised her eyes to meet his; her expression was one of anger. Defiance. The other three trembled, their fear palpable. The youngest of them, a fair chestnut-haired girl, seemed ready to faint. Alun glanced around the clearing and easily found her parents in the circle of lycans—her father was the only male willing to meet his gaze. He was ready for a fight, even though he knew he would never win. The woman clinging to his arm was in tears.

Alun knelt in front of the girl. "What are you called?" he asked, in a soft tone. Her only answer was a choked sob.

"Her name is Elizabeth," Rhianna hissed at him. "She's a *child*. The alpha female must be a woman!"

"Who are *you* to tell the pack leader his business?" challenged the blonde in trousers. She turned to Alun. "Elizabeth is fifteen, hardly a child, but you can see for yourself, she's frightened out of her wits. If you've *any* decency, *diangen*, you'll show a little compassion and choose someone else, before we've two more bodies to burn." She cast a quick glance over her shoulder at the girl's parents.

Alun laid his hands on Elizabeth's arms—she sobbed, pleading softly with him not to choose her.

Rhianna growled; the blonde called him a bastard.

Alun ignored them. "It's gonna be all right," he promised Elizabeth. He stood, pulling her gently to her feet with him. He took the terrified girl's hand and led her back to her parents.

The mother dropped her gaze immediately—the father let out a low, warning growl.

"Don't," Elizabeth begged. Alun wondered if she was pleading with her father not to challenge him or begging him not to kill her father.

But it didn't matter. He let go of her hands. "Fifteen is too young," he said simply. "If I'd known…." He shrugged. He didn't owe them an explanation.

Elizabeth's mother didn't seem to care; she wrapped her daughter into a tight embrace, whispering "thank you" so softly Alun wasn't sure if it was meant for him or not. No doubt both parents had been praying to the Goddess for their daughter's return.

As Alun made his way back to Rhianna and the others, James caught his eye; the younger man smiled. *I'm so proud of you*, his expression seemed to say. Alun smiled back, but he saw how tired James was, the dark circles under his eyes, the pallor of his skin. Humans were so much more fragile than lycans.

Alun stepped behind the blonde woman, the one wearing men's clothing. "Stand," he ordered—Rhianna growled angrily.

The blonde got to her feet, and Alun pressed his nose to the back of her neck. She stiffened, but didn't protest as he inhaled her scent. Only her clenched fists gave away how much she resented his attention. Him. Rhianna was still growling as Alun closed his eyes and sniffed the blonde's skin again, more thoughtfully this time. She smelled of green grass. Lichen. Dark earth. Good smells. She was Half-Moon born and strong. He let out a low growl of approval—of warning. She tensed, but didn't resist as Alun bit down on her neck; it wasn't a soft bite, but he was careful not to draw blood. When he drew his teeth away, he nuzzled her skin, an apology for having hurt her.

"I accept the will of the pack leader," she hissed softly. "But I want you to know that you will have to force me to your bed. And I swear by the Moon herself, I will kill any offspring you produce inside of me before it's ever born."

Alun released her, taken aback by the harsh words, her bitter tone. "I'm sorry you could hate a man you don't know so much that you'd take it out on his unborn babes, but I promise you, it'll never come to that. I *have* a mate."

"So did the last pack leader. That didn't stop him from forcing himself on every female here. Except those ones who went willingly." She eyed Rhianna darkly.

"You *allowed* this?" he demanded of the Lore Keeper.

She shrugged. "It is the pack leader's prerogative to bed whom he wishes, to produce strong offspring."

"*Only* when he doesn't have a mate!" snarled Alun; he made no attempt to mask his anger. His father had *never*... he shook his head to clear it and turned back to the blonde woman he'd just chosen as his alpha—a woman whose name he didn't even know. "You don't know me, so you've no reason to believe me, but I swear to you that whatever went on before… it stops *now*. I don't know how many'll stay—I don't expect many will—but I'll be having words with the Lore Keeper over her behavior." *And not just over this*, he swore silently. "In my birth pack, the Lore Keeper would have stopped any lycan, *even* the pack leader, from taking an unwilling partner to his bed."

"Perhaps your birth pack's Lore Keeper wasn't *female*," Rhianna snapped at him.

"You know that doesn't enter into it," he shot back. "We'll talk later, Rhianna," he promised her. He dismissed the other two females, so they could return to their families and then turned to the woman he'd chose as his alpha. "What are you called?"

"Gwyneth."

"And your family name?"

She stared at him, fresh anger dancing in her hazel eyes—but then she frowned. "You really don't know, do you?"

"How would I? I've never been allowed on pack lands, except by official 'summons', an' not one of you ever saw fit to so much as look at me before tonight."

She swallowed. Nodded. She was as guilty of that as the rest of them. "My name is Scadbury. This is—*was*—my family's land. Percival became pack leader by challenging my father. He was an old man with a young mate and no sons. Only me."

Alun understood what she didn't say; if she'd had brothers, one of them could have challenged Percival and reclaimed their family's estate. Females didn't have the right to challenge, even when the challenge was just. "Where are your parents now?" he asked.

"Percival killed my father. *After* he yielded. The next day, my mother took her own life. I was ten. That was twelve years ago."

"I'm sorry," he told her earnestly. Before she could respond, Alun turned to address the rest of the pack. "I name Gwyneth Scadbury as alpha female," he told them in a loud, clear voice. "An' I name her Caretaker of the pack's lands."

"She's a woman!" Rhianna hissed at him. "Tradition—"

"Is something you're happy to overlook when it suits you," said Alun. "These lands belong to the Scadbury family. It's only right Gwyneth should be Caretaker."

"Human law doesn't apply here," said Rhianna.

"No. Only mine does. Unless *you're* challenging me?" he snarled, hackles raised.

She backed down. "No, my Lord."

"Go and see to the dead, Rhianna," Alun told her. Then he let his gaze fall on each of the lycans in the circle gathered around him. No one met his gaze, no one challenged him—no one seemed especially unhappy about his choices, either. For that, he was grateful; he was exhausted, physically, mentally, and above all, emotionally. "Gwyneth, is there someplace James an' me can get cleaned up proper, get some rest, an' maybe some clothes we can borrow?"

"I'll take you up to the house."

Chapter **24**

WHEN Alun held out his hand, James took it. He leaned into his tall, handsome, Welshman, his mate, and let Alun guide him up the narrow path.

"The manor's up through the woods," Gwyneth said over her shoulder. "It's not far, but we can take the cart if you need it."

Alun didn't give him the chance to say he could walk; he accepted the offer on his mate's behalf and followed where she led. James was too exhausted to argue. Now that it was over, all he could think about was Robin. He squeezed his eyes shut, trying to forestall the tears. He was safe. Alun was safe. They would go home, but Rob... Rob would never go home. James didn't even know where "home" was for the young Irishman. Would anybody even miss him? Surely his friends from the theater would wonder what had become of him, but what of Rob's family? He'd never spoken of them, but he must have someone.

"*Cariad?*" Alun asked softly. "Are you all right?"

Looking up into beautiful black eyes, James wanted to lie; he could see how worried Alun was. Everything still felt so tender and raw between them—which was exactly why he couldn't lie. "No I'm not all right," he admitted. "But... it's not... I just need... a little quiet." He wasn't ready to talk about Rob, and he was grateful when Alun didn't press the issue.

At the edge of the clearing stood an old farm wagon. The big draft horse hitched to the front of it lifted her head and regarded them sleepily as they clambered in back—James was content to let Alun help him. He curled into his lover's arms and closed his eyes.

Gwyneth climbed into the driver's seat and set the big mare walking a sedate pace; the woods were dark, and the path twisted and turned. But the quiet suited James. At last, he found his voice. "Alun... when... when those two men... those two lycanthropes... when they grabbed me... I... I wasn't alone. I... Robin Perris was with me." He waited for Alun's hackles to go up, because if Rob knew—*had known*—Alun, then Alun had to know Rob was a Mary-Anne, a male harlot. *He'll assume I slept with him....* Heat burned in James's cheeks, and fresh tears welled up in his eyes.

Alun's hackles didn't go up. Instead, he smoothed his mate's hair and pressed another soft kiss to his forehead. "What happened, *cariad*?"

"They killed him. Those two... the ones who brought me here. They didn't have to kill him, Alun! They... if they wanted me... they didn't have to kill him! Rob was... he was just this sweet kid!"

Alun held him while he sobbed; he didn't try to tell James it would be all right—James was grateful for that. When his parents died, and then later, his brother, so many people told him it would be "all right." But it wasn't all right. It would *never* be all right again. His parents were gone. His brother.

Robin.

James wished he'd given Rob more of his time, been a better friend, instead of spending all those months avoiding him because of his own stupid guilt. James cried until his whole body ached, until he was sure he was out of tears.

"The ones who attacked you an' Rob, they were acting in good faith on Percival's orders," Alun told him in a gentle tone. "I can't punish 'em for that. I know that don't seem fair, but I promise, James, if they decide to stay, I'll tell 'em they ain't welcome. It's the most I can do."

James didn't understand. Murder was murder. It wasn't as if Robin was a threat to either of the two lycans who attacked them. "They should hang."

"I can't let 'em get taken into human custody."

"I know." He closed his eyes and snuggled into his lover's embrace; there were goose bumps on Alun's arms. "You're cold."

"I'll be all right."

"Wouldn't you be warmer the other way—with fur?"

"I don't want to do that to you."

"I wouldn't mind."

Alun looked at him, not seeming to believe what he was saying.

James straightened and cupped Alun's face in both his hands. He didn't speak, he just met Alun's gaze and held it. A moment later he was looking into a wolf's black eyes. James encircled the giant lupine in his arms and buried his nose deep in the dense fur. He rubbed his face against Alun's coat, covering himself in his mate's scent. James closed his eyes again and became willfully oblivious to everything except the soft beating of Alun's heart and the thick fur under his fingers. He didn't open his eyes again until they arrived at the sprawling manor house. It was bigger than he'd expected, but he didn't get much of a look at it.

Gwyneth pulled the wagon around to the side of the house and led them in through a servants' entrance. Alun remained in his wolf form as she hastened their steps through a series of narrow hallways and back stairs, up to her own bedroom—it was beautiful. Opulant. Far more feminine than James would have expected from a woman who clothed herself in men's attire. "The bath chamber's through that door," she told them. "You're free to make use of whatever you need. You'll have... ample privacy."

James blushed at her words and was glad when she took her leave.

Alun resumed his human form. "It don't matter what they think, *cariad*. By sundown, they'll all be gone anyway. They don't want a *diangen* as a pack leader. An' that don't matter, neither," he said, when James started to speak. "Come on, let's get you into the bath. And I want to look at your arm," he added sensibly.

James nodded; he allowed Alun to pull him into the huge bathroom. James didn't argue when Alun divested him of his tunic, his shirt. "Damn," the lycan muttered when he looked more closely James's injured arm.

"That bad?" James craned his neck to see for himself.

"You'll be all right, I think. Good thing with so much blood is that it's kept the cut clean."

James nodded; it wasn't much of a consolation, but he'd take what he could get. He finished getting undressed while Alun filled the tub with hot water—unlike his house in London, Gwyneth Scadbury's home seemed to have hot water pipes running throughout. Maybe it *was* time to invest in new plumbing, James mused. How nice would it be to simply turn the tap and have a tub full of hot water to soak in at the end of a long day?

A few moments later, Alun helped him into the deep copper tub; the water felt like pure heaven on his aching body. James closed his eyes—and there was a light tap on the bathroom door.

"Erm...," Gwyneth called from the other side.

Heat overtook James's cheeks once more. Unflustered—and still naked—Alun opened the door for her. James sank as far into the tub as he could get without putting his head underwater.

"I'm sure you and... and...." She hesitated.

"James is my mate, Gwyneth."

"Yes. Well. I'm sure you're both hungry." She was carrying a tray heaped high with meat, bread, some cheese. There was a pot of tea and a decanter of rich amber liquor.

Alun thanked her for her generosity, but Gwyneth still lingered, even after he took the tray. "I... none of us knows what to call you," she told him.

"I'm not sure it's gonna matter come sundown, but my name's Alun and that's always been good enough for me."

"You might be surprised about how many are left tomorrow night, Alun. The former pack leader wasn't especially well liked, either. At least with you... well... you seem... loyal." She glanced at James, "even if it is to a human. No offense, Mr. Heron."

James didn't respond, he just peered over the ledge of the tub, waiting for her to leave. When she did, he breathed a sigh of relief and sat back up again. "Doesn't nudity bother *any* of you?" he asked Alun.

The lycan shrugged. He set the tray down on the floor where they could reach it easily. "Why should it? How many wolves you ever seen wearing clothes?"

"You're not a wolf."

"I could prove you wrong." Alun grinned.

James wasn't amused. "You know what I mean."

Alun slid into the tub behind him. "Lycans don't have human sensibilities, James. The body's the body, wolf or man—or woman. It don't matter none. When we see each other, we just see other lycanthropes."

"But...."

"I thought you said that's how you look at me." He sounded genuinely hurt. "You said you see me just the same, no matter what skin I'm wearing."

"I do, but… but I don't look at you the same when you're wearing clothes as I do when you're naked! How could I?"

"An' how *do* you look at me when I'm naked?" he asked, his brows raised inquisitively.

"You know perfectly well what I'm trying to say."

Alun laughed. Then he wrapped his arms around James's midsection and rested his head against his shoulder. "I am sorry, *cariad*," he whispered.

"For what?" James was certain the apology wasn't for laughing at him.

"Everything I put you through t'night. If it weren't for me—"

"Don't, sweetheart." James laid his hands on top of Alun's arms and squeezed them tight. "Don't blame yourself for things you couldn't control."

"I just can't help thinking that if you'd never met me…."

"Don't. *Please*."

"I don't want you to wake up tomorrow morning and realize how much you hate me, James."

"*Never*." James took his lover's hand and moved it lower, so Alun was touching his cock.

"James…"

"I need to be touched, Alun. To be… to be loved. *Please*," he implored, half turning his head so he could look at the other man. "I need… *we* need… to remind ourselves that life goes on, that life… life conquers death. No matter how many people die, *life* still goes on. *Love* still goes on."

Alun shuddered, as if overwhelmed by something. Possibly by everything. He took James's shaft into his hand and stroked its length with strong, supple fingers. "How's that?"

James smiled. "I can almost pretend I'm inside you when you do it like that," James answered. He closed his eyes and leaned back, shifting to give his lover—his *mate*—better access to his body.

"I liked you being inside me," Alun whispered in his ear.

"I did too. But I think I like you being in me, better."

Alun's chuckle was a low, throaty laugh. "Guess we're gonna have to take turns."

"I guess so," James agreed. He moaned softly and leaned back into his lover's touch when he felt Alun kissing his shoulders and neck. Alun's lips were warm, soft; his hand was strong and his rhythm steady. "I could come just from this," James murmured.

"So why don't you?"

"It seems like a waste."

"Come for me, *cariad*, just like this. Let me see it," Alun breathed. He kissed James's neck again, and slid his free hand over his lover's chest. He took hold of one of his nipples, and rubbed it between his thumb and forefinger, gently at first, then harder until James gasped and jolted, and a jet of white cum shot out of the end of his shaft.

"Hell," James swore softly. He was sure he'd never come so hard or so fast in his life.

Alun chuckled. His own erection was poking James in the back, but he didn't seem to be in any hurry to do anything about it. Instead, he took the washcloth and lathered it up. He nudged James forward and ran the cloth gently over his back.

"I love you," James sighed.

Alun laughed some more. "Would that be for jerking you off or scrubbing your back?"

"Both?"

Alun continued to snicker, but when he spoke, his tone was nothing but sincere. "I love you too, James Heron."

"Thank you for that—for still calling me Heron."

"It suits you."

"What, an ugly swamp bird?"

"I think herons're beautiful," Alun told him. "Just like you."

As much as he wanted to, James couldn't argue. He was too tired. Too hungry. He reached over the side of the tub, grabbed a piece of cheese. He chewed without tasting, but he was glad to have something in his stomach at last. He turned and fed a piece to Alun as well, then poured himself a healthy shot of the amber liquor into one of the teacups on the tray. It was rich, smoky… scotch. Not his favorite, but he didn't care. He would have drank just about anything if it would take the edge off of the last twenty-four hours.

When Alun finished washing him, James suggested they switch—Alun wasn't in any more of an arguing mood than he was and turned around without a word of protest. James soaped up the cloth and rubbed it over the lycan's muscular back. He used his free hand to try and get at some of the knots in Alun's neck and shoulders—it felt like Alun was carrying a decade's worth of tension. It reminded James of the last time he'd seen Robin… the last time he ever would see him. He blinked back more tears; he was tired of crying. Of hurting. He reached down for his cup and gulped back the last of his second shot of scotch. He decided against a third, even though he wanted it.

"Alun, I… Rob and I, we were talking, before…." His throat closed around the words.

"Shhh. Don't."

"No, I think this is important," James insisted.

Alun turned to face him, scowling just slightly.

"Rob and I were… we were talking about… about the murders. I didn't tell him about what you said, about thinking it was a lycanthrope," he added quickly, although he hoped Alun would know that already.

"I trust you to keep my secrets, James," he assured him.

"I would never do anything to hurt you. Not on purpose. Hopefully not ever."

"I know. What were you an' Perris talking about?"

"I… *he*… suggested that… that someone might… might do to a woman what was done to that first woman if they wanted to cover up a pregnancy. It made me think about what you told me before, about how during the persecutions, sometimes infants were murdered by their own parents, if… if they were… lycanthropes."

"The dead woman wasn't a lycan."

"I know. Or… I mean I assume you would have told me if she was."

"I would've. I'm still not sure what you're getting at, though."

"You said that having children with humans thinned the bloodlines. So what if a lycanthrope got that first woman pregnant? What if... what if he or somebody else didn't want the baby to be born? I don't know if a coroner would know the baby wasn't human, but if the father or whoever didn't want to take the chance...." He ended in a shrug.

Slowly, Alun nodded. "It... it ain't inconceivable," he admitted, clearly reluctantly.

"We still don't know who that first woman was," James went on. "What if... what if Claire Walker and Emily Harris were only killed to make it *look* like the Whitechapel killer was back? That would at least explain why a lycanthrope would resort to using a knife, even though he wouldn't need one."

"Emily was killed by... she was murdered on Percival's orders, James."

"What? Why?"

"To set me up."

"But... you told me that ruddy bastard made it your job to figure out who was murdering those girls in the first place! Why the bloody hell would he do that and then set you up? What kind of a sick son of a prick—?"

"It was a game. Everything with Percival was a game. An' maybe... maybe there's more to it. I ran into Rhianna after Claire was killed. She had to see something was different about me."

"Different? What was different about you?"

Alun laid his hand over top of James's; the younger man slid his fingers through his, and Alun smiled. "You're what was different about me, *cariad*," he said. "I'd found my mate. Coupled with him. And even though I ran away like a coward, that didn't change nothing."

James looked at Alun's shoulder—his leg. Faint scars were all that remained of the horrible, bloody battle with the dead pack leader. "Percival was afraid of you, wasn't he?"

"He knew I was stronger than him, knew the others might follow me, even though I'm *diangen*. Before he died, he said he always figured I'd challenge him, 'cause I'm full blooded. There's so few of us left—prolly Rhianna's the only other full-blooded lycan any of the pack's ever met. My birth pack was all full-blooded werewolves. Only way a mixed blood got let in was to mate with a pack member—and even then, they got treated different."

James didn't comment; the more he heard about lycanthropes, the more they sounded like humans: elitist, narrow-minded, class-divided, capable of heinous crimes... great love. Alun rubbed his thumb over James's hands; they were both starting to get pruned fingers, but James was reluctant to leave the warm sanctuary of the bathtub. Alun didn't seem in any hurry to get out either. "I would have done anything to protect you, James. Even... even if it meant you leaving me."

James leaned in, and Alun met his kiss halfway; James savored it. He slid into Alun's lap, positioning his entrance against the leaking head of Alun's cock.

"James...," Alun protested, putting an end to the kiss.

"Let me. I want you inside me. I want to feel you come. I want *you*, Alun, and I never want you to doubt how much."

"Then at least let me help," he said, sliding his hand between James's legs, pressing one soapy finger up against his hole.

James groaned when he felt it slide past the tight ring of muscles; he willed himself to relax, and within moments, he had a second finger pressing into him, filling him. Stretching him. James braced his hands on Alun's shoulders, like he had that morning in the kitchen, and tried not to slosh too much water out of the tub as he moved himself against his mate's hand, driving Alun's fingers deeper into him until they touched his prostate. He tilted his chin, giving Alun his throat. Alun took it. He kissed... licked... bit down hard, causing the younger man to cry out. James pressed his neck into Alun's mouth, encouraging him to bite harder still. He lifted off Alun's hand and settled himself onto his cock, taking him fast—hard. It burned; he relished the pain, the pleasure. "I'm yours, Alun. All yours. Always yours. Only yours. I want you. I want you so much...." It became a litany as he rode the lycan, faster... faster.... When Alun bit down on his neck again, James came, his stream shooting between them, coating both their chests in thick white cum. A moment later, he felt a rush of heat as Alun filled him with his seed. It was over far too soon.

But then Alun wrapped his strong arms around him, and nothing else mattered. He brushed the damp hair from James's face. "I'd like you— *us*—to get some rest. Then I want you to go home."

"Without you?"

"I have to see things through here."

"Why can't I stay with you, then?"

"Your Mrs. Dunberry'll worry herself sick if you're gone all day, *cariad*. It'll only be worse when she hears you disappeared off your beat last night. It ain't fair to do that to her."

Reluctantly, James nodded. "How long will you be?"

"A day. Maybe two."

James swallowed hard. "You *are* coming back to London, aren't you, Alun?"

"I promise, James. My home will always be wherever you are."

Chapter 25

ALUN waited until James was safely on his way back to London, with Gwyneth as his escort, before confronting Rhianna. Her home was a tiny hovel deep in the woods. He wondered if Percival had treated her as he did because he knew he couldn't trust her, or if her malice had been spawned by his ill treatment. He supposed it didn't matter. He found the Lore Keeper working in her garden; she looked up as he approached, anger burning in her eyes. "You were supposed to choose *me*," she told him.

Alun frowned. "You set me up for murder—Emily Harris was a friend of mine."

"She was a human whore. Her life means nothing to me—it shouldn't mean anything to you, either."

A low growl rumbled in his throat.

"What would she have done if she'd ever seen you for what you are? Do you think she would have embraced your friendship? Or would she have cried 'monster', raised the alarm to Crown and Church?"

He declined to answer; he knew Rhianna was right. "Why did you manipulate me into challenging Percival?" he wanted to know.

"Because you and I are the only real lycanthropes here. It's our place—*your* place—to lead them, to strengthen the bloodlines. It's why you were supposed to choose *me* as your alpha female not that stubborn, weak-blooded bitch."

Alun ignored the venom in her tone. "Why you?" he asked. Rhianna made no secret of her scorn for him. Why would she want him as a mate?

"Because we're dying out! In the last ten years, only two of the children born into this pack are able to shift shape. Yet the ones who couldn't were still allowed to live. To *breed*. Percival's mate was a sentimental wretch. Gwyneth Scadbury will be no better. She'll never allow you to do what needs to be done. In a few generations there will be no shape shifters left, Alun. Once upon a time we culled our offspring to save them from human torturers; we killed off future generations because we were too afraid of the Inquisition to fight back. Now we must cull those born who can't shift in order to preserve what little future we have left. If we don't, the men who hunted us nearly to extinction will finally win."

Alun's gut churned at her words. "That's madness, Rhianna."

"Is it? Or are you simply too weak to see the truth? Go ahead and couple with that miserable human if it makes you happy—at least you won't pollute your bloodline with bastard children. I suppose that's one blessing to your perversion. But lie with *me*. Produce children with *me*. Give your pack a true lycan heir."

"It was a lycan what murdered that woman on Palmer Street a couple of months ago, wasn't it? He murdered Claire Walker too, but it was that first woman what you wanted dead 'cause she was pregnant."

A wicked smile curved across her face. "You're cleverer than I'd thought."

"What was her name?"

"How should I know her name? She was a human whore, and I wasn't going to have her sullying my bloodline with bastard grandchildren. It's bad enough I've had to mate with mixed-blood wolves all my life. Don't look so surprised, Alun. I've mothered over a dozen children with the strongest lycanthropes I could find. If you were true to your blood, you would have too—and you wouldn't tolerate any of them mating with humans any more than I did. You're a New Moon, like me. If anyone understands what it means to truly be lycan, it should be you."

"I am *nothing* like you," he seethed.

She smirked. "You've been living with the humans too long."

"I want you gone, Rhianna."

She stared at him a moment, as if not comprehending. "What do you mean, *gone*?"

"I am removing you as Lore Keeper and banishing you from pack lands."

Her eyes widened. "You can't! You're untrained—uninitiated. You *need* me."

"You made me pack leader, an' now you're gonna live with what you've done—*all* of what you've done. I want you off this land by sundown. An' if I ever find the bastard what killed Claire and the other girl, he'll pay the price with his own wretched blood."

"You would choose those human harlots over a lycanthrope?"

"Killing like that's more than enough grounds to mark a wolf *diangen*. So's condoning it."

"You wouldn't dare!"

"Don't test me."

ALUN spent the afternoon exploring the woods on four legs; he swam in the lake, he hunted rabbits. He missed his mate, sorely. By the time he returned to the manor, barely an hour before sundown, Gwyneth was back. She reported that James had been delivered home safe and sound. "Though I can't vouch for what condition he'll be in after his housekeeper is through with him," she added with a smile.

Alun chuckled; he was glad Gwyneth had worn a dress to drive James back home. He could well imagine what Mrs. Dunberry would have said if the good Lady Scadbury had been wearing trousers when she arrived. Then he told his alpha female about his encounter with Rhianna. "Did anyone else know she had a son—that he'd killed those girls?" he wanted to know.

"If anyone did, you can be certain they were in Percival's inner circle. They're sure to be long gone by now."

Alun snorted. He was sure the entire pack was long gone by now.

ALUN sat, with no small amount of reluctance, on the same roughhewn, wooden chair Percival had used as his "throne." Gwyneth sat in a slightly smaller chair next to him, her legs tucked up under her—she was back in trousers and a waistcoat. A low table sat between them; they shared a bottle of wine she'd brought from the manor. Alun wondered how long they should wait; no one was going to show up. But then two men joined them, carrying logs for the fire.

Since Alun and Gwyneth had started a small fire already, the newcomers piled the wood they'd brought up near the fire pit and sat down on the ground near it. Neither of the men spoke to him—or to Gwyneth, for that matter—though they occasionally glanced anxiously in Alun's direction. As soon as he tried to make eye contact, they looked away.

One by one, more lycans joined the circle; some brought firewood, others brought wine and food to share. The offerings were simpler than the previous night's banquet, but each item was dutifully presented to the pack leader before being offered to anyone else. Alun accepted what he was given graciously, even though his stomach was too knotted for him to be able to eat more than a few bites.

Gwyneth leaned over and whispered, "Percival wouldn't touch anything *anyone* brought him for almost a full year."

Alun scoffed. "Afraid they'd poison it?"

"Wouldn't you be?"

He shrugged. He didn't sense anything more than nervous uncertainty in those who approached him. He was *diangen*, but he was also a full-blooded lycan; the former made him an outcast, while the latter ensured him respect, even if it was borne solely out of fear.

"For what it's worth," said Gwyneth, "none of these people are like that." As if to prove her point, she reached across and tore a chunk of bread off the piece he wasn't really eating anyway.

Alun chuckled. "By all means, help yourself."

She gave him a startled look—then she grinned. It was the first he'd seen her smile; he decided he'd like to see it more.

"You've got a strange sense of humor, Alun," she said.

Alun started to respond. He looked up when he noticed Elizabeth and her parents joining the circle; there was a young boy with them.

"Elizabeth's little brother, Stuart," Gwyneth told him, before Alun could ask.

"How many children are there?"

"We have a few families—perhaps a dozen children. Percival didn't like children at the pack's bonfires, especially the ones not born 'true'—

able to shift shape—so none attended. Not many women came, either, but that was for other reasons."

Alun nodded; he could well imagine what those reasons were. Elizabeth brought her family's contribution to the feast up to the alphas. "Mum made this for you," she said softly, putting the small pie on the table. "I hope you like apple."

"It's my favorite," Alun assured her. He could hear Elizabeth's heart hammering in her chest, but the girl looked up, met his gaze—then dashed back to her parents like a frightened rabbit.

"Their fear has more to do with you being full blooded than... than your choice of mates, Alun," Gwyneth told him softly. "The only full-blooded lycan most of us have ever seen before was Rhianna and... well, she did little to make us easy about full bloods."

Before Alun could answer, tell her that he didn't imagine his "perversion" sat real well either, another young couple entered the clearing. The hair on the back of Alun's arms stood on end. They were both New Moon born, the first ones to join the circle tonight—and he was certain they hadn't been at last night's bonfire, either. They had a child with them, a little girl about five years old. She trailed fearlessly along with her father when he brought a wheel of cheese over for the pack leader's approval. The man seemed even more nervous of him than the rest of the pack—but the little girl grinned at him. Alun smiled back, then her father shooed her back to her mother with a weak apology to the alphas. He was gone himself only a moment later, having never even looked up at Alun.

"Richard and Natalie Pierce, and their daughter, Abigail," Gwyneth told him their names. "Richard and Natalie are New Moons—but you knew that, didn't you?"

He nodded. "Are they the only ones?"

"Rhianna didn't like competition. Richard and Natalie moved to London only a few months ago. Alun... men Rhianna didn't like had a way of getting... injured. Women she didn't like came under Percival's scrutiny more than the rest of us. It's a wonder those two stayed at all."

"You've never lived on your own. You don't know what it's like."

"I wasn't exactly in favor with the pack leader."

"But you never lived alone."

"No. I never lived alone."

"If you had, you'd understand."

She only nodded. "That's everyone."

Alun wasn't surprised Gwyneth already knew who was staying and who had left.

He stood up, and silence fell over the clearing. Alun looked around the circle of lycans gathered before him, taking in each of their faces—noting with relief that Nigel and Alex were nowhere to be seen. He hadn't expected them to stay, but he was just as glad there wouldn't be a confrontation. Even without his promise to James, he wouldn't have allowed them to remain.

Counting a dozen children, there were thirty-two lycans present, and they were all looking to their new pack leader, though what they were looking for, he wasn't sure. *They prolly don't know themselves*, he reckoned. It didn't look like anyone had much of an appetite; they'd all helped themselves to food, but very little of it had been eaten. There were nearly as many women as there were men and far more Half Moons than Full. Alun was surprised any of the Full Moons had stayed—but assuming none of them challenged him, he was glad to have them. He didn't know if there were other packs nearby, but if there were and they coveted his pack's lands, *this* would be a very good time to try and take it. If that happened, he would need every Full Moon he had to defend their territory. *His pack?* he wondered. When had he started thinking of this as his pack?

Alun threw back his head, raising his voice to the sky. One by one, the rest of the pack joined his song. They were hesitant at first, but soon their courage grew, until even the children were singing—howling. Alun grinned; that was as it should be. When the song died away, Alun glanced back over his shoulder at Gwyneth; she shot him a wry smile. He suspected he had her to thank for there being so many lycans still there, though he wasn't sure he really wanted to *thank* her. It would have been so much easier if no one had stayed.

He turned back to his pack. There seemed to be a glimmer of hope sparking in a few of them, replacing some of the dread and fear he'd felt earlier. "I don't rightly know how Percival did things." Alun cursed silently as his voice crackled. He cleared his throat. "It's been a long time since I was part of any pack. But when I was, my father was a good leader. We had our differences—I'm sure you can figure what they were. I ain't gonna hide what I am, or pretend to be nothing I'm not. I came to London almost ten years ago as a *diangen* wolf. I'm still *diangen*. My mate is human. Male." He looked around the circle, particularly at those who hadn't been there last night. It was impossible to guess what they were thinking, but nobody looked surprised. He hadn't expected he would be telling them anything they didn't already know, he just wanted his pack to hear it from him. "James is a part of my life. He *is* my life. You don't have to like it, or him, or even me, you just have to accept that it's the way things are." He paused, waiting, watching. When the pack remained silent, he went on. "I know things happened here that weren't right, but it's *over*. What matters now is what happens *today*. Tomorrow. Next year—the year after. We're responsible, all of us, for where we go from here, an' what kind of future we make for ourselves."

Behind him, Gwyneth threw back her head and howled her approval; the rest of the pack was quick to join in.

EVEN though all Alun wanted was to get home to his mate, he stayed. He ate. They all ate. The rest of the pack began to talk quietly amongst themselves, occasionally casting glances his way, but always looking away quickly when he tried to catch their eye. Eventually, he gave up, and settled for watching the children play around the fire. He wasn't aware that a smile had stretched across his face, or that the parents of those children were watching him with intense interest. Some looked worried, others relieved.

The sound of footsteps approaching his "throne" drew Alun's attention from the children. It was Richard Pierce. His head was lowered, his eyes downcast; his fear was palpable. Alun took in the cut of his clothes, the cloth—Pierce wasn't a rich man, but he had more money than Alun ever had. He was probably a merchant or maybe a skilled tradesman; certainly he belonged to the middle class. But that was in the human world. Here, Pierce was nothing, he had nothing that his pack leader didn't permit him to have. It was a sobering realization for Alun.

When Pierce's gaze rose briefly, questioningly, Alun nodded, and Pierce knelt in front him, unbuttoning the top button of his shirt. He tilted his head, offering his throat in submission. Alun blinked, startled—then he leaned forward and took Pierce gently by the shoulders. The man was shivering; it wasn't the cold. Alun laid his teeth against his throat, biting down only hard enough to have it felt, but not so hard as to bruise skin. Pierce's heart pounded, his fear turning to terror.

Unsure what the actual protocol was—he couldn't remember from his youth—Alun held the frightened man for several seconds, then released him and sat back. Pierce lowered his head again. His breath was ragged.

"Gwyneth tells me you an' your family're new to London," said Alun, when the other remained mute. It looked like Pierce had used up all his courage in coming over.

"Yes, Sir," he eventually whispered.

"'Sir' is something humans call each other."

Color blossomed in Pierce's cheeks. "Wh-what should I... we... call you?"

"My name's Alun, an' that's always suited me fine." He said the same thing he'd told Gwyneth earlier.

Pierce nodded. He fidgeted.

"Was there something you wanted?"

"I... my wife and I, we're both New Moons. Spirit Dancers."

"I know."

Pierce swallowed hard and nodded. "You... you've not said... that is...if you'd let us stay...."

"I said any who could abide me as pack leader was welcome."

"But we're New Moons. Rhianna...." He looked around nervously—apparently word hadn't yet circulated that she'd been banished. Either that or no one believed she was really gone.

"Rhianna is no longer a member of this pack," Alun told him. "Which makes you and your mate doubly welcome—though you would've been welcome, anyway," he promised.

Pierce blinked. "I don't understand. She's the Lore Keeper."

"Not anymore."

Pierce drew in a ragged breath. "Natalie—my mate—it's because of her that we're still here," he admitted softly. "She had a good feeling about you, said she knew you'd be different."

Alun's chuckle was rueful. "You'll have to give her my thanks," he said anyway.

Pierce nodded again. He hesitated. He fidgeted some more.

"Sometimes it's easier to just say what's on your mind than to sit there fretting 'bout how to make it come out right," Alun told him gently.

"You... you're... *diangen*. It... it's because... humans call it contrasexual, don't they?"

"Yes." Alun made the effort to keep his tone even.

"Would you accept another *diangen*? Someone like you, someone who didn't do nothing else wrong?"

"I assume you're not talking of yourself."

"No, Sir... Alun," he corrected himself, hastily. "Thad and Natalie grew up together—I came into the pack later, but I'll vouch for him. He's a Full Moon, he's got a temper, but he's *never* hurt anyone. When Thad was exiled, me and Natalie went with him."

"Is he in London?"

Pierce nodded. "Percival made his life a living hell."

He snorted. "Of that I have no doubt." Alun asked if there were any other wolves in the city who didn't belong to the pack.

"I... I don't think so. But I wouldn't know, Natalie and me... we weren't exactly in Percival's inner circle." He licked his lips nervously, casting a quick glance toward the shadows.

"All right. I'll meet your friend, an' make my decision 'bout him after I do." *Goddess*, he swore silently. He'd been pack leader for less than a day, and already he was making decisions.

"Thank you." But he continued to hesitate.

"Tomorrow," Alun told him. Because tonight, all he wanted to do was get home to James.

"Thank you," the other man said again. "We own a leather shop—I own it. Percival said...." He shook his head. "Thad works for me. If you ever need anything—"

Alun waved it aside. "If I ever need anything, I'll pay for it," he insisted—he didn't need Gwyneth to tell him that Percival had taken whatever he wanted from the Pierces the same way he took what he wanted from everyone else. Alun got the name and address of the shop and promised to come by the next day, late in the afternoon, and prayed to the Goddess that James would be understanding.

One by one, the rest of the pack came up to him, as if their courage had been bolstered by witnessing Pierce's audience. Each member of the pack offered Alun his throat; he accepted, learned their names, and tried to put them at ease, but as the hour grew late, there was only place he wanted to be....

JAMES woke when the bedroom door opened; he didn't have to open his eyes to know who it was. He smiled and rolled over to greet Alun properly.

"Sorry to wake you," his lanky Welshman whispered, leaning in.

James met his kiss happily. "I'm not sorry. Not sorry at all." He kissed Alun again. "How... how did everything go?" he asked at length. Alun looked weary to the bone; it was nearly dawn.

"Over thirty stayed. Rhianna weren't one of 'em. I told her she had to leave by sunset."

"And she went? Just like that?"

"She didn't have choice. James... she confessed her role in... in all what's happened," he said hesitantly. "She didn't know the name of the first woman, but you were right about why she died."

"And the killer...?"

Alun shrugged.

James stared at him, unable to believe Alun's only answer was a shrug. "Did you even *try* to make her tell you the killer's identity?"

"His name don't matter, James. He could never be brought to the kind of trial you want. It's over."

"Somewhere out there, that girl's parents are staring out into the darkness wondering where their daughter is! It won't be over for them until they know what happened to her."

"I'm sorry, *cariad*. It could be she don't got parents. Nobody's come forward, have they?"

James drew his knees up to his chest. It wasn't just that girl's parents he wanted to give closure to. "I couldn't find Rob," he said, fresh tears pricking at his eyes. "I only wanted to give him a proper funeral. I don't think he's got anyone, at least no one who could afford to bury him properly. I went 'round and saw some of his friends, but I didn't know how to tell them that... that his body just vanished. How does a body just vanish! I asked at all the hospitals, and I sent telegrams everywhere else I could think of."

Alun wrapped his arms around him. "I'm sure…." His voice caught in his throat, surprising James. He hadn't gotten the impression Alun liked Rob all that much. "He can't stay missing forever, *cariad*."

James wasn't sure about that. Dr. Stodderley said sometimes bodies never turned up, went to some kind of black market. Human cadavers were in high demand amongst medical students. The physician promised to check his own sources and let James know if he heard anything, but he wasn't too hopeful. Neither was James. "I quit my job, Alun," he told his mate softly, changing the subject.

"Why?"

James smiled. "I didn't have much of a choice. I couldn't very well tell anyone where I was or why I 'walked off' my post again. So instead of trying, I went in and told them I was through." He was only grateful he hadn't run into Inspector Lamont. "I managed to get this before I left," he added, reaching over to the bedside table. He handed Alun his purse, the one Stanwix and Mills had confiscated. Claire Walker's crucifix was still in it.

Alun turned the small gold pendant over in his hand. "How…?"

James smiled. "Let's just say that if they ever find out I nicked it, I'm in a world of trouble."

"Why would you…?"

"I figured you must've had that pendant for a reason, something important."

The lycan nodded. "Claire has a daughter. I promised her I'd get this to her."

James gave him a questioning look.

"Her spirit. I saw her spirit. I know you don't believe—"

"It doesn't matter. You do. There were all sorts of things my mother believed that my father never did. He still loved her."

Alun slid the pendant carefully back into his battered old purse. "Thank you, *cariad*."

Epilogue

JAMES gazed out the big front window in wonderment at the falling snow; it looked like they were going to have a white Christmas, after all. Not that Alun, it turned out, celebrated Christmas, but he was willing to have a tree and other trimmings, if it made James happy. Hanging mistletoe in every doorway of the house had helped the younger man make his case. They were constantly catching each other for quick kisses, usually while Mrs. Dunberry tried very hard to pretend she disapproved. Alun might yet be unconvinced that the housekeeper actually liked him, but James knew better.

Although London had settled back to normal, James would never look at his city the same way again, especially after Alun took him to meet the corvidthropes—the were-ravens—who lived in the Tower of London. According to Alun, the corvids knew everything that happened in the city. They confirmed the same thing Alun's new Lore Keeper, Natalie Pierce, had told him: there were no lycanthropes in the city of London save those already accounted for. It was a shallow comfort to James; there was still a killer out there, somewhere, there was just nothing he could do about it. His only consolation was that no more murders had been attributed to Jack the Ripper, at least none credibly so—not that that prevented Inspector Lamont from walking down their street from time to time. Thankfully, he was nowhere in sight, tonight.

James turned from the window; he smiled at the sight of his mate, fussing over the candles on the Christmas tree, trying to get them perfectly spaced.

"I still don't understand all this. You're a atheist," the lycan grumbled when he noticed he was being watched.

"There's nothing particularly religious about evergreens. Besides, that's not the point."

"There's a point?"

"Yes, there's a point." James crossed the distance between them and wrapped his arms around Alun. "The point is being thankful for everything we have." He leaned in, and Alun met his kiss halfway.

And the doorbell rang. James frowned. It was late. Dark out. He hadn't seen anyone on the street when he'd been standing at the window. "I'll get it," he told Alun. "You finish here."

As soon as James opened the door, the cheery "Happy Christmas" died in his throat.

Standing there in the lamplight was a slight young man with a mop of curls tucked up under his scarlet cap. He had the brightest green eyes James had ever seen and wore a purple velvet coat and a long red scarf.

"Happy Christmas, James," the young man said, in a lilting Irish accent.

"Rob?" It couldn't be! His knees started to buckle. A moment later, Alun was standing behind him, holding him up.

Bright emerald eyes darted from James to Alun and back again. "I… I didna mean to intrude, I jus'… jus' wanted to… to see you. To say 'Happy Christmas' to… to both of ya."

It was Rob's voice. His face. His hair. His eyes. But… Rob was *dead*! James saw them kill him. He barely noticed the tears falling from his own eyes. "Robin? Is… *how*…?"

"I—I'm sorry," Rob stammered. "Maybe I shoulda come sooner or… or not at all. I… I'm sorry to've troubled you. Good night—"

James pulled away from Alun and wrapped his arms around Robin's shoulders before he could turn away. He felt so real. So warm. "Don't you dare," he wept. "Don't you dare go *anywhere*."

Robin held him tight. "I'm sorry, James."

"Don't be sorry, just… just come in, please." He straightened, wiping the tears from his cheeks.

"I shouldn't—"

"Don't be silly, come in!" James urged—but Robin stayed where he was. James cast a glance back toward Alun; it was impossible to tell what the lycan was thinking, but his gaze was darker than usual. "I… I think you might know each other," James began awkwardly.

"We're *acquainted*," Alun glowered.

Rob swallowed hard.

James opened his mouth to ask—to *beg*—Alun to please be a little more hospitable, but then Alun's eyes softened all on their own. He huffed out a breath. "James is right, Robin. Come in out of the cold. Stay for a while."

"I...." Robin still hesitated.

Alun held out his hand. "It's good to see you again," he said in a tone that sounded sincere, at least to James.

Rob flashed a tight smile as he accepted Alun's hand. "It's good to see you too," he answered, and stepped in out of the night.

HELEN BARBARA PATTSKYN remembers writing her first short story in the second grade—it wasn't very good, but it was a good start! Growing up as an only child being raised by her grandmother, she preferred to spend time alone in her bedroom reading, writing, drawing rather than playing sports or hanging out, like most kids her age.

She started writing fanfiction in her early twenties, in response to the dreaded "it didn't really happen" third season of television's *Beauty and the Beast* and has been writing it ever since. It was only a few years ago that she entered the world of M/M slash—and she hasn't looked back since. As one of her readers put it, "Boys kissing is hot."

In addition to being a writer, Helen is an artist and tarot reader. She shares her life with a wonderful man, an occasionally wonderful teenager, two cats who graciously allow her to live in their house, and a spoiled rotten xolo dog. She can be found hanging out at science fiction conventions in her home state of Michigan.

Visit H.B.'s website: http://helenpattskyn.com. You can also e-mail her at thylacine.yawn@gmail.com.

RHIANNE AILE

BETRAYED

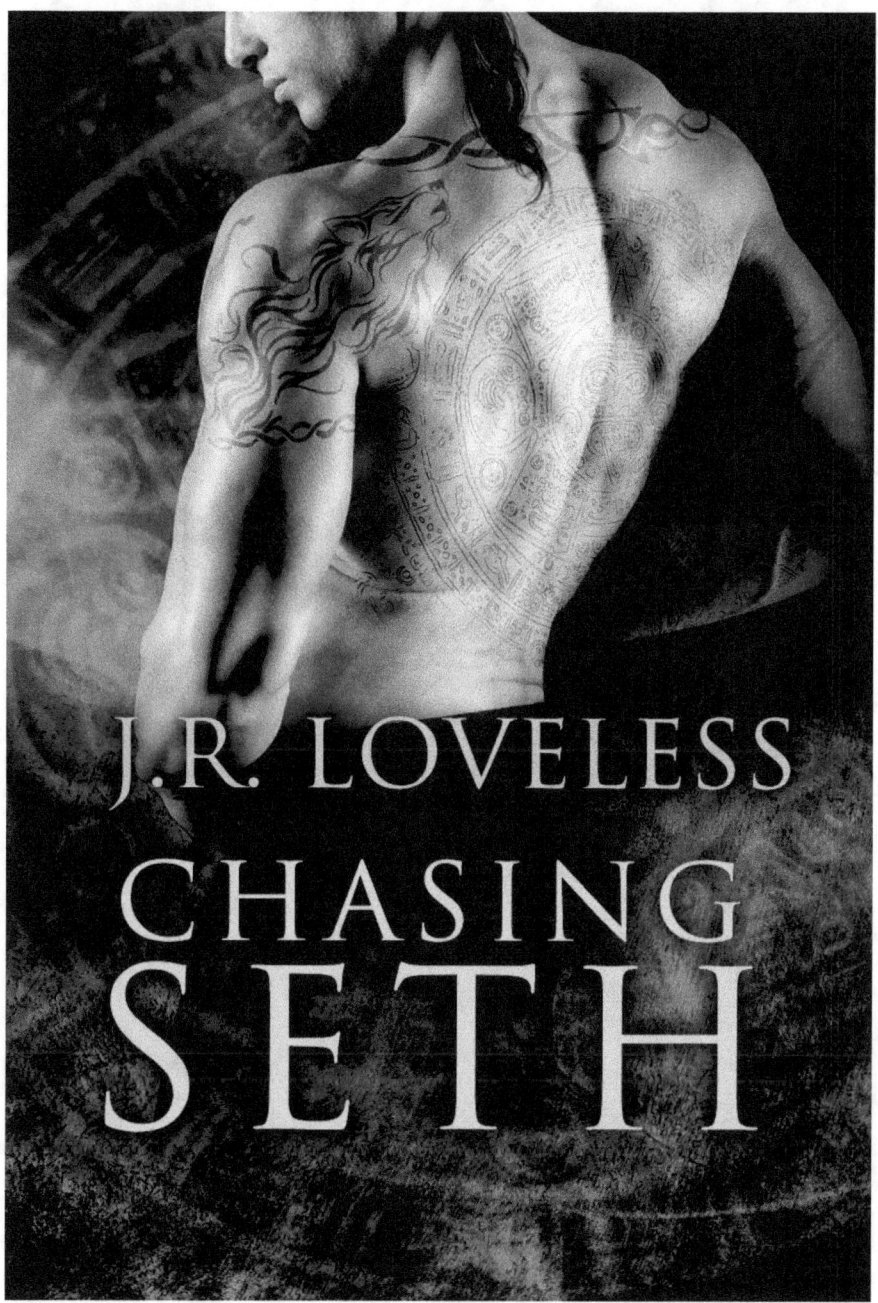